J. J. Connington and The Murder Room

>>> This title is part of The Murder Room, our series dedicated to making available out-of-print or hard-to-find titles by classic crime writers.

Crime fiction has always held up a mirror to society. The Victorians were fascinated by sensational murder and the emerging science of detection; now we are obsessed with the forensic detail of violent death. And no other genre has so captivated and enthralled readers.

Vast troves of classic crime writing have for a long time been unavailable to all but the most dedicated frequenters of second-hand bookshops. The advent of digital publishing means that we are now able to bring you the backlists of a huge range of titles by classic and contemporary crime writers, some of which have been out of print for decades.

From the genteel amateur private eyes of the Golden Age and the femmes fatales of pulp fiction, to the morally ambiguous hard-boiled detectives of mid twentieth-century America and their descendants who walk our twenty-first century streets, The Murder Room has it all. **>>>**

The Murder Room
Where Criminal Minds Meet

themurderroom.com

J. J. Connington (1880–1947)

Alfred Walter Stewart, who wrote under the pen name J. J. Connington, was born in Glasgow, the youngest of three sons of Reverend Dr Stewart. He graduated from Glasgow University and pursued an academic career as a chemistry professor, working for the Admiralty during the First World War. Known for his ingenious and carefully worked-out puzzles and in-depth character development, he was admired by a host of his better-known contemporaries, including Dorothy L. Sayers and John Dickson Carr, who both paid tribute to his influence on their work. He married Jessie Lily Courts in 1916 and they had one daughter.

By J. J. Connington

Sir Clinton Driffield Mysteries
Murder in the Maze (1927)
Tragedy at Ravensthorpe
  (1927)
The Case with Nine Solutions
  (1928)
Mystery at Lynden Sands
  (1928)
Nemesis at Raynham Parva
  (1929)
  (a.k.a. *Grim Vengenace*)
The Boathouse Riddle (1931)
The Sweepstake Murders
  (1931)
The Castleford Conundrum
  (1932)
The Ha-Ha Case (1934)
  (a.k.a. *The Brandon Case*)
In Whose Dim Shadow (1935)
  (a.k.a. *The Tau Cross Mystery*)
A Minor Operation (1937)

Murder Will Speak (1938)
Truth Comes Limping (1938)
The Twenty-One Clues (1941)
No Past is Dead (1942)
Jack-in-the-Box (1944)
Common Sense Is All You
  Need (1947)

Supt Ross Mysteries
The Eye in the Museum (1929)
The Two Tickets Puzzle (1930)

Novels
Death at Swaythling Court
  (1926)
The Dangerfield Talisman
  (1926)
Tom Tiddler's Island (1933)
  (a.k.a. *Gold Brick Island*)
The Counsellor (1939)
The Four Defences (1940)

The Sweepstake Murders

J. J. Connington

An Orion book

Copyright © The Professor A. W. Stewart Deceased Trust 1931, 2014

The right of J. J. Connington to be identified as the author of this work has been
asserted in accordance with the Copyright, Designs and Patents Act 1988.

This edition published by
The Orion Publishing Group Ltd
Orion House
5 Upper St Martin's Lane
London WC2H 9EA

An Hachette UK company
A CIP catalogue record for this book is available from the British Library

ISBN 978 1 4719 0605 3

www.orionbooks.co.uk

CONTENTS

CONTENTS

Introduction
by
Curtis Evans

During the Golden Age of the detective novel, in the 1920s
and 1930s, J. J. Connington stood with fellow crime writers R.
Austin Freeman, Cecil John Charles Street and Freeman Wills
Crofts as the foremost practitioner in British mystery fiction of
the science of pure detection. I use the word 'science' advisedly,
for the man behind J. J. Connington, Alfred Walter Stewart,
was an esteemed Scottish-born scientist. A 'small, unassuming,
moustached polymath', Stewart was 'a strikingly effective
lecturer with an excellent sense of humour, fertile imagination
and fantastically retentive memory', qualities that also served
him well in his fiction. He held the Chair of Chemistry at Queens
University, Belfast for twenty-five years, from 1919 until his
retirement in 1944.

During roughly this period, the busy Professor Stewart
found time to author a remarkable apocalyptic science fiction
tale, *Nordenholt's Million* (1923), a mainstream novel, *Almighty
Gold* (1924), a collection of essays, *Alias J. J. Connington* (1947),
and, between 1926 and 1947, twenty-four mysteries (all but
one tales of detection), many of them sterling examples of the
Golden Age puzzle-oriented detective novel at its considerable
best. 'For those who ask first of all in a detective story for exact
and mathematical accuracy in the construction of the plot',
avowed a contemporary *London Daily Mail* reviewer, 'there is
no author to equal the distinguished scientist who writes under
the name of J. J. Connington.'[1]

Alfred Stewart's background as a man of science is reflected
in his fiction, not only in the impressive puzzle plot mechanics
he devised for his mysteries but in his choices of themes and

depictions of characters. Along with Stanley Nordenholt of *Nordenholt's Million*, a novel about a plutocrat's pitiless efforts to preserve a ruthlessly remolded remnant of human life after a global environmental calamity, Stewart's most notable character is Chief Constable Sir Clinton Driffield, the detective in seventeen of the twenty-four Connington crime novels. Driffield is one of crime fiction's most highhanded investigators, occasionally taking on the functions of judge and jury as well as chief of police.

Absent from Stewart's fiction is the hail-fellow-well-met quality found in John Street's works or the religious ethos suffusing those of Freeman Wills Crofts, not to mention the effervescent novel-of-manners style of the British Golden Age Crime Queens Dorothy L. Sayers, Margery Allingham and Ngaio Marsh. Instead we see an often disdainful cynicism about the human animal and a marked admiration for detached supermen with superior intellects. For this reason, reading a Connington novel can be a challenging experience for modern readers inculcated in gentler social beliefs. Yet Alfred Stewart produced a classic apocalyptic science fiction tale in *Nordenholt's Million* (justly dubbed 'exciting and terrifying reading' by the *Spectator*) as well as superb detective novels boasting well-wrought puzzles, bracing characterization and an occasional leavening of dry humour. Not long after Stewart's death in 1947, the Connington novels fell entirely out of print. The recent embrace of Stewart's fiction by Orion's Murder Room imprint is a welcome event indeed, correcting as it does over sixty years of underserved neglect of an accomplished genre writer.

Born in Glasgow on 5 September 1880, Alfred Stewart had significant exposure to religion in his earlier life. His father was William Stewart, longtime Professor of Divinity and Biblical Criticism at Glasgow University, and he married Lily Coats, a daughter of the Reverend Jervis Coats and member of one of

Scotland's preeminent Baptist families. Religious sensibility is entirely absent from the Connington corpus, however. A confirmed secularist, Stewart once referred to one of his wife's brothers, the Reverend William Holms Coats (1881–1954), principal of the Scottish Baptist College, as his 'mental and spiritual antithesis', bemusedly adding: 'It's quite an education to see what one would look like if one were turned into one's mirror-image.'

Stewart's J. J. Connington pseudonym was derived from a nineteenth-century Oxford Professor of Latin and translator of Horace, indicating that Stewart's literary interests lay not in pietistic writing but rather in the pre-Christian classics ('I prefer the *Odyssey* to *Paradise Lost*,' the author once avowed). Possessing an inquisitive and expansive mind, Stewart was in fact an uncommonly well-read individual, freely ranging over a variety of literary genres. His deep immersion in French literature and supernatural horror fiction, for example, is documented in his lively correspondence with the noted horologist Rupert Thomas Gould.[2]

It thus is not surprising that in the 1920s the intellectually restless Stewart, having achieved a distinguished middle age as a highly regarded man of science, decided to apply his creative energy to a new endeavour, the writing of fiction. After several years he settled, like other gifted men and women of his generation, on the wildly popular mystery genre. Stewart was modest about his accomplishments in this particular field of light fiction, telling Rupert Gould later in life that 'I write these things [what Stewart called tec yarns] because they amuse me in parts when I am putting them together and because they are the only writings of mine that the public will look at. Also, in a minor degree, because I like to think some people get pleasure out of them.' No doubt Stewart's single most impressive literary accomplishment is *Nordenholt's Million*, yet in their time the two dozen J. J. Connington mysteries did indeed give readers in Great Britain, the United States and other countries much diversionary reading pleasure. Today these works constitute an estimable addition to British crime fiction.

After his 'prentice pastiche mystery, *Death at Swaythling Court* (1926), a rural English country-house tale set in the highly traditional village of Fernhurst Parva, Stewart published another, superior country-house affair, *The Dangerfield Talisman* (1926), a novel about the baffling theft of a precious family heirloom, an ancient, jewel-encrusted armlet. This clever, murderless tale, which likely is the one that the author told Rupert Gould he wrote in under six weeks, was praised in *The Bookman* as 'continuously exciting and interesting' and in the *New York Times Book Review* as 'ingeniously fitted together and, what is more, written with a deal of real literary charm'. Despite its virtues, however, *The Dangerfield Talisman* is not fully characteristic of mature Connington detective fiction. The author needed a memorable series sleuth, more representative of his own forceful personality.

It was the next year, 1927, that saw J. J. Connington make his break to the front of the murdermongerer's pack with a third country-house mystery, *Murder in the Maze*, wherein debuted as the author's great series detective the assertive and acerbic Sir Clinton Driffield, along with Sir Clinton's neighbour and 'Watson', the more genial (if much less astute) Squire Wendover. In this much-praised novel, Stewart's detective duo confronts some truly diabolical doings, including slayings by means of curare-tipped darts in the double-centered hedge maze at a country estate, Whistlefield. No less a fan of the genre than T. S. Eliot praised *Murder in the Maze* for its construction ('we are provided early in the story with all the clues which guide the detective') and its liveliness ('The very idea of murder in a box-hedge labyrinth does the author great credit, and he makes full use of its possibilities'). The delighted Eliot concluded that

Murder in the Maze was 'a really first-rate detective story'. For his part, the critic H. C. Harwood declared in *The Outlook* that with the publication of *Murder in the Maze* Connington demanded and deserved 'comparison with the masters'. 'Buy, borrow, or – anyhow – get hold of it', he amusingly advised. Two decades later, in his 1946 critical essay 'The Grandest Game in the World', the great locked-room detective novelist John Dickson Carr echoed Eliot's assessment of the novel's virtuoso setting, writing: 'These 1920s [. . .] thronged with sheer brains. What would be one of the best possible settings for violent death? J. J. Connington found the answer, with *Murder in the Maze*.' Certainly in retrospect *Murder in the Maze* stands as one of the finest English country-house mysteries of the 1920s, cleverly yet fairly clued, imaginatively detailed and often grimly suspenseful. As the great American true-crime writer Edmund Lester Pearson noted in his review of *Murder in the Maze* in *The Outlook*, this Connington novel had everything that one could desire in a detective story: 'A shrubbery maze, a hot day, and somebody potting at you with an air gun loaded with darts covered with a deadly South-American arrow-poison – *there* is a situation to wheedle two dollars out of anybody's pocket.'[3]

Staying with what had worked so well for him to date, Stewart the same year produced yet another country-house mystery, *Tragedy at Ravensthorpe*, an ingenious tale of murders and thefts at the ancestral home of the Chacewaters, old family friends of Sir Clinton Driffield. There is much clever matter in *Ravensthorpe*. Especially fascinating is the author's inspired integration of faerie folklore into his plot. Stewart, who had a lifelong – though skeptical – interest in paranormal phenomena, probably was inspired in this instance by the recent hubbub over the Cottingly Faeries photographs that in the early 1920s had famously duped, among other individuals, Arthur Conan Doyle.[4] As with *Murder in the Maze*, critics raved about this new Connington mystery. In the Spectator, for example, a reviewer hailed *Tragedy at Ravensthorpe* in the strongest terms, declaring of the novel: 'This is more than a good detective tale. Alike in plot, characterization, and literary style, it is a work of art.'

In 1928 there appeared two additional Sir Clinton Driffield detective novels, *Mystery at Lynden Sands* and *The Case with Nine Solutions*. Once again there was great praise for the latest Conningtons. H. C. Harwood, the critic who had so much admired *Murder in the Maze*, opined of *Mystery at Lynden Sands* that it 'may just fail of being the detective story of the century', while in the United States author and book reviewer Frederic F. Van de Water expressed nearly as high an opinion of *The Case with Nine Solutions*. 'This book is a thoroughbred of a distinguished lineage that runs back to "The Gold Bug" of [Edgar Allan] Poe,' he avowed. 'It represents the highest type of detective fiction.' In both of these Connington novels, Stewart moved away from his customary country-house milieu, setting *Lynden Sands* at a fashionable beach resort and *Nine Solutions* at a scientific research institute. *Nine Solutions* is of particular interest today, I think, for its relatively frank sexual subject matter and its modern urban setting among science professionals, which rather resembles the locales found in P. D. James' classic detective novels *A Mind to Murder* (1963) and *Shroud for a Nightingale* (1971).

By the end of the 1920s, J. J. Connington's critical reputation had achieved enviable heights indeed. At this time Stewart became one of the charter members of the Detection Club, an assemblage of the finest writers of British detective fiction that included, among other distinguished individuals, Agatha Christie, Dorothy L. Sayers and G. K. Chesterton. Certainly Victor Gollancz, the British publisher of the J. J. Connington mysteries, did not stint praise for the author, informing readers that 'J. J. Connington is now established as, in the opinion of many, the greatest living master of the story of pure detection. He is one of those who, discarding all the superfluities, has made of deductive fiction a genuine minor art, with its own laws and its own conventions.'

Such warm praise for J. J. Connington makes it all the more surprising that at this juncture the esteemed author tinkered with his successful formula by dispensing with his original series detective. In the fifth Clinton Driffield detective novel, *Nemesis at Raynham Parva* (1929), Alfred Walter Stewart, rather like Arthur Conan Doyle before him, seemed with a dramatic dénouement to have devised his popular series detective's permanent exit from the fictional stage (read it and see for yourself). The next two Connington detective novels, *The Eye in the Museum* (1929) and *The Two Tickets Puzzle* (1930), have a different series detective, Superintendent Ross, a rather dull dog of a policeman. While both these mysteries are competently done – the railway material in *The Two Tickets Puzzle* is particularly effective and should have appeal today – the presence of Sir Clinton Driffield (no superfluity he!) is missed.

Probably Stewart detected that the public minded the absence of the brilliant and biting Sir Clinton, for the Chief Constable – accompanied, naturally, by his friend Squire Wendover – triumphantly returned in 1931 in *The Boathouse Riddle*, another well-constructed criminous country-house affair. Later in the year came *The Sweepstake Murders*, which boasts the perennially popular tontine multiple-murder plot, in this case a rapid succession of puzzling suspicious deaths afflicting the members of a sweepstake syndicate that has just won nearly £250,000.[5] Adding piquancy to this plot is the fact that Wendover is one of the imperiled syndicate members. Altogether the novel is, as the late Jacques Barzun and his colleague Wendell Hertig Taylor put it in *A Catalogue of Crime* (1971, 1989), their magisterial survey of detective fiction, 'one of Connington's best conceptions'.

Stewart's productivity as a fiction writer slowed in the 1930s, so that, barring the year 1938, at most only one new Connington appeared annually. However, in 1932 Stewart produced one of the best Connington mysteries, *The Castleford Conundrum*. A classic country-house detective novel, Castleford introduces to readers Stewart's most delightfully unpleasant set of greedy relations and one of his most deserving murderees, Winifred Castleford. Stewart also fashions a wonderfully rich puzzle plot, full of meaty material clues for the reader's delectation. *Castleford* presented critics with no conundrum over its quality. 'In *The Castleford Conundrum* Mr Connington goes to work like an accomplished chess player. The moves in the games his detectives are called on to play are a delight to watch,' raved the reviewer for the *Sunday Times*, adding that 'the clues would have rejoiced Mr. Holmes' heart.' For its part, the *Spectator* concurred in the *Sunday Times*' assessment of the novel's masterfully constructed plot: 'Few detective stories show such sound reasoning as that by which the Chief Constable brings the crime home to the culprit.' Additionally, E. C. Bentley, much admired himself as the author of the landmark detective novel *Trent's Last Case*, took time to praise Connington's purely literary virtues, noting: 'Mr Connington has never written better, or drawn characters more full of life.'

With *Tom Tiddler's Island* in 1933 Stewart produced a different sort of Connington, a criminal-gang mystery in the rather more breathless style of such hugely popular English thriller writers as Sapper, Sax Rohmer, John Buchan and Edgar Wallace (in violation of the strict detective fiction rules of Ronald Knox, there is even a secret passage in the novel). Detailing the startling discoveries made by a newlywed couple honeymooning on a remote Scottish island, *Tom Tiddler's Island* is an atmospheric and entertaining tale, though it is not as mentally stimulating for armchair sleuths as Stewart's true detective novels. The title, incidentally, refers to an ancient British children's game, 'Tom Tiddler's Ground', in which one child tries to hold a height against other children.

After his fictional Scottish excursion into thrillerdom, Stewart returned the next year to his English country-house roots with *The Ha-Ha Case* (1934), his last masterwork in this classic mystery setting (for elucidation of non-British readers, a ha-ha is a sunken wall, placed so as to delineate property boundaries while not obstructing views). Although *The Ha-Ha Case* is not set in Scotland, Stewart drew inspiration for the novel from a notorious Scottish true crime, the 1893 Ardlamont murder case. From the facts of the Ardlamont affair Stewart drew several of the key characters in *The Ha-Ha Case*, as well as the circumstances of the novel's murder (a shooting 'accident' while hunting), though he added complications that take the tale in a new direction.[6]

In newspaper reviews both Dorothy L. Sayers and 'Francis Iles' (crime novelist Anthony Berkeley Cox) highly praised this latest mystery by 'The Clever Mr Connington', as he was now dubbed on book jackets by his new English publisher, Hodder & Stoughton. Sayers particularly noted the effective characterisation in *The Ha-Ha Case*: 'There is no need to say that Mr Connington has given us a sound and interesting plot, very carefully and ingeniously worked out. In addition, there are the three portraits of the three brothers, cleverly and rather subtly characterised, of the [governess], and of Inspector Hinton, whose admirable qualities are counteracted by that besetting sin of the man who has made his own way: a jealousy of delegating responsibility.' The reviewer for the *Times Literary Supplement* detected signs that the sardonic Sir Clinton Driffield had begun mellowing with age: 'Those who have never really liked Sir Clinton's perhaps excessively soldierly manner will be surprised to find that he makes his discovery not only by the pure light of intelligence, but partly as a reward for amiability and tact, qualities in which the Inspector [Hinton] was strikingly deficient.' This is true enough, although the classic Sir Clinton emerges a number of times in the novel, as in his subtly sarcastic recurrent backhanded praise of Inspector Hinton: 'He writes a first class report.'

Clinton Driffield returned the next year in the detective novel *In Whose Dim Shadow* (1935), a tale set in a recently erected English suburb, the denizens of which seem to have committed an impressive number of indiscretions, including sexual ones. The intriguing title of the British edition of the novel is drawn from a poem by the British historian Thomas Babington Macaulay: 'Those trees in whose dim shadow/The ghastly priest doth reign/The priest who slew the slayer/And shall himself be slain.' Stewart's puzzle plot in *In Whose Dim Shadow* is well clued and compelling, the kicker of a closing paragraph is a classic of its kind and, additionally, the author paints some excellent character portraits. I fully concur with the *Sunday Times*' assessment of the tale: 'Quiet domestic murder, full of the neatest detective points [. . .] These are not the detective's stock figures, but fully realised human beings.'[7]

Uncharacteristically for Stewart, nearly twenty months elapsed between the publication of *In Whose Dim Shadow* and his next book, *A Minor Operation* (1937). The reason for the author's delay in production was the onset in 1935–36 of the afflictions of cataracts and heart disease (Stewart ultimately succumbed to heart disease in 1947). Despite these grave health complications, Stewart in late 1936 was able to complete *A Minor Operation*, a first-rate Clinton Driffield story of murder and a most baffling disappearance. A *Times Literary Supplement* reviewer found that *A Minor Operation* treated the reader 'to exactly the right mixture of mystification and clue' and that, in addition to its impressive construction, the novel boasted 'character-drawing above the average' for a detective novel.

Alfred Stewart's final eight mysteries, which appeared between 1938 and 1947, the year of the author's death, are, on the whole, a somewhat weaker group of tales than the sixteen that appeared between 1926 and 1937, yet they are not without interest. In 1938 Stewart for the last time managed to publish two detective novels, *Truth Comes Limping* and *For Murder Will Speak* (also published as *Murder Will Speak*). The latter tale is much the superior of the two, having an interesting suburban setting and a bevy of female characters found to have motives when a contemptible philandering businessman meets with foul play. Sexual neurosis plays a major role in *For Murder Will Speak*, the ever-thorough Stewart obviously having made a study of the subject when writing the novel. The somewhat squeamish reviewer for *Scribner's Magazine* considered the subject matter of *For Murder Will Speak* 'rather unsavoury at times', yet this individual conceded that the novel nevertheless made 'first-class reading for those who enjoy a good puzzle intricately worked out'. 'Judge Lynch' in the *Saturday Review* apparently had no such moral reservations about the latest Clinton Driffield murder case, avowing simply of the novel: 'They don't come any better'.

Over the next couple of years Stewart again sent Sir Clinton Driffield temporarily packing, replacing him with a new series detective, a brash radio personality named Mark Brand, in *The Counsellor* (1939) and *The Four Defences* (1940). The better of these two novels is *The Four Defences*, which Stewart based on another notorious British true-crime case, the Alfred Rouse blazing-car murder. (Rouse is believed to have fabricated his death by murdering an unknown man, placing the dead man's body in his car and setting the car on fire, in the hope that the murdered man's body would be taken for his.) Though admittedly a thinly characterised academic exercise in ratiocination, Stewart's *Four Defences* surely is also one of the most complexly plotted Golden Age detective novels and should delight devotees of classical detection. Taking the Rouse blazing-car affair as his theme, Stewart composes from it a stunning set of diabolically ingenious criminal variations. 'This is in the cold-blooded category which [. . .] excites a crossword puzzle kind of interest,' the reviewer for the *Times Literary Supplement* acutely noted of the novel. 'Nothing in the Rouse case would prepare you for these complications upon complications [. . .] What they prove is that Mr Connington has the power of penetrating into the puzzle-corner of the brain. He leaves it dazedly wondering whether in the records of actual crime there can be any dark deed to equal this in its planned convolutions.'

Sir Clinton Driffield returned to action in the remaining four detective novels in the Connington oeuvre, *The Twenty-One Clues* (1941), *No Past is Dead* (1942), *Jack-in-the-Box* (1944) and *Commonsense is All You Need* (1947), all of which were written as Stewart's heart disease steadily worsened and reflect to some extent his diminishing physical and mental energy. Although *The Twenty-One Clues* was inspired by the notorious Hall-Mills double murder case – probably the most publicised murder case in the United States in the 1920s – and the American critic and novelist Anthony Boucher commended *Jack-in-the-Box*, I believe the best of these later mysteries is *No Past Is Dead*, which Stewart partly based on a bizarre French true-crime affair, the 1891 Achet-Lepine murder case.[8] Besides providing an interesting background for the tale, the ailing author managed some virtuoso plot twists, of the sort most associated today with that ingenious Golden Age Queen of Crime, Agatha Christie.

What Stewart with characteristic bluntness referred to as 'my complete crack-up' forced his retirement from Queen's University in 1944. 'I am afraid,' Stewart wrote a friend, the chemist and forensic scientist F. Gerald Tryhorn, in August 1946, eleven months before his death, 'that I shall never be much use again. Very stupidly, I tried for a session to combine a full course of lecturing with angina pectoris; and ended up by establishing that the two are immiscible.' He added that since retiring in 1944, he had been physically 'limited to my house, since even a fifty-yard crawl brings on the usual cramps'. Stewart completed his essay collection and a final novel before he died at his study desk in his Belfast home on 1 July 1947, at the age of sixty-six. When death came to the author he was busy at work, writing.

More than six decades after Alfred Walter Stewart's death, his J. J. Connington fiction is again available to a wider audience of classic-mystery fans, rather than strictly limited to a select company of rare-book collectors with deep pockets. This is fitting for an individual who was one of the finest writers of British genre fiction between the two world wars. 'Heaven forfend that you should imagine I take myself for anything out of the common in the tec yarn stuff,' Stewart once self-deprecatingly declared in a letter to Rupert Gould. Yet, as contemporary critics recognised, as a writer of detective and science fiction Stewart indeed was something out of the common. Now more modern readers can find this out for themselves. They have much good sleuthing in store.

1. For more on Street, Crofts and particularly Stewart, see Curtis Evans, *Masters of the 'Humdrum' Mystery: Cecil John Charles Street, Freeman Wills Crofts, Alfred Walter Stewart and the British Detective Novel, 1920–1961* (Jefferson, NC: McFarland, 2012). On the academic career of Alfred Walter Stewart, see his entry in *Oxford Dictionary of National Biography* (London and New York: Oxford University Press, 2004), vol. 52, 627–628.
2. The Gould-Stewart correspondence is discussed in considerable detail in *Masters of the 'Humdrum' Mystery*. For more on the life of the fascinating Rupert Thomas Gould, see Jonathan Betts, *Time Restored: The Harrison Timekeepers and R. T. Gould, the*

Man Who Knew (Almost) Everything (London and New York: Oxford University Press, 2006) and *Longitude,* the 2000 British film adaptation of Dava Sobel's book *Longitude:The True Story of a Lone Genius Who Solved the Greatest Scientific Problem of His Time* (London: Harper Collins, 1995), which details Gould's restoration of the marine chronometers built by in the eighteenth century by the clockmaker John Harrison.

3. Potential purchasers of *Murder in the Maze* should keep in mind that $2 in 1927 is worth over $26 today.

4. In a 1920 article in *The Strand Magazine,* Arthur Conan Doyle endorsed as real prank photographs of purported fairies taken by two English girls in the garden of a house in the village of Cottingley. In the aftermath of the Great War Doyle had become a fervent believer in Spiritualism and other paranormal phenomena. Especially embarrassing to Doyle's admirers today, he also published *The Coming of the Faeries* (1922), wherein he argued that these mystical creatures genuinely existed. 'When the spirits came in, the common sense oozed out,' Stewart once wrote bluntly to his friend Rupert Gould of the creator of Sherlock Holmes. Like Gould, however, Stewart had an intense interest in the subject of the Loch Ness Monster, believing that he, his wife and daughter had sighted a large marine creature of some sort in Loch Ness in 1935. A year earlier Gould had authored *The Loch Ness Monster and Others,* and it was this book that led Stewart, after he made his 'Nessie' sighting, to initiate correspondence with Gould.

5. A tontine is a financial arrangement wherein shareowners in a common fund receive annuities that increase in value with the death of each participant, with the entire amount of the fund going to the last survivor. The impetus that the tontine provided to the deadly creative imaginations of Golden Age mystery writers should be sufficiently obvious.

6. At Ardlamont, a large country estate in Argyll, Cecil Hambrough died from a gunshot wound while hunting. Cecil's tutor, Alfred John Monson, and another man, both of whom were out hunting with Cecil, claimed that Cecil had accidentally shot himself, but Monson was arrested and tried for Cecil's murder. The verdict delivered was 'not proven', but Monson was then – and is today – considered almost certain to have been guilty of the murder. On the Ardlamont case, see William Roughead, *Classic Crimes* (1951; repr., New York: New York Review Books Classics, 2000), 378–464.

7. For the genesis of the title, see Macaulay's 'The Battle of the Lake

Regillus', from his narrative poem collection *Lays of Ancient Rome*. In this poem Macaulay alludes to the ancient cult of Diana Nemorensis, which elevated its priests through trial by combat. Study of the practices of the Diana Nemorensis cult influenced Sir James George Frazer's cultural interpretation of religion in his most renowned work, *The Golden Bough: A Study in Magic and Religion*. As with *Tom Tiddler's Island* and *The Ha-Ha Case* the title *In Whose Dim Shadow* proved too esoteric for Connington's American publishers, Little, Brown and Co., who altered it to the more prosaic *The Tau Cross Mystery*.

8. Stewart analysed the Achet-Lepine case in detail in 'The Mystery of Chantelle', one of the best essays in his 1947 collection *Alias J. J. Connington*.

CHAPTER 1: HELL'S GAPE

WENDOVER received his winnings mechanically, pushed back his chair a few inches, and glanced in turn at the two remaining tables where play was still going on.

Though no bridge-fiend, he liked a good game; and tonight, as he reflected ruefully, the game had not been good. His partner, old Thursford, had let him down badly once or twice. Besides, like everything else, bridge needed a proper environment if the last drop of enjoyment was to be squeezed from it. Wendover's memory conjured up a picture of his smoking-room at Talgarth Grange on a winter's evening: the green table under the cunningly shaded lights; a big fire blazing on the wide hearth; gleams on the old panelling, here and there in the dimness; a glass of decent whiskey to hand; a thread of blue-grey smoke spiralling up from a good cigar at one's elbow; and, for contrast, the rain swishing or pattering on the window-panes behind the heavy curtains. Add three old friends who knew each other's play to a nicety, and the Wendover standard of enjoyable bridge was reached. No fear of being let down by one's partner; no need for angry post-mortems: physical comfort and mental concentration each reinforcing the pleasure of the other.

Of course he could hardly refuse to help Halstead out of his difficulty. This informal bridge-club — two tables — met once a week at Halstead's house; and naturally, when Halstead had a guest, an extra table had to be got together somehow, if the visitor wasn't to be left at a loose end. Wendover was glad enough to lend a hand there. Still, he didn't care much for playing with strangers; and most of the men there that night were hardly even acquaintances of his. Wendover knew his host well enough; but Halstead's friends came from another circle and mainly from a different generation.

He had found himself landed at a table with old Thursford, young Mackworth, and Halstead's guest, Willenhall. Old Thursford had drunk stiff whiskey-and-soda throughout the evening and had grown more and more disagreeable as the alcohol dissolved his thin coating of late-acquired manners. Young Mackworth, whom Wendover hardly knew, turned out to be a talkative player — a type for which Wendover had no love. Willenhall seemed to combine a naturally good card-memory with occasional fits of absent-mindedness, which lent more than a touch of uncertainty to his game. It was the first time that Wendover had come across him, but he had taken a faint liking to this rather shy and gentle-mannered personality. Willenhall's touch of diffidence was a pleasant contrast to old Thursford's whiskey-fed boorishness.

When Wendover, having noted the progress of the games at the other tables, brought his eyes back to his own, he found Willenhall patiently waiting to attract his attention.

"Halstead tells me that you're an authority on the sights worth seeing, round about here, Mr. Wendover; and he advised me to ask you about some of them. That kind of thing interests me . . ."

He paused, as though leaving Wendover to take up the subject. Wendover had no hesitation. Halstead was comparatively a newcomer to the district and took little interest in its antiquities; but Wendover had been born and bred on the ground. Anchored by his small estate, he had been content to devote himself mainly to the good of the countryside, and he prided himself that there was little he did not know about places or people within a radius of thirty miles. He was by no means averse to letting a stranger see that there were things worth a visit in the neighbourhood.

"What's your particular line of interest?" he asked. "Archaeology, geology, the picturesque, or something in the historical line? We ought to be able to find something for you, especially if you don't mind a walk or two off the beaten track."

Willenhall made a gesture of polite deprecation.

"I'm not a specialist in anything, I'm afraid. Just inquisitive, with a liking for seeing what's worth seeing in a district. I carry a kodak round with me and snap anything that takes my fancy. Architecture, natural curiosities, geological features: all that sort of thing's grist to my mill."

Wendover reflected for a moment or two while he searched his memory for curiosities. Old Thursford, obviously bored by the turn of the conversation, poured out another half-glass of whiskey for himself. Mackworth got up and walked over to the next table to watch the play.

"Let's see," Wendover began ruminatively. "If you happen to be up in the Heatingham direction, you'll find the remains of a fair-sized abbey there. You might try your camera on that. One fragment forms the south wall of the present village church. Some other bits of walls and an archway standing by itself are in fair condition. The place was a Benedictine Priory, founded not long after the Conquest, they say; but these remains belong to a transitional style: Norman arcades outside and a

Pointed arcade inside. You'll see when you get there. The key of the place is kept at the shoemaker's shop in the village; you've only got to ask for it and he'll give it to you."

Willenhall took out a pocket-book and jotted down the particulars.

"That's just the kind of thing I'm looking for," he said, gratefully. "Can you think of anything else?"

"Let's see . . . Oh, if you want something to photograph, there's a circle of standing stones out on the Greenthorpe road, on the right-hand side, about a quarter of a mile after you pass the Stag Inn. You can't miss them. They call them the Twelve Apostles, but you needn't hunt for the twelfth; it's gone long ago, before my time."

"Thanks very much. By the way, have you any caves or things of that sort? I have a flash-light apparatus, and I rather like exploring caves, apart from photographing them."

Wendover shook his head discouragingly.

"There used to be one rather good limestone cave: Jack's Hole, they call it. But it's ruined now, unfortunately. A lot of beanfeasters went up there one day — a lot of scum decanted from a motorbus. I suppose it was rainy, or they found time hanging on their hands. Anyhow, they spent the afternoon amusing themselves by shying stones at the stalactites and generally doing as much damage as they could. Wrecked the place, practically, so far as all the finer tracery was concerned. It's hardly the sight it once was."

"I don't think I'd care to see it if it's in that state," Willenhall confessed. "A bit depressing to see damage of that sort, when one thinks of how many centuries it took to build the thing up. I hate vandalism."

4

"So do I," Wendover agreed heartily. "Let's see, what else is there that you'd find worth your while? Oh, yes, if you like natural curiosities you shouldn't miss seeing Hell's Gape. That is, if you don't mind a bit of a walk. It can't be got at by car."

"Hell's Gape?" Willenhall echoed. "That sounds interesting. What is it?"

"Oh, you needn't expect brimstone," Wendover warned him with a smile. "The name sounds suspiciously like one of these local corruptions, the more so since there isn't any picturesque legend tacked on to the thing. Hell's Gape was the original form, I expect. It's a geological curiosity, a big chasm in some volcanic rock. I've never seen anything quite like it, elsewhere. Quite worth seeing. I'd certainly advise you to go and have a look at it."

"Hell's Gape," Willenhall jotted down. "I'll make a point of seeing it. I'm likely to have some time on my hands soon. It seems Halstead will have to leave me to my own devices; he's got some business in hand which has turned up unexpectedly."

Wendover had smiled at some thought which crossed his mind, and he felt it polite to account for his amusement.

"Hell's Gape almost led to ill-feeling in the district, at one time," he explained. "The local Field Club visited it one day, and it led to ructions among them. If it won't bore you, I'll explain the points and you can verify them when you go up to it yourself. It seems that the Gape is at the edge of a terrace of volcanic rock formed by a lava-flow in the old days. Some time or other, a split formed near the edge of the terrace, so that this chasm opened up between the main bulk of the terrace and the outer slice. This is what I mean."

He picked up the pack of cards, and held them upright on the table.

"That represents the original terrace of rock. Now if I let loose the last few cards at one end of the pack, naturally they tend to fall away and come down flat on the table."

He suited the action to the word.

"Obviously, if anything stopped the fall of the cards after they'd begun to tilt away from the main pack, you'd get a chasm on a small scale between them and the main pack."

"Clearly," Willenhall confirmed.

"Well, as I was saying, the local Field Club went up there one day to have a look round. It's a fearsome-looking place. The cleft's about sixty or seventy feet deep if you measure down the north face. Just a sheer cliff from top to bottom on that side. You could flick the ash off your cigar at the top and see it hit the rocks at the foot. The chasm's quite narrow, only fifteen or twenty feet wide at the most; and at one place it narrows to about three feet or so. It's light enough at the one end, but as you go down it and the walls get close together, it grows gloomy. I don't know why, but it always struck me as a disagreeable place on a dull day. Kind of entrance-to-the-dragon's-den look about it, somehow. It's certainly impressive to clamber along some three hundred feet of it and see the strip of sky getting narrower overhead as you go forward."

Wendover paused to light a cigarette.

"The detached bit has been weathered badly in places. The top of it is a series of huge jagged fangs of rock jutting up from the main body of the fragment. Very picturesque. You ought to take a few snapshots of it from various viewpoints. However, I just wanted to give you some notion of it. The President of the Field Club had his ideas about it all cut and dried. By his way of it, the ground under the outer edge of the original terrace had subsided a bit and then, when its support was withdrawn, the rock had cracked under the strain, forming the chasm. And to back that, he pointed out that the indentations on one side of the chasm corresponded with the bosses on the other. He was rather a pompous old bird, and he laid all this off as if it were a bit of divine revelation. It seemed all right, you know. But unfortunately one fellow in the party spotted that the bosses on the slice were higher than the corresponding indentations on the main block, which meant that the slice had been heaved up, somehow, when the chasm was formed, instead of slipping downward. Earthquake shock was his explanation. They began to take sides on the question; and when these scientific fellows get across each other they seem to lose their tempers. Anyhow, they came home in two different parties; and it was a long time before things cooled down. So if you find a third explanation, I hope you won't bruit it abroad and start the whole affair over again."

"I'll certainly pay the place a visit," Willenhall decided. "It must be well worth seeing, from what you say. How do you get to it?"

"Oh, if you let me know when you think of going up, I'll give you directions, so that you'll have them fresh in your mind. There's no use explaining it just now. Let's see if I can think of any other things you ought to see."

Wendover was able to remember a number of other points of interest in the neighbourhood, all of which the visitor noted down on his list. They were interrupted by the stoppage of play at the next table, where an animated post-mortem broke out between two of the players.

Wendover glanced across with a sardonic look on his face.

"It's a curious thing," he commented. "The people who seem keenest on post-mortems as an educational pastime are usually the ones who learn least from them. They seem to do a lot of talking, but mighty little listening. Oh, by the way, Blackburn!"

A middle-aged man at the next table swung round in his chair.

"Yes?"

"Care for a round on Tuesday?"

Blackburn shook his head.

"Sorry. I've got to get across to the Continent. Fix it up later on, perhaps?"

"Going by air, as usual?" Wendover inquired, more from politeness than for information. Blackburn, he knew, had a preference for flying when he had to cross the Channel.

"Yes. I can't stand the sea-passage. I expect to be back again a week today. Book you for a round the day after that, if you like."

Wendover nodded his agreement.

The third table had broken up, and one of the players came over from it. A physiognomist would have detected a faint but unmistakable resemblance between him and the old man sitting at Wendover's table. The short, sturdy figure; the pale-blue eyes, cold and yet watery-looking; the predatory curve of the rather thick nose; the full cheeks and broad jaw; the crop of coarse hair, fair in the one and silver in the other: there the likeness was plain enough. In mouth and figure they differed. Under his heavy moustache, old Thursford's full lips betrayed a decline which had not yet showed itself on his nephew's face; and as he wallowed in his chair he formed a complete contrast to the springy appearance of the younger man. As Harry Thursford came up to Wendover's side, his uncle gave him a glance which showed that he had no high opinion of his nephew.

"Lost much?" he demanded abruptly.

"Three pounds or so," Harry admitted curtly.

He turned slightly away from his uncle, as though to speak to Wendover, but the old man refused to take the hint. Instead, his eyes lighted up angrily. He had reached the quarrelsome stage when every statement is regarded as a covert insult.

"Three pounds or so!" he repeated with drunken contempt. "H'm! it's just as well I made you a partner, if that's the way you play. You youngsters 've no brains. No brains, I say! You've been all cockered up, good money spent on you, livin' on the best and never been up against it. An' you take it all for granted — yes, for granted. And what's it all come from? Just because you'd the luck to be born in the right cradle. Luck, that's all! If you'd been born in the gutter, my lad, you'd ha' stayed there, stayed there all your life, you would. You'd never 've had the guts or the brains to scramble up on to the kerb, even. No, there you'd have stayed, down there in the gutter. That's where you'd have been — in the gutter. So don't you put on airs. You've nothing to put on airs about, nothing! Can't even play cards without losing; and I made £400 on the Exchange this afternoon, just with brains. If you'd been born a little ragged boy in the gutter, you wouldn't be making £400 in an afternoon. You'd be on the dole, my lad, like a lot of other skrimshankers. On the dole, you'd be, and glad to draw it at the bureau, too. There was no dole in my day, I can tell you. In my day, if you hadn't brains you just starved. That's what you'd have been — a ragamuffin in the gutter. You ought to be damned grateful, *damned* grateful, for all that Providence did for you. You didn't do much for yourself, let me tell *you*."

He stared with tipsy malignity at the younger man and seemed on the verge of adding further insults. Apparently he thought better of it, however; for instead, he picked up his tumbler and drank clumsily. Willenhall, obviously uncomfortable, fiddled with his pencil and made some pretence of being engrossed in his pocketbook entries. Wendover, with a blank expression, ignored the whole affair. Harry Thursford made no reply to the tirade, though the muscles of his jaw obviously tightened under the skin. It seemed clear to Wendover that scenes of this sort must be common enough between the two men in private. Harry's expression suggested that he was inured to his uncle's peculiar manners.

Fortunately there came a diversion. In ordinary circumstances, Mackworth's company was not altogether welcomed except by those who shared the same hobby. In his private life, his primary interest was wireless; and it was impossible to be in his presence for five minutes without learning that fact in the plainest possible manner. Even in that short time he generally managed to make clear that only one side of broadcasting had any attraction for him. He belonged, in fact, to the group of humanity designated as "dial-twisters," "station-hunters" and "DX-hounds." Programmes, as such, had only the slightest interest for him; in fact, there was no record of his ever having listened to one for an hour on end. What he sought in wireless was the joy of reaching out over the world for a signal. A fragment from a politician's speech, the weather report from Stockholm, jazz from Poland, a bar or two from an opera in Rome, a few words of a Berlin talk, or the midnight chimes from

Copenhagen: they all had exactly the same value to Mackworth. They indicated simply that he had "got the station"; and there his interest in them ceased.

In itself, this craze of his would have been harmless; but he was possessed by all the propagandist zeal of a Hot-Gospeller where his hobby was concerned. "What! Not got a wireless set? You don't know what you're missing. Come up some night and hear mine." Wendover, out of kindliness, had once been seduced into accepting this invitation; and he looked back on the evening with a shudder, even after the lapse of years.

Mackworth's conversation had been memorable. "This is Toulouse. . . . Sounds like an accordion solo. . . . These three strokes on the gong are the interval signal, you know. . . . Now he's bawling out advertisements. No good listening to that, is there? We'll try somewhere else. . . . That's the Berlin metronome you hear now. A bit dull, what? We'd better try elsewhere. . . . Vienna, now. Sounds like somebody with a bad cold giving a talk on something or other. No, I don't understand German. You'll find what it's all about if you look up the programme in *World-Radio;* it's lying on the floor beside your chair. . . . Here's Milan coming in well: sounds like opera or something. I'm not very keen on that sort of stuff; are you? . . . We'd better hunt somewhere else. . . . Ah! hear that chime? Pretty, isn't it? That's the interval signal from Budapest. Just wait a jiffy and you'll hear the announcer saying 'Rah-dio *Budapest!'* One learns a lot from wireless; I used to call it Buda*pest* before. That fellow's got one of the clearest voices on the ether. . . . And now, while we're up at this end of the scale, we'd better have a dash at letting you hear the Ljubljana cuckoo. . . . H'm! Pity! No good tonight, I'm afraid. Where's Ljubljana? Somewhere in the Balkans — Yugoslavia, if that helps. . . . And now we'll switch over on to the long waves and try for a couple of Russian stations, just to let you hear what the set can do in that direction."

It had strained Wendover's politeness to its limits to sit through the remainder of the evening; and since then he had evaded Mackworth whenever he could manage to do so. Tonight, however, on seeing him approach their group, he was almost prepared to hail him with joy as a possible saviour of an awkward situation.

The unconscious rescuer played his rôle well. Coming up to the table, he tapped young Thursford on the shoulder.

"How's your wireless doing, these days, Harry?" he demanded, his face lighting up as he saw the chance of airing his hobby after the enforced abstention while play was going on.

"Oh, so-so," Harry answered, with a wary glance towards his uncle. "I picked up St. Louis last night on 275 metres. Got KDKA, too, in a storm of atmospherics. Heard the announcer all right, though, at one stage."

Mackworth's white teeth showed in a smile of mock-pity.

"No good trying for America on the medium waves nowadays. It's a pure waste of time. What you want, Harry, is a short-wave set. It brings in the stuff as clear as a bell. Look here! Last night I got W9XF, W3XAL, W8XK, W2XAF, and W2XAD. Hardly any fading at all."

"Change from the last time I sat up to listen to your set, then. Nothing *but* fading, that shot."

"I can't help it, if you're a Jonah," Mackworth protested. "I got the whole of that lot on the loudspeaker, anyhow. Buenos Aires, too, very clear indeed. And I've struck something worth hearing on the twenty metre band: two amateurs using C.W. One's in Macao; t'other's in Guam. A bit of a thrill to pick *them* up."

Harry Thursford nodded his agreement. This last item seemed to have stirred his curiosity.

"All right! I'll drop in, one of these nights, and give your set another chance. Fix up the date later on. I'm a bit busy just now."

He took the opportunity to edge out of the group, lest his uncle should be moved to a fresh denunciation. Mackworth, in search of new converts, turned to the tall stranger at his elbow.

"Are you keen on wireless?" he demanded.

Willenhall shook his head.

"Not a bit, I'm afraid," he confessed, politely. "I haven't even a crystal set."

"You miss a lot," Mackworth said, in genuine commiseration. "You ought to take it up. Don't judge it from listening to other people's sets. I know I wasn't keen on the thing until I got a set of my own. Still, if you'd care to listen to mine . . . any night you like?"

Willenhall's cautiously vague reply committed him to nothing.

CHAPTER II: THE SYNDICATE

"Going, are you, Mackworth?" the host demanded, as the wireless fanatic wished him goodnight. "Stop a minute or two, will you? Care to take a ticket in a raffle?"

Mackworth shook his head.

"Can't stop," he explained. "There's something on in Schenectady this evening that I want to hear."

"You don't mean to pretend you're going to listen to a bit of the programme?" Halstead demanded. "That won't wash, you know. We know your habits."

Mackworth fidgeted and consulted his watch.

"I can't stay, really, Halstead. America's coming over extra well this evening. I picked up a station or two before I came here. I really must go."

"Oh, all right, then."

When Mackworth had gone, Halstead turned to the remainder of his guests.

"Here's a sporting proposition," he said, raising his voice so as to attract the attention of everyone in the room. "Blackburn tells me he's got some tickets for the big Sweep and he's willing to let some of you in, if you like. Anybody care to subscribe? They're ten-shilling tickets, you know."

With a gesture, Blackburn stopped his host and took the explanation on his own shoulders.

"The fact is: I've got a few more tickets than I actually want for myself. What I thought was: Why not form a small syndicate? Let someone else into the thing. Naturally, I want to stand in myself. Say nine tickets among the lot of us. If one of the nine tickets wins, we divide in equal shares. That seems fairer than selling a separate ticket to each man, doesn't it?"

He exhibited a small book of tickets as he spoke. Wendover, out of curiosity, reached over and secured it.

"As a magistrate, I suppose I ought to confiscate these things," he pointed out with a twinkle in his eye. "Strictly illegal, if I'm not mistaken. How did you manage to import them into this innocent country? I had an impression that the Customs officials were questioning everybody on landing here, and confiscating any tickets they could find in the luggage."

"They didn't confiscate these," Blackburn pointed out. "I'm not going to explain how I got them. And if your conscience is stirring, perhaps I'd better have . . ."

He held out his hand for the tickets, but Wendover stepped back slightly out of reach and waved him aside.

"I've never seen one of these things before. Don't be afraid, Blackburn; I just want a glance at them."

He flipped the booklet open and began to read fragments from the wording on the green tickets inside.

" 'THE DERBY, to be run at Epsom Downs,' and so forth. . . . 'For prizes, see reverse.' . . . 'To be drawn in public under the supervision of General Somebody-or-other . . . on May 30th.' . . . Ah! Observe this caution. 'Subscribe only through a Business House, Bank, Friend, or Trusted Acquaintance whose address and credentials are known to you.' Where are your credentials, Blackburn? . . . 'Ticket participates in Draw only when Counterfoil received with Remittance.' . . . A neat combination of soldierly brevity and commercial caution, that . . . And now what about the other side?"

He turned over the leaf and continued.

"I see they've gone back to the big-prize system again, this time. . . . 'After deduction of audited expenses, as sanctioned under the Act, 75% of the money received from the sale of tickets, calculated under the Act, will be distributed as Prizes. The balance, 25%, will be paid to the Hospitals.' . . . That ought to be a tidy sum of money?"

Blackburn nodded.

"There's a big rush at the last moment, usually," he said. "The latest estimates put the total cash from ticket sales at well over £2,000,000. That means a million and a half in the Prize Fund, roughly."

"Phew!" Wendover ejaculated. "That'll be a nice nest-egg. Now let's see. The drawer of the winning horse gets 30% of the prize-money; the second horse's ticket takes 15%; and the third horse brings in 7½%. Why, on that basis, the fellow who draws the winner will scoop in something like half-a-million sterling! For the second horse, it's a quarter of a million; and even a ticket for the third horse would be worth over £100,000."

He ran his eye down the provisions on the back of the ticket.

" 'Drawers of all other horses not declared forfeit for on or before the Tuesday of the week before the Race divide . . .' "

"It works out somewhere round about £2000. Perhaps a bit under that figure, for each horse drawn," Blackburn volunteered. "Besides that, there are three hundred and sixty cash prizes in the Draw, each worth about £1500 or so."

"And then there's your little commission for peddling

the tickets," Wendover pointed out slyly. "I see it mentioned here. What does it mean to you if you happen to sell a ticket for a horse that gets placed?"

"A thousand."

"No wonder you've turned ticket-smuggler at that rate," Wendover commented. "Now let's see some more. Ah! 'In any event the sum of £25,000 is guaranteed as a minimum, and has been deposited at the Bank of . . . and so forth . . . in the names of the Trustees.' Considering the way money poured in for the earlier Sweeps, that's a very safe offer. H'm! Here's something else. . . . 'Prizewinners are the persons named on the Counterfoils drawn. Should the Race not take place, the Prize-Money (less the Cash Prizes) will be divided equally amongst the drawers of horses; the Cash Prizes will be distributed as drawn.' That seems fair enough. Then there's a warning. 'Prizes unclaimed within six months will become forfeit to the Hospitals.' And, finally, 'Acknowledgments of subscriptions will be sent to sellers for issue to Subscribers. Subscribers should notify Hospitals Committee direct of failure to receive acknowledgment. Draw lists will be posted to "Sellers" abroad and Particulars issued to the Press of all countries.' By Jove, they must have a big staff to tackle that part of the thing."

Wendover handed the book of tickets back to Blackburn.

"Well, I don't mind standing in with the rest, if you're in earnest about it."

"I'm a bit surprised at you," said a nervous, disapproving voice from the group. "I don't think a Justice of the Peace should lend his countenance to a thing that's known to be illegal — like this."

Wendover's eyebrows lifted a trifle. He knew his critic

only slightly, and he resented the implied aspersion on his conduct.

"What's the harm, Mr. Kirkham?" he asked in a lazy tone. "I've taken a ticket in the Derby Sweepstake at one of my clubs every year since I was elected. Nobody ever suggested that there was anything wrong with that. The police never troubled us in the matter, nor do they interfere with the other half-million Derby Sweeps that are run every year. I don't see any moral difference between my club sweep and this one, except that in this case part of the money goes to hospitals. The fact that the prizes are bigger in this one has nothing to do with the case on the moral side, surely."

"Lotteries are illegal," snapped Kirkham.

"So are games of chance," Wendover pointed out. "I saw you get a grand slam tonight, which meant that you made a few pence on the game. It was pure chance that the deal gave you anything higher than a six in your hand; and then no play on earth would have let you make your grand slam. On that basis, bridge is a game of chance like any other, and yet you're quite content to collect your winnings at the end of it. These distinctions are a bit too fine for me."

"There's no resemblance between these cases," Kirkham objected angrily.

Wendover refused to argue further. Instead, he turned to Blackburn as though tacitly inviting him to go on with his proposals.

"Well, apparently Mr. Kirkham doesn't want to join," Blackburn acknowledged suavely. "Anyone else care to take a hand?"

"I'm going to join," old Peter Thursford broke in, with a glance of vinous contempt in Kirkham's direction. "I'm not one of your mealy-mouthed lot. I've done

a bit of gambling myself, in my day; and I never thought
the worse of myself for doing it. No, never a bit the
worse, and you can take my word for it. What's wrong
with gambling, if the stakes are on the table, eh? What's
wrong with it? A lot of old wives' chatter, all this sort of
talk. D'you think you're a better man nor me? Eh? Do
you? You don't? Then what're you setting up as a judge
for? What right 've you to go putting on airs, eh? That's
what I ask. That's a plain question, isn't it? What 've
you ever done that gives you the right to be superior,
eh? Just tell us that, will you?"

He applied himself to his tumbler again. Kirkham
had nothing of the stuff of martyrs in his composition.
It was one thing to register what he thought was a gentle-
manly protest. It was quite another affair to be involved
in an argument with a tipsy man. With a glance at his
host, he seized the opportunity to retreat from the room
while Peter Thursford was busy with his whiskey.

Blackburn glanced round the remainder of the party.
Harry Thursford caught his eye.

"I don't mind, if you want a Jonah in your syndicate.
I've never drawn a winning ticket yet, in anything."

"Right. You, Checkley?"

Wendover studied the avaricious mouth of Checkley
with a certain sardonic interest. Quite plainly it dis-
played the mental conflict in Checkley's mind. A ten
bob sprat might catch a fortune; but then ten bob was
ten bob. Was it worth it? Wendover had no more than
a nodding acquaintance with Checkley, but the man's
reputation for meanness was common property. A second
or two passed. Would he risk it?

"How much does each of us stand to win if we draw
the winner?" Checkley demanded doubtfully, as though
to gain further time to make up his mind.

"About £50,000 apiece if we all go in," Blackburn drawled, with slow emphasis upon the figures. Evidently he also was amused by the internal struggle.

The concrete statement seemed to tip the scale in Checkley's mind.

"All right, then. I don't mind risking ten bob."

Blackburn nodded and turned to a young man whose rather apathetic air was belied by the alertness of his eyes.

"You, Coniston?"

"Oh, count me in, certainly."

"Halstead, what about you?"

Halstead shook his head.

"No. I've sworn off all that sort of thing years ago. No moral scruples in the matter; but I've grown sick of holding dud tickets. My sanguine soul always counted on winning something, and the bump of the disappointment rankled a bit, if you see what I mean. One gets tired of seeing dreams go west, even if they're only little ones."

"Count you out, then."

Blackburn ran his eyes over the group, singling out those who had not yet spoken. His glance rested on two hot brown eyes under a shock of dark red hair.

"You, Falgate?"

"Oh, all right," Falgate agreed morosely. "It seems a pity to stand out."

"Mr. Willenhall, would you care to take a share?"

Willenhall blinked, as though he had not expected to be invited and had been taken by surprise at the request.

"Certainly, if you wish it," he answered in a tone which only his politeness saved from being one of complete indifference.

"That leaves you, Redhill," Blackburn pointed out.

Tommie Redhill was young Thursford's closest friend.

"Oh, count me in," he agreed at once. "If Harry scooped the pool and I were left out in the cold, things would never be the same. He'd suspect me all the time of wanting to borrow a fiver."

Blackburn had jotted down each name as it came in; and he now took the precaution of reading over the list: —

"Wendover, two Thursfords, Checkley, Coniston, Falgate, Mr. Willenhall, Redhill — and myself, of course. That makes a syndicate of nine. You won't join, Halstead? Ten of us would make evener figures Save calculation, if we happen to win. No?"

Halstead shook his head with a smile.

"No, I'm done with sweepstakes, really."

"Very good, then. We ought to have some sort of agreement, I think. Only businesslike to put it in writing now."

He went across to a table, tore a couple of sheets from a marker, and found the backs blank.

"This will serve. Now how about the wording? How would this do? 'The undersigned agree that the Derby Sweepstake tickets numbered G/B:B.8811 to G/B: B.8819 inclusive are to be held jointly by them and that any Prize won by any one or more of these tickets shall be equally divided among the holders when the prize-money is distributed. Counterfoils are to be filled in in the name of . . .' There are nine of us: call it the Novem Syndicate? That's not likely to be duplicated by anyone else."

"As well that as anything else," Wendover acquiesced. "It doesn't much matter what you call it, since we're not likely to win anything."

"That's agreed then?" Blackburn inquired. And as no one dissented he continued his draft. " 'In the name of the Novem Syndicate.' That's that. Now I'll read it over again. If no one objects then, it stands."

He repeated the phraseology hurriedly, but nobody seemed to find anything in the wording to criticise. Then Blackburn again bent over the table and made a fair copy of the document in his precise handwriting.

"I suggest we sign both copies. One of them can be kept by a member of the Syndicate. I propose Mr. Wendover. He's the only one of us who's a J.P. so that makes the selection easy — and appropriate, since we can all shelter behind him if the Law gets busy. The second copy I'll hand to Halstead to put in his safe. He's a disinterested party — a sort of stakeholder for us. Are we agreed?"

"That seems fair enough," Jack Coniston confirmed. "A lot of fuss about nothing, though, it seems to me. We're not likely to catch much."

He took out a pen and signed each of the documents. The rest of the new Syndicate followed in turn. When all had signed, Blackburn handed one copy to Halstead and passed the other to Wendover, who placed it in his pocket.

Willenhall had watched the proceedings with an expression which blended detachment and curiosity. It seemed as though he had been speculating on some question or other; and when he broke the silence in a faintly diffident tone, the trend of his reflections betrayed itself.

"So if one of our tickets wins the first prize, we shall get about £50,000 each. It sounds a big sum." He swung round to Checkley. "Er . . . Mr. Checkley, what would fifty thousand pounds mean to you, if you don't mind my putting the question?"

Checkley, taken aback by the sudden inquiry, stared resentfully at his interlocutor almost as though Willenhall had been trying to borrow money.

"What does it mean to me? It means £50,000, of course. What else would it mean?"

"Exactly," Willenhall confirmed in his gentle voice. "What else would it mean? You won't spend your money before you get it, evidently, Mr. Checkley, even in imagination."

A rather wistful smile took away any possible offence from his remark.

"And you, Mr. Coniston, what would £50,000 mean to you, if we happened to win?"

"I could buy a racing car I've had my eye on," Coniston answered with a grin which showed that he took no umbrage at the question. "Or go in for aeroplaning on my own, instead of having to hire a bus at so much a hop. Run round a bit. Give the girls a treat. It wouldn't run the length of a floating palace with copper funnels, but one might manage to pick up something more moderate in the yacht line. I'd have a good time and I expect some other people would have a good time as well, at my expense."

Willenhall nodded reflectively, as though he were weighing up the value of Jack Coniston's ideas. He turned to Peter Thursford.

"And you, Mr. Thursford? What does £50,000 suggest to you, if you don't mind telling us?"

Rather unexpectedly, old Peter seemed pleased at being questioned. He hitched himself forward heavily in his chair and tapped the table to emphasise his opinion.

"What does £50,000 mean to me, eh? What does it

mean to me? Well, some old fellow or other — you'll remember his name, maybe; it's slipped my memory — anyhow, he used to crack up Wine, Woman, and Song. Huh! Song? He can keep his songs — a lot o' ruddy caterwauling, songs are. Wine? Whiskey's good enough for me; it's all a man wants. But women? He was right there; he was dead right. £50,000 would buy a lot o' those goods. Lot o' bluff to be had for £50,000, I can tell you. But you want to be careful. Some o' your money buys women — and when you've bought 'em, they spend the rest of your money for you, if they get the chance. That's how it goes, unless you keep a tight hand on 'em. Well, no woman ever got the better o' me; you can kiss the Book on that!"

His last sentence seemed to recall something which set him wheezing and chuckling in his chair.

Willenhall gave him no chance to expatiate further. His glance caught young Redhill, who was examining old Thursford with an amused curiosity not untinged with contempt. As Willenhall's gaze fell on him, Redhill looked up.

"You want my pipe-dream to add to the bunch?" he said in an indifferent tone, returning Willenhall's glance with expressionless eyes. "Wasn't it Rockefeller who said that a poor man with only $100,000 needn't despair of making money if he gave his mind to it — or words more or less to that effect? So I suppose even a poor man with only £50,000 might make something out of it, either in politics or the financial side, if he set about things properly. It might be interesting, in some ways. I've often wondered what it feels like to be a big pot."

Wendover began to feel his liking for Willenhall fading bit by bit as this catechising went on. It dawned on him that probably the man collected psychological data in the same spirit as he took snapshots of out-of-the-way objects on the countryside. He hankered after curiosities of the mind, perhaps, as well as after gazing-stocks in the physical world. By Wendover's rather simple code, this probing and questioning seemed to go more than a little over the bounds of good taste. That sort of thing might be all right in some circumstances; but for a stranger to do it . . . Unconsciously, Wendover shook his head. Not the sort of thing he'd have thought of doing.

As Redhill finished his impersonally-worded contribution, Falgate's eyes turned to Willenhall with an expression in which a tinge of hostility seemed to lurk.

"Me?" he said, without waiting to be asked. "I'm not strong on pipe-dreams. But if £50,000 comes my way, it'll be useful enough to . . . extend my business a bit."

The almost imperceptible halt in the last sentence was enough to catch Wendover's attention. He had heard rumours. It was not for extension that Falgate needed the money. It was to shore up a business already tottering under the strain of the trade slump. And there was more behind it than that, if all tales were true. Falgate was an impulsive devil, always ready to take the quick way out. A sinking business coupled with heavy and injudicious speculations may land a man in Queer Street. £50,000 would come very handily to Falgate at this moment. He had almost blurted that out in so many words, and had just managed to change the meaning at the last moment. That was a fair index of how near the surface it lay in his thoughts.

And Falgate seemed to have other troubles on his shoulders — the kind that even £50,000 can't cure. That Langdale girl . . . Wendover almost shook his head again. He preferred not to poke his nose into things which weren't his affair; and the business of Viola Langdale was one which he had left alone, except for stray talk which he could not help hearing. But Falgate's views on Viola's engagement to Harry Thursford would perhaps have given Willenhall some extra curiosities of psychology to add to his collection, if he could have got them.

Willenhall's eye travelled round the group until it lighted on the seller of the tickets. Blackburn shrugged his shoulders at the mute interrogation.

"I've only one pipe-dream. I'm not so keen as I was. I'd be glad to drop out of the race: settle down. If one had £50,000, the tax collector could singe one's feathers pretty deep without hurting the skin. That's how I look at it."

Willenhall's nod suggested that he sympathised with this view more than with the others.

"And you?" he asked, turning to Harry Thursford.

"What would I want if I had £50,000?" Harry speculated, with a grin which showed perfect teeth. "Why, more, of course. Nobody's ever content with what they have; and I don't suppose I'd be different from the rest."

"That's common sense, anyhow," Checkley broke in.

He had been listening with scarcely-veiled contempt to the various opinions he had heard, and now his thin-lipped mouth curved in a faint grimace of derision.

"You've all been talking as if £50,000 capital meant an Arabian Nights' dream. When you take off the taxation, it comes to an income well under £2,000 a year. That's all. Of course you'd want more if you could get it."

Something in the tone annoyed Wendover.

"Why?" he demanded.

Checkley was taken completely aback.

"Do you mean to say you wouldn't want more?" he asked, not taking the trouble to conceal his scepticism.

"What would I get out of it?" Wendover retorted. "As I am at present, I have the things that suit me. I smoke the tobacco I like. I wouldn't change for a more expensive brand simply because I had a bigger income. Why should I? And other things are much the same. I've no wish to alter my scale. It suits me. I'd have more money to give away, if I wanted to. That's the only difference, so far as I can see. Nothing to get excited about, surely."

"We haven't all got your income," Checkley rejoined rudely.

"That doesn't alter the fact that your generalisation isn't sound," Wendover answered, placidly.

"Then why do you take a ticket?" Checkley persisted.

"Why do I take a ticket in my club sweep? Because it gives me some slight amusement. It's always interesting to see if one draws a horse or a blank. One doesn't expect to win. Nobody would be more surprised than I, if I did win. It might even be embarrassing, from my point of view, if all one hears is true about these things."

"Anybody's welcome to embarrass me on these terms," Checkley scoffed. "There's a lot of embarrassment in £50,000, isn't there?"

Wendover was saved from a reply. The door opened; a fair-haired girl in an opera-cloak came in. For a moment she seemed dazzled by the lights; then, after a rather cavalier greeting to her host, she turned to her brother.

"I dropped in to pick you up, Harry, in case you hadn't got the two-seater tinkered up."

Wendover noticed her cool scrutiny of her uncle. It seemed as though she were gauging his condition. Obviously she was used to seeing him in his present state and was merely calculating how much trouble he might give before they got him away.

"It was only a sooted plug, just as I told you," Harry Thursford explained. "I knew it would be all right."

"Well, if it's here, that simplifies things. I've got Viola and Di in the car outside, and it was going to be a bit awkward. You can take Viola to her hutch in the two-seater."

Then Wendover heard her add in an undertone:

"What's he like tonight? Di can sit beside me in front; and we'll shove him in by himself at the back. That'll be O.K."

"You'd better manage him," Harry suggested in the same tone. "He's got across me tonight. He's at the 'little ragged boy' stage."

It seemed a known index, for Enid Thursford's brows knitted at the sound of it.

"As bad as that? Oh, well, Di can sit beside me, in case he's in one of his enterprising moods. I do get sick of him."

She turned to old Thursford, and raised her voice.

"Come along, Uncle. I've got Diana and Viola out in the car. Don't keep them waiting."

At the sound of the girls' names, Peter Thursford's watery eyes brightened. He hoisted himself laboriously from his chair.

"Quite right. Mustn't keep 'em waiting. Nice girls."

He walked off, heavily but quite steadily, towards the cloak-room. His example gave the impetus to a break-up of the party. Wendover, as he moved off with the rest, could not help reflecting on the kind of life Enid Thursford must lead under the roof of her uncle. He liked to think the best of people; but old Thursford seemed to have no redeeming points. No wonder a decent girl was sickened by him. And even a decent girl was bound to be coarsened by continual contact with him. Wendover thought of the cynical way Enid had reviewed things and the crudeness of the bait she had flung out on the spur of the moment in order to get the old man off the premises without argument. A rum view of life a sensitive girl would pick up in that environment. And it wasn't likely she would remain sensitive for long. There was no escape for her, except at the cost of giving up the things which a young girl naturally wanted. Enid Thursford had no money. Evidently she preferred to hold on to what she had, even if she had to pay for it by living in her uncle's house.

CHAPTER III: TICKET NUMBER G/B:B.8816

WITH an income more than sufficient for his simple tastes, no profession to occupy him, and an easy-going temperament, Wendover's chief temptation was to idle away his time. It was so fatally easy to spend the day pottering about with trivial affairs and to end up in the evening with nothing definite to show for the wasted hours. He was shrewd enough to recognise that this sort of life, pleasant as it was, would lead him in the end to mere boredom. The best safeguard against that was to institute a definite routine which would keep him up to the mark. His natural tendency towards order and tidiness, both mental and physical, helped to ease the pressure of his self-imposed system. He never became a slave to his time-table, but he came to a stage when the recurring things of the day were always taken in a certain order.

When breakfasting alone, he made it a rule to read his letters first, and then turn to his newspaper. A friend, obviously, was of more importance than the Dalai Lama or the affairs of Mozambique. This morning he picked up the pile of letters and turned over the envelopes incuriously until the glimpse of a characteristic handwriting caught his attention.

Sir Clinton Driffield, Chief Constable of the County, was one of Wendover's most valued friends. They met infrequently. Their correspondence was spasmodic. But they had the knack of taking up the thread of intimacy instantaneously, even after the lapse of months. Wendover enjoyed the semi-sardonic tinge of Sir Clinton's talk; he liked that half-ironic nickname "Squire" which only the Chief Constable used; he sympathised with Driffield's preference for realities as against the desk-work which bulked so large in his official duties.

Another interest drew them together. Wendover had a fancy for criminology, and more than once he had played the part of a not inefficient Watson in cases which had cropped up. Sir Clinton held the view that in the catching of criminals, it should be a case of "All hands to the pumps." He was quite ready to sink the Chief Constableship and give practical assistance to any subordinate who might be in difficulties with a case. But it was characteristic that few hints of these activities filtered out to the public. If the criminal was captured, the subordinate got the credit.

Wendover tore open his letter and, as he read it, his face betrayed his unexpected pleasure. Like all Sir Clinton's communications, it was laconic.

Dear Squire,

If I can get off for a week-end soon, could you put me up? Fresh air and some exercise are my simple needs. If you can take me in, I'll let you know the precise date as soon as I can arrange it.

C. D.

"If he says a week-end, he means a week-end," Wendover reflected. "Pity he can't stay longer. Still, it's better than nothing."

He skimmed through the remainder of his letters without finding much to interest him. Then, propping his *Times* in front of him, he began his breakfast.

It was Wendover's belief that *The Times* was an infallible touchstone in a world of quack educational ideas. If a man had enough knowledge of the world to read through a single copy of the paper and understand all that he read, then — by Wendover's standards — that man belonged to the educated class. If he failed to pass this test, even though he were crammed to the back-teeth with classics or science, he was no better than a barbarian living amid a civilisation which he could not appreciate.

Naturally, with these views, Wendover took his daily dose of *The Times* seriously. His practice was to turn first to the middle page for the latest news; and then, starting afresh at the racing and cricket intelligence, work his way step by step through the remainder of the paper until he ended up with the financial columns at the back.

On this particular morning, his attention was arrested on page 8. By this time, his personal interest in the Sweepstake had almost passed out of his mind; and it was the heavy type "RESULT OF THE DRAW" which took his eye to the three closely-printed columns. "PRIZE FUND OF £1,451,830," he read, though without any eagerness. He was familiar with the rationale of the Draws, and merely glanced rapidly down the descriptive section to see if anything out of the common had occurred. Evidently it had all been stage-managed as usual: the procession of nurses, the sacks of counterfoils, the big drum into which they were tipped, the glass cylinder with the names of horses, the loudspeakers to broadcast the chairman's address, the General supervising the draw.

Wendover's eye travelled down to the auditor's report:—

Total money subscribed	£2,070,515
Prize fund	£1,451,520
Drawer of winning horse	483,840
Drawer of second horse	241,920
Drawer of third horse	120,960
Seventy-nine other horses, starters and nonstarters, each	1,839

The hospitals, he discovered, would net just above half-a-million sterling from the Draw. H'm! At least that money would be well spent. But what about the winner of the first prize? If that went to some poverty-stricken wretch, as it might easily do, the chances were that it would drive him clean off his rocker.

He glanced at the next heading: "DRAWERS OF FANCIED HORSES" and immediately below it his eye caught the name: "Novem Syndicate" in the body of the paragraph. Almost incredulously he read the news that the Syndicate had drawn Barralong.

With a lifetime's experience of blanks drawn in other sweeps, Wendover's first thought was that a mistake had been made. He could hardly persuade himself that for once he had been lucky. Sweeps, as he knew them, were all of the one pattern: you took a ticket, and some-one else got the money. It seemed a reversal of the normal order that he should actually have drawn a horse. These things didn't happen in real life. He picked out the item in the actual list of the Draw. There it was, beyond dispute. "BARRALONG.—Novem Syndicate. (G/B:B. 8816)." When he had convinced himself that there was no error, his first sensation was one of pure astonishment and it was not till much later that he gave any thought to the financial aspect of the affair.

Barralong, he remembered, was priced at 7 to 1.

Aswail, the favourite, stood at 2 to 1; and there was Netsuke at 11 to 2 as well as one or two others more fancied than Barralong. If he had been betting on the Derby himself, Barralong wasn't the horse that would have carried his money.

Still faintly incredulous, he turned back to the list of the Draw, and felt slightly relieved that no address had been put on the counterfoil. Blackburn had shown good sense there.

"But I expect somebody will ferret it out," he reflected with distaste. "It's not the sort of publicity I'm keen on, I must say."

It was all very well to have one's private satisfaction over drawing a horse for once in one's life; but to have one's name blazoned in the newspapers as a member of the Syndicate, to have reporters on the doorstep, inquiring about one's sensations, and to be deluged with begging-letters . . . Wendover, now that the first flush was over, began to regret a success which might prove to be a source of irritation.

He dismissed the whole affair from his mind without much effort and went on with his leisurely breakfast. After he had left the table, a cigarette helped him through the remainder of *The Times;* and then he was free for the next items of his routine: his meagre business correspondence and some odds and ends connected with the working of his estate. When these had been dealt with, he had the best part of the morning still before him.

As he put away the last paper, he glanced out of the window. Sunshine and high-sailing clouds suggested that he had spent enough time indoors; and, casting round for something to do, he bethought himself of Sir Clinton's letter. Why not stroll down to the post-office and send a wire, instead of writing a note? There was really no urgency, but he wanted some objective in his walk, and that would serve as well as another.

He had hardly got beyond his lodge gates and onto the high road when a car slid up behind him and stopped at his side. Falgate's over-tired eyes and drawn features appeared at the open window of the driving-seat.

"Seen the result of the Draw, Wendover? It seems we've drawn Barralong."

"So I gather," Wendover answered, trying to manifest more interest than he really felt.

Evidently there was going to be no escape from discussing this infernal Syndicate's affairs from now on until the race was run. His gardener had offered congratulations when he passed him on the drive, and now here it was again.

"I don't fancy Barralong much," Falgate went on in an aggrieved tone. "My money's on White Starlight. I suppose all we'll see will be the £1800 for drawing a horse at all. That's not much help when it's split up among nine of us. Two hundred per skull."

"The big figures are giving you an inflated notion about money," Wendover suggested with a smile. "Look at it this way. If you'd put your ten bob on Barralong, and *if* Barralong had won, you'd have got about seventy shillings at the present price. Now you get £200 for your ten bob, win or lose. I see nothing to complain about."

"A fat lot of good £200 is," Falgate said, rudely.

"Two hundred pounds is £200, as your friend Checkley would say," Wendover pointed out philosophically.

He disliked this cavilling at what was, after all, a gift from the gods. But a glance at Falgate's face brought him round into a less unsympathetic mood. The man looked worried to death. That hint about having backed White Starlight suggested possibilities in the background. It might mean nothing much. On the other hand, suppose that Falgate, finding his business foundering under him, had taken to the Turf in the hope of recouping himself by heavy betting? Then, if White Starlight didn't crawl home . . . A man doesn't sneer at a windfall of £200 if he has plenty of money. In that case, £200 means very little, one way or the other. But Falgate, if rumours were true, hadn't plenty of money. He needed cash. And if he sneered at £200, then evidently £200 was a drop in the bucket compared with his needs.

Falgate hesitated, as though he had something more to say. Then, apparently he changed his mind, for with a curt nod he let in his clutch and the car slid away. Wendover, with a faint shrug at his own imaginings, walked on to the post-office.

Here again he had to listen to talk about the Draw. The brisk old lady behind the counter was something of a favourite of his, and her rejoicings over his luck were obviously genuine, without the faintest tinge of jealousy. That someone in the neighbourhood had been successful appeared to be quite enough for her; and the fact that her own ticket had got nothing did not seem to worry her. And yet, as Wendover reflected, £200 would have meant a good deal more to her than it apparently did to Falgate.

As he was filling in his telegram form, the door opened and a dark-haired girl in a leather jacket and golfing skirt came in. She nodded to the postmistress and then, catching sight of Wendover, she turned to him with a smile.

"I see your Syndicate's drawn Barralong, Mr. Wendover. I expect you're being snowed under with congratulations. I'd like to add mine to the lot."

"Thanks very much," Wendover answered. "The news seems to have got abroad somehow. I don't quite see how, for our names weren't given."

"Oh, neither they were. I'd forgotten that. But my future uncle-in-law got the results of the Draw in last night's paper and he's been boasting about it ever since. All the countryside knows, by this time, I expect. Of course I heard about it myself from Harry."

"H'm! I'd rather not have had the advertisement," Wendover admitted rather ruefully.

It was reasonable enough that young Thursford should have told Viola Langdale. Since they were engaged, it was her affair almost as much as his. But old Peter Thursford might have kept his mouth shut instead of bragging all over the place as if there was any special credit in drawing a horse in a sweep. This explained why his gardener had offered his congratulations, and how the postmistress had the news. Wendover had a vision of having to shake hands with the whole village in turn as he came across them.

He looked up to find Viola Langdale watching him quizzically.

"You don't like being the Village Hero?" she asked. "Cheer up! There are nine of you on the premises and the public attention is divided. Besides," she added with a faint sneer, "Harry's good uncle will lap up more than his share, so you'll get off easier. He's very proud of himself. It's wonderful what confidence a little money gives some people. I wish I had some more of it."

"Confidence?" Wendover asked in a faintly ironical tone.

Lack of self-confidence was the last thing Viola could have been charged with.

"No, of course not. Money, I meant. Think of what one could do with £50,000. I've been thinking of nothing else for the last few hours. Fact! I couldn't get to sleep until I'd spent about half of it. As good as a Hollywood super-film — and much cheaper. I dropped off into a doze just as I was telling the third chauffeur to bring round all the Rolls-Royces, if there were as many, so that I could pick out the one I wanted for the day."

"To drive to the rainbow's end and dig up the crock of gold there, I suppose."

Viola Langdale was a girl about whom Wendover never felt over-sure. Outwardly she was feminine enough. She looked her twenty-seven years, but not a day older. She could carry her clothes so that even her shabby golfing-kit showed her off to advantage. Plenty of men had tried to catch her fancy in the years since she was twenty; and her looks alone would have accounted for that. And yet, somehow, Wendover had a feeling that, either by the exaggeration of some quality or by the nimiety of another, she diverged ever so slightly from what he regarded as normal femininity. Her conversational frankness suggested that she was throwing her mind open to inspection; but it was the calculated frankness of the conjurer displaying his trick cabinet for examination by his audience. "Examine it as much as you like, ladies and gentlemen; it's all in plain sight." And yet the skilfully-contrived mechanism escapes the investigator. Wendover didn't like girls who were as complicated as all that.

Viola bought a book of stamps at the counter and then, as Wendover handed in his telegram, she nodded towards the miniature car at the door.

"I'm going up to the links. Can I give you a lift?"
Wendover shook his head.

"No, thanks," he decided. "I doubt if I'd find any-one to play with."

As they came out of the post-office together, he eyed the shabby little four-year-old car. "All the Rolls-Royces, if there are as many." Viola's pipe-dreams dealt with material things, evidently; and that made the con-trast between them and the present reality all the more glaring. She had a tiny income, just sufficient to scrape along on by living in the house her parents had left her. Within limits, of course, she could live as she liked; there was no one to interfere with her. And in some ways, if all tales were true, she had made the limits wide enough. But on the financial side her bounds were nar-row, and it was no wonder that she wanted more.

He opened the car door for her and she slipped neatly into the driving-seat. When she drove off, he watched the tiny car for a moment or two as it receded down the road. Well, he reflected, no doubt Harry Thursford knew his own business; but Viola Langdale had been engaged to three different men before, without men-tioning other affairs. In Harry's place, he would have been inclined to wonder if the fourth man was any like-lier to keep her than the other three had been. Either she went into these things very lightly or else . . . She had certainly turned Falgate down when he began to get into business difficulties.

Wendover disliked thinking about that sort of thing where a girl was concerned. Instead, he turned to an-other mental picture: Viola with her worn suède golf-jacket and her dingy little car, keeping a footing among her richer friends as best she could, and covering all her difficulties with that bright, hard smile. One could guess what it cost her in secret economies, especially in a period of changing fashion in evening gowns. If she betrayed a trace of cynicism at times, it was hardly surprising.

As he passed the local druggist's, Wendover almost ran into Willenhall, who was just coming out of the shop with a kodak in his hand.

"I suppose you've seen the result of the Draw?" Willenhall inquired after they had greeted each other. "I don't know how you feel about it, but I must confess I'm more surprised than anything else. One never expects to get anything in these affairs."

Wendover was not ill-pleased to find someone sharing his own feelings.

"I expect your next sensation will be annoyance," he said, with a smile. "The names of the Syndicate have leaked out, it seems, and we're likely to attract more attention than we'll care about, from all I can see."

Willenhall nodded, as he slipped his kodak into his pocket.

"So I gathered just now. I went into a shop to buy a new cable shutter-release. This one's frayed a bit and I'm uneasy about it holding out. Unfortunately they hadn't one in stock. While I was buying some fresh films, the druggist congratulated me most effusively. I couldn't make out how he knew anything about it."

"Old Thursford has been spreading the news," Wendover explained.

Willenhall did not seem surprised to learn the source of the information.

"He struck me as rather a talkative old gentleman," he commented with an ironical look. "By the way, I must thank you for your hints about the neighbourhood. I've been up at Heatingham Abbey and found it most interesting. In fact, I used so many films on various bits of it that I ran out of stock."

"You haven't been up to Hell's Gape yet, have you?"

"Not yet; but I mean to see it before I leave. I'm staying for a week or ten days longer, so I shall be able to pick a fine day. From what you told me, I'd better choose a time when the light's good."

"If you can manage to get there in the morning, I think you'd find the conditions at their best," Wendover advised, after thinking for a moment or two. "If I remember right, the shadows of the rock-fangs fall rather well about that time. You'd get something that would make a picture as well as a photograph."

"Thanks, I'll bear that in mind."

Wendover felt no desire to prolong the interview. His opinion of Willenhall had improved slightly again. At least he hadn't made a fuss over their luck in the Draw but had taken it in a sportsmanlike fashion.

"Well, anything more I can do for you in the matter of the local antiquities? If you want any more information, I'll be glad to give you what I have."

Willenhall thanked him, but seemed to think that he had enough to keep him occupied for the present.

CHAPTER IV: DISASTER IN THE AIR

No sooner had the names of the Syndicate leaked out than Wendover's breakfast-table was encumbered with an unaccustomed pile of letters which embarrassed him considerably. The mere reading of them ate into his mornings. The sad tales which reinforced the inevitable appeal for financial assistance lacerated his feelings. If he sent a cheque in reply, he had an uneasy feeling that he was being swindled by a professional beggar; and if he withheld his donation, he could not altogether persuade himself that he had not refused a genuine application. At last he bethought himself of the Charity Organisation Society. They could sift the cases for him and distribute his subscriptions to the deserving ones.

What they could not do, however, was lessen the size of his morning post. No one can breakfast in comfort with a pile of a hundred letters in front of him. So his cherished routine had to be broken through. The letters were deposited in another room; and he began his breakfast and his *Times* simultaneously.

This morning, as he opened his paper and turned as usual to the middle page, a heading caught his eye: —

AIR LINER CRASH

ONE PASSENGER KILLED

The E.D.G. air liner Domodossola, due at Croydon at 2.25 P. M. yesterday, crashed on the Belgian coast, owing to engine trouble. Two passengers were severely injured. Mr. Edmund Blackburn, another passenger, was killed instantaneously. Mr. Blackburn was a member of the Novem Syndicate which drew Barralong in the Hospital Sweepstake.

"Poor chap!" Wendover murmured to himself. "That's awful luck. And all because he wanted to avoid the discomfort of a Channel crossing. It's fortunate he hasn't got a wife waiting for him here."

His acquaintance with Blackburn was of the faintest. There was no feeling of personal loss in Wendover's mind. His sympathy was purely a humanitarian one. Dreadful, to think of a man being shot out of existence like that! But at least he hadn't suffered. "Killed instantaneously."

Wendover tried to put the matter out of his mind and to concentrate on the rest of the morning's news; but his effort was only partly successful. The picture of that shattered aeroplane insisted on surging up before him. Dashed precarious, this modern existence! Every new advance seemed to open up fresh avenues leading down to death. If your gas-pipes went wrong, you might die of suffocation in your sleep. If the electric wiring fused, you might be burned alive in your bed. Or a tramway cable might electrocute you in the street. As for motors, there was the daily death-roll staring you in the face if you opened a newspaper. And aeroplanes. . . . Poor Blackburn! Modern man lived a very hazardous life. And then Wendover smiled faintly at the recollection that thirty years ago people were actually knocked down and killed by horse-traffic! They must have been a slow-moving lot in his young days.

He forced himself to complete the perusal of *The Times* and then retired to his smoking-room to wrestle with the pile of letters which awaited him. A rapid sifting extracted all those addressed in known handwritings; and these he dealt with first. When they had been disposed of, he settled down rather gloomily to the task of slitting envelopes and glancing at the openings of the contained letters, so that nothing private should be sent on to the Charity Organisation Society offices.

He had just got into the swing of this, when to his annoyance he was interrupted.

"Mr. Checkley wishes to see you, sir, if you are not engaged."

Wendover, letter-opener in hand, looked up from his task.

"Show him in," he directed the maid, after a moment's hesitation.

He could not imagine what had brought Checkley there at this hour of the morning. It could not be a mere friendly call, for Checkley hardly knew him — had never been in his house before, as a matter of fact. Obviously it must be this damned Syndicate cropping up again. But why the Syndicate should suddenly become an urgent affair he could not conceive.

He rose to his feet as Checkley entered the room. Somehow Checkley's little black eyes and avaricious mouth reminded him of a baby crocodile.

Checkley wasted no time in needless conversation.

"You've seen the news?" he demanded. "Blackburn's crash, I mean."

If there was any regret in Checkley's tone, Wendover failed to catch it. Checkley evidently had an interest in Blackburn's death, but whatever that interest was, it had little to do with normal human sympathy.

"A dreadful affair," Wendover commented.

"Yes, of course," Checkley agreed, perfunctorily.

44

"By the way, I suppose you have that copy of the memorandum we made about the Sweep tickets? I ought to have copied it at the time, but I hadn't an opportunity. D'you mind if I have a glance at it now, if you have it anywhere handy?"

Rather disgusted by Checkley's behaviour, Wendover confined his reply to a nod of acquiescence. The paper was in his safe, and he was able to lay his hands on it at once. Checkley seized it eagerly and ran his eye down the document.

"Yes," he said at last, in the tone of a man who has found his beliefs confirmed. "It seems all right. I'll take a copy of it now. That'll save bothering you again."

Wendover produced some sheets of writing-paper and pushed aside the piles of envelopes so that Checkley could sit down at the desk and make his copy.

"You're getting them too?" said Checkley contemptuously, as he pointed to the mass of letters. "I chuck mine straight into the fire as soon as I've made sure what they are. Infernal cheek these people have, with their squalls for help."

"They are a nuisance," Wendover admitted in a colourless tone.

He disliked Checkley's methods so much that he even began to feel inclined to defend the begging-letter writers.

Checkley, having finished his copying, pushed the original document aside and turned round to his host.

"There's another thing I wanted to see you about. I've had an offer for a half-share in our ticket for Barralong. Redhill tells me that he's had an offer too, for a one-third share in it. What do you think? If Barralong comes in nowhere, then we'd make something by closing with these offers, of course. But if Barralong's placed, we'd be a lot worse off in the end."

"Barralong's not likely to be placed," Wendover opined.

"You think not?" Checkley seemed doubtful. "Then you think we should come to terms with these people?"

"No," said Wendover, bluntly, "I don't. If you're going to bet at all, then you ought to do it in a sportsmanlike way. I never hedged a bet in my life; and if this isn't hedging, it comes so close to it that I can't see the difference."

Checkley seemed completely taken aback by this view.

"You mean you wouldn't take either offer? I don't see your point. What's the good of chucking away money if you think Barralong isn't going to be placed?"

Wendover, in his turn, was at a loss. It is extremely difficult to formulate one's ideas of sportsmanship on the spur of the moment, especially for the benefit of someone who evidently cannot sympathise with them. He chose the easy way of dogmatic statement.

"I went in for a pure gamble. You're proposing a commercial transaction. I don't care about mixing up commercial methods with sporting affairs. That's my position."

"Well, I can't see it," Checkley answered grumpily. "It seems a queer way to look at the thing. However, we're all in the same boat, and if you object, that's an end of the project."

Then a thought seemed to strike him which put the matter in a fresh light.

"You can't prevent me dealing as I like with my own share, of course. I can sell part of my chance in that, if I like. That doesn't affect anyone else."

"So long as you don't implicate me, you can do as you please," Wendover admitted. "You're free to play any tricks you may fancy, so long as they don't infringe the terms of that original document there."

"I'll think over it," Checkley announced, after pondering for a second or two.

As Wendover showed no desire to retain him, he took his leave immediately. When he had gone, Wendover picked up the copy of the agreement from his desk with the intention of putting it back in his safe.

"When Checkley's time comes, he'll offer the Angel of Death a cheque to let him off — and probably plead for five per cent. discount," he prophesied, half-humorously.

As he glanced idly at the nine signatures to the document, it struck him once more that most of these people belonged to a circle different from his own. They cared nothing for the countryside or the country people. They represented the new trades and factories which were springing up like mushrooms south of the old industrial block in the Midlands. They had cast their eyes about for districts where the rates were low; and where one came, another followed.

Wendover, with an inherited prejudice in favour of agriculture, had viewed the invasion with a faint latent hostility. He liked things that were stable and permanent. These invading things weren't like the old staple trades: coal, iron, shipbuilding, and so forth. They were all based on flimsy articles, or next door to that.

There was poor Blackburn with some office gadget or other; and Redhill with his under-capitalised place in Stanningleigh turning out fancy brands of enamel; Falgate over in Ambledown with his acetate silk factory (which might not last much longer); and Mackworth

47

with his ZZZ Sauce. And in their train had come Coniston with his motorbuses; and old Thursford with his cinemas. (Not forgetting young Thursford's ten per cent. partnership.) And finally Checkley's venture in toffee. These people quite obviously didn't think along the same lines as himself. One might accept them as neighbours, but one stuck to one's own group when it came to choosing friends.

His eyes fell again on the document in his hand. Why had Checkley been so eager, all of a sudden, to make sure of the precise wording? There it was, in simple enough language: —

The undersigned agree that the Derby Sweepstake tickets numbered G/B:B.8811 to G/B:B.8819 inclusive are to be held jointly by them and that any Prize won by any one or more of these tickets shall be equally divided among the holders when the prize-money is distributed. Counterfoils are to be filled in in the name of the Novem Syndicate.

He read it twice before fathoming Checkley's motive.

"So that's what he wanted to be sure about?" Wendover ejaculated aloud in his disgust.

He restored the document to his safe, and then with a sigh returned to his letters.

CHAPTER V: THE INJUNCTION

DERBY DAY added another novelty to Wendover's experiences. He had been surprised to find himself drawing a horse at all; but that was nothing in comparison with his astonishment when he heard, over the wireless, the result of the race: —

1. ASWAIL
2. BARRALONG
3. SILVER RAIN

He certainly had not fancied Barralong. Not even his involuntary personal interest in the horse had sufficed to persuade him that it had a sporting chance of a place. As a prophet, he had to admit, he had not shone; and he was fain to console himself with the recollection that a three weeks' spell of blazing weather had made the turf like iron. Evidently Barralong had done better in these conditions than might have been the case in more normal circumstances.

The Syndicate stood to win £241,920; say, somewhere between twenty-five and thirty thousand pounds each. Wendover was not the kind of man to be thrown off his balance by a sum of this sort. He had not been posing when he had said that it really meant very little to a person with simple tastes, like himself. He didn't intend to go in for a more expensive brand of cigar simply because it *was* more expensive; and other things were much the same as cigars in that respect. He would be able to do more for his tenants without stinting himself; the local hospital wouldn't object to a gift or two; and he might be able to carry through one or two long-planned improvements on the estate, which had been precluded by the increasing pressure of taxation.

On the morning after the race, his mail swelled suddenly to dimensions which drove him to despair. Every beggar in the Kingdom seemed anxious to have a share in the bonanza. But as he turned over the pile of envelopes before settling down to tackle them methodically, his attention was caught by one which bore a firm's name on the flap: Dyce & Monyash. Wendover knew them well enough: old-established solicitors in Ambledown. Wondering what business they had with him — for his own affairs were in the hands of another firm — he tore open the envelope and glanced over the letter.

4th June

Dear Sir,

MR. EDMUND BLACKBURN'S ESTATE

We are acting for the Trustees of the above estate, and in examining the papers of the late Mr. Blackburn we found some Sweepstake tickets and memoranda relating thereto. Apparently you hold a note of agreement on the matter, of which we have no copy. As we understand that one of these tickets has obtained a large money Prize, may we ask you to send us a copy of the form of agreement in your possession, so that we may know how the matter stands?

Yours truly,

DYCE & MONYASH

Wendover read the letter through a second time. Of course, Blackburn had possession of the winning ticket.

Wendover had forgotten that fact completely. And now the legal sharks had got their teeth into the business, the whole aspect of it would change. What had, originally, been a roughly-drawn agreement between gentlemen would now become something which might have to be interpreted by lawyers. It might even be dragged into court, if they weren't careful. He had a shrewd idea of how Checkley read it; and he had a conviction that Dyce & Monyash would not be likely to agree with Checkley's views, when they saw the actual wording. The solicitors would naturally want to do the best they could for their client. Checkley, unless Wendover misread him badly, would be equally anxious to do the best for himself; and if he insisted on his "rights" he could act on his own behalf whether the rest of the Syndicate agreed with him or not. In that case, the Novem Syndicate's affairs would get a publicity even wider than they had already obtained. Wendover shrugged his shoulders rather disgustedly as he thought of it.

In the meanwhile, he transcribed the agreement and sent off the copy to Dyce & Monyash. That part of the business, at least, was straightforward. But obviously he could not go on acting for the Syndicate without some authority. He went to the telephone, rang up each member of the Syndicate in turn, and explained the situation. It amused him to note the different ways in which the news was received.

Jack Coniston was indifferent. "Why shouldn't they see the agreement? I don't see it matters a damn. It's not likely they'll make a squall over the Lottery Act. And that ticket's our property. They can't mislay it, or anything of that sort."

Old Peter Thursford was profane in his fury at the

idea of any lawyer daring to put his finger into the pie, and meddle with "a plain agreement between a lot of gentlemen." Wendover could hardly get him to promise to pass the news on to his nephew.

Tommy Redhill, dragged away from a consultation with his mixer, seemed slightly resentful from his tone; but whether the resentment was due to the interruption or to the nature of the news, Wendover failed to determine. Tommy was too cool a person to give himself away like old Thursford.

Falgate was not so cautious. Without reaching the heights to which Peter Thursford had soared, he made no bones about his annoyance at this new factor in the affair. "Damn their eyes! I suppose this means we'll be held up somehow or other until they've got a few dozen letters written at six and eightpence a shot. Once a thing gets into the hands of lawyers, it's months before anything can be pushed through. They've got the ticket, you say? Then they have the whiphand of us, I suppose. We can't do anything without them. Good Lord!" The rasp in his voice made it clear that he had some urgent objection to any delay; and Wendover, recalling Falgate's betting on White Starlight, inferred that he might be in urgent need of cash to pay his losses. If that were so, it was no wonder that he chafed when this unexpected intrusion of Dyce & Monyash might mean procrastination.

Willenhall could not be reached on the telephone. He was out on some expedition or other, and Wendover had to content himself with inquiring when he would be back.

Checkley received the news with obvious suspicion. "I don't like it. I'm not sure you should have given them a copy. The less we have to do with lawyers, the better. I think . . . Oh, well, if they have the ticket, I suppose you had to. Still, I don't like it. Don't do anything more till we get together and talk the thing over. It doesn't do to give ourselves away."

"Well, they asked a civil question and I gave them a civil answer," Wendover pointed out. "We've nothing to conceal, surely."

"No. No, of course not. Still, the less said the better. That's my view."

Wendover had little doubt about the next move which Dyce & Monyash would make, so he was not surprised next morning to receive a second letter from them. The promptness seemed to belie Falgate's premonitions. There was no need for the solicitors to hurry. They held the trump card in whatever game was to be played. Without the ticket, the Syndicate was powerless. If they approached the Sweepstake authorities for payment, Ticket G/B:B.8816 would have to be produced to substantiate their claim. Without it, no money could be collected. Dyce & Monyash would know that well enough.

"Checkley won't like this," Wendover reflected rather sardonically as he read the solicitors' letter.

5th June

Dear Sir,

MR. EDMUND BLACKBURN'S ESTATE

We are in receipt of your letter of yesterday's date, enclosing copy of the agreement entered into by the members of the Novem Syndicate.

We note that "any Prize won by one or more of these tickets" (i. e. the tickets numbered G/B:B.8811 to G/B:-B.8819 inclusive) "shall be equally divided among the holders when the prize-money is distributed."

According to the official list, the Novem Syndicate has obtained the prize for the second horse, Barralong, with the ticket numbered G/B:B.8816; and under the clause in the agreement which we quoted above, one-ninth of the prize-money belongs to the estate of the late Mr. Edmund Blackburn.

Acting under the instructions of the late Mr. Blackburn's Trustees, we have to point out that we should be associated with the representatives of the Novem Syndicate in the collection and division of the prize-money accruing under the agreement.

We shall be glad to have your confirmation of this at your convenience.

Yours truly,
DYCE & MONYASH

"If Checkley has his way, it'll be a while before they get their confirmation," Wendover commented, as he glanced again over the document. "Well, I can't handle this off my own bat. It's a matter for the whole of the Syndicate."

He pondered for a time over the possible courses, and finally decided to call a meeting of the Syndicate members at his house, and to invite the solicitors to come and discuss the matter without prejudice. Having arranged a time with the lawyers, he summoned the Syndicate members half an hour earlier, so that they might have an opportunity of talking matters over beforehand among themselves.

At the Syndicate meeting it became clear at once that there were four different points of view. Checkley, Falgate, and old Peter Thursford formed one camp and made no bones about their views. They meant to see that, by hook or crook, the share originally belonging to Blackburn should be split up among the eight remaining survivors of the Syndicate. Checkley constituted himself the protagonist of this trio.

"These lawyers are just trying it on. They haven't a leg to stand on, but they think we're soft. The agreement's plain enough. It wasn't drawn exactly to cover this case, but it covers it all right for all that. Besides, supposing we were fools enough to give in, where does the money go? I've made inquiries about it. Blackburn left all his estate to his brother — a fellow simply rolling in money. He doesn't need this cash; he's got more than he knows what to do with already. It's not as if Blackburn's heirs were poor devils without a stiver, though even that wouldn't make a rap of difference to the rights of the case. This claim is just a bit of damned graspingness. They're trying it on to see if they can get something for nothing."

"I agree with Checkley," Falgate chimed in. "Why should we give up money to feather the nest of a fellow who doesn't need it as much as we do? Besides, I read the agreement as favouring Checkley's interpretation."

When old Peter Thursford spoke, Wendover was agreeably surprised. He had not understood how Halstead ever invited such a ruffian to his house. Apparently, however, Peter sober was a very different person from Peter under the influence of too much alcohol. He spoke now with firmness and something which might almost be called quiet dignity.

"If I thought this claim was just, gentlemen," he said, "I should be the first to admit it. But it isn't a just claim; it's an imposition, to my way of thinking. And I refuse to be imposed on by any pack of lawyers. It's not the money. I don't need the money. But no man swindles me, while I have my senses."

"What about you, Redhill?" Wendover demanded.

Tommy Redhill's hard clean-shaven face was one factor which enabled him to keep his own counsel. Without the faintest suggestion of posing, he could appear sphinxlike. Not a flicker of emotion crossed his features unless the brain behind them voluntarily dictated it. And his manner of speech suggested the same watchfulness. He rarely used the first person singular when putting forward an opinion, so that it was difficult to be sure whether he was giving his own views or merely voicing, for the sake of argument, the ideas which might be held by someone else.

"There's a good deal to be said for Mr. Thursford's view," he said in a tone which suggested almost complete indifference to the whole matter. "No one likes to feel he's being bounced out of something he's entitled to, least of all when the man behind the bouncer doesn't need the money. Who's doing the bouncing in this case, though? Is it this lawyer fellow, or is it the rest of us here? It's a matter of interpreting a phrase, and neither side's likely to agree with the other. There's no compromise possible, for either Blackburn's share goes into the Syndicate's pocket or it doesn't. There's no middle course."

"You, Coniston?" Wendover inquired, as Redhill finished his inconclusive survey.

"Oh, I don't give a damn either way," Jack Coniston admitted frankly. "Complicated affair, apparently. I don't profess to be impartial or anything of that sort, of course. I'd just as soon have the money as not. How much is it, by the way?"

Checkley had the figures ready.

"The Syndicate nets £241,920 in any case. Divided among eight, as it ought to be, each man's share's

£30,240. Divided among nine, as this lawyer wants, it means only £26,880 per share. Each of us stands to drop £3,360."

"Thanks. I hadn't bothered to work it out," Coniston resumed. "Well, what's three thousand, after all? Even at the worst we'll do pretty well out of the thing. Why not let him have it?"

"Chuck away £26,000 — nearly £27,000?" Checkley ejaculated in angry incredulity. "That's a silly notion, Coniston."

"You think so? P'raps you're right. It was just an idea. Then if we shouldn't do that, and if Redhill's objecting to a compromise, there's nothing for it but to dare our legal pal to do his worst. That way, at any rate, we'll find out how we stand, for I expect he'll drag us to court over it."

Wendover glanced across at Harry Thursford and raised his brows interrogatively.

"Me?" Harry inquired. "Oh, I'm all for leaving it to the legal sharks to tell us what we meant. You see, it's going to come to that anyhow. They've got the ticket. We can't draw the cash without the ticket. They won't give up the ticket unless we pay 'em one-ninth share. Why not take an action against 'em for recovery of ticket or whatever it ought to be? That would put things straight, wouldn't it?"

"Yes, and hang the whole business up long enough for the prize to become forfeit to the Hospitals," Falgate pointed out sulkily.

Tommy Redhill seemed struck by this point.

"There's a way round that," he suggested. "Suppose this lawyer finds there's nothing doing. What's his obvious move? If you read the papers about these previous disputes about prizes, the next move's obviously for

him to go to the High Court with an injunction to prevent the prize being paid over to the Syndicate. That'll
hang the business up for a bit, but it won't endanger
the prize-money, so far as one can make out."

"There's something in that," Harry Thursford admitted. "I remember two or three cases like that in the
papers."

"What's your view?" Wendover asked, turning to
Willenhall, who had still to give his opinion.

Willenhall seemed in some doubt about the exact
words to use. Evidently he felt that he was on shaky
ground and wished to put things tactfully.

"Personally, if it were purely my own affair, I'd be
inclined to surrender with a good grace. But that, I admit, would not necessarily be the proper course, since
I don't know how we stand either legally or in equity.
The point was never dreamed of when the agreement
was drafted; we all know that. And on that account I
don't press for a surrender of the money. I'm hardly in
a good position to do so, for if we give it up, it won't
make much difference to me financially, whereas it may
mean more to some members of the Syndicate. I don't
like to advocate a course which might hit them harder
than it would hit me. I think you understand what I
mean?"

"Hear! Hear!" Checkley agreed *sotto voce*, but it was
clear that his approval was elicited by Willenhall's policy
rather than by any recognition of its thoughtfulness.

"I feel much the same as Mr. Willenhall," Wendover
said, in a businesslike tone. "The fact that I don't need
the money makes me very disinclined to take any line
which might be to the detriment of less fortunately-
placed members of the Syndicate. The general feeling
seems to be against conceding anything until we're sure

of our ground. Am I correct in that? Very well, suppose we have Mr. Monyash in and tell him so."

Mr. Monyash, when he entered, did not make a favourable impression upon those who had not met him before. Though only middle-aged, he seemed like a survival from a past age when lawyers lived in air-tight offices with cobwebbed windows. An amateurishly-shaven chin hung above a collar which looked as though it had seen ten days' hard service. His tie had loosened and crept towards the right, for forty years of experience had still left him incapable of achieving a decent knot. His hands looked as though he had come straight from grubbing among the office archives; and Wendover unconsciously drew in his breath at a glimpse of nails in heavy mourning.

Mr. Monyash advanced to the table, seated himself deliberately, drew out some papers, searched again in his pocket and extracted horn-rimmed spectacles which he placed on his nose. Then, with an air of a chairman opening a meeting, he remarked:

"I suppose, gentlemen, that you've agreed to take the reasonable course?"

"Of course," Jack Coniston threw out with an engaging grin. "What we want to know now is whether you're reasonable enough to think that it's reasonable. See what I mean?"

Mr. Monyash evidently did not relish this flippancy.

"I think that is hardly the spirit, hardly the spirit," he protested. "Mr. Wendover, perhaps you would be so good as to explain the decision you have arrived at. I do not think a matter of this importance should be handled as if it were a joke, a mere joke."

"I can put it in a nutshell, Mr. Monyash," Wendover answered, with his eyes fixed upon Mr. Monyash's nail-tips, which exercised an unpleasant fascination upon him. "The Syndicate does not agree with your interpretation of the agreement."

Mr. Monyash seemed surprised. He adjusted his spectacles, picked up the paper, and examined it several times as though he expected to find something on it which evaded him.

"It seems plain enough, quite plain," he said at last, with a final glance at the document. "The prize-money is to be distributed among the holders. The late Mr. Blackburn was a holder. Therefore his share is part of the assets of his estate. That seems quite clear, very clear indeed."

Checkley could not repress himself.

"The prize-money isn't to be divided among the holders. It's to be divided among the holders-when-the-prize-money-is distributed. Mr. Blackburn isn't a holder. He's dead. He can't be a holder-when-the-prize-money-is-distributed. Besides, his interest lapsed with his death. There's nothing in the document about his heirs, successors, or assigns. He dropped out, when he died."

"We don't read it so," said Mr. Monyash, with simple dignity.

"Then what do you propose to do?" Wendover asked politely.

Mr. Monyash made a gesture which brought his finger-nails into prominence.

"We shall consider what steps to take," he stated, with the air of one charged with great decisions. "We might present the ticket and secure the whole of the prize-money, after which we should, of course, hand over one-ninth of it to each member of the Syndicate. Without the ticket, Mr. Wendover, you are quite helpless, perfectly impotent, if I may point that out."

"If you attempt to cash that ticket, I'll have you charged with embezzlement," Checkley broke in angrily. "You can't act in our name without our authority, and you haven't got that."

Ignoring Checkley's outburst, Tommy Redhill leaned forward with a gesture to attract Monyash's attention.

"Here's a suggestion," he said, in his usual impersonal way. "Suppose you hold on to the ticket as security, and that you go to the High Court for an injunction to prevent the people who are running the Sweep from paying over the prize to the Syndicate without your client getting his share. The High Court will settle the rights and wrongs of the business on the evidence, without any fear or favour. It may take a few weeks, but that doesn't matter much."

Falgate shook his head at this, but Redhill ignored him.

"If that suggestion does not satisfy your client," he continued, "then it's evident that this is a mere blackmailing business and not a serious proposition. The Syndicate's quite prepared to let it be a friendly action and not a fight, for the simple reason that you haven't a leg to stand on. Your client had better move for an injunction at the earliest moment, for if he doesn't, other steps may be taken which wouldn't suit him so well. Is that quite clear — plain enough?"

Mr. Monyash seemed hardly to know what to do. It looked as though Tommy Redhill had stolen his thunder. Evidently the last thing he had expected was the challenge to move for an injunction.

"We had already considered, carefully considered, this course," he explained. "It was, naturally, in our minds . . ."

"But your client would rather have the money without the fuss, eh?" old Thursford interjected with a chuckle. "Well, sir, my view is that he'll get the fuss without the money. We're not ashamed to go into court over the affair, if he is."

"I am afraid you take things in the wrong spirit," Mr. Monyash protested with a smile which seemed slightly awry. "We are quite prepared to go into court if necessary, and, if I may say so, we expect to win our case."

"We'll go into court with clean hands, anyhow," old Thursford retorted, with a rather unfortunate choice of metaphor.

Mr. Monyash seemed quite unaware that he had suffered a thrust.

"I regret that I shall have to report to my client that you will not come to an agreement on our terms," he said, rising. "I had hoped that you would be more reasonable, much more reasonable."

"I'm afraid we differ on a question of definition," Wendover replied courteously as he also rose from his chair. "You'll move for this injunction, then? I take it that as it's purely a formal matter, you'll keep us informed of your procedure?"

"I have no power to pledge my client to any course of action," Monyash pointed out. "In any case, it may be necessary to ask the High Court for leave to issue summonses out of their jurisdiction upon members of the Syndicate. That has been done before in a somewhat analogous case."

And with this parting shot, he collected his belongings and departed.

"Seems to be rather a muddle," Coniston commented cheerfully, as the door closed behind the solicitor. "And yet none of us saw anything wrong with the agreement when we signed it. Just shows how the unexpected pushes in."

Harry Thursford had apparently been thinking over the problem.

"What evidence is there to produce if the High Court asks for our interpretation of the document?" he inquired. "There's nothing in writing to show that we have an understanding on the point, even now."

Checkley fastened upon this immediately.

"That's quite right. We ought to have it down in writing, as a sort of guarantee of good faith. Better late than never. How would this do? 'We, the members of the Novem Syndicate, are agreed that the prize-money due to us on account of Ticket No. G/B:B.8816 is to be divided equally among . . .' How would you phrase it?"

" 'Among those of us who are still alive when the cash is actually paid over by the Trustees of the Prize Fund.' How would that do?" Harry Thursford suggested.

Checkley jotted down the complete sentence and examined it for a moment.

"We'd better leave no loophole," he said, doubtfully. "What about another clause: 'and that no other person whatsoever is entitled to any share in the prize-money aforesaid.' That seems to make it as clear as it can be. Nobody could mistake what our intentions were."

"I don't see much point in it," Wendover interjected. "No court will bother about our intentions. They'll interpret the document purely on its wording."

"Still, I think we ought to know where we actually stand and to put that on record," Checkley insisted. "There's no harm in signing this, is there? It's merely a statement of what we've actually agreed to just now."

Rather to Wendover's surprise, Willenhall supported Checkley.

"It seems to me," he said, "that Mr. Checkley's draft goes no further than we've already gone in our statement to Mr. Monyash, a few minutes ago. We dealt with him on the basis that we were agreed upon this particular interpretation of the position, and I don't see any harm in having that interpretation put down in writing. Would you mind reading over the wording again, Mr. Checkley?"

"Here it is," Checkley said, and he read from his draft. " 'We, the members of the Novem Syndicate, are agreed that the prize-money due to us on account of Ticket No. G/B:B.8816 is to be divided equally among those of us who are still alive when the cash is actually paid over by the Trustees of the Prize Fund and that no other person whatsoever is entitled to any share in the aforementioned prize-money.' That seems shipshape."

"I've no objection to signing it," Willenhall agreed, pulling out his fountain pen and holding out his hand for the paper.

"Oh, I don't mind signing either," Jack Coniston concurred. "One never knows, in these days. The whole lot of you might die of spotted fever, and leave me almost a quarter of a millionaire. And if I draw the spotted fever, you fellows are welcome to my share in the cash. I shan't want it myself."

"Some people have gruesome minds," Tommy Redhill pointed out objectively as he put his signature to the note. "You'll sign, Harry?"

He passed the paper to Harry Thursford, from whom it went the round of the other members of the Syndicate.

CHAPTER VI: DEATH AT HELL'S GAPE

"Don't let me interfere with your simple pleasures, Squire," said Sir Clinton Driffield as Wendover groaned audibly at the sight of the letter-laden table in the smoking-room. "I'll amuse myself with the papers while you go on with your good works. It'll be time enough for our tramp when you've waded through them. And, by the way, if you come across any specially fine examples of the begging-letter writer, just pass the things over, please. It all helps to keep one abreast of one's profession."

He picked up *The Times* and began to read it, while Wendover sullenly fell to his task of slitting envelopes and glancing at the contents. The post had been heavy that morning, and the task of sifting grain from chaff was a wearisome one. But by this time Wendover was in good practice, and Sir Clinton was inwardly amused to see how rapidly the work could be done. A flick with the paper-cutter, a rustle as the paper was withdrawn from the envelope and opened out, another rustle as it went to join one or other of the sorted piles, and then flick again, as a fresh epistle was slit open. The sounds succeeded each other so rapidly that they merged into an almost steady rhythm, interrupted only when Wendover came across one of the rare personal documents in the mass.

Sir Clinton put down *The Times* at last and picked up, instead, one of the weekly reviews. As he opened it and glanced idly over the pages, his eye was caught by a local name.

"Hullo! Another branch of industry sprung up here since my last visit," he commented aloud.

"What's that?" Wendover demanded, looking up from his task.

Fresh local industries had no charm for him, and he wondered what new invasion was to be expected next.

"Oh, only a little 'un," Sir Clinton reassured him. "Here's the news. 'Literary Typewriting carefully and promptly executed. MSS. 1s. per 1,000 words. Carbon copy 3d. per 1,000. Miss V. Langdale, Azalea Cottage, Steeple Talgarth.' "

"That's not new," Wendover said, with a faint sigh of relief. "Viola Langdale's been on that tack for quite a while. I don't think she makes much of it, though, or she wouldn't have as much time on her hands as she has."

Sir Clinton nodded and returned to his reading. Wendover's paper-cutter continued its work, but suddenly the rhythm of the sounds at the table was interrupted. The Chief Constable, unconsciously roused by the break, glanced up from his paper to find Wendover staring at a document in his hand, with an expression of amazement on his features. He turned and caught Sir Clinton eyeing him.

"Here's something in your line," he suggested, skimming the letter through the air to his guest, who retrieved it as it landed at his feet. "What do you think of that? Some people have a weird sense of humour."

The Chief Constable unfolded the document gingerly so as not to leave his finger-prints on it. Wendover watched his face, but Sir Clinton showed nothing in his expression as he read over the typewritten lines: —

You boys of the Novem Syndicate think you've got away with the money. But some of us mean to have our share.

You will bury ten thousand pounds (£10,000) in small notes in a tin box behind the third milestone beyond the village on the Ambledown road next Friday night at midnight and then go straight home. Don't hang about or it will be the worse for you. We have eyes that can see in the dark and we can run like the devil so we can catch you if you try to play tricks.

The money must be in old notes and not in new notes which could be traced and the notes must not be marked in any way. They must all be of small denominations.

If you try any games or if you don't fork out the money we shall bump off one of you and after that it will be twenty thousand pounds (£20,000) so just you be careful. We don't stick at anything and no one can catch us.

A copy of this is being sent to each of you so just you take warning and do as we order or else the Lord have mercy on your souls.

This is all for the present from

Yours truly
THE BLACK HAND

p.p. Big-headed Ben the Gunman

"Some kids amusing themselves," Wendover grumbled. "Look at the phrasing: 'We have eyes that can see in the dark' and 'we can run like the devil.' This is one result of old Thursford's work in bringing the movies to the village. These kids have evidently absorbed the film atmosphere and got intoxicated by it. All that stuff about the third milestone at midnight and the rest of it. A good hiding is what they need."

"You might chuck the envelope across," the Chief Constable suggested. "H'm! Local post-mark — 7.30 P. M. Cheap paper and envelope is what one might have expected, but this seems good enough stuff. I'd have looked for more dirt on the paper if the Black Hand is to be taken literally. Well, I'll pass this on to our old friend Inspector Severn and let him lay a trap at the third milestone tonight, just in case of accidents. He'll be pleased to make the writer run like the devil, I'm sure."

He stowed letter and envelope away in his pocket; and then, with a glance at the desk, he inquired:

"Take you much longer to finish up that lot, Squire? I see you're nearly through."

"Not more than ten or fifteen minutes."

Sir Clinton looked at his watch.

"Well, when you've finished, suppose we take some sandwiches and a flask with us and cut out lunch today. I confess I want a longish walk rather badly."

Wendover reflected for a moment or two, after consulting his own watch.

"What do you say to a tramp over the moors? Plenty of fresh air up there. We might look in at Hell's Gape on the way home. A man was asking me about it some time back, and that reminded me that I haven't seen it for years myself. I'd rather like to pay it a visit, just to refresh my memory; and we may as well have some sort of object in our walk."

Sir Clinton nodded a careless assent and buried himself again in his papers whilst Wendover set himself to finish his examination of the remaining letters.

The walk proved to be all that Sir Clinton could desire. The day was sunny without being too hot; and when they left the road for paths and hill-tracks a cool breeze blew across the uplands. They ate their sandwiches beside a streamlet whose tiny falls made a soothing background to their talk, and the softness of the turf betrayed them into lingering there rather longer than they had intended.

"Fairly lonely, up here," Sir Clinton commented after they had walked for a while. "We've hardly met a soul since we left the road."

They had come to the crest of some rolling upland and could look around them over a stretch of country.

"There's only one road comes anywhere near here — you see a bend in it down yonder," Wendover pointed out. "It's just waste land round about; stuff that no one could make anything out of. There are one or two isolated cottages scattered about in it, here and there, and that represents the whole population on the heights."

He gazed round in great content. Though a sociable man in the main, Wendover at times had a liking to get away from his fellows and to feel that he had left the crowd behind him. This deserted tract of land gave him the sensation he wanted. Plenty of elbow-room, just earth and sky as far as one could see in this undulating country. Suddenly his keen eye picked up an object farther down the slope.

"Somebody else out for fresh air," he said, pointing the thing out to his companion. "Looks like one of these little cars a bit off the road. It must be somebody out for a picnic, scattering papers and bottles all over the place, probably."

He turned slightly and pointed again.

"See that spinney across there, Clinton? Hell's Gape

is just beyond that, on the farther slope. It'll take us . . . let's see . . . about three-quarters of an hour or so to get over there."

"We shall probably drop straight into your picnic party, if they've left their car and gone up the hill," Sir Clinton conjectured. "You'll be able to give them a few words about litter as we pass, if you feel so strongly about it as all that. We'd better be moving now."

Ten minutes later, his prophecy was fulfilled. In a ferny nook they stumbled upon the two picnickers. Harry Thursford was stretched at full length on the grass, his cap tilted over his eyes to ward off the sun. Beside a tiny pool, Viola Langdale was busy rinsing cups and plates and repacking them in a tea-basket. Wendover, despite his confirmed bachelorhood, had a soft place in his heart for a pretty girl; and he was sentimental enough to be rather touched by this preliminary sketch of domesticity. Harry Thursford was quite capable of washing up the cups; but Viola would insist on doing it herself. And this picnic-party would leave no litter, that was one thing.

Attracted by the sound of their footsteps, Harry Thursford looked round and rose to his feet.

"We hardly expected visitors to drop in," he said, as he brushed some grass-blades from his jacket, "but we might be able to stand you some tea, if you're thirsty," he added hospitably.

"This is Sir Clinton Driffield," Wendover explained by way of introduction. Then, as Viola looked up, he added. "Thanks for the offer, but we've had a picnic of our own only a short while ago, Miss Langdale. Please don't trouble about us."

Viola came forward with that efficient smile in which

Wendover always imagined he saw a touch of hardness.

"Gorgeous day, isn't it? We've been up here since
midday and the time seems to have passed like light-
ning."

"You've picked a nice spot," Sir Clinton said, with
an appreciative glance round the little dell.

"Oh, we often come up here. One can run the car
off the road a good distance so that no one touches it,
and then this place is within easy reach. Sure you won't
have some tea? It's no trouble to get it."

Sir Clinton shook his head.

"No, thanks. We've got a good walk in front of us,
and I don't think we should stay. Mr. Wendover's taking me up to have a look at Hell's Gape."

Harry Thursford's fine teeth showed in a smile.

"Hell's Gape's evidently popular today." He glanced
at his watch. "However, I don't expect you'll come
across Willenhall up there if it's as late as all that. He
asked me to show him the Maiden's Well down by the
road there, so we walked up together in the morning;
and then I put him on the road to Hell's Gape and
waited here for Miss Langdale. He'll be gone long ago,
though."

"If you'd thought about it, I could have brought both
of you up in my car," Viola pointed out.

"Willenhall said he wanted a walk," Harry explained.

"You must have hustled him off pretty quick. I'd
like to have seen him. He grows on one, rather. The
first time I saw him, I thought he was a complete dud;
but it's just that shy manner of his. I don't think he
liked me, quite. I offered to let him take my photograph
to add to his museum of local curiosities; and he didn't
quite know how to take it. He got a bit embarrassed,

as if he thought he ought to turn a compliment and was sure he'd make a hash of it if he tried. So I'd like to leave a better impression."

"What did you expect him to say?" inquired Wendover amusedly.

"Oh, I hadn't a notion. He looks like one of those men who've never had much to do with women and don't quite know how to take them. I rather like that sort. One never knows what they'll say next, out of sheer inexperience."

"I think we'd better be moving on," said Wendover hastily, in mock perturbation. "If we stay any longer, there's no saying what you might extract from my inexperience. Coming, Clinton?"

Viola made a gesture to bring him to a halt.

"Wait a moment. Are you coming back this way after you've been up at Hell's Gape? (If I say that name again, I shall yawn!) If you are, we'll still be here when you get back, and I daresay we might just manage to squeeze you into my car and give you a lift home, if that's any use to you. It'll be a tight fit, but I believe we could pack four in at a pinch."

"My fear for your springs is greater even than my desire for your company," Wendover retorted with intentional extravagance. "No, it's very kind of you, but I think we'd better get home on our feet. We came out for exercise, and we ought to stick to our programme. Thanks very much for the offer, though."

"Very well, if you won't you won't," Viola agreed. "We'll see you when you come back."

Sir Clinton and Wendover took their leave and turned their faces towards the ridge beyond which lay Hell's Gape. When they were well out of earshot, Sir Clinton turned to his companion.

"That's the girl of the typewriting advertisement, isn't it?"

"Yes."

"Apparently she won't be typing much longer. They're engaged, aren't they?"

"Yes, but how did you . . . Oh, I suppose you saw her ring? Yes, they're engaged."

Sir Clinton eyed Wendover for a moment.

"You don't seem very sure about it, to judge from your tone," he commented.

"I'm not," Wendover admitted frankly. "Young Thursford may manage to keep her, but if the engagement's broken off, it won't be her first experience in that line."

"As freakish as all that?" Sir Clinton inquired. "I should have said she was a person who knew her own mind. She struck me as rather a cool card, in that short acquaintance."

"You've put your finger on it," Wendover said grudgingly. "At least, it looks suspiciously like it. And yet I can't help feeling a bit sorry for the girl, somehow. She's devilishly hard up — look at that typewriting advertisement, for instance."

"You're the poorest hand at explaining things, Squire. From your confused remarks I gather that she's hard up, that she's rather mercenary, perhaps, that she's been engaged once or twice and found it convenient to get out of her entanglements. And, finally, that she's not one of your pets. Pull yourself together and tell a plain story. The girl rather interested me."

"Well, I never know what to make of her," said Wendover, crossly. "I don't much care for girls who pretend to put everything in the shop-window, when all the time you can guess that the real things in stock are quite different. That's the impression I get of her, and I've known her for years."

"You make me more interested. Proceed. We've a longish walk in front of us."

Wendover looked slightly uncomfortable.

"I'm not going to crab the girl, but the outside facts are common knowledge," he said at length. "She was left devilish hard up and she's had to learn by experience the exact difference between eleven-pence three-farthings and one bob. Not an exhilarating experience for an ambitious girl, that. She's got looks above the average, a good figure, and she can set off her clothes: quite sound assets for a girl. First of all she got engaged to a youngster, but he took to lifting his elbow a bit too high, and she broke that off. Quite right, too. He was a young rotter. Perhaps that taste of love's young dream soured her a bit, though on the surface she didn't show much. Anyhow, some time after that, she got engaged again to a fellow a bit older than herself with a fair amount of capital. Like a fool, he took to speculating during the big slump and went burst. That engagement was broken off, too. I don't altogether blame her. My impression was that she'd got caught on the rebound from the first affair; felt lonely, you know; and took the second fellow to fill the void somehow. Then, by the time the smash came, she'd discovered he wasn't quite her type, and she was glad to get out of it. Then the new factories began to spring up round here, and a fellow named Falgate arrived to start one of them. She got engaged again and it looked all right. Only, he's one of these quick-tempered devils and she's the kind that loses her temper inside but keeps cool on the outside, so that you never know there's much wrong until the whole affair blazes up at once. Falgate's business began to go wrong, and I expect his temper got no sweeter. She was probably getting sick of it for a good while before the explosion came over some trifle or other. Anyhow — another engagement gone. Falgate was badly cut up; one couldn't help guessing that. She didn't show anything; she never does. Perhaps she regretted what had happened, but one couldn't have told it from the surface. Then young Thursford — the fellow you saw just now — stepped in and made the running. He wasn't a catch. I gather he's only a sort of ten per cent. partner in old Thursford's business and he could just keep a wife in bare comfort without frills. However, Viola's getting up towards the thirties now, and she must be growing deadly sick of continual pinching. She took young Thursford on, though I must say the keenness seemed all on one side. However, her ship seems to have come home, this shot."

"How?" Sir Clinton inquired.

"Oh, this damned Sweep. He stands to win somewhere over £25,000 like the rest of us. That'll always help in housekeeping."

"I see they've planted an injunction on you, or something like that, in the High Court, though."

"There's nothing in it, really," Wendover explained. "That's only a question of the value of each person's share. It's got nothing to do with the actual prize, except that the cash is held up for a while until the Court makes up its mind on a point."

In a few words he put the situation before Sir Clinton.

"So in any case young Thursford stands to win £25,000," the Chief Constable mused when he had heard the whole story. "Then, if the girl's out of money, I suppose he's got her safe enough?"

"I don't know that she's that, entirely," Wendover protested in an evident desire to be fair. "From one or two things I've seen, I believe she could have twisted old Thursford round her finger if she'd thought of nothing but cash. He was always on her skirts for a while, until at last she fended him off pretty bluntly. She could have had him without the trouble of bringing him up to the scratch; but she took his nephew instead. The result is that the old man hates his nephew like poison."

Sir Clinton seemed to have lost interest in the subject. He made no reply to Wendover's remarks, and they walked on for a time in silence until they topped the ridge for which they had been making.

"Go easy, Clinton," Wendover cautioned, as the Chief Constable began to move down the further slope. "There's a sheer sixty-foot drop just in front there. That tree's just at the edge of the chasm."

As they descended the gentle declivity, Sir Clinton's eye caught something lying in the turf ahead.

"Your friend Willenhall must be somewhere about still," he said, as he pointed out the object. "There's a kodak on the grass."

"He must have left it behind, surely. He can't have spent all that time up here," Wendover surmised. "We'd better salvage it and I can send it across to him tonight."

Sir Clinton gave a nod of assent and descended to the edge of the chasm.

"Very picturesque, these pinnacles on the other side," he said, looking across at them. "They've got a nasty look about them, somehow, all the same. Rather like the tusks in some monster's jaw. I shouldn't care to be up here on a misty day, Squire. Rather risky, with this place completely unfenced."

His eye travelled down the sheer rock-fangs, and he leaned over the edge to see down into the depths of the ravine.

"There's somebody down there, Squire!"

Wendover craned eagerly forward at the tone.

"It's Willenhall," he said, aghast. "Poor devil! He must have slipped on the edge here and fallen right on those rocks."

And without waiting a moment, he drew well back from the rim and began running along the edge of Hell's Gape towards the place where the chasm ended and a grassy slope allowed access to the lower levels.

The mere sight of the body had convinced Sir Clinton that Willenhall was dead. That being so, there was no need for hurry. He gave a cursory glance round the place on which he stood, and then, in a leisurely fashion, made his way along in Wendover's tracks.

"Don't touch anything," he called, as Wendover reached the end of the precipice and began to descend the scarp beyond.

CHAPTER VII: ENTER INSPECTOR SEVERN

THE floor of Hell's Gape was mainly of earth; but here and there the rugged tops of sunken boulders showed through the soil. It was on one of these that Willenhall had apparently struck when his fall ended.

No expert was needed to decide that life was extinct. The head injuries alone were enough to show that death must have been practically instantaneous. Wendover was glad enough to turn away from the ugly sight while Sir Clinton, without actually handling the body, made a superficial examination.

"It might have been worse, Squire," he said at last, as he rose to his feet again. "He was killed outright and didn't suffer. If he'd been crippled in the fall and not completely finished, the chances are that he might have lain here till he died of starvation and pain, unless someone like ourselves happened to come along."

"Poor devil!" said Wendover, rather shakily. "I wish I'd never thought of recommending this place to him. It was I who put it into his head to come here, you know. I wish I hadn't."

"If we're going to search as far back as that," Sir Clinton pointed out brutally, "then you'd better blame his parents for bringing him into the world at all. Or the people who leave a place like this unfenced at the top. Don't get morbid about it, Squire. You're not responsible."

"I don't suppose I am," Wendover admitted. "But still I wish I hadn't suggested the place to him."

A thought seemed to cross Sir Clinton's mind.

"You knew him. There's no chance that it was suicide and not accident, is there? He didn't look under the weather, or anything of that sort, did he, when you saw him last?"

"Not a bit," Wendover assured him. "He was an easy-going fellow who didn't look as if he'd a trouble in the world."

"It might have been a case of vertigo at the sight of the chasm, of course: the terror of heights — I forget the medical name for it," Sir Clinton went on. "A lot of people suffer from that and may not know it till they get a bad attack in a place like this. But that's hardly our affair just now. We'll need to get some assistance and have the body removed before dark."

"I'll go, if you like," Wendover volunteered.

Obviously one of them would have to stay by the body until help came; and Wendover, who had known Willenhall, had no desire to be that one. It was better to have something to do, rather than sit beside that shattered wreck and worry over a piece of unfortunate advice.

Sir Clinton had his plans cut and dried.

"Very well, then, Squire. Get off down to where those two were picnicking. They said they'd be there till we came back, so you'll catch them, all right. Get them to run you down in the car — that girl's better out of the way, if we've got to bring the body down. Go to Inspector Severn, if you can find him, and tell him about the affair. He'll get the police surgeon and we'll need a motor-ambulance sent up the road to the place where Thursford and Miss Langdale had their car. We probably can't get the ambulance farther up than that. We'll need a stretcher and some bearers to come up here and take the body down to the ambulance. If you can manage it, bring Severn and the surgeon back with you in your own car; then we won't be bothered with a crowd, at the start. By the way, is that crabbed little fellow Alloway still police surgeon?"

Wendover nodded in confirmation.

"Oh, well, he won't waste time," Sir Clinton said drily. "I remember he gave me the impression of wanting to get on to the next job before he'd quite finished with the first one. A hustler, if anything. Well, you'd better hustle too, Squire. You're not likely to be back here under an hour and a quarter at the earliest."

He pulled his cigarette-case from his pocket as he spoke and glanced at the contents.

"I've enough to see me through. Now, off you go."

Wendover set off at once, climbed the crest, and made his best speed down the valley beyond; and all the way he was haunted by the mental picture of that shattered wreck in Hell's Gape. Clinton had taken the thing very coolly, he reflected. But Clinton's interest in it was purely professional — a case of accidental death within the bounds of his district. Besides, Clinton hadn't known Willenhall alive. But Wendover couldn't pretend to the same aloofness. He could hear Willenhall's soft, diffident voice putting these fatal questions which had led him in the end up on to the heights behind and to death. Wendover knew quite well that he had merely tried to do the man a kindness; he could hardly have refused the information; he was absolutely blameless in the affair; and yet . . . "Oh, damn! I wish it hadn't happened so! Poor devil!" Then again the picture of the distorted body would cross his mental vision, and once more the whole train of thought would run through his mind again. He knew perfectly well that his ideas were baseless, a mere perturbation resulting from the shock at the sight of Willenhall's corpse; and yet he was pursued by that tormenting thought of responsibility even as he denied it to himself.

At last he came in sight of the picnic-place; and to his relief he was able to make out the two figures there. Fortunately they had held to their plans and had not gone home. That meant so much time saved. He took out his handkerchief, waved to attract their attention, and was cheered when an answering wave showed that they had seen him. How was he going to break the news, with the girl there? No use upsetting her, of course. Better say there had been an accident and that they needed help to get Willenhall down. And as his mind passed to the fresh problem, the other phase of the affair dropped from his mind, leaving him cool again.

At the sight of his evident excitement, they had come out to meet him, and when he came near enough Viola called to him.

"Has there been an accident? Where's Sir Clinton?"

"Driffield's all right. It's Willenhall that's hurt."

Harry Thursford blundered in with a direct question:

"Is he killed, man? What's happened?"

Wendover frowned meaningly at him at a moment when Viola turned her eyes towards Hell's Gape.

"He's fallen over the cliff up there. I've left Sir Clinton to look after him. We'll need help to bring him down."

"I'll go up now," Harry Thursford volunteered.

"No," Wendover restrained him. "We'll need an ambulance sent up here and some stretcher-bearers, before we can shift him. You'll be more use helping to collect them than you would be up there."

81

He turned to the girl.

"Can you drive us down?"

For once, Viola's coolness impressed Wendover in her favour. She wasted no time in useless questioning but hurried back to her car, turned on the petrol and had the engine running almost as soon as they reached her side.

"Jump in!" she ordered.

Harry Thursford slipped in beside her; Wendover crammed himself into the tiny back seat; and before they had closed the doors, she had the little car on the move and was driving it gently over the turf towards the road. Once there, she opened the throttle and made the best speed possible.

Harry Thursford seemed to have taken Wendover's warning, for he put no further questions about the accident.

"What do you want me to do?" he demanded.

"If Miss Langdale will drop us at the police station, I think we can manage. Or, no, would you mind waiting for me and taking me up to the Grange after that? I'd better bring my own car in case we want more men than we can cram into the ambulance."

"I'll bring mine, too," Harry volunteered.

"It won't be needed," Wendover objected.

He remembered that Sir Clinton had no desire for a crowd.

"Well, I'll come along in it, anyhow," Harry persisted.

Viola confined her attention to her driving; and Wendover was again favourably impressed. Most girls would have found difficulty in refraining from futile inquiries. On the other hand, most girls would have found time to say at least a word of sympathy or pity for the victim. What one gained on the swings, one evidently lost on the roundabouts, in Viola's case. There was a streak of hardness alongside her coolness.

When they reached the police station, a car was standing at the door and on the pavement a small group of villagers had assembled and were eagerly discussing something which seemed to cause excitement. Wendover got out; brushed past them; and as he entered the station he was relieved to see the tall figure of Inspector Severn come out of one of the rooms, closing the door behind him.

"Oh, Severn! There's been a bad business up at Hell's Gape. The Chief Constable's sent me down to get an ambulance, and some stretcher-bearers, and the police surgeon. . . ."

"That's all right, sir," Severn replied, to Wendover's amazement. "I've telephoned over to Ambledown for the motor-ambulance. It ought to be here any minute now. And I've rung up Dr. Alloway. He's coming up with us. And luckily I've been able to lay my hands on enough men to carry a stretcher. It's all arranged."

"But . . . How the devil do you know anything about it?" Wendover demanded.

Severn made a gesture towards the room behind him.

"Mr. Checkley's in there. He brought the news just a few minutes ago. It seems to be a nasty affair. He's a bit worked up over it — been sick. It must have been an ugly sight, I gather. Terrible smash after a fall of that height."

Wendover nodded. He didn't want to think of that sight again himself, just then.

"Sir Clinton wants you to bring the ambulance up the road past the Maiden's Well and park it. I'll show you the place. Then we can take the stretcher on from there. He's up at Hell's Gape himself."

"Oh, on that side?" Severn seemed suddenly enlightened. "I was just wondering why you hadn't come across Mr. Checkley yourself. But that accounts for it. He went up to the Gape from the other side, the west, starting off the by-road there by Brookman's farm; and I expect he came back the same way. You came along from the east, I take it, and so you didn't run across him. He must have been a bit ahead of you at the Gape, and got away again before you put in an appearance. I gather he didn't stay long on the premises," he added with a sardonic expression.

Wendover made a slight gesture of understanding. He could quite imagine that Checkley would not want to linger in Hell's Gape that afternoon.

"I'm going off to get my car, now," he explained to Severn. "I'll come back here on the way up, and I can take four of your people if you want transport. Sir Clinton's not keen on a crowd, for obvious reasons; so you needn't rope in more help than we absolutely need."

With a nod to Severn, he made his way out of the police station. Viola, he found, had turned the car while he was inside, so that there was no delay. In a few minutes they were at the door of the Grange, where Wendover, after thanking her warmly, turned pointedly away in the direction of the garage, as a hint that he preferred to be unaccompanied. Harry Thursford did not appear to take the hint. He followed Wendover along the gravel sweep and, when they were out of earshot of the little car, jerked out an inquiry.

"He's dead, isn't he?"

"Yes. A terrible affair," Wendover admitted.

"I saw you didn't want to say too much before Viola," Harry Thursford continued in a cautious tone. "Quite right; no use giving her nightmares by describing it. But I guessed he was done for. By the way, you might give me a lift. It'll save my going for my own car. I'd like to bear a hand, you know. I knew the poor beggar. In fact, I suppose I was the last person to see him alive. I might be useful."

Wendover, rather disgusted at what seemed suspiciously like morbid curiosity, declined bluntly.

"I can't take you. I've told the Inspector he can count on the seats in my car."

"Oh, well, then I suppose I must get my own."

And as Wendover went into his garage, Harry Thursford, with a movement of suppressed ill-temper, turned back to the little car, spoke a few words to Viola and then got in beside her. Wendover, busied with his own motor, did not see them drive away.

At the police station, Wendover found Severn on the pavement, talking to the police surgeon who was waiting there with his car in obvious impatience. At a word from the Inspector, two constables got into the back of Wendover's car; Severn himself took the seat next Wendover; and they moved off at once, followed by the surgeon in his own motor.

"The ambulance has gone on in front," Severn explained. "You'll be able to get ahead of it, I expect, and we can show them where to stop."

Wendover nodded and pressed harder on the accelerator as they began to climb a long slope.

"Did you think of telephoning to Mr. Halstead?" he asked, remembering suddenly that someone should get in touch with Willenhall's relations.

"He's out of town today, but we're trying to get him

with a trunk call to find out the deceased's home address," Severn reassured him.

Wendover found that the formal phrase stirred him uncomfortably. At eleven o'clock that morning there had been a Mr. Willenhall; now it was "the deceased" that they had to deal with. To divert his mind from that lugubrious line of thought, he turned to a fresh subject.

"What about Mr. Checkley? Is he all right again? Pulled himself together?"

"He's gone off home," Severn explained. "After he'd had a drink he seemed a bit better. But there's no doubt he'd had a bad shake-up by what he saw up there. He looked mighty white about the gills. Two visits to the police in one day seem to be more than his nerves can stand," he added with a grin.

"*Two* visits?" Wendover queried, out of politeness, for evidently Severn had thrown out a bait which he wished to be taken.

"Well, the first one was really a 'phone-call," Severn admitted. "He rang us up this morning, early, to complain that his office had been burgled last night. I sent a man round, of course, to look over things. It's nothing serious: all that seems to be missing is three one-pound sample tins of coffee and a few shillings out of the petty cash box. The salient clues were a window smashed to get at the catch and a filthy handkerchief dropped on the floor, the kind of handkerchief you might expect to find on a gutter-brat who'd got it as a christening-gift and used it ever since. I expect it was used to hold the catch when the window was opened, for my man found no clear fingerprints round about there. Kids know too much nowadays," the Inspector concluded, gloomily.

"There was no attempt to open the safe, then?" Wendover inquired.

"They don't keep coffee or the petty cash in the safe, and that was what was wanted, apparently. No, the safe wasn't touched in any way. Besides, Mr. Checkley says there's nothing in the safe even if it had been opened, except his books. He keeps no cash on the premises overnight if he can help it; which is wise enough, seeing that his place could be entered as easy as winking except when a constable's actually passing on the pavement beside it."

His eye caught something on the road, a considerable distance ahead.

"I see the ambulance in front, there. If you'll blow your horn twice when you come up behind it, they'll draw in and give you the road. I gave them instructions when they started."

In a few minutes, Wendover's car overtook the ambulance on a hill and, with some little difficulty, managed to pass it on the narrow road.

"That's all right," said the Inspector, as they drew ahead. "Hullo! Somebody in a hurry, behind us, surely."

Wendover glanced at his driving-mirror and recognised Harry Thursford's big two-seater which was roaring up the slope behind them.

"I don't propose to let him pass," he said, as he turned his eyes to the road in front. "That's a pertinacious young devil if you like, Inspector. I've given him more than one plain hint that he isn't wanted; and yet here he comes, shoving his nose in as if he were indispensable. Some people have neither tact nor decency. I know Sir Clinton doesn't want a public meeting up yonder."

Severn craned out of the window and looked back.

"It's young Mr. Thursford right enough," he confirmed. "I'm afraid he'll just have to come along if he wants to. It's a public road, and we can't stop him. Queer how this rubber-neck business grips some people; and the uglier the sight, the keener they seem on getting a free peep. But most likely he's just trying to make himself useful," he added, in a tone which betrayed a complete contempt for amateur assistance in any shape or form.

It did not take them long to reach the point from which the stretcher-party had to start on foot. Wendover parked his car on a level bit of turf. Alloway, arriving almost immediately after them, drew up alongside; then came Harry Thursford's car; and finally the ambulance rolled up and disgorged two more constables. Wendover constituted himself guide, and they set off immediately in the direction of Hell's Gape.

Harry Thursford attached himself to Wendover and Severn; but he had the sense not to talk as they tramped along. Wendover had no desire for conversation. He was bracing himself to meet the ugly sight he had seen earlier in the day. Severn ignored the volunteer completely. Dr. Alloway, apparently fuming over some grievance, trudged along in silence, a few yards behind the others. The constables with the stretcher brought up the rear.

Wendover directed the march so that instead of following the line that he and Sir Clinton had taken in the morning, the party crossed the crest immediately above the grassy scarp and were able to descend directly to the end of Hell's Gape without disturbing the ground on the edge of the precipice from which Willenhall had fallen. Sir Clinton was sitting on a boulder just outside the mouth of the chasm but at sight of the figures straggling down the slope, he rose to his feet and came forward to meet Severn.

"Mr. Wendover's told you all about it?" he asked. "I've left everything untouched, so you can look round for yourself now. There'll be an inquest, and I don't want to be dragged to it if that can be avoided. Mr. Wendover can testify to our finding the body; and you can do the rest, I think."

Severn understood that the Chief Constable had no desire to be dragged away from his normal work to give unnecessary evidence. He agreed at once to the proposal.

"I'll fix that with the coroner, sir. It'll be all right."

Alloway, with a curt nod to Sir Clinton in passing, moved over to where Willenhall's body was lying.

"Wait a moment, Doctor," the Chief Constable suggested. "I think we might as well take a photograph of the body before you shift it. It may give the coroner's jury a clear idea of the state of affairs; save them a tramp up here, perhaps, to look at the lie of the land."

He turned to one of the constables.

"Just go up on top there" — he pointed to the lip of the chasm — "and get a kodak that's lying on the grass. Carry it by the handle. And don't trample round too much in getting it."

As the man set off, Sir Clinton turned to Severn.

"A bit like seething a kid in its mother's milk: taking a picture of a man's corpse with his own camera. Still, I think we ought to have a record. I know exactly where the kodak was lying, so there's no harm in shifting it now."

When the constable returned with the camera, Sir

Clinton took it from him and examined the dial at the back.

"Number 4," he read. "He's obviously taken three photographs on this spool and he may have taken a fourth without winding the film forward after the last one. We'd better be on the safe side and start ourselves on No. 5."

He screwed the handle, which worked rather stiffly, until No. 5 appeared. Then, choosing first one aspect and then another, he took two photographs of the body and its surroundings.

"You'd better keep the kodak in your charge," he said, handing it to Severn when he had finished. "By the way, you're a photographer yourself, I remember."

Severn was obviously pleased to find that the Chief Constable had recollected that.

"In that case," Sir Clinton suggested, "I think you'd better develop these yourself and save needless formalities with a photographic expert. You can manage that all right?"

"Easily enough," Severn assured him. "I see your point. It saves dragging someone else in to give formal evidence of the developing."

"And I think," Sir Clinton added, "that it would save trouble if you develop the roll as one film, without cutting it; and keep it intact as a single exhibit, instead of cutting off the separate exposures. You'll be able to fake up a printing-frame so that you can get prints from the various negatives, even if they aren't separated?"

"Oh, easily enough, sir. No difficulty with that."

"I think I'd leave that film in the camera and take it out in your dark room," Sir Clinton advised. "From the way the handle turned, it felt as if he'd put the film in slightly off the straight; and that corrugates the edges a bit. You might get fogging along the edge of the roll if you took it out. There's no need to risk that."

Alloway was fidgeting in the background, evidently anxious to start his examination and get it over. At a gesture from Sir Clinton he fell to work.

"You'd better have a look round at the top of the cliff," Sir Clinton suggested to Severn. "There's nothing more we can do here until Dr. Alloway's made his examination. Suppose we climb up yonder."

He led the way up the escarpment, accompanied by the Inspector. Wendover followed, and Harry Thurston also attached himself to the party in obvious curiosity.

"This is where his camera was lying," Sir Clinton explained to Severn, indicating the place as he spoke. "I've looked over the ground, but there's not much in the way of traces. He seems to have gone over the edge somehow — which is a fairly obvious inference," he added, with a smile. "So far as I can make out, he must have fallen from this bit of the cliff-top — here — but there's nothing to show how he slipped."

"He might have had his camera in his hand and been taking a photograph," Harry Thursford suggested. "If he was watching his viewfinder and moving to and fro to get exactly the picture he wanted, he might have stepped over the edge without looking where he was going."

"That's so," Severn admitted grudgingly. "You don't see the ground at your feet in a viewfinder. And one does get concentrated on the picture so that one doesn't pay much heed to where one's stepping. It's just possible."

Sir Clinton shook his head.

"Try again," he said decidedly. "When you feel yourself falling, your instinct makes you grip tight on any-thing you have in your hand; and if it's loose, it falls with you. Willenhall's kodak would be down below, if he'd been photographing at the moment when he went over the edge."

"That's true," Harry Thursford admitted, rather ruefully. "I hadn't thought of it in that way."

Sir Clinton turned to Severn.

"Another thing you can rule out. He wasn't leaning on his stick at the brink. His stick's over yonder, well back from the cliff; and most likely he laid it down when he began to work with his camera, and needed both hands."

Severn walked across and examined the stick.

"I see it's got an iron spike in the ferule. There aren't any holes in the turf that might suggest anything from that, sir?"

"No, none, so far as I could see," Sir Clinton replied. "I had a fair amount of time on my hands while I was waiting here, and I went over the ground minutely along the edge of the cliff. He didn't use his stick there."

He glanced down into the chasm.

"Dr. Alloway's still busy. There's just one thing more up here: one of these metal sandwich-cases."

"I noticed it, amongst the grass near his stick," Severn answered. "It's open and the paper's unfolded from one of the sandwiches. Looks rather as if he'd just started on his lunch and had got up to look over the cliff when . . . It may have been an attack of vertigo that made him stagger."

"Possibly," Sir Clinton admitted, without claiming that he himself had thrown out the same suggestion to Wendover earlier in the afternoon. "There doesn't seem much to go upon, one way or another. We may as well go down. You can have another look round later on, if you want to."

Severn hesitated for a moment and then picked up the stick and the sandwich-case, as though satisfied that he had seen all that was to be seen. Wendover guessed that, since Sir Clinton had spent the best part of an hour on the ground and had detected nothing, the Inspector was not optimistic about unearthing much by a further search. Severn had worked hand-in-hand with the Chief Constable before, and had come out of that experience with a very modest estimate of his own detective ability when compared with that of his superior.

They descended again to the open space at the end of Hell's Gape. The doctor was still busy with his examination, halting at intervals to jot down something in his pocket-book. As they stood waiting for him to finish, Sir Clinton turned to Harry Thursford.

"You'll probably be called as a witness at the inquest," he pointed out. "As a matter of form, it may be necessary to trace out Willenhall's movements in the forenoon. You can carry the tale up to the time he left you to come up here. About midday, that was, wasn't it?"

"I'll put it as near as I can for you," Harry volunteered. "We walked up together to that little dingle where you found us picnicking this morning. I'd arranged to meet Miss Langdale there at 12 o'clock. Willenhall didn't stop. He went straight on towards here. I waited about ten minutes, I should guess, before Miss Langdale turned up. She's usually punctual to a minute and she's been up to that place often, so I expect she was just on time. That would mean that Willenhall left me about ten to twelve or a quarter to, perhaps. I can't put it closer, because I didn't look at my watch then; but it's a fair guess, I think."

"It's about a twenty-minute walk up from the road," Severn interposed. "That means that he would reach here shortly after twelve."

"Unless he dawdled a bit," Sir Clinton pointed out. "He was a person with a turn for the picturesque, Mr. Wendover told me once. A man of that sort might turn aside here and there from the direct route and waste time."

"He certainly didn't hurry while he was with me," Harry put in. "And I remember he was a bit finicky about his snapshots. He put me through it about how the sun fell on these pinnacles and what time he was likely to get the shadows of them on the cliff face. I did what I could to help him, of course; but as I've only been up at this damned place once before, and that was years ago, I couldn't tell him much more than that it ran north and south, with the pinnacles on the south side. Quite likely, when he got here, he found that the shadows didn't come just where he wanted them."

"And sat down to eat his lunch to pass the time?" Severn suggested.

Sir Clinton turned and looked into the mouth of the chasm. The sun was westering now, and its rays shot slant-wise into the Gape, throwing triangular shadows of the great rock-fangs upon the vertical face of the northern cliff.

"That's very striking," Sir Clinton said in a tone of frank admiration. "I've never seen a place quite like this before. It looks a bit grim, even in this sunshine. In the twilight, it must be on the edge of awe-inspiring, I should think. The kind of place that would make you wonder what might come creeping out on you from the abyss. You'd be quite prepared for a prehistoric monster."

He seemed to ignore the sinister group in the foreground and let his eye run over the rugged walls of the chasm as if in pure aesthetic pleasure. Then, rather irrelevantly, he observed:

"I've often wondered about that miracle of Isaiah's."

Severn was completely at sea.

"What miracle, sir?"

Wendover, with more experience in following the line of Sir Clinton's thoughts, saw the reference. He glanced up at the long triangular shadows.

"You mean the Dial of Ahaz?"

"Yes. You ought to read your Bible, Inspector. Try the Second Book of Kings, amongst the last four or five chapters, and you'll find it. It's just before the bit about 'Berodach-baladan, son of Baladan, king of Babylon,' which always sticks in my mind on account of the names."

Severn would obviously have liked more enlightenment; but at that moment Alloway snapped his bag as though to show that he had finished his work. Sir Clinton walked into the chasm, followed by the others. As they entered it, they felt as though the sun had suddenly passed behind a cloud. By contrast with the brilliant sunshine a few yards away, the cleft seemed almost in twilight.

"Not much difficulty about this," Alloway pronounced abruptly. "Skull's badly fractured; he seems to have come down on his head. Two ribs broken on left side, by this ridge on the rock, I expect. Internal injuries as well, probably. They'll have to wait till I get a P. M. done. The damage to the head's quite enough to cause immediate death."

"Can you estimate how long he's been dead?" Severn inquired.

"Eh? Not accurately. Body temperature's now 74°. But the air's warm and the ground's cool. A bit hard to guess what the rate of cooling's been in a case of this kind. Anywhere between two and six hours might fit. I shouldn't care to go closer than that."

"You can't suggest any reason for his fall?" Severn pursued. "Vertigo, or something like that?"

"My dear man, I'm not a clairvoyant. I don't think he had an epileptic seizure, though it's possible, of course. But if you ask me to diagnose whether his head was swimming or not, it can't be done. Not by me, at least. His family doctor might know if he was subject to that sort of thing. I don't."

Severn, accustomed to Alloway's brusque manner, took no offence. The doctor picked up his bag.

"That's all I can do here. I'll arrange with you later about the P. M. There'll be an inquest, of course? All right. I must get away."

With a cavalier nod, he walked out of the cleft and began to climb the escarpment.

"You'd better see if there's anything in the pockets," Sir Clinton suggested to Severn.

Rather gingerly, the Inspector set to work, noting down each article in his pocket-book as he came across it.

"Take the jacket-pocket that's uppermost, first of all. Two rolls of film, unexposed. Two more rolls, been exposed, evidently. They're six-exposure rolls, all of them. That's all there. Breast-pocket, a note-case with some notes and postage-stamps in it. A letter with a type-written address and the local post-mark."

"Let's have a look at that before we go any further,"

96

Sir Clinton directed, holding out his hand for the envelope.

"This will interest you, Wendover," he remarked after a glance at the contents. "It's a carbon copy of that threatening letter you got in this morning's post. Listen to this, Inspector."

He read the document aloud for Severn's benefit; then, without comment, returned it to its envelope.

"Anything else in the pockets?"

"A cigarette-holder and a penknife in one, a petrol lighter in another, and a fountain-pen in the left upper pocket. That's all in the waistcoat. Right-hand trouser-pocket: small bunch of keys and a few coppers. Hip-pocket: a gold cigarette-case," Severn reported.

He snapped his fingers, and a constable came forward and helped him to turn the body into a fresh position.

"Left-hand jacket-pocket, nothing but a flask with a silver cup on the butt of it. Flask's smashed, of course, in the fall. Seems to have been whiskey and water in it, apparently, but it's all run out. Trouser-pocket, some loose silver. That's the lot."

"Not much of a haul, so far as information goes," Sir Clinton commented, though without any disappointment in his tone. "Want to have another prowl round, Inspector, before we pack up and go?"

"You've told me everything you've found yourself, sir?"

Sir Clinton nodded.

"Well, in that case, I think I'll let it go at that," Severn decided. "I haven't seen anything myself, beyond what you'd found; and I don't suppose I'd spot anything fresh if I looked again. If you're quite satisfied now, we'd better make our way back."

Sir Clinton agreed. Severn gave orders to his constables. The body was lifted onto the stretcher and the mournful little procession filed out of the jaws of the chasm into the sunlight beyond. As they emerged, Wendover glanced back into the gloom of the ravine.

"Not many people will want to linger about here in the dusk after this," he reflected. "It was ugly enough before. Now it'll have the name of being haunted as well. It looks it."

At the crest of the slope, Sir Clinton paused and began to examine the landscape. The stretcher-party continued its way down the farther descent, but Wendover, Thursford and the Inspector halted with the Chief Constable.

Below them, on their right, they could see Alloway's figure receding steadily towards the tiny grey spot which marked the position of the ambulance. On the left, the crest bent slightly northward and concealed the further horizon.

"What's beyond that?" Sir Clinton demanded, turning to Wendover.

"Much the same sort of country. Half an hour's walk would bring you to a road. There's an isolated farm there: Brookman's Farm. It's on the far side of the road and a bit back from it. That's the nearest inhabited place round about here, though there are scattered cottages farther up the road."

"Mr. Checkley came up that way, sir," Severn put in. "He was really the first person to find the body."

In a few words he explained to Sir Clinton how the news had been brought to him.

"Luckily, he left things alone," was Sir Clinton's comment, when the Inspector had finished.

Harry Thursford had kept silent for a long time;

but now, to Wendover's annoyance, he began to specu-
late on the manner of the tragedy.

"I suppose it *must* have been a sudden attack of
giddiness," he opined. "There wasn't anything up on
the edge there that he could have stubbed his toe on or
tripped over. It's plain turf right up to the rim of the
drop. Or d'you think he may have been kneeling down
and bending over to get a flower, or something, on the
cliff face?"

"There weren't any flowers there. I looked," said
Sir Clinton in a discouraging tone.

"He couldn't have lost his balance in a gust of wind,
and toppled over the edge?"

"Not in a dead calm," Wendover objected. "There
hasn't been a breath of wind since the morning."

"That's so," Harry confirmed, after reflection. "So
it wasn't that. Well, unless he turned giddy, I don't see
how it happened. It's a bit mysterious, isn't it? I mean,
hundreds of people must have been up there at one time
or other out of curiosity, and yet none of them fell over.
Why should he? He couldn't have been trying to shin
down the rock-face, because there was an easy grass
slope to get down by, in plain sight."

He shrugged his shoulders with the air of one who
abandons a problem which he finds too difficult.

Sir Clinton had apparently seen all that he wanted.

"We may as well go down now," he suggested, setting
the example.

Wendover joined him. Harry Thursford, not caring
to attach himself to the two friends, had to drop into
step with the Inspector, who followed at a few yards
distance. No one seemed much inclined to talk; and
almost in silence they made their way back to the place
where the cars had been parked. Alloway's was gone;

but the ambulance was still standing by the roadside along with the two others. As Sir Clinton appeared, the constables rose from the grass where they had been sitting, and awaited orders.

"You've put the stretcher in?" Sir Clinton asked.

"Yes, sir."

Sir Clinton glanced round the group and then at the cars, as though estimating numbers.

"We're a bit short of room now," he commented. "Eight of us to get home somehow. One on the ambulance . . ."

"I've got a dickey-seat," Harry Thursford broke in.

Sir Clinton seemed relieved.

"Oh, then that's all right," he said. "One constable on the ambulance with the driver; the other three with you; and the rest of us can get into Mr. Wendover's car."

And without giving anyone time to question this arrangement, he motioned Wendover to get in and then took the seat beside him. The Inspector jumped in behind; and Wendover, glad to be quit of Harry Thursford and his speculations, started the engine and drove off at once.

When they had gone a hundred yards or so, Sir Clinton turned round to Severn.

"It looks a plain enough affair. An attack of vertigo would fit the facts, obviously. And yet . . ."

"You don't think it was an accident?" the Inspector queried.

"I've no opinion, one way or the other," Sir Clinton admitted frankly. "But just to be on the safe side, I think you'd better develop the whole lot of these exposed films and see what's on them. Handle them carefully and don't cut the negatives away from each other.

One never knows what may turn up. We might want proof of the order in which they were taken; and if they're kept intact, it's easier to see which came first on each roll. Once you start cutting, you'd have to number them, and so on."

"Very good, sir. I'll attend to that."

"And you may as well be able to produce everything at the inquest, backing-paper, spools, and labels. It's as well to be thorough when one starts."

"I'll see that's done, sir. By the way, I suppose it's that threatening letter we found in his pocket that's making you doubtful about it being a pure accident?"

There seemed to be a hint of mischief in the faint smile which crossed Sir Clinton's face at this remark.

"I'll rely on you to form your own opinion on that letter, after you've gone into the matter a bit more thoroughly," he said, in a serious tone. "Once you've done that, we can compare notes. I don't want to prejudice you by telling you what I think about it."

"Well, of course, in its form it's a blackmailing demand," the Inspector admitted. "Question is, was it meant as anything more than a joke?"

Sir Clinton evaded a direct answer.

"As Saint Paul observed to Timothy: 'They that desire to be rich fall into a temptation,' " he quoted.

"Then do you think . . . ?" the Inspector persisted.

"I'll tell you exactly what I think," Sir Clinton said, with an unusual display of frankness. "I think there's a lot of money going to change hands over this affair, as Mr. Wendover can tell you. And I agree with Saint Paul that the love of money is a root of all kinds of evil. But there isn't a scrap of evidence that I can see which shows that Willenhall didn't come to his death by a pure accident."

CHAPTER VIII: THE INQUEST

THE possible composition of the coroner's jury had given Wendover some qualms. The Novem Syndicate had attained a national notoriety owing to its success in the draw; and the inquest on Willenhall would be reported in many of the bigger newspapers merely because he had been one of the members. Obviously the whole of the Syndicate's affairs would be dragged into the limelight in the course of the inquiry. That was almost unavoidable. But if one of the jurors proved to be a fussy and inquisitive fellow, he might insist on asking questions which had no real connection with the case; and Wendover had no desire for more publicity.

However, as he glanced from face to face, he heaved a faint sigh of relief. He knew every man of them, and none was likely to show the slightest initiative. It was a jury which would depend entirely upon the coroner and be quite content with the information which was vouchsafed to it.

His glance passed to some of the other people in the room. The coroner he knew: a man who would extract all the information which was necessary but who would not turn himself into a *juge d'instruction* and fish for irrelevant details. Wendover nodded to Halstead, young Thurston, Checkley, Alloway, and the Inspector, who had obviously been called as witnesses. In the background he caught sight of Mr. Monyash, who was cleaning his nails with a toothpick to pass the time. Beside him was a clean-shaven alert stranger whom Wendover put down as the legal representative of Willen-hall's relatives. Monyash, Wendover suspected, was holding a watching brief on behalf of Blackburn's trustees. The death of Willenhall paralleled that of Blackburn, so far as the original Syndicate agreement went; and Monyash could not know of the subsequent arrangement which had been made. Probably he had come merely to keep an eye on the proceedings in the interest of his clients.

After a few words of explanation, the coroner called Halstead as the first witness.

"You have identified the body as that of Mr. Godfrey Willenhall?"

Halstead had evidently been coached as to the evidence he was to offer.

"Yes, I identified the body as that of Mr. Willenhall. Mr. Willenhall was a bachelor living at 29a Cyprus Mansions, Kensington, where he had a service flat. He had private means and engaged in no business, so far as I am aware. He was a quiet, retiring man, of very simple tastes. I have known him for a number of years. We met mainly in town when I happened to be in London. I never met any relative of his except a married sister and her husband."

"He was staying with you at the time of his death?"

"Yes. Early in May, I invited him to come here on a visit. He was interested in local curiosities — old churches, historical sites, and that kind of thing — and he was quite anxious to spend some time here exploring the neighbourhood. No particular length of visit was arranged, but it was understood that he would be here for some weeks. He arrived on May 20th."

"You had some idea of when he was likely to leave, though?"

"I believe he meant to go off this week, sometime. There was nothing definitely arranged. That is merely my impression. I was quite glad to have him as a visitor. I was engaged during the day, and he spent the time wandering about the district, photographing things which took his fancy. He was interested in photography."

"Here is a kodak camera. Can you identify it as the property of the deceased?"

Halstead examined the instrument.

"It's a No. 1A Kodak, the same as I use myself occasionally. To the best of my knowledge this is the camera belonging to the deceased, but I really cannot swear to it being his. I never examined his camera closely."

"The deceased was a member of a Syndicate, the Novem Syndicate, which drew the second horse in the Hospitals Sweep?"

"That is so."

"You were not a member of this Syndicate yourself?"

"No, I had no interest in the matter, unfortunately. I was offered a ticket, but refused it."

"You had no business dealings with the deceased?"

"None whatever, in any shape or form. Our relationship was purely of a friendly nature."

"On the morning of June 13th — the day of his death — the deceased received a letter by the first post?"

"Yes, he got it at breakfast time and passed it across to me. It was a carbon copy, not a ribbon copy, and it was signed 'Big-headed Ben the Gunman.'"

"You identify this as the document you mention?"

Halstead glanced at the paper which the coroner handed to him.

"That appears to be the document which I saw. It is

in the same terms, at least, so far as I remember them."

The coroner took back the paper and read the letter to the jury.

"What impression did you form of this document?"

"Mr. Willenhall laughed at it and said something about 'Boys will be boys,' I remember. Neither of us took it seriously."

"Do you take it more seriously now?"

"No," said Halstead frankly, "I don't. I put it down to practical joking or to some boy who has been to the pictures oftener than's good for him."

"You can't regard it as likely to throw any light on the deceased's death, then?"

"Not in the slightest. That's my opinion, merely."

"The deceased was not worried by it?"

"Not at all. He laughed over it and put it in his pocket merely as a curiosity."

"Did he give you any indication of his plans on the morning of his death?"

Halstead shook his head decidedly.

"No. I had no idea what he meant to do."

"Did you ever detect any tendency to vertigo in him?"

"He never mentioned anything of the sort to me. I believe you can suffer from giddiness as a result of indigestion, but so far as I know his digestion was all right. He didn't complain of it."

The coroner seemed satisfied with this evidence, but just as he was about to dismiss the witness, his eye was caught by Monyash's companion, and this seemed to remind him of a question which he had not put.

"Just one more point, Mr. Halstead. During your acquaintance with Mr. Willenhall did you ever see anything which might suggest that he had suicidal tendencies?"

"Never," Halstead declared emphatically.

"And as he was living on a private income, you saw no signs of business troubles?"

"None."

"In conversation with you, did he ever say that he speculated?"

"No. In fact, when we did discuss financial questions I remember that he always argued in favour of gilt-edged stocks. He was quite averse to speculation; and if you are suggesting that he may have had heavy losses, I can only say that I got no hint of any such state of affairs."

The coroner made a gesture which showed that he accepted this without ado. Halstead went back to his seat, and his place was taken by a fresh witness, Josiah Napton, the village druggist.

"The deceased used to purchase his photographic films at your shop, didn't he?" the coroner inquired.

"Yes, he used to come in every second day or so to buy some. He also had his films developed by me and prints made from them."

"Do you recall any other purchases which he made?"

"I don't remember any other purchases, but once he came in asking for a new shutter release cable. I couldn't supply it from stock; and he said he thought his present one would last until I could order one for him."

"When did he purchase films from you last?"

"On the morning of his death. He came into my shop about a quarter to ten and bought four spools for his kodak."

"You never saw his camera, I suppose?"

Napton shook his head.

"No, he never showed it to me. He bought spools for a No. 1A, so it must have been that model that he had."

"Are you sure about the time of his last visit?"

"I am, fairly. I had an appointment with a traveller from one of the wholesale firms at ten o'clock that morning. He came just as Mr. Willenhall was going out, and I remember I said something to him about being more eager than usual — just a little joke, you understand — and it turned out his watch was wrong. So I gave him the right time from my own watch. That's how I'm fairly sure of the time when Mr. Willenhall left my place."

The coroner seemed to have no further questions for this witness. Harry Thursford was the next person summoned to give evidence.

"You had an appointment with the deceased on the morning of his death?" the coroner began.

"Yes. I had offered to show him the Maiden's Well. It's not far off the road, but a stranger might easily miss it, and I volunteered to take him to it. We arranged to meet at Crowland Corner and I had a note from him — here it is — fixing 10.45 A. M."

The coroner took the note and read it through aloud for the benefit of the jury.

June 12th.

Dear Mr. Thursford,

Thanks for your offer to show me the road to the Maiden's Well, and to point out the way to Hell's Gape afterwards. If we meet at Crowland's Corner at 10.45 A. M. it will suit me very well. Thanks for your kindness.

Yours sincerely
G. WILLENHALL

"Was he on time when you met him?"

"I was there first," Harry Thursford explained. "But he did not keep me waiting. I looked at my watch just before he came round the corner, and it was between twenty and a quarter to eleven then."

"There are several roads from here up to Crowland's Corner?"

"Yes, there are a couple of short cuts and there's the main road as well. By the short cuts it's about a mile and a half or a mile and three quarters, I should think; along the main road it's about four miles, owing to the way the road curls round the Talgarth Grange ground."

"Which route had he taken?"

"I really can't say," Harry admitted. "The short cuts join the main road a bit before Crowland's Corner. He came along the main road to meet me, but for all I know he may have come by one of the short cuts — either the one near the lake or the other one — and dawdled a bit by the way, taking photographs. All I really know is that I met him at Crowland's Corner at about a quarter to eleven. I didn't ask him which way he had come up."

"From what you saw of him, would you say he was a good walker?"

"I should say that he'd had plenty of practice and was very fit," Harry answered in a decided tone. "He was a fast walker, if anything. I should think four miles an hour would be his normal pace on a road."

"What happened when you met?"

Harry reflected for a moment or two.

"We stood about for a few minutes, looking at the view from there. He got me to point out various places to him, down below. We talked about this and that, and then we moved on up the road. It's about a mile — or rather less, I think — to the place where you turn off to the Maiden's Well. We left the road there . . ."

"That would be about eleven o'clock, then?" the coroner interjected.

"About then. It's a quarter of an hour's walk to the Well — there or thereabouts. I sat down while he poked about a bit with his camera and took some photographs. At a guess, I'd say we were about ten minutes or a quarter of an hour at the Well. Then we made our way back to the road again. After that we dawdled up the hill. I was in no hurry, as I had an appointment at noon, and I didn't want to hang about as I'd have had to do if I hurried. I remember I looked at my watch when we left the Well and it was just about half-past eleven then, unless I've made a mistake. We walked slowly up from there, and when we got to the turn-off for Hell's Gape, I showed him the way and let him go off at once. I didn't press him to stay, because my fiancée had arranged to meet me there at midday, and to tell the truth I didn't want to run the risk of his joining our picnic. Miss Langdale arrived about five minutes after he'd gone."

"You didn't see him making his way up to Hell's Gape?"

Harry Thursford shook his head.

"No. From where we were sitting, the trees come in the way and you can't see the track up towards the Gape."

"What happened after that?" the coroner asked.

"Miss Langdale and I sat there for some time. We had a picnic. She'd brought some lunch up in her car. Just after we'd finished lunch, Sir Clinton Driffield and Mr. Wendover turned up. That was at a quarter past two, for I happened to look at my watch then. They talked with us for a few minutes and then went on towards the Gape."

"You and Miss Langdale remained behind, of course?"

"Yes. The next thing was Mr. Wendover coming back with the news that Mr. Willenhall had had an accident, a serious accident. He didn't say he was dead. We three went off for assistance, in Miss Langdale's car."

"What time was that, can you remember?"

"It was five minutes to three. I looked at my watch carefully then, for I had an idea that the time might be important. I made a note of it later on."

The coroner nodded as though terminating that part of the subject.

"You are a member of this Novem Syndicate, I believe?" he demanded.

"Yes."

"Have you received a copy of this threatening letter which has already been communicated to the jury?"

"Yes, all of us seem to have got one. Mine was a carbon copy like that sent to Mr. Willenhall."

"Did you mention it to Mr. Willenhall?"

"Yes, we discussed it. Not very seriously. We thought it rather a joke. I don't take it very seriously even now. It's rather rumly phrased if you look at it."

The coroner evidently felt that he was allowing Harry Thursford to wander from the point. Abruptly he switched off on to a new subject.

"You did not notice any signs of vertigo in the deceased that morning?"

Harry Thursford reflected carefully before answering.

"No," he said at length, "I can't say I did. I suggested at the Maiden's Well that he might get a good snapshot by climbing up the rock-face a bit and he put the idea aside. He may have been afraid of turning giddy; but he certainly didn't say so. I got the idea that his artistic ideas and mine didn't agree and that he thought poorly of my notion. That was what I thought at the time."

This seemed to satisfy the coroner, for he allowed Harry Thursford to stand down. Checkley was called next; and as he gave his evidence, Wendover noticed that he must have prepared it well beforehand, for he had very little hesitation at any point.

"You are a manufacturer of confectionery, Mr. Checkley?" the coroner began, evidently leading up to some point which Wendover could not forecast at the moment.

"Yes. My main line's Checkley's Kreematic Toffee. I run one or two side-lines as well. Checkley's Ginger Crunchers is one. Checkley's Orchard Refreshers is another. I'm on the look-out for new ideas in the confectionery line."

Wendover was slightly disgusted by what he took to be an attempt on Checkley's part to advertise his wares in connection with a case which was bound to receive wide publicity.

"Damn the fellow," he reflected, biting his moustache. "He'd turn a funeral into an advertisement pageant if he got half a chance. I suppose he's out for cheap publicity; hopes this puff will be reproduced in the reports. Why doesn't the coroner sit on him?"

But the coroner seemed to have no intention of doing so. In fact, he appeared inclined to encourage Checkley.

"Then naturally a hint of something fresh in the way of a recipe would attract your attention at once?"

"I'd be on to anything like that, straight away."

"You received a suggestion on these lines from the deceased?"

"I did. He wrote me a note about it."

"Thank you." The coroner held out his hand and took the sheet of paper which Checkley held out. "I see that it is typewritten, like the one which Mr. Thursford produced in the course of his evidence. I had better read it for the benefit of the jury:—

June 12th.

Dear Mr. Checkley,

It occurs to me that as a manufacturer you might be interested in new recipes for sweetmeats. In my walks round the district I happened to light on something which might be worth your attention.

I chanced to stop at a small cottage off the road to ask for a drink of water as I was very thirsty. The old lady asked me into her house and I noticed a large glass jar filled with a rather attractive-looking sweetmeat. In casual conversation I learned that the sweetmeat was of her own make prepared from an old family recipe and flavoured with herbs which she collects. She sells it locally to a very small clientele under the name of Herb Suckit which I take to be a corruption of the old word "sucket" for a sweetmeat.

Being anxious to repay her kindness to me I purchased a small quantity. And as she assured me that it was excellent for quenching thirst I tried some of it on my way home and found it novel and attractive in taste.

It occurs to me that by putting you in touch with my late hostess I might do a service to both of you. I cannot direct you to her cottage as I did not ask her name and the route I followed was rather intricate but I could find my way back there without difficulty.

Tomorrow I have arranged to pay a visit to Hell's Gape and shall be coming down from it by the path which leads on to the road near Brookman's Farm. If you care to meet me there with a car I shall be very glad to guide you to the cottage so that you may judge for yourself whether the thing appeals to you or not. I shall be at Brookman's Farm at 1.30 P. M.

Yours faithfully
G. WILLENHALL

The coroner, having finished reading the letter, put it down on the table before him and turned to Checkley.

"You received this letter by the post?"

"Yes. First post on Saturday, June 13th. Saturday's a half-day at my factory, so I'd no difficulty about keeping the appointment. I went up to Brookman's Farm, arrived there just about half-past one. There was no sign of the deceased, so I waited a while. After twenty minutes or so I got bored doing nothing. It occurred to me I might as well leave the car and walk up the hill to meet the deceased. I didn't see any sign of him, so I walked on and on, expecting him to appear at any moment. Finally, I got so near the Gape that I thought I might as well go the whole way before turning back. It crossed my mind that he might have sprained an ankle or something like that. I got up to the Gape, and found the body of the deceased on the floor of the Gape. He was obviously dead, which was a great shock to me. It made me quite sick. I looked at my watch as I came away in search of assistance. It was then twenty past two. I touched nothing about the deceased. I did not go up to the top of the cliff. My whole idea was to get away again and summon help. I went straight back to my car and drove down at once to the police station here, where I met Inspector Severn. I told him what I had found and left him to do the rest. After that I went home. I had had a very bad shock, coming upon the thing unexpectedly like that."

"Your impression was that he had fallen from the cliff?"

"Of course. The injuries I saw couldn't have been caused in any other way that I can think of."

The coroner appeared to have come to the end of his inquiries except for the familiar question:

"You received a copy of this threatening letter which has already been mentioned several times?"

"Yes, I did — a carbon copy."

"Did you attach any importance to it when you received it?"

"None whatever. And I don't attach any importance to it now."

"You think it merely a joke?"

"A very silly sort of joke," amplified the witness, with a sneer.

When Checkley was dismissed, Wendover found himself called by the coroner. Just as he had feared, the whole story of the Novem Syndicate was dragged out: the formation of it at the bridge-party, the complications resulting from Blackburn's death, the new agreement, and the application to the High Court. While concealing nothing, Wendover took care to make his evidence as colourless as possible so as to give very little chance to the sensational press, if they chose to deal with the case. After this side of the matter had been thrashed out, the coroner turned to the actual tragedy, and Wendover described his meeting with Harry Thursford and Viola Langdale, as well as the succeeding events up to the time when the body was brought away in the ambulance.

The coroner produced a kodak camera and asked Wendover if he could identify it as Willenhall's.

Wendover shook his head.

"I can't identify it definitely," he admitted as he turned it over in his hands. "If it belonged to Mr. Willenhall, I should expect to find the cable of the shutter-release badly worn."

He pressed the stud, opened out the front, and examined the part.

"This shutter-release cable is very badly worn. To that extent, I feel inclined to say that this is Mr. Willenhall's camera. But that is as far as I can go."

The coroner asked Harry Thursford to come forward and look at the instrument.

"I had Mr. Willenhall's camera in my hands for a minute or so at the Maiden's Well," Harry explained. "I noticed that the leather was worn about the red window and a bit had been gouged out of the edge near there, probably by the camera falling at one time. Also, there was a scratch on the autographic flap. This camera has all these points, and I'm practically certain that this is Mr. Willenhall's instrument. But that's as far as I care to go. These kodaks are all standardised and although I noticed the flaws I've described, I only had the thing in my hands for a moment or two, and I'd no particular reason for paying special attention to it."

The coroner indicated that the jury could make up their minds on the point. As they would see shortly, the camera was important. He would call their attention to the fact that two witnesses had mentioned the defective cable which the camera obviously had; and another witness had identified it by a totally different piece of evidence. He ordered the kodak to be passed to the jury so that they might examine the features for themselves. While they were looking it over, he went on with his examination of Wendover.

"You received a copy of this threatening letter, I believe, Mr. Wendover?"

"Yes. The ribbon copy of it was sent to me. I attached no importance to it. Sir Clinton Driffield, the Chief Constable, was staying with me at the time and I showed it to him. He seemed to take the same view of it as I did — that it was a boy's prank — and he proposed to get Inspector Severn to set a trap for the author. I handed the letter to Sir Clinton to give to Inspector Severn."

The coroner produced a paper and showed it to Wendover.

"Yes, that's the letter I got," Wendover swiftly confirmed.

"You don't attach any importance to this letter in connection with Mr. Willenhall's death?"

"None whatever. If you read the letter, you'll see that it demands £10,000 to be paid within twenty-four hours of the letter's being posted. No blackmailer who meant business would make an absurd provision like that. Further, it threatens that 'if you don't fork out the money' one of the Syndicate will be murdered. But Mr. Willenhall came to his death half a day before the expiration of their time-limit; it was on the midnight of the day of his death that the money was to be handed over. It seems to me that there's nothing more than a coincidence there — a rather gruesome coincidence, I admit, but nothing more than that."

"The jury will take a careful note of the point you've made, Mr. Wendover. It certainly throws some clear light on the subject and helps us to assess this letter at its proper value."

Wendover was glad to escape and made way for Alloway, the police surgeon, who gave technical evidence as to the injuries which Willenhall had sustained.

"Did you examine the contents of the stomach?" the coroner asked after Alloway had finished his account.

The police surgeon's habitual air of a man with a grievance was intensified by this inquiry.

"There was nothing abnormal in the stomach contents," he snapped. "So far as I could see, he'd had nothing since his breakfast and the digestion seemed quite normal."

"Then, so far as you could see, he hadn't been taking a dose of a drug which might have made him giddy and so caused him to fall from the cliff?"

"I found nothing of the sort."

"You didn't find anything in his flask?"

Alloway's air of irritation grew even more marked.

"His flask was smashed in the fall. There was nothing left in it except a drop or two of his whiskey."

The coroner seemed to attach little importance to his own suggestion, which he had apparently thrown out on the spur of the moment.

Wendover, reflecting on the scene, was struck by the way in which individuality vanished when people began to give evidence. They all sounded very much alike in their language. He remembered that he had noted this point in reading short-hand notes of murder trials; and was interested to find it confirmed by practical experience. All witnesses seemed to be divested of their normal turns of speech and to express themselves in the plainest and simplest possible way, so that there was a strong common resemblance between the different testimonies. That gave a slightly inhuman touch to the affair, he observed. It was like the uniformity which one might expect from robots rather than the diversity of normal human beings.

When the coroner called Inspector Severn to give evidence, Wendover brought his attention back to the case before him. He knew Severn well and had experience of his thoroughness in a case which had been staged in his own boat-house. In this affair of Willenhall, however, he did not see much chance for Severn's exhaustive methods. The Inspector had come into the case even later than Wendover himself and had seen no more than he had seen in the later stages. It seemed difficult to imagine that he had anything fresh to contribute. And yet his knowledge of the Inspector's mannerisms gave him a hint that this evidence would be different from that of the other witnesses.

Severn opened his statement with a description of Checkley's arrival at the police station with the news of the Hell's Gape tragedy. He then passed lightly over the intervening events until he reached the point when the Chief Constable had led them to examine the ground at the top of the cliff.

"The following articles," he explained, "were found within a few yards of the point from which the deceased must have fallen. First, there was a sandwich-case lying open on the grass, with one of the packets in it partly unrolled as though the deceased had just begun his preparations for lunch. This is the sandwich-case" (he held it up) "which is of the normal pattern, made to pack flat after the contents have been used. The second article was a walking-stick with a steel point on the ferule, like an alpenstock. That has been identified by several persons as the stick which the deceased always took

118

with him on his walks. Finally, there was this kodak, which we have every reason to assume to be the one used by the deceased in his expeditions."

He held up the camera which had already been shown to Wendover and Harry Thursford.

"When Sir Clinton Driffield picked up this kodak, there was in it a roll-film of six exposures. Three of these had already been exposed, and the dial indicated No. 4. After I arrived on the scene, Sir Clinton Driffield screwed the spool forward to No. 5. On this No. 5 and on No. 6 section, he took two photographs of the body of the deceased as it lay before it had been in any way disturbed. These two photographs give a clear picture of the body and its surroundings. With the coroner's permission, I shall exhibit them to the members of the jury."

At a sign from the coroner, he passed the two prints to the foreman and waited whilst the jury had inspected them. When he had received them back again, he continued his narrative.

"In the pockets of the deceased, we discovered two rolls of film which had been exposed in the camera and two other rolls with the seals unbroken, which had evidently not been used. Each roll was a six-exposure roll; so that including the three exposures on the roll in the kodak itself, there was evidence that the deceased had taken fifteen photographs."

Severn produced a bag which he had brought with him, and from it took three long strips of developed negatives.

"I developed all five rolls of film, keeping the strips intact so as to preserve the relative positions of the various exposures. Two of the films — those with the makers' seals unbroken — yielded nothing on development.

I didn't expect anything on *them*, of course; but it's well to be thorough."

He held up the three strips of film on which the negative pictures could be seen.

"These are the three remaining strips: one from the camera and two from the pocket of the deceased. As you will see in a moment, they were all taken that morning by the deceased, and it is possible to establish the order of the exposures. I have marked the three films respectively Exhibits A, B, and C. Exhibit A is the one which was first exposed; then comes the second roll used by him, Exhibit B; and finally the roll taken from the camera itself, on which he had taken three pictures before his death, Exhibit C. Each roll contains six exposures in order, so that by numbering these 1, 2, 3 . . . etc. I can refer to a particular film without having to trouble the jury with detailed description."

He dipped into his bag again and produced a number of strips of bromide prints taken from the various negatives. One of these sets he handed to the coroner, the others he passed over to the jury.

"These positives are taken from the negatives I showed you; and for convenience I have numbered the prints according to the scheme I mentioned. For example, if you look at Exhibit C, No. 5, you will find one of the photographs of the body taken by Sir Clinton Driffield. The exposure before that is blank — that is, Exhibit C, No. 4 — because Sir Clinton screwed the film one space forward before taking the picture lest the deceased had used No. 4 and had not screwed the film on before his death."

Wendover, examining the jury, could see that they handled the photographs with a blend of curiosity and awe. By some queer association of memory, there drifted into his mind the spell from Ingoldsby's *Hand of Glory:* —

> Open lock, To the Dead Man's knock!
> Fly bolt, and bar, and band! —
> Nor move, nor swerve, Joint, muscle, or nerve,
> At the spell of the Dead Man's hand!
> Sleep all who sleep! — Wake all who wake!
> But be as the dead for the Dead Man's sake!

Here, in a different sense, was the spell of the Dead Man's hand. It was almost as though Willenhall had reached out from beyond the grave to bring his own testimony as to his fate. These photographs, the last he had ever taken and the results of which he was never to see, might throw some light upon his doings up to the very moment when disaster overtook him. Wendover felt the thrill that comes from half-guessed mysteries, and he could see that something of the same fascination was over the jury as they handled these records made by the dead.

"If you'll look at the first photograph — that is, Exhibit A, No. 1 — you will find that it's a picture of a stile, with a glade beyond," Severn began prosaically. "No. 2 shows the lake in Mr. Wendover's grounds, taken from the side nearest the village. No. 3 shows the lake again, taken from the end. You can see Mr. Wendover's boat-house if you look carefully. Then No. 4 is a bit of wood-path. No. 5 shows the lake again, taken from the far side and from a good distance away up the slope. No. 6 shows the Maiden's Well, with Mr. Thursford standing beside the rock. These photographs show that the deceased took the short cut on his way to Crowland's Corner. I've made inquiries, but I can't learn that anyone met him on the way. As you know, that track through the Silver Grove grounds is not much used; and we happen to have been unlucky to the extent that no one happened to be on it that morning. However, the photographs themselves tell the tale plain enough, as I'll make clear in a moment or two."

Severn picked up a fresh strip of photographs.

"If you'll be good enough to turn to Exhibit B, you will find the continuation of the story. The deceased took out the old film, put it in his pocket, and inserted this fresh roll. On Exhibit B, No. 1 exposure shows the Maiden's Well again. No. 2 shows the Well from a different aspect, with Mr. Thursford sitting down just at the brink of the pool. No. 3 is practically the same picture. You can see that Mr. Thursford has changed his position very slightly. Exposure No. 4 shows the Well again, taken quite close up. That finishes the exposures he made at the Well. The next one, No. 5 on the same strip, shows Hell's Gape, a view taken from the edge of the cliff, looking down into the chasm. Exposure No. 6 shows Hell's Gape again, taken from between two of the spikes of rock on the south side. That finishes the six exposures on that roll. He took that out of the camera, put it in his pocket, and inserted a fresh film — Exhibit C — which contains the last three photographs he took."

Wendover, who could not see the details of the prints which the jury were handling, was on tenterhooks to hear Severn's description of this ultimate set of exposures. Here, if anywhere, the truth would be found. And from his own eagerness he discovered that in his inmost mind he was still doubtful if Willenhall had actually met with an accident. Some of the evidence given that morning had made him prick up his ears; and yet he could not say that he had any very definite suspicions. Simply, he felt, the thing might not be so obvious as it looked at first sight.

"Exhibit C, No. 1," Severn continued, "shows the mouth of Hell's Gape. Exposure No. 2 is the same, taken from a slightly different viewpoint. Exposure No. 3 — the last which he took — is a picture of the chasm taken from the top of the cliff, as in No. 5 of Exhibit B, but from a slightly different standpoint. Then comes the blank exposure, No. 4, and the two photographs, 5 and 6, taken by Sir Clinton Driffield.

"From these photographs taken by the deceased himself at Hell's Gape, it is simple enough to reconstruct his movements round about the place. He came to it by a route which landed him at the brink of the precipice. There he took B.5. He then walked down the scarp and past the mouth of Hell's Gape on to the south side, where he seems to have clambered up the rocks until he could look into the Gape through one of the gaps between the spikes of rock on that side. He took B.6 from that position. Then he must have gone back to the mouth of the Gape, changed his film for a new one, and then taken C.1 and C.2. He then climbed up the scarp to the top of the cliff again, took C.3 from that point, and settled down to begin his lunch. Something must have drawn him to the cliff-edge after that; and evidently he fell in."

Wendover was a little disappointed by this tame ending. He had expected something rather more refined from the Inspector. Anyone, he reflected, could have developed the negatives and produced this bald commentary on them. The whole evidence left them almost where they were before it was given.

The Inspector had not finished, however.

"I have some further evidence which may not be of much importance in the present case, but I think the jury is entitled to hear it. Following up a hint given me by Sir Clinton Driffield, I have been able to establish fairly closely the actual time of the disaster. Saturday, June 13th, the day of Mr. Willenhall's death, was bright and sunny; and if you examine the prints which I have put in evidence, you will see that all of them show sharply-defined shadows at some point or other in the pictures."

Wendover smiled covertly when he heard this. Evidently the Inspector had turned up the Second Book of Kings and discovered the meaning of the Dial of Ahaz.

"On June 13th," Severn continued, "the sun rose at 4.43 A. M. and set at 9.17 P. M. at Greenwich. The figures in the almanac are exactly the same for the following day, Sunday, June 14th. That's to say that a photograph taken at 11 A. M on the 14th would show practically the same shadows as one taken at 11 A. M. on the 13th. It occurred to me that in this way it would be possible to check the times at which these various photographs were taken and so confirm the evidence of witnesses at the inquest — or even determine times when there was no independent witness on the spot."

Wendover had to admit that Severn had got more out of the Dial of Ahaz than he himself had. He hadn't thought of this application of the shadow in the cleft to which Sir Clinton had drawn their attention.

"June 14th turned out to be another bright, sunny day, with sharp shadows, just like the day before," Severn pursued, with something of the air of an artist displaying a masterpiece. "The important point was obviously Hell's Gape, but as I had to walk up there in any case it occurred to me that I might just as well follow up the route taken by the deceased and check the times at which each of the photographs was taken by him.

"I procured the actual camera belonging to the deceased, as well as a supply of films. I took a constable with me, and we started out rather earlier than the deceased did, so as to arrive at the scene of his first photograph in ample time. I had with me prints of the various negatives taken by him. If you will look at Exhibit A, No. 1, you will notice that the shadow of a tree just touches the extreme end of the second step of the stile, whilst another tree-shadow terminates in the middle of the path up to the stile. I had no difficulty in identifying the viewpoint from which the deceased took his photograph. I stationed myself there, with his camera, waited until the shadows fell into the exact position — so far as I could judge — of the shadows in the photograph. I noted the time and made an exposure, so as to have a permanent record."

Severn dived again into his bag and produced a packet of bromide prints. After asking the coroner's permission, he distributed these to the members of the jury.

"These prints come from three separate rolls of film with six exposures on each roll except the last, which has five on it. They run parallel to Exhibits A, B, and C, so I have lettered them Exhibits X, Y, and Z. Thus the picture taken by the deceased on Exhibit B, No. 5 corresponds to the picture taken by myself and indicated by Exhibit Y, No. 5."

He glanced from face to face among the jury to make sure that they had followed this. Apparently satisfied that he had made himself clear, he continued.

"I think, if you compare Exhibit A, 1, with Exhibit X, 1, you will be satisfied that for all practical purposes they are the same picture, so far as the shadow-positions are concerned. Since Exhibit X, 1, was taken at 9.59 A. M. on June 14th, it is safe to say that Exhibit A, 1, was taken by the deceased within a minute or two of 10 A. M. on June 13th."

He paused to give the jury time to examine the details of the two photographs. When they had satisfied themselves, he continued.

"As soon as this photograph had been taken, I hurried on to the next site and repeated the process, making an exposure when the shadows in the actual scene were in the position shown in the photograph taken by the deceased. By a comparison of Exhibit A.2 with Exhibit X.2, you will see that the coincidence in detail between the two prints is quite good. I do not wish to contend that the times are exact to a second, but I think the evidence is good enough within, say, five minutes. That second photograph was taken at 10.05 A. M. I shall not trouble you with the figures as I go along, but shall give you them all together later.

"Exhibit X.3 shows the lake with the boat-house in the distance, Exhibit X.4 is the wood-path picture, and Exhibit X.5 shows the view of the lake in the distance. I gauged the time in its case from the shadow on the broken hummock on the right of the picture.

"The next series of pictures shows the Maiden's Well, where there were plenty of shadows to work upon. Exhibit X.6 corresponds to Exhibit A.6, and I made the constable pose in the same position as Mr. Thursford in the original photograph. The same was done in the cases of Exhibits Y.2 and Y.3, which correspond to the original pictures B.2 and B.3.

"I now come to the first picture of Hell's Gape, taken from the top of the cliff — Exhibit X.5, which corresponds to the deceased's first picture B.5. The shadow thrown by one of the rock-pinnacles across the floor of the chasm was what I used as a gauge, and the time could be fairly closely estimated on account of the broken character of the floor of the Gape. It came out, as near as I could make it, at 12.45 P. M., and I do not think that estimate is more than a minute or two out, at the most. The irregularities on the floor of the chasm are as good as the degrees on a sundial — better, perhaps.

"If you will pass now to Exhibits C.3 and Z.3, you will find that they are practically identical. Here again I used irregularities on the floor of the chasm as a gauge in estimating time. Z.3 was taken at 1.45 P. M., so that the deceased must have taken his last photograph within a few minutes of a quarter to two on June 13th. It was after that that the disaster happened. How long after it, one cannot tell from the photographs, of course. It may have been a minute or two, or it may have been longer. At least, it was before 2.45 P. M., when Sir Clinton Driffield and Mr. Wendover arrived at the Gape and found the body."

Checkley interrupted suddenly.

"Before 2.20 P. M., you mean. That was when I found the body."

Severn made an apologetic gesture.

"Of course. What I wish to make clear is that the death occurred later than, say, half-past one, according to the evidence of these photographs."

Checkley seemed satisfied with this. Wendover, knowing the Inspector's craving for accuracy, wondered whether the slip had been made deliberately with some ulterior purpose. He concluded, however, that in all probability it was a genuine lapse of memory on Severn's part.

"There was one final test which could be applied to this method," Severn went on. "Sir Clinton Driffield took two photographs of the body, which appear in the series as Exhibits C.5 and C.6. I had made a note at the time when these photographs were taken. I found the viewpoints without difficulty, avoided consulting my watch so as to be quite unbiassed, and when the shadows came near the proper position I got the constable to lie down in approximately the same position as that occupied by the body when we found it. When the shadows were exactly right, as far as I could judge it, I made the two exposures, which correspond to C.5 and C.6 You will find them indicated by Z.5 and Z.6 in my series. Exhibit C.5 was taken by Sir Clinton at 4.05 P. M. Z.5 was taken by me at 4.09 P. M. as I found by looking at my watch immediately after making the exposure. That checks up the method as being accurate within five minutes in this particular case; and although the conditions here were specially favourable owing to the irregularity of the ground surface, still I think the method is vindicated within reasonable limits."

He picked up a sheet of paper before going further.

"This is the list of the times at which I estimate the deceased took the various photographs which have been put in in evidence.

A.1. Stile and Glade	9.59 A. M.
A.2. Lake (nearest side)	10.05 A. M.
A.3. Lake (with boat-house)	10.10 A. M.
A.4. Wood Path	10.25 A. M.
A.5. Lake (distant view)	10.30 A. M.
A.6. Well (Mr. Thursford standing)	11.18 A. M.
B.1. Well	11.22 A. M.
B.2. Well (Mr. Thursford sitting)	11.25 A. M.

B.3. Well (Mr. Thursford sitting)	11.25 A. M.
B.4. Well (close view)	11.30 A. M.
B.5. Hell's Gape (from top of cliff)	12.45 P. M.
B.6. Hell's Gape (from pinnacle side)	1.00 P. M.
C.1. Hell's Gape (mouth of chasm)	1.10 P. M.
C.2. Hell's Gape (mouth of chasm)	1.15 P. M.
C.3. Hell's Gape (from top of cliff)	1.45 P. M.
C.4. Blank film	
C.5. Body (taken by Sir C. Driffield)	4.05 P. M.
C.6. Body (taken by Sir C. Driffield)	4.05 P. M.

I don't claim more than approximate accuracy for these times, but I've made a rough calculation to show how near the true time one might come if circumstances were favourable.

"Suppose you have a tree that throws a shadow 30 feet long. The tip of the shadow is describing a circle with a circumference of 180 feet. (I'm not taking into consideration the variation produced by the rise and fall of the sun in its path across the sky; all I want to give is a very rough result.) Theoretically, the shadow of the tree-top would travel 180 feet in 24 hours. That's 90 feet in 12 hours, or 90 inches an hour — say an inch-and-a-half per minute. A four-minute difference between two photographs would be represented by a shift of the shadow through six inches on the ground. That's quite appreciable in these photographs. With even a fifteen-foot shadow the measurement can be made without much error; and at this time of year, round about noon, a twenty-five foot tree will throw a fifteen-foot shadow. Most of the trees I used as gauges are much higher than that."

The coroner consulted his notes.

"The times you estimate for the snapshots taken at

the Maiden's Well concord very fairly indeed with the times Mr. Thursford gave in his evidence," he pointed out. "According to him, he and the deceased reached the Well at about 11.15 A. M. and left it again about half-past eleven, whilst your estimates place the photographs as being taken at the Well between 11.18 A. M. and 11.25 A. M. That's a very striking agreement, when the difficulties are taken into account. And on that basis, it seems established beyond doubt that the deceased did not die before half-past twelve at the earliest. It may not be a matter of much practical importance, but the jury will be glad to have had the information. It's always well to feel that every available piece of evidence has been elicited."

"There's just one further point which can be inferred from these photographs," Severn went on, when the coroner paused. "When I traced out the route which the deceased must have followed in order to take the series of snapshots A.1 to A.5, it became quite clear how he had managed to put in a whole hour on the short-cut which he could have covered in less than half an hour if he had pushed straight ahead. The sequence of the pictures showed that he had wandered about a good deal over the ground and hadn't kept to the path."

The coroner evidently knew that Severn had now reached the end of his evidence, for he allowed him to stand down without further questions. Wendover, glancing round, saw Harry Thursford engaged in a whispered conversation with Halstead, evidently on the subject of the Inspector's testimony, since they were both intent on the bar of shadow cast across the floor by an upright in the window.

"Damned ingenious," Wendover heard Harry comment in undisguised admiration.

The coroner frowned in Harry's direction and then, glancing at his notes to refresh his memory, he began to sum up the evidence.

"That completes the evidence which it is proposed to submit to you," he explained. "You have heard how the deceased came to pay a visit to this district, and of his hobby of photography. Evidence has been submitted to show how he chanced to become a member of this rather notorious Novem Syndicate and how, had he lived, he would have participated in the division of a considerable sum of money owing to the success of that Syndicate in the Hospital Sweep. I do not propose to comment upon the various arrangements entered into, among themselves, by the members of that Syndicate. Part of these arrangements is at present *sub judice* in a Court of Law; and although that Court is not within our jurisdiction, still I feel it inadvisable to discuss the matter here. You have heard the evidence, and I shall leave it at that.

"You have learned that the deceased, in common with some other members of this Novem Syndicate, received a threatening letter. It was pointed out to you by one witness that the deceased's death occurred before the expiry of the time-limit fixed in that letter. It is for you to make up your minds whether or not to attach the slightest importance to this threatening letter."

From the coroner's tone, it was evident that he himself regarded the letter as of no account in connection with the case.

"Further evidence which you have heard," the coroner continued, "has enabled you to follow the movements of the deceased from the time he left the village until almost the very moment when he came by his death. I need hardly remind you of how neatly the evidence of independent witnesses has dovetailed together, nor do I need to recapitulate the evidence in detail, as it is fresh in your minds. If you have any questions which you wish to ask, I shall be glad to hear what they are. If you do not wish any further information, you should withdraw and consider your verdict."

The jury conferred for a few minutes. Finally the foreman announced that they had agreed unanimously on a verdict of Accidental Death. They desired to express their sympathy with the relations of the deceased man.

As the little gathering dispersed, Wendover found himself in proximity to Checkley and Harry Thursford. Checkley was obviously relieved to have got the affair over with so little loss of time.

"It's a good thing they didn't drag the business out into the afternoon," he remarked, as they came through the door. "I've lost a morning over it, as it is."

He paused, evidently irked by Wendover's slightly disgusted expression. Then his avaricious turn of mind got the better of his prudence, and he let his real thoughts slip out unguardedly:

"It's an ill wind that blows nobody any good. This means we get £34,000 apiece instead of only £26,000."

"I'm rather sorry for poor Willenhall," Wendover interrupted in an icy tone.

"Oh, so am I, of course; so am I," Checkley hastened to assure him. "Sad case, and all that. But after all, I hardly knew the man. There's no use in being hypocritical about it, is there? Most likely I'd never have seen him again. One must keep some sense of proportion in these things. If one wept over every acquaintance one loses, the handkerchief trade would be looking up."

Harry Thursford exchanged a glance with Wendover.

Evidently he also disliked Checkley's crude reflections.

"That let's me out," he said, acidly. "I won't need to buy a fresh dozen of handkerchiefs for *your* funeral, Checkley. The present stock will see me through the business when it comes."

Over Wendover's shoulder he caught a glimpse of Severn leaving the building, and his face lighted up with interest.

"I say, Inspector," he hailed.

Severn, bag in hand, came up to the group.

"That was deuced cute work of yours," Harry Thursford went on. "I'd like to offer my congratulations on it. I never thought one could get so much out of a pack of snapshots. Amazingly neat, it was, I thought. Until you worked it out, I never realised how quick a shadow creeps along; and yet, of course, what you said was O.K."

"It wasn't altogether my own notion," Severn confessed. "It was a word or two from the Chief Constable that put me on the track, really. Of course, once one got the hint, there wasn't much in it except following the thing up."

"I'd like to get to know him," Harry angled ingenuously with a side-glance at Wendover. "He must have a lot of yarns worth hearing, I should think, if one could get him started. The Maze case was before my time, and I'd like to hear the ins and outs of it."

"Mr. Wendover could tell you about that," the Inspector pointed out. Then, with a sudden change of subject, he turned to Wendover.

"You haven't parted with a share in *your* share of the ticket, by any chance?"

Wendover shook his head.

"Not I. Mr. Checkley wanted something of the sort but I refused."

Severn swung round to Checkley.

"I'm rather curious on the point, Mr. Checkley. It's this matter of these threatening letters that I've got to look into. One has to hunt about for all sorts of trifles," he added, half-apologetically, "just to see if one can make anything fit in."

Checkley glanced at Wendover and laughed rather nervously.

"I don't mind telling you, though the joke's against me now," he admitted. "I parted with a quarter-share in *my* share before the race was run. They gave me £2,000 for it. When Barralong came in second, their quarter-share was worth £6,500. Now, with two of the Syndicate gone, it's worth £8,600. However, even as things are, I rake in £27,875 as against the original ninth share of £26,880. But I wish I'd taken your advice" — again he glanced at Wendover — "and not hedged the bet. You've done better out of it than I have."

Quite obviously he was vexed by the knowledge that Wendover had made a bigger profit on the same chances.

"Whom did you sell the share to?" Severn inquired casually.

"Ask another," Checkley replied with a shrug. "They made a lot of talk about secrecy, hush-hush business, and so forth. I got the idea that it was a firm of bookies doing a bit of reinsurance for themselves. Naturally they wouldn't want that to leak out; it might have spoiled their game a bit. All I know is that I met a Commissionaire at an hotel in London; he fished out an envelope with £2,000 in notes in it; and when I'd passed them over a bank counter and seen they weren't flash stuff, I signed a typed agreement to hand over the cash to bearer when the prize-money's divided. Two of the bank clerks witnessed my signature. The cash was all right. That was the main thing from my point of view. It might have been some new brand of the confidence trick, you see. They can collect their share when the money comes in, unless they forget about it, which isn't likely."

Severn seemed interested in this curious transaction.

"Would you know the Commissionaire again?"

"I doubt if I'd recognise him. I had to keep my eye hard on the cash."

The Inspector seemed still slightly inquisitive.

"And you haven't a notion who the principal was?"

"Not the foggiest," Checkley protested. "What did it matter to me? The cash was all right."

Suddenly an idea seemed to flash into his mind and he blurted it out unconsciously.

"It might have been one of the Syndicate, for all I know."

"It wasn't I," said Wendover, freezingly.

Harry Thursford apparently read a danger-signal in Wendover's eye; and to avoid open unpleasantness he good-naturedly threw himself into the breach on the spur of the moment.

"Tommie Redhill's in the cart as well as you, Checkley. Worse, in fact. He sold a third of his share for £2,100 first of all. Then, by-and-by, he heard some rumours about Barralong that put him in a panic, so he sold another third of his share for £1,500, and then another half of what he'd got left for £800."

Checkley's mental arithmetic was almost instantaneous.

"That means he gets under £10,000 out of it —

£9,810 exactly," he reckoned, with hardly-suppressed maliciousness.

"Is that all? Hard lines," Harry Thursford said in a tone of regret. "Anyhow, what I was going to say was that his gang played the same hush-hush game. He doesn't know who they are until they choose to come down on him for the cash. If I were in Tommie's shoes, I'd be inclined to collect the spondulicks and then hop it for Patagonia or the Isles of Javan and Godire — somewhere outside extradition limits, anyhow."

The Inspector smiled rather sourly at this suggestion.

"It's none so easy to get beyond the reach of an extradition warrant nowadays," he declared. "And generally we manage to get our oar in at an earlier stage."

"Passports are a rank nuisance, nowadays," Harry commented, in an aggrieved tone.

Severn returned to the original subject.

"I suppose you don't know of any other member of your Syndicate who's sold part of his share?" he inquired of the company generally.

"Falgate may have. He's hard up," said Checkley, crudely.

"So they say," the Inspector admitted, cautiously. "You don't know whether Mr. Coniston's been doing a deal, too? Or your uncle?" he added, turning to Harry Thursford.

"Neither of 'em have, so far as I know. You'd better ask 'em to be sure, though."

"I suppose so," Severn agreed without any apparent eagerness.

CHAPTER IX: THE MOTOR TRAGEDY

INSPECTOR SEVERN, returning home after midnight from a visit to a friend half-way across the country, listened to the steady thrum of his motorcycle, which gave him the illusion of companionship. It was a dark night, for the new moon was due in a couple of days; but he knew every turn of the road and was more engrossed with his own thoughts than with the outer world. He gazed down the bright alley of his headlight beam and gave himself up to reflections which of late had become almost habitual in his unoccupied moments.

Severn took humanity as he found it. Unfortunately for humanity, the Inspector's professional work brought him more into contact with the seamy side of society than with the better part; and as a result, he was rather inclined to look critically at certain things which other people accepted at face value.

All the evidence in his possession, he had supplied to the coroner's jury. In this particular case, he could see no reason for keeping anything up his sleeve; and, so far as the evidence went, he was quite prepared to admit that the verdict of Accidental Death was a sound one. On the facts before them — and it was on these facts alone that they were sworn to give their decision — they could hardly have reached any other conclusion. If he had been on the jury himself he would have taken the same course. The affair at Hell's Gape was just the sort of thing which is bound to occur, sooner or later, if a dangerous place is left completely unfenced.

And yet, the Inspector reflected more than once, Sir Clinton was right when he pointed out that a lot of money would change its destination because Willenhall had died up there at the Gape; and when money could change hands in that way, there was always an incentive to help it on the road. The more Severn thought over the affair, the less he liked the look of it; and yet he frankly admitted to himself that he had no real grounds for suspicion. Accidents do happen. The air-liner tragedy was an obvious accident, unconnected in any way with the operations of the Novem Syndicate. The disaster at Hell's Gape had been examined by unbiassed people with all the evidence before them, and they had pronounced it to be accidental. If the Syndicate had never existed, no one would dream of suspecting a crime in the Willenhall case, any more than they would attribute the air-liner crash to criminal manœuvres.

Yes, true enough. But taking humanity as Inspector Severn found it, one couldn't drop the Syndicate out of the picture completely. The Syndicate stood for money, money in such sums that it could not be ignored. And there was no use burking the fact that murder had been done in the past for very much less money than this. Severn disliked uncertainty, even in small things; he was prepared to take endless trouble in clearing up doubtful points. And here, he felt, the whole thing was doubtful. On the face of it, Willenhall's death was accidental. Against that, he had only this undefined misgiving that things weren't quite what they appeared to be on the surface. Quite obviously, there was no data to go on. The whole thing might be a mare's nest. Still . . .

Whenever he resolved to drop the affair, another factor surged up from the back of his mind and altered his decision. The Chief Constable, in rather cryptic language, had hinted that Severn should satisfy himself that the affair had really been above board; and by doing so, Sir Clinton had betrayed that he himself was not altogether easy in his mind on the subject. Quite apart from official credit, Severn had a strong desire to gain his Chief's approval. It was a personal and not an official affair, the hankering of a minor artist to gain the recognition of a connoisseur whose opinion was of real weight. If he could make head or tail of this affair, prove it to be crime or accident beyond all doubt, he knew that he was sure of something which he reckoned higher than official promotion.

Severn was nearing home when he was roused from his reverie by an incipient side-slip. Since he came over this by-road on his outward journey earlier in the evening, a heavy local thunder shower had fallen, and now the road was greasy. Roused to a more conscious notice of things about him, Severn slowed down slightly and drove with caution.

It was well for him that he did so. As he slid round a corner — the first on an S-bend — he came upon a scene which caused him to jam on his brakes regardless of the risk of side-slip. His cycle slid on the treacherous surface and it was only by luck that he saved himself from coming down. As soon as he was on his feet, he swung his cycle round to bring the headlight to bear, hitched the machine on to its stand, and ran forward to where the hedge had been ripped away and the wheel of an overturned car showed beyond the gap.

The big saloon, travelling at high speed, had mounted the bank, torn through the hedge, and lurched into the field beyond, turning topsy-turvy as it fell. Pulling out his pocket-torch, Severn got through the gap in a moment and bent over the wreck. No sound came from the car. As he went round to the front, the Inspector saw the driver's body half-through the wind-screen, where he had been thrown by the shock. The shattered glass had inflicted terrible wounds on the face and neck, but by the light of his torch Severn recognised Jack Coniston. To judge by the quantity of effused blood, a carotid artery or jugular vein had been injured. It needed no expert eye to estimate the seriousness of the injuries; and when Severn, with some difficulty, had succeeded in reaching the body, he found that he was too late to help. The Novem Syndicate had lost another member.

There might have been passengers in the back of the car. The Inspector went round to the window and flashed his torch into the interior. With a sigh of relief he discovered that Coniston had been alone. Only some rugs lay in the back of the car, and these Severn secured, in order to cover Coniston's body. As he reached for them, a peculiar tang in the atmosphere of the car caught his nostrils. A smell of burning? Then he'd have to get the body out as best he could, before the whole thing went ablaze.

But there seemed to be no sign of combustion, when he came to look closer; nor was the odour at all like that of burning oil or of petrol. It had a peculiar catchy quality which both these fumes lacked. It was familiar, and yet uncommon: the sort of smell one doesn't meet with every day. . . .

"Fireworks!" Severn ejaculated suddenly, as he identified it at last. "Gunpowder!"

A suspicion shot through his mind, only to be discarded instanter.

"Suicide? Not with Coniston. There's no reason for it."

He pulled out the rugs, covered the body, and then, walking over to the bank, sat down to think.

If it *were* a case of suicide, it could be established easily enough. The wound would be on the body, and the pistol was bound to turn up, either in the car or by the roadside. He could afford to let that business stand over for the present.

Accident? Coniston was notoriously a fast driver, and the road at this point was treacherous. Severn had his own recent experience to tell him how easily a side-slip might happen at that very spot. And on an S-bend at high speed, a car might easily get out of control on a greasy surface. Accident was possible. But then accident wouldn't serve to account for gunpowder fumes inside the car.

Severn tried to persuade himself that he was reasoning the affair out logically; but all the while he knew quite well that his conclusion had leaped ahead of his ratiocination.

Murder!

He had seen one of these "accidents" before and had been left in doubt over it. This time, he would make certain.

He rose to his feet and went across to the car to examine the windows round the driver's seat. Evidently they had been up at the time of the crash, but the glass was so shattered that he was unable to make much out of his search. If a shot had been fired into the car, the subsequent impact had destroyed any obvious traces of the bullet-hole. By piecing the stuff together later on they might be able to prove something; but in the dark it was not worth attempting.

Struck by a fresh idea, the Inspector climbed over the bank again and descended into the road. Suppose that someone had held up the car and shot Coniston through the open door, then re-started the car and let it rush to destruction.

A careful scrutiny of the wheel-tracks convinced him that this solution would not fit. For fifty yards before the disaster-point, the tracks of the tyres ran steadily almost as if drawn by an artist. There had been no nerveless hand at the wheel when they were made. Nor was there the faintest sign that the car had been stopped and re-started with the slightest slip of the driving wheels on the greasy surface. Coming to the spot where the side-slip had occurred, Severn could see at a glance that the car had been at full speed when it reached that point. The length of the side-slip track and its slow sag towards the ditch were sufficient to show that the car had travelled a long way forward in the time that it took for the wheel to slide sideways. Besides, the ripping away of the stout hedge for twice the length of the car was evidence enough in itself that the speed had been high. Always thorough, however, Severn returned to the car and satisfied himself that the gear-lever was in top. When he put the whole of the data together, it seemed plain enough that there had been no hold-up. The car had come along the road at full speed up to the moment of the side-slip.

If Coniston had been shot, then, it must have been done while his motor was at high speed. Even a crack shot would find a feat of that sort difficult, if not impossible except by chance.

And if he had been killed in this way, how came there to be fumes of gunpowder actually inside the car?

And if the shot had been fired by someone in the car with Coniston, how did the assassin manage to escape from a car travelling at full speed and on the verge of instant disaster?

"I'm damned if I see through it," the Inspector exclaimed aloud in his annoyance at being so completely baffled.

He had no intention of leaving the spot until assistance of some sort arrived. For all he knew, some crucial clue might be amongst the débris; and it would never do to leave the wreck to be pawed over by the first passerby. A police patrol would pass the place in an hour or so, he knew; and he resigned himself to wait for that, if nothing turned up earlier. In the meanwhile, he dipped his handkerchief in Coniston's blood, hung it over his cycle lamp, and so improvised a danger signal. He wheeled his motorcycle about a hundred yards up the road and propped it on its stand, facing oncoming traffic; then, returning, he posted himself at the corner where he had side-slipped, so as to be in readiness to hold up traffic on that side. Satisfied that he had thus guarded the tracks of Coniston's car from obliteration by motors which might arrive, he sat down to wait.

Assistance came long before he had expected it. He had hardly settled down to watch when the lights of a car appeared; and at the sight of the red light the driver apparently slowed down and crawled cautiously along, while the Inspector hastened to meet him.

Dazzled by the headlights, Severn could not at first recognise the motorist, but a familiar voice hailed him as he walked up to the car. Tommie Redhill's cool accents were easily recognisable.

"Hullo! What's this?" he demanded. "Has there been a smash?"

"Mr. Coniston's car's gone off the road."

"I thought so," Tommie Redhill commented, unexpectedly. "Is he hurt?"

"Killed."

"Poor devil! I was afraid something had happened."

Severn, completely at sea with this, did not know what to think.

"What made you think that?" he asked brusquely.

"Silly thing to go driving full tilt at night on roads like this. I didn't like it; and when he didn't get home on time, I thought I'd come along and make sure he hadn't come to any harm."

This sounded like Double-Dutch to the Inspector. Coniston had been driving homeward when the disaster occurred; Redhill had followed him up; and yet Redhill professed to know that Coniston hadn't reached home. Then a possible explanation crossed his mind.

"Were you ringing him up?"

Tommie Redhill evidently shook his head, then put the thing into words.

"No, it was simpler than that. We had a bet on."

The Inspector saw that evidently the explanation might be complex, and he decided to postpone it to a more convenient moment.

"Look here," he explained. "The first thing to do is to get assistance. Will you turn round and drive back for a sergeant and a couple of constables? The sergeant lives at 7 Milton Lane. If you knock him up, he'll rout out the constables. They've all got push-bikes and can get up here themselves. Or, if it's no trouble to you, would you mind bringing them up in your car, and then you can tell me what all this is about. I can't make head or tail of what you're saying," he concluded irritably.

"Very well. I'll see to it," Tommie Redhill acquiesced

at once. "But about poor Jack? Hadn't we better see if we can't do something for him, before we start off?"

"There's nothing you can do for him," Severn retorted grimly.

"Quite dead, you mean? Killed at once, was he? Good Lord! what a business!"

"I shouldn't want to see him, if I were you," the Inspector said in a significant tone. "It's been a very ugly smash."

"Poor Jack! I suppose the glass . . . He'd have done better to use triplex stuff, but he always had some prejudice against it. I suppose he never believed he'd be in a smash. Few of us do, at the back of our minds. How did it happen?"

"I'll tell you about it when you get back," Severn promised hastily. "The first thing's to get assistance. I can't leave the wreck till someone relieves me."

"Why not? If he's dead? . . . Oh, I see. All right, I'll be back again as quick as I can. Mind standing clear while I reverse?"

He turned his car, and without more ado set off down the road by which he had come.

"That's a mighty cool card," the Inspector reflected as he watched the red tail-lamp vanish into the night. "Most people would have been thrown out of gear a good deal by news like that."

But after all, when he thought it over, Redhill's behaviour was much what one might have expected from him. He was well-known for his coolness. Once there had been an alarm of fire in his little enamel factory, and Redhill, a cigarette between his lips, had shepherded his workgirls out of danger with such convincing calm that a nasty panic had been avoided by the sheer force of his personality. He had even gone back into the blazing building to make sure that no one had been overlooked. A man who was prepared to take big risks like that was obviously not the kind of person to be rattled even by the news of a ghastly accident. And, apparently, when he came upon the scene he was already prepared for some mishap.

Severn's training had taught him never to grow impatient when gathering information; and now, knowing that he would get Redhill's story very shortly, he refused to worry himself about its nature. He took up his post again and waited stoically for the arrival of his reinforcements.

Redhill was rather longer than the Inspector had bargained for; but by this time it was late, and no cars arrived to cause trouble. Severn was not a nervy person, and this vigil beside Coniston's corpse did not disturb him. He lit his pipe and passed the time by reviewing the data which he had collected during his hasty inspection of the wreckage; but any probable solution of the affair failed to present itself to his mind. That whiff of gunpowder fumes refused to allow itself to be fitted into any plausible theory.

At last the lights of Redhill's car appeared; and Severn hastened forward to give orders to his subordinates. Until dawn, he decided, traffic had better be diverted from that section of the road. Once they had light enough, the wheel-tracks could be measured; and after that a guard over the wrecked car would suffice to keep things undisturbed. When he had issued his instructions and seen his men in their allotted positions, he returned to Tommie Redhill's car.

"Jump in, Inspector," Tommie suggested, opening the door at his side. "It's as cheap sitting as standing, if you want to ask any questions."

Severn had extinguished his pipe when the police arrived, and he refused Tommie Redhill's offer of a cigarette. He stepped into the car, however, and took his seat while Tommie switched on the roof-lamp.

"Now what do you want to know?"

"I'd like to know how you came to follow up Mr. Coniston's car," Severn said in a neutral tone. "This isn't your road home, Mr. Redhill. Your house is on the other side of the village."

"That's simple enough," Tommie Redhill explained frankly. "Some of us were at the Thursfords' tonight, and as we were coming away there was some talk about cars and driving. Poor Jack Coniston took a bet that his new car could cover the distance between Thursfords' and his own house, up beyond here, in six minutes, door to door. That's pretty good going, considering the rises here and there and the twisty road. But he won a hill-climb with the car the other day and he was very sure he could pull it off, even including the standing start and the slow-down at the other end."

Tommie Redhill threw away the stub of his cigarette and took a fresh one from his case. When he had lighted it, he resumed.

"The arrangement was that when he pulled up at his own door he was to switch on the light in the porch. With glasses, one can see his porch from the Thursfords' garden, which made it easy enough to time him. He was allowed five seconds extra for the switch-on. We saw him start off and waited till the time was up, but no light appeared. After about ten minutes, it seemed funny; but of course the car might have gone wrong. At the end of a quarter of an hour, it looked rum when no light had been switched on, so I left the rest of them and came up here to see that everything was all right.

In coming up, I got a bit anxious and began imagining that something had happened to him; so it wasn't altogether a surprise when I dropped on you here and learned that there had been a smash. It was a risky thing to try, with the roads like this; but Jack was very confident of his driving, always. Poor beggar! He was such a good sort, too. Always so cheery."

"There was no one in the car with him?" the Inspector demanded, cutting short Tommie Redhill's tribute.

"No, of course not. He was going home."

"Had you been drinking?" Severn asked, bluntly.

"Nothing to speak of, unless you'd call a couple of two-finger nips, drinking. That's all I had myself."

"Who else was there tonight besides yourself?"

"Coniston, myself, Miss Hathern, Miss Langdale, Miss Ridgeway, Miss Thursford, of course, and her brother, and Checkley. That's eight, isn't it? We had two tables of bridge to start with. Old Peter Thursford wasn't there. Out at a Masonic dinner, or something, I gathered."

The Inspector paused for a while before putting any further questions, as though he were turning things over in his mind. Then he fastened upon a phrase which Redhill had used.

"You played bridge 'to start with.' What did you do after that?"

"A couple of rubbers happened to finish together at the two tables. Nobody wanted to start afresh, and there was some talk, just general conversation of no particular interest. By and by Checkley got his oar in and wanted to try some experiments: deal out a set of cards on the table; one person fixes his mind on a particular card; another person draws a card. Checkley wanted to make out that by telepathy or something the proper card was drawn oftener than probability allowed. At first he got quite good results, and it looked interesting; but after a bit his average fell off badly and there seemed to be nothing in it."

"Then you turned to something else?"

"Yes. Checkley started on hypnotism. He's a trifle mad on that subject. He offered to have a shot at hypnotising somebody. Miss Langdale volunteered to let him try with her; but Harry Thursford objected, so that dropped. I let him try to hypnotise me with the help of a silver spoon, but it was a complete wash-out. Then Jack Coniston offered; and it seemed to come off with him. Checkley got him to crow like a cock and put his jacket on outside-in and burn himself with a cold poker. But poor Jack was a bit of a humourist always, and not a bad actor; and I had a suspicion that he was pulling Checkley's leg by pretending to be hypnotised, simply. Checkley was quite serious about it, though."

Hypnotism was a subject which the Inspector had never studied. He had always felt a certain scepticism about the whole thing, a feeling which had disinclined him from troubling to learn anything about it. One heard stories, of course; and he had a vague recollection that in some rather ugly foreign cases hypnotic phenomena had been alleged to lie behind crimes. But he had never seen a case of actual hypnotic trance, and to his practical mind "seeing was believing." When a thing was so out-of-the-way as all that, one would want to see it with one's own eyes before one swallowed it.

And yet, despite this subconscious prejudice, Tommie Redhill's half-contemptuous narrative roused ideas in the Inspector's mind. Suppose you *could* hypnotise a man and get him under your control, how far would your influence go? Could you make him do something which, in his normal state, he would refuse to do? Could you make him lose control of his car? Or could you make him step over a cliff? Had you to be present when he did the things you ordered him to do? Or could you give him his instructions for some hour further on in the day? In fact, could you contrive a crime which would look exactly like accident or suicide and yet be perfectly safe from suspicion because you were not on the spot at the actual moment when your victim went to his death? There was the case of Smith, the Brides-in-the-Bath murderer. Severn remembered a theory — which he had dismissed at the time as sensational rubbish — to the effect that Smith hypnotised his victims and suggested that they should drown themselves while in their baths. Could there be anything in the stuff after all?

"What happened after that?" he asked Redhill.

"Oh, nothing much. It was getting late and we began to think of making a move. Outside, where the cars were standing, there was some talk about the hill-climb. Poor Coniston was very full of his car, and Harry Thursford had been at the hill-climb and backed him up. Coniston, — I don't quite remember how it started — but Coniston said he could get home in record time with the car tuned up as it was. Checkley offered to bet that he couldn't do it in seven minutes, and when Coniston took that, Checkley tried to hedge by making a second bet on six minutes. Harry Thursford made a side-bet with Checkley on the six-minute run. Then Coniston started off, after Harry Thursford had gone into the house and brought out an opera-glass and a pair of race-glasses for us to watch for the light in Coniston's porch. I hadn't any bet, so I was acting as referee. That was really all that happened, so far as I can remember."

He paused, as though trying to recall anything further; but found nothing to add.

"How did you come to find out about it?" he asked.

Severn gave him a very brief account of his own entry on the scene.

"Are all these people still waiting at Thursfords'?" he inquired when he had finished. "I shall probably have to see them and get their evidence. The coroner will want that."

"No, most of them will be gone by this time. Nobody was anxious to have the girls there when old man Thursford got home from his Masonic dinner, probably well lit up. He's a bit . . . awkward, on these occasions. Miss Langdale went off in her own car while we were arguing about the bets. Checkley started just before I did; and he took Miss Ridgeway with him. She lives in the same direction. I promised to go back and pick up Miss Hathern, after I'd seen that poor Coniston was all right; but probably Harry Thursford will have run her home by now."

The Inspector considered for a moment or two.

"You'd better get off home now, Mr. Redhill," he suggested. "I'm going to take my motorcycle and go round by Mr. Thursford's house. If they've gone to bed, there's no harm done. If not, I can get what I want while their memories are clear, and avoid having to rake this nasty business up afresh again tomorrow."

"Oh, very well," Tommie Redhill acquiesced. "Sure you don't need me for anything? It's no trouble to go along with you. No? Very well, I'll push off, then."

When Severn reached the Thursfords' house, he found one of the ground-floor windows still lit up; and in answer to his ring, Enid Thursford came to the front door. Evidently all the maids had gone to bed earlier in the evening.

"I'm Inspector Severn, Miss Thursford," the Inspector said by way of introduction, as he was not sure if she knew him. "Is your brother in? I'd like to see him for a moment."

Enid Thursford had evidently recognised him, for she opened the door wider and invited him to come in.

"My brother will be back in a few minutes, I expect. Won't you come in and wait for him?"

She led him into a room; and the Inspector's apparently incurious glance took in the two bridge-tables, littered with cards and markers, the tray with decanters and soda, the cigarette smoke, and the general disarrangement of the furniture. Enid, evidently rather puzzled to know on what footing she ought to meet this unexpected visitor, picked up a cigarette-box and proffered it to him.

"Care to smoke while you wait for my brother, Mr. Severn?"

The Inspector, however, declined with regret. Abdullahs did not often come in his way; but business was business and he did not care to smoke when paying an official domiciliary visit.

"I've really come on rather a serious matter," he admitted, as he made a gesture of refusal. "I'm sorry to say that Mr. Coniston's got mixed up in a smash, a rather bad smash."

Enid was obviously taken aback by the news.

"Oh, I hope he isn't hurt — not badly," she exclaimed. "I thought they were taking a risk with that bet."

Severn had got his cue now, and he meant to get as much information from the girl as he could, before her brother arrived. Independent evidence was worth more than what one got by questioning two people in presence of each other.

"I'm afraid Mr. Coniston's rather badly hurt," he confessed. "He had a side-slip and went off the road. You say he had a bet on? That would account for it. I couldn't make out why he was driving so fast on a slippery road."

"Is he very badly hurt?" Enid returned to the point which Severn especially wanted to avoid.

"He's being looked after. I really don't know the extent of the damage," the Inspector assured her, correctly if disingenuously.

He turned and stared pointedly at the decanters.

Enid followed his eyes and saw the veiled suggestion.

"Oh, you think that?" she said, rather sharply. "You're quite wrong. I happened to notice that Mr. Coniston didn't drink much. He never does. He had one glass of whiskey and soda which was mostly soda, for I saw him pour it out. The second time, Mr. Checkley happened to be filling his own glass over yonder, and Mr. Coniston passed him his tumbler to get it filled too. When he got it back, he said to Mr. Checkley: 'You've made this a bit stiff,' and he didn't seem to like it. He was perfectly sober, if that's what you want. If he's had an accident, it wasn't on *that* account."

Severn nodded to indicate that he accepted her statement without reservation.

"Could you tell me exactly what happened before he started?" he asked, partly with the idea of testing her memory.

"They made this silly bet, that it would take Mr.

Coniston seven minutes to get home. Mr. Checkley bet him that he couldn't; and when Mr. Coniston took it, Mr. Checkley made another bet that he couldn't do it in six minutes; and Mr. Coniston took him again. Somebody else — my brother, I think — made a bet with Mr. Checkley also."

"Can you remember what the sums were?"

"Oh, five shillings, I think."

"And as soon as the bets were made, Mr. Coniston drove off?"

"No. Somebody asked for a cigarette and Mr. Coniston pulled out his case, I remember. Or perhaps someone asked him for one. I forget. Anyhow, he pulled out his case and one or two of us helped ourselves from it. I took a cigarette from it as it passed round. I remember when he got it back again he said we were a lot of wolves because we'd only left him one for himself. I'm telling you that just to show you I do remember things fairly well, so that when I say Mr. Coniston had only those two drinks, you'll be prepared to believe it. I don't want you to get the least idea that he wasn't thoroughly fit to drive."

"I quite understand that," the Inspector interposed hastily.

"Well, then, that was all that happened. We lit our cigarettes, Mr. Coniston offered me a light and then lit his own. And then Mr. Redhill gave him the word to start. I want you to be quite clear that there was no stirrup-cup business or anything of that sort."

The Inspector was faintly perplexed by this insistence on the drink question. Then he remembered old Peter Thursford's habits and thought he saw light. Naturally, with an example of that sort before her every day, Enid Thursford would be apt to lay stress on the point when it was brought up. If she found her relative indefensible, probably it made her more touchy when a suggestion was made about one of her friends.

The rattle of a latch-key made itself heard through the open door and Harry Thursford came into the room.

"Got back, Tommie?" he said, as his eye lighted on the visitor. Then, realising his mistake, "Oh, it's you, Inspector? I though it was Mr. Redhill. Didn't look closely, because I expected to find him here."

Then, in very apparent surprise, he inquired:

"What brings you here at this time of night?"

Severn gave him the same explanation as he had given already to Miss Thursford. Harry, with more acuteness than his sister, guessed that something lay behind the Inspector's carefully veiled phrases.

"You'd better cut up to bed, Enid," he suggested. "The old man will be back shortly and you're better out of the road after a Masonic dinner. I can handle him."

When she had gone, he turned to the Inspector.

"A bad smash, you say? D'you mean he's done for?"

Severn nodded.

"Poor beggar! Poor beggar! I was pretty sure it was bad news by the way you wrapped it up. Good of you not to let my sister know. These things aren't good for a girl to hear at night. Time enough in the morning for that. Poor Jack! A real good sort. You know, it's damned hard to realise it, somehow. You're quite sure? I can hardly believe it."

"I found him," the Inspector explained. "There's no question about it."

"Let's hear about it," Harry demanded. "Now she's

gone, you needn't wrap it up, you know. Poor chap!"

Severn gave him a brief account of the tragedy.

"Had he been drinking much while he was here?" he asked bluntly as he concluded his story.

"Jack Coniston? He never was drunk in his life. What put that into your head?"

"One has to ask that sort of thing; it's just a formal question."

"Well, the answer isn't formal. He was at my table tonight and he had one very weak glass of whiskey and soda. Then, later on, Mr. Checkley filled up his glass for him — to suit his own taste, I expect — and Coniston complained that it was too strong. But you can take it as Gospel that it wasn't strong enough to turn anyone's head. He was as sober as a judge when he left here. I've a fair experience in that line, and I can tell when a man's had even a very little too much. You can score that off the sheet."

CHAPTER X: THE STICK

THE day after Coniston's death was a busy one for Inspector Severn. As soon as it was light enough to make investigation possible, he reached the scene of the disaster and began his examination of the ground, the body, and the car.

In the daylight, the wheel-tracks were easier to examine; and on the greasy road it was possible to follow the trail of the car for a considerable distance back from the point where the side-slip had begun. But the most careful search failed to reveal any sign that the motor had been stopped and re-started. It seemed beyond doubt that the car had been travelling at high speed at the previous corner in the road; and after that it had gone on without a check to the place where the smash had occurred.

Turning next to Coniston's body, the Inspector made a most careful search for a bullet-wound, but without success. Nor did the later examination by the police surgeon reveal anything except the cuts produced by the broken glass of the wind-screen. A suspicion of Severn's led to the chemical investigation of the stomach contents by an expert; but here again a blank was drawn. No traces of any drug could be found.

Under the Inspector's eye, the interior of the car was searched with the utmost care. A half-smoked cigarette with a cork tip was the only find. The Inspector had no difficulty in identifying it as the stub of an Ardath cigarette, which was the brand Coniston had always smoked. The cigarette-case in the pocket of the body was empty, which confirmed Miss Thursford's evidence about the scene at the door when Coniston started on his fatal dash. But there was no sign, either in the car or along the road, of any firearm.

Determined to carry thoroughness to the extreme, Severn had the cigarette-stub examined for traces of a drug; but here again the experts reported only a negative result. Clearly enough Coniston had not been doped by means of his tobacco.

The steering-wheel was examined for finger-prints, but the only fresh ones detected were those of Coniston himself; and as these were unsmudged except at the point where his hand had been jerked from the wheel at the moment of the accident, it seemed clear that no one wearing gloves had been manœuvering the car.

Severn laboriously reassembled the broken glass of the windows in the hope of detecting something abnormal. He was still haunted by the idea of firearms. If a shot were fired into a car, it would make the driver swerve even if it did not strike him directly. The smashing of the glass about him would be sufficient to take his attention momentarily off the road. But there was no bullet in the car, nor did the glass of the windows, when pieced together, give the slightest indication that a shot had traversed it. Severn looked in vain for the rounded hole which a bullet makes in a sheet of glass; and his search for lead splashes such as the pellets of a shot-gun might leave was equally abortive.

By every test he could apply, Coniston's death seemed purely accidental.

And yet, how did accidental death fit in with that whiff of gunpowder?

The Inspector gained no further enlightenment from questioning the remaining members of the bridge-party. Viola Langdale confirmed Redhill's story about the hypnotic experiments; but she gave Severn the impression that Coniston had been pulling Checkley's leg and had not really been hypnotised at all. She was quite positive that Checkley could not have suggested anything to Coniston without being overheard by those who were standing round while the thing was done. The Inspector had been careful not to hint that the hypnotic experiment had any connection with the tragedy. He had succeeded in getting his information mainly by appearing as though he wished to test the preciseness of her recollections on a minor point.

Viola could give no details about the final incidents of the evening. She had driven off in her own car at the moment when Coniston's success in the hill-climb had come into the conversation and had not even heard of the betting until after the disaster. As to Coniston's condition, she was emphatic that he had not been under the influence of drink, even in the slightest degree.

Diana Hathern's evidence carried the matter further than Viola's, for she had been present when Coniston started. She was in doubt as to whether Coniston had been really hypnotised or not. If not, then his acting had been extraordinarily good, she thought. She, also, had heard everything that Checkley had said, and her account of the affair left no room for foul play at that point, apparently. Her description of the betting incident tallied closely with those which Severn had obtained elsewhere. Checkley had made three bets, two with Coniston and one with Harry Thursford. While the talk about these transactions had been going on, Harry Thursford had asked Coniston for a cigarette and, with a joke, had passed the case round the group. She had taken a cigarette from it and passed it to Enid Thursford, who had also helped herself to one. Mavis Ridgeway, she thought, had refused the offer, and then Harry Thursford had taken one and passed back the case to Coniston, who had grumbled at the greediness of the company and had lit the remaining cigarette himself. The cigarettes were cork-tipped, and before taking one she had asked what brand they were. Coniston had told her they were Ardaths. She was positive that Coniston was perfectly sober when he started.

Mavis Ridgeway confirmed most of this, but had nothing further to tell.

The Inspector did not question Checkley about the hypnotic affair, but so far as the later stages were concerned Checkley confirmed what had already come to light. He remembered Viola driving off before the bets were discussed, and he recalled that he passed Coniston's cigarette case to someone — he thought it was Miss Ridgeway. He was smoking at the time and did not take a cigarette out of the case himself. So far as he knew, Coniston was perfectly sober when he started. As to the drink he had poured out for Coniston, it was just the same as his own — three fingers, perhaps, at the outside. Nothing out of the way, certainly. Coniston had complained that it was too stiff; but Coniston was very abstemious.

This evidence left Severn very much where he had been before. He decided that when he appeared at the inquest he would be very circumspect. It was reasonable to keep something up his sleeve, in case the affair should turn out eventually to be foul play; and when he came to testify, he said simply that he thought he had noticed a faint smell of burning, but on examination had found no fire in the car. That gave the coroner's jury the facts, and it was for them to make what they could out of them, in his view.

As he expected, the verdict was one of Accidental Death.

Unfortunately for the Inspector's peace of mind, it was a verdict in which he disbelieved completely. And yet, so far as he could see, there was no way of getting behind it. Barring that whiff of sulphurous fumes, there was not one scrap of evidence, except facts which pointed to pure mishap.

He had to confess in his own mind that if Coniston had not been a member of the Syndicate, no tittle of suspicion would have arisen. Jack Coniston was the last man to make enemies. Cheery, approachable, always good-tempered, and incapable of any meanness, he had money enough to be generous and not sufficient to excite envy. He was well-liked wherever he went. To imagine anyone plotting against him in revenge was almost incredible.

But Jack Coniston *was* a member of the Syndicate, and that put the whole thing in a different light. If there had been foul play, it was clear enough that the person aimed at was not Jack Coniston, private individual, but Jack Coniston, No. 3 of the Novem Syndicate, whose death meant that still more money would trickle into the hands of the surviving members. That was the only credible motive in the background in this case. Willenhall was a stranger, and for all one knew, he might have had private enemies; but Coniston had been on the spot long enough to be well known, and the idea of private revenge in his case was merely absurd. He was a member of this accursed Syndicate; there was the rub. Three "accidental" deaths out of nine people within a month: that was far too high an average for probability.

At last, however, the Inspector was forced to give up the Coniston problem in sheer despair; and he turned back, perforce, to the death of Willenhall. If the two events were linked together — as he was firmly convinced they were — then the solution of one problem would probably lead to the clearing up of the other; and in view of the complete dearth of evidence in the motor case, the catastrophe at the Cape seemed to offer a better chance.

Not over-hopefully, Severn re-examined his notes on the matter; but for all his conning, they suggested nothing fresh. It was easy enough to have suspicions. He had plenty of suspicions, if it came to that. But it was a different thing to find clues which could really be followed up. There seemed to be nothing to take hold of in the business.

In something like despair, he turned once again to the photographs; and, determined that this time he would miss nothing, he scrutinised each of them through a magnifying glass. The first series yielded nothing; but he had expected that. The second roll's contents proved equally barren of any hint, although he spent immense pains in the reviewing of each picture, inch by inch, in the case of the two exposures made at the Gape. Rather despondently he turned to the final set of three. The two prints showing the mouth of the Gape were sterile like the rest. He laid them aside, and put the final picture — the one taken from the cliff-top — under his lens; and suddenly, in the magnified image, a tiny detail sprang to his eye, a thing so small that it had completely escaped his notice during his earlier examinations.

"That's it!" he exclaimed aloud in his excitement at the discovery.

Putting the positive with the others, he sought out the strip of film containing the corresponding negative and subjected that in its turn to a minute examination with his lens, lest he should have been deceived by a flaw in the film. Then, to make doubly sure, at the first convenient opportunity he made an enlargement of that particular picture on bromide paper.

Then, satisfied at last, he sat down to consider the best course to pursue. The detail was a very minute one indeed; and he was just a shade doubtful if an ordinary person would be able to make out without prompting, the precise nature of the original object. His first inclination was to show it to one of his subordinates; but on consideration he rejected this course. No matter how well-disciplined a force may be, there is always danger of leakage; and this was a case in which any leakage might be dangerous. The least whisper would be magnified by gossip over the whole countryside; for once the fact came out, people would not be slow in hinting at names; and then there would be trouble of a most unpleasant kind, whilst the actual criminal would be forewarned. Anything would be better than that. And then, as he considered the difficulty, a name came to his mind.

Wendover was the very man he wanted. He had a sound judgment; he knew the facts and the place; he was a close friend of the Chief Constable; and he would keep his mouth shut. There would be no breach of confidence where he was concerned.

Much relieved by this happy thought, Severn went to the telephone and rang up the Grange to make an appointment for that evening. Then he packed up the photographs and put them under lock and key.

It was just after Wendover's dinner-hour that Severn arrived at the Grange, laden with his exhibits. He was shown into the smoking-room, where he found his host.

"Have some coffee before you produce the hand-cuffs?" Wendover invited. "They're bringing me mine. Or would you rather have a whiskey and soda?"

The Inspector, recalling that Wendover's whiskey was a pre-war stock, chose the second alternative.

"That relieves my mind," said Wendover, chaffingly. "If this were a domiciliary visit of the unpleasant type, I know you wouldn't take a drink. Have a cigar? Or would you rather have your pipe? There's a tobacco-jar over there if you care about it."

The Inspector postponed his business for the moment.

"I don't care about going round saying: 'Hush! Hush!' and all that sort of thing, Mr. Wendover; but I'd rather wait till your maid's brought your coffee and cleared out again. What I want to consult you about is strictly confidential, you understand? I've come to you because I can trust your judgment and I know you won't talk. One whisper of this business might cause the devil's own bother."

"I won't chatter," Wendover promised. "By the way, before I forget about it, here's another specimen to add to your archives. It arrived this morning, and I was just going to send it over to you when you rang up."

He felt in his pocket, produced a letter in its envelope, and handed it across to the Inspector.

"Postmarked last night at the local office," Severn noted as he examined it. "It's another threatening letter, isn't it? Same kind of envelope and paper as the last one, I see. Ribbon copy again, too. They seem to give you the best specimen always. Letter itself undated, like the last one. Let's see what they say: —

That's two of you bumped off now. No need to mention names. Haven't you got any sense or must we go on a bit further with the job before you get on to the idea that we mean business?

Whenever we put one of you in the bone-yard the rest of you collect a bigger share of the pool and if you think you'll get this for nothing you're off the rails.

This time it will be thirty thousand pounds (£30,000) that you will have to pay. It will have to be in small notes (old ones) the same as you ought to have used last time and you can plant it at the old place the day after tomorrow at midnight. Don't try any fresh stuff on us and remember that if you don't pay this time somebody else will be bumped off and by then it will cost you fifty thousand pounds (£50,000) to save your skins.

You are giving us a lot of trouble and we are getting tired of you.

Yours truly
THE BLACK HAND

p.p. Big-headed Ben the Gunman"

The Inspector pondered over the document for a moment or two after he had read it. The maid came in with Wendover's coffee, and then returned with whiskey and soda for the guest. When she had gone, Severn looked up.

"I'll keep this," he said, tapping the document. "What do you think of it yourself, Mr. Wendover?"

"I'm damned if I know what to make of it," Wendover replied in a rather irritated tone. "The first time, I thought it was simply some cinema-struck kids amusing themselves. I'm not sure even yet that it's not that. But if it's a joke, it's growing a bit gruesome, and the jokers would be none the worse for a lesson. And if it isn't a joke, then it ought to be looked into."

"You're not thinking of paying?" demanded the Inspector.

"*I*'m not," Wendover assured him emphatically.

"But some of the rest of the Syndicate are?" Severn suggested, catching the hint of Wendover's emphasis.

Wendover hesitated for a moment as though not sure whether he should say anything further.

"Well, there's nothing particularly confidential about it, and I don't see why I shouldn't tell you," he confessed at length. "Some of them are getting cold feet over the business, so far as I can judge. At least, that's my impression of the state of affairs and I give you it merely for your own information. Old Peter Thursford is going about with an aged and formidable-looking revolver in his pocket, swearing that he's able to look after himself; but his young nephew seems to me growing a shade white about the gills. Of course, the agony's being drawn out a bit by the delays over this High Court business. Young Thursford has insisted on a meeting of the Syndicate in a day or two, presumably to discuss the whole affair."

"If you pay and let the matter drop, you're compounding a felony," the Inspector pointed out.

"I'm not going to pay," Wendover retorted. "I wasn't over-keen on joining this Syndicate at the start. I did it more out of mere politeness than anything else. But now I'm in it, I stay in it; all the more since this kind of thing started. I'm not going to be frightened out of my position by threats."

Quite obviously Wendover's pride had been touched

by the mere suggestion that he might show the white feather. So far as the money went, the affair made little appeal to him; but now that he seemed to have got into a position of possible danger, a streak of obstinacy in his character forced him to stand by his guns. He would have despised himself if he had turned tail and cleared out of the business, even though common sense favoured that course.

"I'm glad I came up this evening," the Inspector confessed. "If that's the state of affairs, I think you ought to know what I've found out now, though I'm telling you it absolutely in confidence. It may alter your views."

Wendover shook his head decidedly, but refrained from interrupting his guest. Severn produced his photographs and laid them on the table beside him.

"What do you think of Coniston's death coming on top of the aeroplane crash and the business at Hell's Gape?" he asked, with a keen look in Wendover's direction.

"A curious coincidence," Wendover replied.

"With the accent on the adjective? That's how I felt about it myself. But the plain truth is that I haven't been able to rake up a single bit of evidence to prove that it was anything more than an accident. If it was a criminal business, it was managed by a pretty sharp man who left nothing to take hold of. But if it was more than accidental, then the Hell's Gape affair was probably more than a mishap, too. That's how I looked at it; and I've spent all my spare time puzzling over it to see if I couldn't make something out."

He drew the small table between himself and Wendover, picked up one of the photographs, and offered his host a magnifying glass.

"I don't want to bias you by describing the thing in

any way," he explained. "I've got an idea that it's a certain object, and I want to see if you can recognise it as that, without being prompted in any way whatever. I'll point to it with my pencil — there! — and now I want you to look at it through the glass and see what you make of it."

Wendover took the glass and bent over the print to examine it. The Inspector did not hurry him; and Wendover, impressed by the caution which Severn had shown, took his time over the scrutiny. At last he looked up and the Inspector saw in his face that his own guess had been confirmed and that Wendover also had grasped the import of the discovery.

"I'll tell you what I see," Wendover said, picking up the glass again to refresh his impression. "It looks to me very like the extreme tip of a walkingstick, just the ferule and about an inch of the wood. There's too little of the stick itself showing for me to make out what pattern it is. But there's one thing quite plain. It's got the ordinary tubular brass ferule on the stick-end. Is that what you made of it?"

Instead of answering, the Inspector pushed an enlarged version of the picture across the table. Wendover examined it in turn.

"That shows it fairly well. In the original it's very small; but once you get your attention called to it, I think it's plain enough. I don't think I'd have noticed it if you hadn't drawn my attention to it, since it's such a minute detail in a small-scale photograph; but I'd be prepared to swear now that it's that and nothing else."

"You might just verify it on the negative," Severn suggested, pushing the film over to Wendover.

"Yes, I can see it all right. Now hold on a moment. I

want to see where this leads to, if I can, without your help."

"That was the last photograph that Willenhall took at the Gape," Severn explained.

"And Willenhall's own walkingstick had an alpenstock point, so this must be the stick of a second person who was there when that snapshot was taken."

"Yes," said Severn. "And that person apparently had his reasons for not offering himself as a witness at the inquest."

CHAPTER XI: A, B, C, AND D

WENDOVER did not even pretend to be surprised by the Inspector's innuendo.

"To put it in plain language, No. 2 was the murderer, you mean?" he asked.

Severn nodded gravely.

"Yes. And that stick-point in the photograph represents the murderer's one mistake. He must have imagined that his stick was too near the camera to appear in the picture. Or he may not have noticed it was there at all when the snapshot was taken. If it hadn't come out on the film, there wasn't a shadow of evidence to prove that Willenhall wasn't alone when the affair happened. Now we know a second man was on the spot, and the whole affair's altered."

Wendover picked up the print and the magnifying glass again and made a prolonged examination of the tiny detail.

"It's no good," he said reluctantly, as he put them down again. "There isn't enough of the stick showing. If there had been another inch or two, one might have seen something on that to identify it by. But so far as that photograph goes, it might be any kind of stick, barring an ebony one."

"That's true," the Inspector admitted, undepressed. "But it's no good grousing because one hasn't got everything, especially when something like this turns up. Look what that single film's proved. First of all, Willenhall wasn't alone at the Gape. Second, he was alive at

1.45 P. M. that day. Third, the man who was with him carried a stick. That's a fair amount to expect from any single snapshot, and I don't feel inclined to grumble because the murderer wasn't kind enough to write his name on a postcard and send it to me."

"It's just as well that I was in the company of the Chief Constable all that day from breakfast-time up to the moment when we discovered the body," Wendover commented, in a half-serious tone. "Otherwise you might have suspected I had a hand in it, since I'm a member of the Syndicate."

"It's my business to suspect everybody now," the Inspector retorted, rather grimly. "But you've got a clear alibi, so there's no use wasting suspicion on you, Mr. Wendover. To tell you the truth, that's one reason why I've consulted you. You're in the Syndicate and know all about it and yet you're absolutely clear of this affair."

"Well, you can say what you like. You know it won't go any further."

Severn picked up his glass and took a small drink before beginning.

"Probably you've thought of a good deal of this yourself," he commenced tentatively. "If you don't want it, just say so. But it would be a help to me if I put it into words; help to clear it up and make it more precise in my own mind, you understand. I've had to keep it to myself, and it's quite on the cards that I've missed some obvious point just by thinking round it too much. One gets blind spots, sometimes."

"I'm interested," Wendover interjected, concisely.

The Inspector acknowledged this with a gesture.

"Motive's the obvious thing to tackle, first of all," he continued. "In this case, there's no difficulty. Who would want to kill this man Willenhall, a stranger in the place and a harmless person, so far as we've been able to ascertain from every source we've tried to tap? Nobody had any grudge against him that we can learn anything about. And who would want to kill young Coniston, a very well-liked man, good friends with everyone, and quite popular in his own circle? So far as we've gone, there isn't a hint of anything in the way of a private grudge in the background in either case. That notion's absurd, anyhow, because you'd have to find a murderer with a strong animus against two men who were strangers to each other until a week or two ago; or else you'd have to suppose that two murderers happened to start business simultaneously. The thing won't stand a moment's examination. I looked into it, because one has to be thorough. But it's simply preposterous.

"It's plain to anyone that what linked those two people together was this Syndicate of yours. And it's the Syndicate, and only the Syndicate, that starts suspicion about the whole affair. People fall over cliffs, and nobody thinks much of it except their relatives. People get killed in motor accidents every day. It's only when you put the two things together, and add the Syndicate, that anyone would think twice.

"Now here's the state of affairs from the money side."

He pushed a small sheet of paper over to Wendover.

TOTAL PRIZE-MONEY £241,920

9 sharing   Value of share = £26,880
.......Blackburn's death
8 sharing   Value of share = £30,240
.......Willenhall's death

172

7 sharing   Value of share = £34,560
                            ......Coniston's death
6 sharing   Value of share = £40,320
5 sharing   Value of share = £48,384
4 sharing   Value of share = £60,480

"I haven't carried it any further," the Inspector commented grimly. "What I want you to notice is that it's what you might call an accelerated increase. Blackburn's death made only a difference of £3,400 in the value of the share. Willenhall's death made a further increase of £4,300. When Coniston dropped out, the value of each remaining share in the Syndicate jumped by £5,800; and a share that was worth £26,000 at the start had now grown to £40,000, which is a fairly tempting amount to some people. The next jump would be one of £8,000, and the one after that would be £12,000 — a pretty tidy lot of money in itself.

"Now if I can see that, the murderer must have seen it too. He'd a more direct interest in it than I have. And what I want to drive home is that progressive rise and its possible bearing on the whole affair.

"It's a risky enough business to commit a single murder. If you commit two, the risks are more than doubled. If you commit three murders, the chances of detection go leaping up. Smith, of that Brides-in-the-Bath case, might have got off scot-free if he hadn't gone beyond his second murder. He took too big a risk when he tried the same game a third time.

"But here, with your Syndicate, the prizes go leaping up in parallel to the risk: £4,300 the first time, £5,800 next time, and the next jump, if it came, would be £8,000. Carry on, and if the risk of detection grows, so does the prize you'll get if you win. For every extra risk you take, you get a bigger and bigger cash return if you pull it off."

Wendover listened to this exposé as though the Inspector had been expounding a problem in algebra. From his attitude, no one could have guessed that he himself ran any risk of being the victim who might cause a future "leap-up" in the dividends of the Syndicate.

"That's very ingenious," was his only comment, as Severn paused.

"My idea," the Inspector pursued, with a certain gruesome enthusiasm, "is that it was Blackburn's death that put the murderer on to the idea originally. He must have reckoned out how much more he was going to get, owing to the air-mail crash; and that likely suggested the idea of improving things still further. It was sort of thrust under his nose, you see.

"But at that time, the thing was a practical impossibility. The interval between the race and the payment of the prizes was far too short to allow of any campaign of murder which had a ghost of a chance of success. Then came that injunction in the High Court; and the usual legal delays. That was what gave him his chance. But even so, it meant quick work. For one thing, he couldn't be sure that Dyce & Monyash mightn't withdraw their opposition in the High Court, and then the whole thing would be closed immediately.

"Suppose that the idea was in his head when the injunction was launched, what would his obvious line be? A set of plain murders would be a bit too crude. The motive would stick out all over a series of crimes of that sort, done in rapid succession as these would have to be. Far too risky, even with big stakes. No, he must have looked round for something better; and then he must have hit on the idea of a set of 'accidents' — things which on the face of it didn't suggest murder at all: a fall over a cliff, a motor smash, things of that sort.

"If that was his line, then Willenhall was obviously bound to be the first victim. Why? Because he was only a visitor and might go off at any moment back to London, where there would be less chance of dealing with him. I'm pretty confident I'm right there. Well, you know what happened to Willenhall. And if it hadn't been for all this money in the background, Willenhall's death wouldn't have excited a whiff of suspicion, not one. Certainly not in my mind; and I don't mind owning up to that.

"Whoever this beggar is, he's a smart devil; that I don't deny. I'm not one to underestimate my opponents. The question is: who is he? I don't know who he is; but I can make a guess at who he isn't. He isn't anybody without some interest in that Syndicate of yours, direct or indirect. That's as plain as the nose on my face.

"Now turn to the Syndicate and you find the thing's more complex than it looks at first sight. You're beyond suspicion yourself. Blackburn, Willenhall, and Coniston are dead. That leaves five of the original Syndicate still to be dealt with. But there's more in it than that; for some of these people have sold parts of their shares, and in that way a fresh set of individuals have got a footing in the scheme. You heard about these transactions yourself. Who were these mysterious beggars who bought their way into the Syndicate? Nobody knows. They're simply not on the map. And yet their stake in the affair is quite a respectable one. I've gone into that side of the thing also, and here's how it stands."

He passed a second sheet of paper across to Wendover.

	Shares Sold	Value of present interest
WENDOVER	None	1 Share £40,320
P. THURSFORD	None	1 Share £40,320
H. THURSFORD	None	1 Share £40,320
FALGATE	None ?	1 Share ? £40,320
CHECKLEY	$\frac{1}{4}$ Share to A.	$\frac{3}{4}$ Share £30,240
REDHILL	$\left\{\begin{array}{l}\frac{1}{3}\text{ Share to B.}\\ \frac{1}{3}\text{ Share to C.}\\ \frac{1}{6}\text{ Share to D.}\end{array}\right\}$	$\frac{1}{6}$ Share £ 6,720

Holding of A.	$\frac{1}{4}$ Share	£10,080
Holding of B.	$\frac{1}{3}$ Share	£13,440
Holding of C.	$\frac{1}{3}$ Share	£13,440
Holding of D.	$\frac{1}{6}$ Share	£ 6,720

TOTAL HOLDING OF A, B, C, & D £43,680

"That's the best I can make of it," the Inspector said in a guarded tone. "I've really no information about Falgate's holding. He may have parted with some of his share, or he may not. When I tried to pump him about it, he as good as damned my eyes and told me to mind my own business. In which he was quite within his rights," Severn added, magnanimously. "The subject seemed a sore one, I gathered."

"Ah?" Wendover interjected absent-mindedly.

He was apparently devoting his attention to the list and paying only casual regard to what the Inspector said.

"I don't wonder at that," Severn continued. "It's no secret that he's hard up and that this prize-money would come in very handy. But he can't touch it immediately on account of this High Court affair and what's more, he can't borrow on the strength of it, either. That's where the shoe pinches, I expect."

"Why can't he borrow?" Wendover demanded, with a sudden recrudescence of alertness.

"Because of that second agreement of yours," Severn explained with a certain pride in his acuteness. "What's his security? The chance of collecting his share of the prize-money. But suppose he dies before the day of divvying up; where does the moneylender come in? He'd get nothing. The only way to manage it would be for Falgate to take out a short-term life policy to cover that risk. But insurance companies aren't fools, and you can bet that by this time they know that Falgate's life isn't just a perfect spec. There was that evidence at the inquest on Willenhall to begin with, threatening letter and all; and there's the general look of the affair now, after Coniston's death. The local agent of any company would know all about that. I don't say they mightn't insure him, but they're as sharp as I am, and *I* wouldn't give him a policy just at present, as a matter of business. He must be pretty hot at having signed that second agreement without seeing just where it was going to land him."

Wendover did not feel called upon to make any comment on this side of the affair. Instead, he picked up the share list.

"I see what you mean about this business, now," he said. "It seems that these outsiders, whom you call A, B, C, and D, have got shares running up to £13,440 in two cases; so that their interests are quite valuable enough to make them a factor, possibly."

"I meant a bit more than that," said Severn in a serious tone. "You're looking at it on the basis that there's Mr. A. with a £10,000 holding, and Mr. B. with a £13,-000 holding, and Mr. C. with another, and Mr. D. with a £6,000 holding. But supposing that it's a case of Mr.

ABCD, a single individual, with a holding of £43,680? That would put the thing in a different light, wouldn't it? His share would be the biggest of the whole lot, then. And if one assumes that somebody will commit murder for £40,000, then it's no less likely that somebody else will do it for £43,000."

Wendover looked up, startled by this fresh idea.

"You mean that this mysterious outsider . . ."

"Has the biggest motive of the lot, if the prize-money's at the root of the whole business," the Inspector completed the phrase. "And that would account for all this mystery-mongering over the transactions in the shares, wouldn't it? I don't quite see my way through the collection of the cash by Mr. ABCD without his identity coming out. That looks difficult to me. But he's got a document that makes it practically 'Payable to Bearer,' you remember; and I don't deny that a smart fellow might manage it without leaving traces behind him."

"It's not exactly a bearer bond," Wendover agreed. "But perhaps there might be some way of managing it, as you say."

"I'm not worrying my head over it just now," Severn confessed with a faint shrug, "for that's all hypothetical stuff. For all I know, A, B, C, and D, may be entirely different people. I'm just trying to cover every possibility, no matter how odd it looks at first sight."

Dismissing the matter, he turned to a fresh aspect of the affair.

"There's one thing more," he explained, producing a fresh set of photographs from his pocket and laying them in front of Wendover. "Here are prints of the snapshots showing the Maiden's Well. Just look at these three with Mr. Thursford in them. Do you see anything interesting in them?"

Wendover scanned the three prints for a few moments and then shook his head.

"Do I need the glass to see it?" he asked finally.

"No, it's in plain sight," the Inspector assured him. "Or, rather," he corrected himself quickly, "it isn't in plain sight at all."

Wendover, enlightened by the last phrase, examined and compared the three snapshots.

"I see what you mean, I think. Thursford has no stick with him. Is that it?"

"That's it," Severn confirmed. "And here's another point. Mr. Checkley came up the hill from his car. Would he be carrying a stick? Not likely. And these are the only two people we've any trace of, who saw Willenhall — alive or dead — after he took the short cut up through the Silver Grove grounds. It's that last bit of evidence that makes me so interested in this Mr. ABCD."

Wendover was quick to see the implications of this.

"The murderer had a stick with him. Thursford had no stick, according to the prints. And I don't remember his having any stick when we came across him that afternoon, either, which confirms that idea. Checkley had no stick, obviously, since he came in his car. But Thursford might have seen the murderer pass, if he came from the east. Or Sir Clinton and I would have seen him fairly easily from the high ground before we came down to where we met young Thursford and Miss Langdale. A man moving over that sort of country catches the eye at once. And he didn't pass Checkley on the road at Brookman's Farm, or Checkley would have remembered it. That means the murderer didn't reach the Gape from the east, north, or west. He must have come up on the pinnacle side, evidently. It's open ground there; but he'd be hidden from all of us by the slope which makes the north side of the Gape."

But while Wendover was uttering this reasoning, his intimate mind was busy with another aspect of the affair, and suddenly a great flood of relief went through him.

Now that his mind was at ease, he was able to admit to himself that he had harboured suspicions about both Checkley and Harry Thursford. They were obviously without any definite foundation on fact, and he had never admitted to himself that he believed them in the slightest. Nevertheless, they had got a lodgement in his brain and had lurked there despite his determination to expel them. Now he was glad to drive them out completely; and as he cast them away, he recognised how completely irrational they had been. Harry Thursford had been the last person — barring the murderer — to see Willenhall alive; Checkley had been — again barring the murderer — the first person to find the body. These had been absolutely the only grounds for suspecting the two; and Wendover was rather ashamed to recognise it now.

His relief had other grounds as well. There was no use burking the fact that these fatalities had thrown a cloud of suspicion over the whole personnel of the Syndicate. It wasn't merely young Thursford and Checkley. Every surviving member of the group gained by these deaths and ran the risk of being branded by his fellows as the criminal. He himself was the only one who was absolutely beyond doubt. He had seen some of the results when two of the Syndicate came together by chance since Coniston's death. There was a certain constraint, a sidelong mutual inspection, a kind of armed neutrality verging almost on semi-hostility in some cases. "Is this the murderer?" He himself had felt it, though he had done his best to overcome it. It was no wonder that members of the Syndicate did not seek each other's company, when even a casual meeting was made odious by this indefinite malaise. "Is this fellow planning that I'm to go next?"

But if the Inspector's surmise was a sound one, then all this mutual suspicion was groundless. The real criminal was outside the circle of the Syndicate, hidden behind the veil of these mysterious transactions in the shares. That increased the risk of his success, unfortunately. It might have been possible to avert danger when the assailant must be one of five people; but when the blow could come out of the dark, the chance of parrying it was a good deal less. One could be on one's guard against Checkley or old Peter Thursford or Redhill, because one knew them; but "Mr. ABCD" was an unknown quantity against whom it would be difficult to provide.

The Inspector gathered up his photographs and stowed them away in his pocket.

"There's just one more thing that strikes me," he said, as he did so. "Whoever's at the back of this business has very good local information. Blackburn's death was public property, and there's nothing in that. But the man who tipped Willenhall over the edge of the Gape must have known the ground and must have had means of finding out when to go up there at the right moment. And Coniston's affair — however it was managed — points to very minute local knowledge, too. I shouldn't be surprised to find that Mr. ABCD is very much on the spot."

Wendover pondered over this unpleasant inference for a moment or two without replying.

"What about the threatening letters?" he suggested finally.

"There was local knowledge there, too," Severn admitted at once. "You remember in the first one that the place to cache the notes was laid down — the third milestone on the Ambledown road. Well, I've been there. It's a good place. Very hard to set a watch on it without being spotted. There you've got local knowledge again. The other milestones would have been no good for the job."

"Then you think these threatening letters were meant to be taken seriously after all?"

The Inspector refused to commit himself directly.

"Suppose Mr. ABCD wrote them. Suppose you fell into the trap and paid up. He'd be so much in pocket. But that wouldn't hinder him going on with his original scheme, would it? That's just a guess. One has to look at all sides of a thing like this."

CHAPTER XII: NECK OR NOTHING

WENDOVER had called a meeting of the Syndicate, since Harry Thursford insisted upon it; but as he glanced round the room he reflected that he had seldom seen a more uncomfortable assembly. To look at these people, no one would have supposed that they had come together on business which meant thousands of pounds into their pockets. They were scattered about the smoking-room, each slightly isolated from his neighbours, and no one seemed inclined to talk to anyone else. The miasma of mutual suspicion had worked upon them all until even casual conversation would have been mere pretence.

Falgate, with a cigarette drooping from his lips, sat hunched forward in his chair, frowning at the fireplace. Checkley, looking more like a baby crocodile than ever, darted glances here and there, examining his neighbours surreptitiously with bright, unwinking eyes. Harry Thursford, over at the window, was obviously in a state of acute discomfort, like an unpracticed speaker waiting for the chairman to call upon him. Even Tommie Redhill's imperturbability seemed to be wearing a trifle thin. Only old Peter Thursford seemed to rise superior to the influence. He was sober; and, as was usual when he was sober, he had a certain dignity which no one would have suspected from a glance at him in his cups.

"We're here at Mr. Harry Thursford's request," Wendover explained formally. "Perhaps he'll be good enough to give his reason for wanting a meeting."

He looked across at the figure by the window as he spoke.

It cost Harry Thursford a considerable effort to begin. Although he had obviously been rehearsing mentally up to the last moment, Wendover's summons seemed to have caught him unawares, without an opening sentence ready in his mind. He moistened his lips uneasily; and then, with something of a hangdog air, he groped for a preamble.

"It's this way," he began, and then stopped abruptly as the eyes of the others turned in his direction.

"I've been thinking," he tried again, haltingly, as though he had to pick his words carefully and was too nervous to be sure of his choice. "I've been thinking over this whole business. It's no good pretending, is it? We're all thinking the same thing, and it's time somebody said it straight out. We'd all be glad to see this Syndicate wound up and everything settled. That's my feeling about it, anyhow. We've gone and tied ourselves in knots with these damned agreements. We should never have made them. The thing drags on and on, and these lawyers will spin it out for long enough yet, now they've got their claws on it. Meanwhile . . ."

He evidently shied at putting into words the thing which overshadowed the whole of them.

Then, leaving his phrase unfinished, he came direct to his proposal.

"Why not do a deal with Blackburn's trustees? Let them take their ninth share if they want to. If we offer that — and perhaps their costs up to date into the bargain — they'll withdraw their opposition in the High

Court. The whole affair will be squared up and the distribution of the prize-money can be tackled immediately. We'll get done with the whole business. That's what I mean."

He stopped abruptly, evidently relieved to have finished, and glanced round the room to see the effect of his words.

Falgate lost no time in lending his support to the suggestion.

"That seems a sound proposition," he said with a certain eagerness. "Let's cut the loss, square up the whole affair once and for all, and get the money now."

It cost Wendover little trouble to interpret Falgate's motive. If he was in deep waters financially, the main thing he needed was immediate cash; and this scheme of Harry Thursford's offered the chance of that, even if it meant a certain loss in paying off the Blackburn share. But with Harry Thursford himself, Wendover was not so sure. There had been both nervousness and vehemence in his voice as he made his proposal, and he was obviously desperately anxious to know how it would be received. "He's lost his nerve over the affair. A bad case of cold feet," was Wendover's slightly contemptuous judgment. "For two pins, that young man would admit that he's afraid of being the next of us to go."

Harry Thursford's face had relaxed slightly when Falgate gave his support, but it grew strained again when Checkley put in his oar.

"I'm not quite sure about it," Checkley began, in a tone which belied his words. "Of course, I daresay we'd all be glad to have this business settled. It's dragged on far too long. But when it comes to cutting losses, one wants to know just what one's cutting. There are six of us here; as things stand, we get £40,320 each. If we concede Blackburn's share, then we only get £34,560 apiece. That's a drop of about £6,000 capital for each of us. £6,000 is a fair sum, a very fair amount. It's equal to £300 a year income. One can't go flinging £300 a year away without thinking about it."

Wendover found himself voicing a fresh suggestion.

"If we concede that Blackburn's trustees have any standing in the affair at all," he said, "then it seems to me fair that we should treat all alike. Willenhall's estate and Coniston's estate ought to profit as well. I admit there's a second agreement; but my own personal feeling is that we should blot that second agreement out altogether, if we begin making changes at all. In equity, I can see no reason why Blackburn's relatives should get a share, whilst the relatives of the other two are left out in the cold. That's how I look at it: either all three or else none."

"But that would mean a drop in the value of our shares from £40,000 to £26,000," Checkley protested angrily. "That's out of the question. I don't mind considering our paying £26,000 — say £4,500 apiece — to Blackburn's trustees to get things settled up and done with as quickly as possible. I think that's carrying generosity to the limit. But to lose £14,000 out of my share! No, no! That's away over the score!"

Wendover surprised a sudden, almost malevolent glance turned on him by Harry Thursford. Obviously Harry had expected to net Checkley with the bait of a speedy settlement made by a comparatively small sacrifice; and Checkley had nibbled at the proposal. But Wendover's amendment had called for a bigger concession than Checkley would ever endorse, and on this rock Harry's scheme was going to founder. As Wendover glanced again at Harry's face, he was confirmed in his earlier judgment. The cub looked more like a rat in a trap than any decent human being ought to do, Wendover reflected, with a tinge of distaste.

Tommie Redhill seemed to feel that it was his turn to state his views; and as he did so, Harry's face grew a shade whiter, for his particular friend gave him not the slightest support.

"There's something to be said for Harry's proposal," he began in a disinterested tone, as though the whole matter lay so far outside his sphere that he could treat it impersonally. "We'd all be glad to be done with this business. But, as Mr. Wendover pointed out, if we go back on our word in Blackburn's case, we'll have to deal with the other two on the same footing. That's incontestable, in mere fairness. But whatever's done, it'll have to be done unanimously. We've no individual rights in the winning ticket and we can take no steps which haven't the approval of every member of the Syndicate."

Wendover glanced at Peter Thursford, who had not yet shown any indication of the side he favoured.

"Gentlemen," Peter began, taking his cue, "I've been surprised by what my nephew has said. It's new to me, I can assure you. My position in the matter's quite plain to me, and I hope to make it plain to you in very few words. I said once before that I don't think this claim put forward by Dyce & Monyash is a just claim. Things may have happened since then . . . Well, you know what I mean, there's no need to put some things into words when we all know what's what. But these affairs have nothing to do with the justice or injustice of the case. We've all signed certain papers and I mean to stand on what I think are my rights in the matter.

I'm not going to be argued or intimidated out of these rights by anyone. I'd be ashamed of myself if I went back on what I've said, merely because somebody . . . because I might be endangering my skin by refusing. I'm not particularly afraid about my skin, gentlemen. And, as I hope I've made clear, my vote goes against any change in our arrangements."

Wendover let his eye range round the group. Harry Thursford had evidently not consulted his uncle before bringing forward his suggestion, and old Peter's blunt refusal to consider the matter seemed to have shaken his nephew even more than what had already occurred. It meant the final turning down of the scheme, since the old man was evidently inflexible in his decision. On Falgate's face also, Wendover could see marked disappointment as the prospect of immediate payment was ended in this summary fashion. Checkley seemed torn between two emotions. Only Tommie Redhill maintained his attitude of polite indifference.

"If Mr. Thursford insists on holding to the agreements, there's nothing more to be said, I suppose," Wendover pointed out. "In any case, there was no general agreement on any of the courses proposed."

Nobody objected, and one or two of the party rose from their seats as though ready to go. But at that moment Harry Thursford broke out in a shrill voice:

"Wait! If you won't take my scheme, I've something else to say. I'm sick of this business. I've had enough of it. It's too risky for my taste. First Willenhall, and then Coniston. And who'll be the next?"

At this blunt utterance of the thing which was in all their minds, his audience stood as though frozen by the vehemence of his cry.

"I don't care what you think," Harry Thursford went

on, "It's not worth it. You've all been pretending that the real thing isn't there at all. But it *is* there. We're getting knocked out, one by one, so that the remaining shares go up each time. Each of us is looking sideways at the rest and wondering who's IT. Most of us wonder how long we'll last. That's the plain truth, isn't it? Well, I've had enough of it. No money's worth it. I'm going to clear out. I resign from the Syndicate. You hear? I take you all to witness that I've got no further share in the business. You can divide my money among you. Do what you like. It doesn't concern me. I'm done with the whole affair from this moment."

Old Peter stared at his nephew with an expression of contemptuous surprise.

"You white-livered young skunk!" he said with deadly quietness.

Harry was evidently too much wrought up to care for the insult.

"Say what you like," he retorted, "You won't hurt me. You can't force me to stay in this damned Syndicate if I choose to clear out. And I'm clearing out, here and now. Understand that? Here and now! It's not worth it, even for a hundred thousand."

Checkley's lizard mouth dropped slightly open as he stared at Harry Thursford. It was evidently difficult for him to realise that anyone could actually relinquish £40,000 when it was almost within his grasp. But when he had assured himself that Harry was serious, his business instincts came to the surface and served to bring the scene back to normal.

"I think that ought to be put in writing," he suggested.

"Oh, I'll do that with pleasure," Harry Thursford agreed in a tone which put new life into the cliché. "As a matter of fact, I've got it written out already."

He pulled a paper from his pocket.

" 'I, Henry Thursford, a member of the Novem Syndicate, do hereby relinquish all rights in the said Syndicate of any kind whatsoever from the present moment onwards.' Is that clear enough for you, Checkley? It is? Well, then, I'll sign it and you can witness it if you like."

Tommie Redhill held up his hand.

"Wait a moment," he said in his equable tones. "This ought to be witnessed by disinterested parties, not by members of the Syndicate. Perhaps a couple of your maids, Mr. Wendover?" Then, turning to Harry he added, "You're a fool to do this. Better think over it a bit. There'll be no second deal, remember. If you sign it, you'll have to stand by it."

"I've thought over it already," Harry answered in a calmer tone. "D'you think I wrote out that paper without thinking about it? I've lost my nerve and all I want is to get clear while there's time. I daresay you think I'm 'a white-livered skunk.' I can't help it if you do. My nerves won't stand it any longer; I can't sleep; I can't eat; I can't do anything except wonder what's going to happen next. I'd be suiciding, if this sort of thing went on."

He halted abruptly as Wendover rang the bell. Nobody else spoke while Wendover gave a few words of explanation to his maids and Harry put his signature to the document. The two witnesses signed and were dismissed.

"That makes each of the remaining shares worth £48,384," Checkley announced with an attempt at casualness which was belied by the rather gloating tone in which he rolled out the figures.

Then his eyes roamed uneasily round the group, as

though he were calculating something less agreeable than the share values. Wendover guessed what was in his mind. Besides the two of them, the Syndicate now contained only Falgate, Tommie Redhill, and old Peter Thursford. And Checkley was probably wondering which of these three he had to beware of in the near future. He would hardly have got the length of inferring the existence of that other sinister factor in the situation, Mr. ABCD. And as he saw Checkley's disquiet, Wendover could have found it in himself to curse the stubbornness which had forced him to stand in with the rest of the Syndicate. The money meant little enough to him. Common sense dictated that he should copy Harry Thursford's example and drop out altogether. And yet he knew quite well that nothing would have driven him to that line of conduct. Something much more important to him than the money was at stake: his self-esteem. While his intellect admitted that Harry had taken the most sensible course, a feeling stronger than intellect prevented him from even thinking of backing out. Besides, were they not all a little inclined to jump to conclusions? But as he assured himself of this, the picture of that ferule drifted across his memory.

Falgate was the first to leave, with a curt nod as he went out of the room. Redhill, evidently not anxious to speak to Harry Thursford at that time, hurried after Falgate.

Checkley, slightly ill at ease, crossed over to where Wendover was standing, and began to make conversation.

"I'm in a bit of a difficulty just now," he began. "You remember that recipe that Willenhall said he'd got hold of — the new brand of sweetmeat that some old woman or other makes? It's damned annoying. It sounded pretty good. He didn't tell me where she lived, and I've raked the whole countryside in search of her, but I can't lay hands on her anywhere. Now you know the district pretty well. Have you ever heard of anything of the sort?"

Wendover shook his head.

"I can't think of anything like it, on the spur of the moment," he admitted. "Of course lots of old ladies in the villages sell sweets."

He spoke rather absentmindedly, for his attention was caught by old Peter and young Harry Thursford, who had come together almost at his elbow. Wendover wanted no scenes, and he waited, ready to intervene in the conversation which he could not help overhearing.

"You've lost more than money over this deal," said Peter, in a tone of jeering satisfaction. "Viola's not likely to want a white-livered thing like you, now that you've got no fortune to settle on her. She's been spending money like water on her trousseau, hasn't she, eh? And who's going to pay for it now? Not you, anyway."

"Shut up," Harry Thursford said savagely, though he kept his voice low.

But old Peter evidently meant to rub it in, and he chose the crudest way of doing it.

"She's a fine girl, is Viola. I like 'em like that, with a slim pair of ankles and neat legs. And supple at the waist. She'll be a bit taken aback when she finds she's got to settle all these bills she's been running up. Well, she won't get stuck. I'll pay them myself if she's nice to me. She's the sort that knows which side her bread's buttered."

"That'll do!" Harry Thursford was evidently on the edge of an outbreak.

"Well, them that lives longest'll see most," Peter replied in a tone of assumed indifference. "*You* ought to see a lot, with the care you take of your skin."

Harry refused to be drawn on this subject. He picked up the document which still lay on the table and handed it over to Wendover.

"You'd better put this in your safe along with the others," he said abruptly, and then, without a glance at his uncle, he left the room.

Old Peter had recovered his grand manner.

"I feel I must apologise for my nephew, gentlemen," he said. "It was a most unseemly exhibition, that. And I hope that you'll take my word for it that it came as a surprise to me just as much as to you. I was quite ashamed that any relative of mine should behave in that way before you all."

"Don't mention it," said Checkley, fatuously.

Peter stared hard at him for a moment, and then, with a dignified inclination to his host, he left the room.

"How happy they'll be at dinner tonight," Checkley surmised with a malicious grin. "And I guess the old man's temper will deteriorate between now and the evening. He's a bit hurt in his pride over the business. And no wonder."

Then, seeing from Wendover's expression that this line of conversation was not welcomed, he returned to his original subject.

"About that recipe, though. You'll let me know if you happen to remember anything that might put me on to it?"

"I'll let you know," Wendover agreed, dismissing his guest with as much celerity as politeness would admit.

When the last member of the Syndicate had departed, Wendover lit a cigar and sat down to gather together his impressions of the meeting. And as he came to think over it, he was surprised to find how varied the behaviour of these five people had been. He leaned back in his chair and tried to fathom the motives behind what he had seen.

Redhill's position was the easiest to understand. His stake was now a small one at the best, and therefore the purely monetary factor had less influence with him than with any of the others. He was a cool-headed fellow, capable of taking a risk without turning a hair if he thought the reward was worth it. His behaviour at the time of the fire at his works showed that well enough. Probably he had sized up the risks in the matter of the Syndicate and had come to the conclusion that they were not so great, after all. Severn had been quite right in saying that the stake was increased with each death in the Syndicate; but quite likely the limit had now been reached and there would be no third tragedy. After all, £40,000 was a very fair sum to most of these people, and probably to Mr. ABCD also, if that mysterious individual had any real existence. It was quite on the cards that there would be no further "accidents." Possibly Redhill had taken that view. And, of course, Redhill had scored a point in Wendover's opinion by the way he had backed up the proposal to include the Willenhall and Coniston estates in the compromise. That showed some decent feelings.

Falgate's motives were not very obscure either. He needed ready cash badly, and was eager to grasp at any project which seemed likely to wind up the Syndicate, even at a loss, so that he might get his hands on the money. To judge by his looks, he must be very near the edge, financially. But Wendover could not quite understand why things should worry Falgate as much as they did. If the worst came to the worst, he could go bankrupt and then, when the prize-money came in, he would be able to pay off his creditors and get the stigma of bankruptcy removed. But perhaps Falgate happened to be one of these people who felt bankruptcy a disgrace, not in itself, but because it implied that they had made a failure of themselves. Possibly some queer distorted idea of business success lay at the back of Falgate's troubles. And then a fresh viewpoint suggested itself to Wendover. Where did Viola Langdale come in? Falgate had been keen enough on her at one time; and, if rumour counted for anything, he had become keen once more, only to find himself forestalled by Harry Thursford. Was it Viola that lay at the back of Falgate's affairs, and not money? Of one thing Wendover was sure: Falgate had got to such a state that fear for his personal safety was not a deciding factor with him.

Checkley was an unpleasant subject. If money had to come into a conversation, Wendover preferred it to be simply "money" without too much stress on amounts. But Checkley was one of these people who couldn't think of cash except in terms of precise figures. Wendover might pay "a tenner or so" for something; but Checkley, he felt sure, would pay the same sum and docket it mentally as "£10 (say ten pounds sterling)." A share in the Syndicate meant £40,000 to Wendover; whereas in Checkley's mind it represented £40,320, no more, no less. And apart from that, Wendover disliked Checkley very thoroughly. That streak of petty maliciousness which showed itself in his grin at Harry Thursford's troubles — the sort of thing the Germans call *Schadenfreude* — was a nasty characteristic of Checkley. And the little beast was obviously torn between a desire for safety on the one hand and a greed for money on the other. Wendover recalled those distrustful glances which Checkley had thrown sidelong at his neighbours. Clearly enough he would be glad to get the Syndicate wound up; but he could not bring himself to make the necessary financial sacrifice.

Peter Thursford was something of an enigma to Wendover. Was he really sincere in all this talk about justice and his rights? Or was that simply a mask for pure greed? When he was sober, he made quite a good impression; but alcohol washed away the surface dignity completely and exposed a very different stratum underneath. In this affair, was he simply taking a risk because he thought it a negligible one, or had he really a contempt for danger because he relied on his own strength? From some things which Peter had dropped at one time or another, Wendover knew that he had roughed it abroad in his early days in places where a man had to rely on his own resources more often than not.

Then there was Harry Thursford. Wendover confessed to himself that Harry had been both a surprise and a disappointment. That yellow streak wasn't at all the thing he had looked for in Harry, from the little he knew of him. And undoubtedly when it did show, it had been very conspicuous. Wendover had seldom seen a man, not actually in immediate physical danger, show up so badly. The young beggar must be very high-strung, though one would hardly have expected that from his normal behaviour. Clean off the rocker with pure funk, apparently. And it must have been a very bad attack, considering what he had to lose by it: forty thousand pounds, and the good opinion of the people who had seen his exhibition. More, perhaps, if old Peter were right in his surmises. It must have been an overwhelming fear that made him give all that up and be so evidently glad to do it.

Suddenly a thought crossed his mind. Was it possible that Harry had got a glimpse of something which had escaped both him and the Inspector, something which convinced the youngster that he would be the next on the list if he stayed in the Syndicate? That might be an explanation of the business. But it hardly seemed likely, after all. Harry, in that worked-up state, would have blurted out anything he had learned, or else gone straight to the police with his information.

Wendover was roused suddenly from his reflections by the maid showing Viola Langdale into the room. As he rose from his chair to greet her, he saw that she was pale under her make-up, so that the lipstick red of her lips showed up more brilliantly by contrast. Her eyes glowed dangerously and two tiny vertical lines furrowed between her eyebrows betrayed an anger which she was holding in check only by an effort.

"Sorry," she apologised, offhandedly. "I couldn't wait, so I got your maid to show me in here at once. I just want to ask you something. You've been having a meeting of your Syndicate, haven't you? Has Harry Thursford backed out?"

Wendover noted her use of the surname. Evidently things had already come to a crisis in this engagement of Viola's.

"He has," Wendover admitted, concisely.

"Ah?" Viola did not seem surprised. "And did he sign some paper or other, to clinch the thing?"

"He did."

"So he meant it," Viola said, more to herself than to Wendover.

She was silent for a moment, then she added, again as if to herself:

"Well, I warned him."

Almost instantly she seemed to recover herself and turned to Wendover with that bright hard smile which he knew so well. Only, this time, the hardness was accentuated and betrayed the effort which she was making.

"Could you give me an envelope, please?"

Wendover crossed the room and picked one from a writing-case. As he turned back, he saw her strip off her engagement-ring.

"Thanks, that will do nicely. And may I borrow your fountain-pen?"

She scribbled an address on the envelope, slipped the ring inside, and gummed down the flap.

"Thanks very much," she said mechanically, as she handed the pen back to Wendover. "Sorry to have troubled you, but I was rather in a hurry."

"I hope you're not in too much of a hurry . . ." said Wendover cryptically.

Viola made no pretence of not understanding him.

"Oh, this?" she tapped the envelope. "No, I've had a night to think over it. And you needn't waste any pity over me, you know. I'm not losing much by it."

Wendover reflected that if Harry Thursford had heard that contemptuous estimate, he might have winced even more than he did under his uncle's epithet.

Viola evidently desired no sympathy. She certainly made no bid for any, but went off at once, her envelope in her hand, as though she were leaving after a formal visit. Wendover accompanied her to the door and watched her get into her weatherbeaten old car. She waved to him as she drove off.

"I don't know that I like her any more for it; but she certainly can keep her upper lip stiff when most girls would be showing how they felt," Wendover mused as he went back to his chair.

It must have cost an effort to keep that stiff upper lip. True enough, as she had said herself, she was not losing much so far as Harry Thursford himself was concerned. Some girls might forgive a man for playing the coward once, but Viola was not that sort. She had too much steel in her character to be patient with weakness in a partner. And clearly, from what she said, Harry had divulged to her beforehand the step he was contemplating. She had warned him of one result; and he had persisted, even at the risk of losing her.

It was not only Harry she was losing. As he slunk out of the Syndicate, he took with him all her visions of fortune. After the dream of wonderful frocks, furs, jewels, and Rolls-Royces, Cinderella had waked again in her worn tweeds and her shabby little car. The struggle to make ends meet and to keep up appearances on a pittance would recommence, all the more bitter for that brief visit to the castle in the air.

Then a recollection of old Peter Thursford's sneer crossed Wendover's memory and set his mind working on a fresh line. Viola had been buying her trousseau. Probably Harry had arranged to settle a good deal of capital on her — she was clear-headed enough to have seen to that. She must have been looking forward to a fair income of her own as soon as they were married. And with that income to meet any bills she might run up on her trousseau, Wendover guessed that she must have spent lavishly. She would want to make up for all those years of secondhand evening dresses, silk stockings that were not quite the best, well-worn gloves, and cheap hats. And now the prospective settlement had gone into thin air, and the bills would come in, far beyond her power to pay.

"She won't get stuck. I'll pay them myself, if she's

nice to me. She's the sort that knows which side her bread's buttered," old Peter had said. And the worst of it was, as Wendover reflected, that old Peter was quite right. Viola did know which side her bread was buttered. She was remarkably free from scruples, if Wendover read her aright. The only thing was that freedom from scruples didn't imply freedom from fastidiousness; and old Peter might discover that too, if he grew too enterprising.

CHAPTER XIII: THE AFFAIR AT THE COTTAGE

VIOLA LANGDALE's tiny villa, Azalea Cottage, lay on the outskirts of the village. Beyond it, the byway on which it stood degenerated into a mere field-track. The house had been the expiring effort of a builder who had gone bankrupt before it was completed, and no one else had taken a site in Speedwell Lane; so Viola was untroubled by any close neighbours. Such isolation might have had its disadvantages; and the policeman on night duty had orders to go down the Lane from time to time and satisfy himself that all was in order.

In theory, these visits should have been paid at irregular intervals, but Constable Tarporley was a man of routine. Every night at 9.15 P. M. he made his way down Speedwell Lane, gossiped for a few minutes with Viola's maid if she happened to be there, and then, duty done, went off to other parts of his beat and did not return again to the Lane until a quarter of an hour after midnight. From the point of view of burglars, this arrangement was ideal; but burglary was not common in the district, so no great harm was done by the constable's time-schedule.

On this particular evening, Constable Tarporley had paid his usual visit at a quarter past nine. As he passed along the breast-high wall which enclosed the garden, he glanced over, expecting to see the maid, who usually chose that hour for watering the rose-beds. It was not her night out, and he had been looking forward to a few minutes' conversation with her. Though not particularly susceptible, the constable was by no means averse to a chat with a pretty girl as a preliminary to a spell of lonely night duty.

Tonight, however, there was no neat figure in the garden, and the roses had evidently been neglected. Constable Tarporley was distinctly put out by this turn of events. He had prepared one or two gems of repartee as he made his way towards the cottage, and he was loath to miss the chance of using them. It occurred to him that Miss Langdale might be at home that evening and that Ruth Lawton might be shy of gossiping with him in full view of the sitting-room windows. Miss Langdale was very seldom at home in the evenings, but tonight might be an exception. Then a stratagem presented itself to his mind. Why not go up to the door and ask for a glass of water? It was a warm night, and there was no harm in the request. Ruth would answer the bell, and they could have their little chat on the doorstep, out of range of the windows of the drawing-room.

The constable pushed open the gate, walked boldly up the short curved path, and rang the bell. Getting no reply, he rang again; but evidently both maid and mistress were out. Mechanically, he tried the front door and found that the catch of the Yale lock had been dropped.

More than a little put out, and now, by force of suggestion, feeling genuinely thirsty, the constable turned away. His eye caught Viola's little motor-shed, which had a separate approach at the far end of the garden, and he noticed that the door of it was closed. Usually Miss Langdale left the shed open when she took the car out, and if she was not back in the early evening, the maid closed it before going to bed.

Giving up hope of his chat, Constable Tarporley walked down the path, closed the little gate behind him, and set off, in a rather bad temper, to inspect the rest of his beat.

At a quarter past midnight, true to his schedule, he was back again at the mouth of Speedwell Lane. The moon had just set, and the night was a dark one for the time of year. The footpath in Speedwell Lane was a bad one, and Constable Tarporley picked his way along it in a leisurely fashion to avoid stumbling. No lights showed through the trees from the windows of Azalea Cottage. True to his routine, the constable moved on towards the garden gate; but just as he approached it, he saw against the faint illumination of the sky the loom of some object partly on the footpath and partly on the roadway. A second glance revealed it as the roof of a saloon car.

The vehicle showed no lights, and Constable Tarporley scented a case. Speedwell Lane was not a highway, but it was a road to which the public had access, and therefore no one had any right to leave an unlighted car on it. Since no light showed in Azalea Cottage, the car obviously did not belong to one of Miss Langdale's visitors.

"Some young spark's brought a girl up here and gone for a walk in the fields beyond," the constable surmised sourly. "And he's switched off his lights so as not to attract attention. Well, I'll have to have a look at his license. Whether he turns up or not, I can get him through the number of his car."

He took a step or two farther forward and then switched on his flash-lamp to examine the car. But as his light fell upon it, he started back with a sharp exclamation at the sight which caught his eye in the beam of his torch. The car had been backed against the wall of the garden, and between wall and motor was an ugly something which had drawn the startled ejaculation from the constable's lips. Pinned there, and horribly crushed, was the body of a man.

Torch in hand, Constable Tarporley hurried forward and examined the corpse. The anguished features were dreadfully distorted; but the constable was able to recognise the victim.

"Why, it's old Mr. Thursford! Lord! Lord! I wouldn't like to die like that!"

For a moment the constable, not a very imaginative man, at the best of times, was shocked into inactivity by the discovery which he had made. But he soon pulled himself together, fought down his feelings, and began to make a further examination. He stepped into the road, went round to the front of the car, and flashed his light on the number-plate.

"It's Mr. Falgate's car!" he said to himself mechanically, as his rather slow mind began to work upon the implications of the evidence before him. The story of the Novem Syndicate had been common talk in the village; and it needed no special intelligence to see something more in this than a mere ordinary motor-smash. For a few moments Constable Tarporley mentally turned the matter over as he stood looking at the bonnet of the car. Mechanically he put out his hand and steadied himself on the still warm radiator.

Seeing no one near the car, the constable had assumed that the driver had gone for help after the smash. Now it occurred to him to search more closely. Flashing his torch into the interior of the saloon, he was amazed to see the figure of a man lying forward across the steering-wheel, as though asleep.

Tarporley went round to the side of the car, opened the door, and shook the figure by the shoulder.

"Here, you! Wake up! . . . Why, it's Mr. Falgate!"

Falgate seemed to rouse himself with difficulty. He stared stupidly in the light of the electric torch, and the constable noticed that he was trembling slightly.

"Drunk!" was Constable Tarporley's succinct diagnosis. "Or else shamming."

He bent forward and sniffed vigorously.

"You've been drinking, Mr. Falgate?"

Falgate made no reply. When the constable's hand was taken from his shoulder, he had dropped back into the driving-seat. Tarporley endeavoured to rouse him by flashing the torch in his eyes, but Falgate paid no attention to it.

"Well, here's a bit of a business," the constable mused aloud. "I've got to get assistance somehow — not that it'll do any good so far as old Thursford's concerned."

It occurred to him to wake up Miss Langdale and her maid. They could be dispatched to bring help while he stood guard over Falgate and the body.

"They must be good sleepers if they didn't wake up with the yell the old man must ha' given when he got that nip, though," Tarporley reflected. "Rum, that is."

Leaving Falgate, the constable walked up to the front door of Azalea Cottage and tried to rouse the inmates by knocking; but his efforts were without result, and he soon came to the conclusion that there was no one in the house. That, at any rate, explained why Peter Thursford's cries had attracted no attention. Tarporley tried the door, out of curiosity, and found it locked as it had been when he tested it earlier in the evening. Evidently there was no hope of securing a messenger;

and as the constable walked back to the car he fell back on the only other alternative.

"Here! Come out of that!" he ordered; and when Falgate paid no attention beyond an incoherent muttering, he hauled him unceremoniously out of the driving seat on to the road.

Falgate seemed completely dazed, and as soon as the constable loosened his grip on his coat-collar, he sat down on the running-board and seemed content to stay there. It was only with the greatest difficulty that Tarporley could get him to move: but at last by supporting his prisoner he was able to lead him along Speedwell Lane towards the main road. As they walked, lighted by the electric torch, the constable noted that Falgate swayed slightly; and it was only with considerable difficulty that Tarporley could get him to keep on his feet. He had all the appearance of an over-tired man who had not enough reserves left to keep himself under control.

A little distance along the main road was a public telephone box; and from it the constable was able to summon reserves. In a short time his reinforcements arrived, followed by an ambulance, in which he took his prisoner down to the station, while the other constables picketed Speedwell Lane to prevent any interference with the scene of the tragedy.

At the station, the names of Falgate and Peter Thursford had at once suggested the Novem Syndicate in which it was well known that Inspector Severn was keenly interested; and a message had been sent to his house as soon as Tarporley telephoned. The ambulance had hardly reached the station before Severn himself appeared.

"You can charge him with being drunk while in charge of a motor-car," he instructed Tarporley, when he had heard the constable's tale. "And he's to be searched before he's put in the cells. After that, I'll go up to Azalea Cottage with you and you can explain things on the spot. You can sit on the carrier of my motorcycle."

Almost before the formalities had been completed, the police surgeon arrived, very much annoyed at being dragged from his bed at that hour of the morning.

"Drunk in charge of a motor? Look at him! Anyone could see he's next door to incapable. You don't need me to tell you that, do you?"

As his examination proceeded, however, he seemed less sure of his initial diagnosis.

"What I can't quite make out," he admitted, "is the state of his eyes. He's been drinking whiskey, and on that basis his pupils ought to be dilated. They aren't. They're a bit contracted, instead. They ought to be sensitive to light. Instead of that, they're a shade below normal. His breath smells of whiskey, as you say. But there may be a tang of something else there as well. He's been doped, perhaps."

"What kind of dope, do you suppose?" Severn asked.

Alloway shook his head doubtfully.

"Ask me another. Not cocaine. Might be morphia; but morphia's damned hard to come by, these days. Might be one of these sleeping-draught stuffs, the kind they put in the sea-sickness cures. I don't know. Whatever it is, he's unfit to be in charge of a motor-car, and I take it that that's what you want certified."

Alloway prescribed medical treatment intended to bring Falgate back to normal as rapidly as possible.

"And now I suppose you want me to go up and see old Thursford's body?" he inquired. "All right. My car's outside. Give you a lift, if you want one."

The Inspector preferred his motorcycle, as he wished to be sure of transit on the way home, and he knew that the doctor would want to get away before he himself had finished his work at Azalea Cottage. Picking up Constable Tarporley, they took the road to Speedwell Lane.

When Falgate's car had been pulled away, Alloway contented himself with a very cursory examination of Peter Thursford's body.

"He seems pretty well smashed up. Breastbone and some ribs gone, apparently. Sort of result you might get if you put a man on the anvil of a steamhammer and pulled the lever. What's the car? Austin Sixteen-Six, is it? Weighs about a ton by the look of it, and accelerates very quick on first speed. Well, if you get a ton-weight moving at ten miles an hour, you can guess the results when it squashes a man. No use guessing at the actual details of the damage till I get a P. M. done."

"How long's he been dead, do you think?" Severn demanded.

"Two or three hours. Not more. That sort of thing can't be estimated to a minute. Say three hours, at a guess. That's fairly safe."

Having completed his work, Alloway climbed into his car and drove off. Severn proceeded to search the body, taking the contents of the pockets into his own charge for future examination. Then, the ambulance having arrived, the body was put on board it and removed.

The Inspector now found himself faced with a ticklish problem. He had no definite proof that the owner of the Azalea Cottage was even remotely concerned in that night's tragedy. Still, he did not feel inclined to assume that Peter Thursford's death at that particular place was purely fortuitous. Speedwell Lane was not a place that old Thursford would normally have chosen for an evening stroll. And in Speedwell Lane, the dead man's objective must have been Azalea Cottage, for there was no other house in the byway. Therefore, common sense suggested, it was advisable to search the house while it was empty and undisturbed. If the search was postponed until after the return of Miss Langdale and the maid, things might get displaced in the meanwhile, either innocently or of set purpose.

The procuring of a search-warrant would take time; and for all he knew, Miss Langdale might return at any moment. Instant search was the obvious policy. But unfortunately, if he entered the house without a warrant, he would be no better than a burglar.

"Damn the consequences!" was Severn's final decision.

He entered the garden and began his investigation at the garage. This had a little window, and by means of his torch he was able to see that Miss Langdale's car was not in the shed.

Going round to the back of the villa, he tried the windows and found them all fastened. But the catches were old-fashioned, and his pocket-knife was sufficient to slip one of them back and give him entrance into the kitchen.

There, everything seemed normal: dishes had been washed up and replaced on the shelves, cloths had been hung up to dry, the fire had been raked out and re-set ready for lighting. Here, at least, there were no signs of a hurried departure. The maid's bedroom told the same tale.

Severn passed to the drawing-room. Here again things were undisturbed and he could see nothing which struck him as important. The flowers in the vases were fresh that day, the one-day clock on the mantelpiece was still going, and Miss Langdale's portable typewriter stood open on a little desk in one corner of the room. Severn noted that the curtains were closely drawn; but as the room faced the afternoon sun, that might have been merely a precaution against the fading of the carpet and the loose chair-covers. He ran his eye over the furniture: two or three easy-chairs, the nest of three tables, several ash-trays, one of which showed signs of having been used, the wireless set, the few volumes in a book-rack, and the folding tea-table stacked in one corner. Then his glance fell on the one disturbed feature in the room: a big chesterfield on which the cushions still bore the impress of someone who had apparently lain down.

The dining-room, to which Severn passed next, was perfectly normal. Here the curtains had not been drawn; but as its windows faced the morning sun, there was nothing in that.

Severn went upstairs and opened the door of what was obviously a spare bedroom from which he learned nothing. Next to that was another room, apparently belonging to Miss Langdale herself. The bed was made up and undisturbed; but when the Inspector's eye lighted on the dressing-table he noted that hair-brushes, hand-mirror, combs, and manicure appliances were all missing. Quite obviously, Miss Langdale had not intended to return that night.

The rest of the house suggested nothing to him and he descended the stair again. At the foot of it, a door caught his eye which he had overlooked before, and on opening it, he found himself in a small pantry containing a store of china, glass, and drawers for knives and forks. It evidently served also as Miss Langdale's modest substitute for a wine-cellar. Severn noted a tantalus with a couple of square whiskey decanters, one of them half-full, which he supposed she kept for her male guests. An incomplete dozen of soda-water pointed to the same conclusion. Vermouth, some liqueurs, and a cocktail shaker completed the catalogue.

The Inspector let himself out of the house as he had entered it, leaving the catch of the window unfastened. So far as he could see, all that he had learned was that the maid's departure had been foreseen and that Miss Langdale herself had gone away for a day or two, whether suddenly or not he could not tell.

CHAPTER XIV: THE LETTERS

On reaching the police station again, the Inspector learned that Alloway's drastic treatment had sobered Falgate sufficiently to make an interrogation of him possible. Before having his prisoner up for examination, however, Severn decided to look over the things which had been taken when Falgate was searched, and also the contents of Peter Thursford's pockets.

Among the papers taken from Falgate he found a typewritten letter which, when he read it, caused him to lift his eyebrows. Apart from this, there was nothing of any apparent importance. The other collection contained a pocket-book; and on opening this, Severn discovered a second typewritten letter which seemed to give him food for thought. At length he had Falgate brought in.

"You're being charged with having been drunk while in charge of a motor-car," he said, curtly. "At the time you were charged, the usual caution was given to you, but perhaps you weren't in a fit state to understand it. I'm not going to question you about that offence. But a man's been killed by your car, and I must have that cleared up."

Falgate, white and sick-looking, received this statement as though dazed.

"What do you mean?" he asked after a pause. "I don't understand."

"A man has been killed by your car," the Inspector

212

repeated patiently. "I want to know how it happened."

"Killed by my car?" Falgate echoed, stupidly. "I don't know anything about that. I didn't hit anyone — at least I don't remember any accident."

Severn had a suspicion that Falgate might not be so bemused as he appeared.

"Have you been drinking much today?" he demanded abruptly.

"No. A couple of drinks, perhaps," Falgate replied, after thinking carefully.

"When did you leave your house this evening?"

Falgate again considered, as though he had difficulty in rousing his memory.

"It was about a quarter past nine," he said finally.

"You took out your car. Where were you going?"

If Falgate proposed to play the forgetful man, Severn resolved that he also could afford to ignore a few things which he knew quite well.

"I was going up to Miss Langdale's house, Azalea Cottage."

"On the chance of seeing her? Or had you made an arrangement to go there?"

"She posted me a note, asking me to go round," Falgate admitted.

His memory seemed to be coming back, and he spoke with less hesitation now.

"You mean you had an appointment? What time were you to be there?"

"At half-past nine."

Severn's face betrayed nothing of the ideas which were passing through his mind. He accepted the reply without comment.

"Perhaps we'd get along quicker if you tell your story in your own way," he suggested.

Falgate sighed rather wearily, but he made no objection. Severn pulled a sheet of paper towards him and prepared to make notes.

"I took out my car at a quarter past nine," Falgate began. "It was broad daylight then. I hadn't the lamps lit since it was long before lighting-up time. I could see perfectly well. I'm sure I hit nobody on the way up. I'm dead sure of that, so there must be some mistake. Nobody stopped me. I went straight up to Speedwell Lane. When I got to the gate of Azalea Cottage, I parked the car. I didn't switch on the lamps, because it was still daylight."

"What time was that?" Severn interrupted.

"That would be a little before half-past nine. Miss Langdale asked me to be there at half-past, and I remember looking at the clock on the dashboard and seeing that I was a minute or two before my time."

"You're quite sure about that?" Severn interjected. "I want to test your memory on details."

"I'm quite sure about it," Falgate answered without heat. "Then I went into the house. . . ."

"Miss Langdale let you in? Or was it the maid?"

Falgate seemed slightly confused.

"Neither of them. Miss Langdale had given me a key of the Yale on the front door."

"When did she give you that?"

"In a letter she sent me, making the appointment. I've got the letter in my pocket."

Falgate made a gesture to take the letter out, but the Inspector stopped him, as though the point was of no interest. It seemed Falgate had forgotten that he had been searched when he was brought in. Probably he had then been too dazed to know what was going on.

"I went into the drawing-room. I know the house

214

quite well. Miss Langdale said in her letter that she might be out when I arrived and that I was to wait for her."

"Did you see the maid?"

"No. The maid must have been out, or else she would have been able to let me in, wouldn't she? I took it that she must be out, since the Yale key was sent in the letter."

"Go on," the Inspector said, as though conceding the point.

"I went into the drawing-room. There was a folding table, a sort of tea-table, right in front of the door in the middle of the room, with a whiskey decanter, a bottle of soda, and a glass on it. I saw a note on it."

"What sort of note?"

"Just a sheet of paper with some typewriting. Miss Langdale hardly ever writes anything with a pen, you know."

"What did the note say?"

"Oh, it was just a scrap to tell me that she might have to keep me waiting longer than she expected, and saying she'd left the whiskey in case I wanted a drink."

"What sort of decanter was it?" Severn demanded sharply.

Falgate looked startled at the Inspector's sudden query. He hesitated for a second or two before answering.

"Oh, it was . . . I don't quite know how to describe it. One of these pot-bellied things, you know, rather like a bedroom water-jug but with a stopper. That's the nearest I can get to it. It had some sort of pattern on it, I think, but I can't remember what the pattern was like. I didn't look at it particularly. I poured out some whiskey. . . ."

"How much did you take? This may be important," Severn cautioned him.

"About three fingers, I should say," Falgate admitted. "Nothing to hurt, with the soda. It was a hot night. I was a bit thirsty."

"Had you any whiskey at dinner-time?"

"Just what one usually drinks at dinner: a couple of fingers, or so."

"Go on."

"I took a cigarette from a box on the mantelpiece, a silver box, I remember. And then I sat down."

"Were the curtains drawn when you went into the drawing-room?"

"Were they? I don't remember. . . . Oh, yes, I do. They weren't drawn, for I remember glancing out to see that the car was all right."

"How had you left your car?"

"Just at the gate, as I'd pulled it up to go into the house. There's no traffic in Speedwell Lane. It was all right there at the wide bit of the road in front of the house. Three cars abreast could get along there, you know. It wasn't obstructing anything."

"And what happened after that?"

Falgate paused even longer than before at this query. He seemed to be racking his brain for an answer and finding none.

"Well, it's dashed funny," he said at last. "I can't remember anything after that, somehow. I've got a sort of memory of a nightmare of some brand or other, so I must have fallen asleep, I suppose. It's funny . . . I can't remember anything. The next thing I really do remember clearly is being damnably sick, and then I found myself here. That's all I can tell you. I can't remember anything more — not a solitary thing!"

Suddenly the Inspector saw an expression of dismay appear in his prisoner's eyes.

"Have I had one of these loss-of-memory turns? The things you hear about in the S.O.S. messages on the wireless? I've had a devilish lot of worry in business lately."

He paused, apparently appalled by a new possibility.

"Have I been running amuck and killed somebody without knowing anything about what I was doing? I don't remember a thing about it, not a thing. Do you think one could do that in one of these fits —amnesia, isn't it? Good God, man! That's awful!"

This suggestion was equally new to the Inspector, but he put it aside for the moment until he had time to think out its bearings.

"Let's get the facts first," he said, soothingly. "When you were at Azalea Cottage, did you see Miss Langdale? Try to remember that."

The commonplace tone seemed to quieten Falgate.

"No," he said, "I don't remember seeing her. The last thing I can recall is sitting down on the chesterfield in her drawing-room to wait for her. I don't remember her coming in."

The Inspector picked up a sheet of notepaper and pushed it across to Falgate.

"Just cast your eye over that and tell me if it's the letter you got from Miss Langdale."

Falgate read the first sentence or two and then gave an affirmative nod.

"Yes, that's it. How do you come to get hold of it?"

"It was in your pocket when you were brought in," Severn explained. "You're sure that's the note you got?"

Falgate glanced again at it, cursorily, and nodded again.

"I'll just read it over to you, to be on the safe side," Severn decided.

He picked up the letter and read as follows:—

Dear Jim,

I know I treated you badly and have no right to expect you to help me. But I am in a dreadful position and I feel sure that for the sake of old times you won't refuse to do something for me when you know how hard I am pressed.

I cannot explain it on paper. Would you drive over here and see me tonight at 10.30 P. M.? I have to go out and can't be sure of being back exactly at that time but I enclose the key of the front door. The maid will be out. Please come in and wait for me.

I can't tell you how grateful I shall be if you will only come. I *must* see you, even if you can't do anything to help.

VIOLA

Falgate listened carefully as the Inspector read. At one point he seemed prepared to interrupt, but Severn stopped him with a gesture and finished the document before allowing him to speak.

"That's the letter," Falgate admitted. "But you made a mistake in your reading. You said '10.30 P. M.' It's '9.30 P. M.'"

Severn made a pretence of consulting the paper.

"It says '10.30 P. M.' here. Look for yourself."

He held the paper out to Falgate and watched the look of surprise which passed over his prisoner's face as he saw the actual figures.

"Never mind. It's a detail," he said hastily. "Now what about this key she mentions? What became of it?"

Falgate seemed rather taken aback by this question.

"The key? I suppose I put it in my pocket after I'd opened the door. I don't remember."

He put his hand into his waist-coat pocket.

"Everything was taken out of your pockets when you came in," Severn explained. "No key was found then."

Falgate's face showed a mingling of misgiving and perplexity in its expression.

"I don't understand this," he said, slowly. "I can't remember . . . but all the same, I'm almost sure . . ."

The Inspector waited for more, but Falgate apparently was completely puzzled and could give no further information.

"You might sign these notes of mine, after reading them over," Severn said, as he was anxious to get to other tasks which awaited him.

Falgate read over the notes, put his signature at the bottom, and the Inspector dismissed him in charge of a constable.

The interview with his prisoner, short as it was, had given him a good deal to puzzle over. He took up the letter which had been found in Peter Thursford's pocket-book and read it again, in the hope of seeing how it fitted into the rest of the facts.

Dear Mr. Thursford,

I have thought over what you said. If you insist then I cannot help myself and must do as you wish.

Bring the money in notes as I cannot have a cheque passing through my account obviously.

Don't come in your car. It would not do to have it standing outside the house so late. Go for a walk first and see that you are not followed as you come here. I am afraid of Harry seeing you. He has been haunting my house for the last week in spite of all I can do.

Reach here at 11.30 P. M. I have let my maid off tonight to stay with friends. I rely on you to be careful.

V. LANGDALE

Severn put the letter down again and began to turn Falgate's case over in his mind. Was the man simply shamming? Or, if he were not shamming, was it a case of temporary amnesia or of dope? Suppose one killed a man while one was suffering from loss of memory, would one be responsible? Or would one be reckoned as temporarily insane at the moment of the crime? Or again, suppose someone drugs a man and under the influence of the drug that man commits a crime, what is the legal position? The Inspector could recall nothing which fitted these cases.

How much, if any, of Falgate's story was true? That was the root of the whole affair, obviously, though even when one had got that length there would still be much requiring investigation.

Three points in Falgate's narrative excited especial suspicion in Severn's mind. First, he had given the time of his arrival at Azalea Cottage as half-past nine o'clock, whereas in Viola Langdale's letter the appointment was made for an hour later. When Falgate's attention had been drawn to the discrepancy, he had been most obviously taken aback. Then again, there was the mislaying of the Yale key. And, finally, came the fact that Falgate had given an impossibly erroneous description of the whiskey decanter. Severn had seen Viola's decanters: square-faced things which no one could confuse with "a bedroom water-bottle" by any possibility. Besides, he now remembered, the tantalus in Viola's pantry had been locked, probably to guard against her maid's visitors being tempted by its contents.

Had Falgate ever been inside Azalea Cottage at all, that night? Wrong time of arrival, wrong description of the decanter, wrong detail about the blinds in the drawing-room: the whole affair sounded a bit cock-eyed, as Severn phrased it to himself. Was it all just a bit of a dope-dream, except for the invitation from Viola?

Then, suddenly, a fresh line of thought opened up. Falgate had convinced the doctor that it was a case of drink or drugs; and Severn had enough faith in Alloway to take that as fairly good evidence. But that evidence failed to establish one thing, which might be crucial.

This was another of these Novem Syndicate "accidents." Severn was absolutely convinced of that. Peter Thursford's death left only Falgate, Redhill, Checkley, and Wendover to share the £240,000 prize-money: a dividend of £60,000 each. That was a clean jump of £12,000 in the value of each survivor's share; and in Severn's opinion, a good many people would commit murder for £12,000 if they thought they could get off scot-free.

"Damn it! I never thought of that," the Inspector ejaculated, almost in admiration at the ingenuity of the idea which had presented itself to his mind as a possible explanation of the tragedy. "Nobody's ever been hung yet for a motor smash. It's the one way you can kill a man nowadays without paying for it in full. Anyone can fill themselves up to the back teeth and go careering about in a motor; and if they happen to knock someone else into Kingdom Come, it's only manslaughter at the worst, and probably not even a dose of hard labour. Suppose Falgate did for old Thursfold in cold blood *and then doped himself* or swallowed a big dose of whiskey, who's to say he wasn't drunk when the 'accident' happened? That's about as neat a notion as I've struck for a month of Sundays."

He leaned back in his chair in almost cordial admiration for the artistry of the conception.

"That method would come off, in the ordinary case, without anyone giving a blink. It's only suspicious this time because of what's gone before. And even at that, it's going to be damnably hard to prove anything. His case will be that he was turning the car and fell asleep at the wheel with the engine running and the reverse in; and that when old Thursford happened to pass behind the car he got waked up, stepped on the accelerator, let the clutch in, and rammed the old boy up against the wall without waking up from his drunken drowse. Well, he thinks he's damned smart, but I'm going to get him all the same. He's tripped on two points already while he was still a bit bemused. It'll be a devil of a job to make the case solid, but he's given me a chance at last."

His thoughts switched over to the two letters which had emerged in connection with the affair. And suddenly a fresh aspect of the situation caused him to wonder if he had not been too hasty, only a moment before. What part had Viola Langdale actually played in that night's work?

She was the person who had summoned both Falgate and the victim to the fatal spot. Whether Falgate's story was a lie or not, her letter pointed to his being at Azalea Cottage an hour before old Peter Thursford was due to put in an appearance. Had that hour been spent by the two of them in putting the final touches to a concerted scheme? The Inspector was free from Wendover's handicap; when it came to a criminal case, he would just as soon suspect a pretty girl as a man. He had no prepossessions in the matter.

Then, ranging back over the three tragedies, he was struck by a point which had never occurred to him before. In none of the cases was any physical strength required. It needs no force to push a man over a cliff when you come upon him unexpectedly. That was Willenhall's case. Then in Coniston's smash, if that was foul play, no physical force had been used. Something subtler had been at work. And, as he now recalled, Viola Langdale had driven off from the Thursfords' house just before Coniston started on his last drive. Finally, here was old Peter's death, and this time the physical force was supplied by the machine. A girl's hand might have launched the mechanical battering-ram which crushed old Thursford like a nut between hammer and anvil. Nothing messy about it, either, like hitting a man on the head with a poker, or anything of that sort. Just the kind of murder one could do in kid gloves — and never have to look at the result of what one had done. After that, if she had doped Falgate, she could lead him out to take her place at the wheel, and then clear off in her own car so as to avoid being called as a witness. Nobody knew when she had gone away. But Severn himself had good reason to suspect that she had been all ready to go, with everything packed up in advance. There had been no sign of haste in that bedroom.

A final sinister detail fitted itself into the pattern, a phrase from her letter. "Bring the money in notes as I cannot have a cheque passing through my account, obviously." On one interpretation, the reason was plain enough: no girl would want to pass a big cheque from Peter Thursford through her banking account. But there was a second interpretation. No bank will honour a dead man's cheque. And no packet of notes had been found when old Thursford's body was searched. Nor were they in Falgate's possession when his pockets were emptied. Falgate could not have known about them unless Viola Langdale had told him.

"This is getting to be a damned complicated business," the Inspector confessed ruefully to himself, as he contemplated the results of his own imagination.

Obviously the only thing which connected Viola Langdale directly with the tragedy was that typewritten letter to Peter Thursford. It was essential to prove that it had been typed on her machine. That meant another visit to Azalea Cottage; and this time things would have to be done more formally. He would have to get a search-warrant. Any excuse would do now: the Offences against the Person Act would serve — administering a drug with intent to commit any indictable offence. And he would have to get hold of that maidservant and find out when she left the Cottage, as well as anything else she had to tell.

He glanced at his watch and found that he would have time to snatch a short sleep before intruding on some magistrate at breakfast in the matter of the search-warrant. Closing his desk, he was preparing to leave, when a constable stopped him.

"I rang up Mr. Thursford's house, as you told me to, and tried to get hold of Mr. Harry Thursford; but he'd gone out earlier in the evening. He'd told his sister — it was Miss Thursford answered the 'phone — that he was going to Mr. Mackworth's. He'd promised to go there to listen to Mr. Mackworth's short-wave set and didn't expect to be home till three or four o'clock this morning. I rang up Mr. Mackworth's and got Mr. Harry Thursford on the phone and told him what had happened. He wanted to know if he could do anything, but I gave him your message. You can see him and his sister any time you like after breakfast."

Severn gave one or two orders and then went home to snatch what sleep he could until the time came for his next moves.

CHAPTER XV: INSPECTOR SEVERN'S BUSY MORNING

THE Justice of the Peace upon whom Severn descended before breakfast-time was surprised by such an untimely incursion; but he made no difficulties about granting a search-warrant. With this document in his pocket, and a constable in attendance, the Inspector set off to make a fresh, and more legal, visit to Azalea Cottage. His only fear was lest Viola Langdale should have returned before his arrival; but when he reached the villa he was relieved to find the place empty. By his instructions, all necessary measurements had been taken and the fatal car had been removed at an early hour, so that Speedwell Lane had returned to its normal aspect.

On entering the house, Severn's first care was to re-examine the drawing-room and to re-check his recollections in the light of Falgate's story.

The folding tea-table was in the corner, just as he remembered it; and the texture of the carpet was not of the kind which takes impressions, so he could find no evidence to show that the table had recently been spread out in the middle of the room. He could find no trace of the typed note which Falgate said had been left for him. The waste-paper basket was empty; and the grate was clear.

On the mantelpiece was a small silver box containing some State Express cigarettes. This confirmed Falgate's evidence; but, as the Inspector reflected, a silver box lasts a good many years, and at one time Falgate had been a habitué of Azalea Cottage and would know that such a box would be on the premises. Better support of his story was a single State Express stub in one of the ash-trays.

Severn carried out a minute search for the decanter which Falgate described, but nothing of the sort was to be found on the premises. The decanters in the locked tantalus could not by any stretch of imagination be supposed to correspond to the description which Falgate had supplied.

Search for the missing Yale key was equally fruitless.

The Inspector then turned to Viola's portable type-writer, an Underwood machine. Rather to his disappointment, the keys yielded no signs of finger-prints. Evidently the machine had been cleaned up since it was last in use.

Severn took a sheet of paper and made impressions of all the characters on the machine, taking care to provide himself with several complete sets for comparison purposes. He also examined the stores of typewriting paper and removed sample sheets of each kind that he found. Among them he found a packet with the embossed address: AZALEA COTTAGE, which corresponded exactly to the paper on which the letters to Falgate and Peter Thursford had been typed.

Another visit to the bedroom upstairs satisfied him that Viola's departure had been no hurried flight but a prearranged affair. He looked in vain, both there and in the bathroom, for toothbrush, toothpaste, bath-sponge, safety razor, or any other toilette accessories which might easily have been overlooked in a hasty packing-up. Bedroom slippers and dressing-gown were also absent. Everything pointed to things having been done in a leisurely fashion quite different from a last-moment rush.

Satisfied at last that he had made his search a thorough one and that nothing useful had been overlooked, he quitted the villa again, leaving the constable on guard.

The Thursfords' house was his next objective, and there he asked to see Harry Thursford. When he was shown in the morning-room, however, he found Enid Thursford there also. Neither of them showed any signs of affliction at the death of their uncle. If they had any emotion, it was evidently relief that they were at last free from that personality which had been a daily irritation to them. The Inspector, who had a shrewd idea of what life had been under Peter's regime, wasted no time in cheap sympathy, but plunged immediately into business.

"Did either of you see Mr. Thursford at dinner last night?" he asked, by way of opening his inquiry with something definite.

"We both saw him then," Harry answered shortly.

"One of us had always to stay and dine with him," Enid explained. "He wouldn't be left alone. Last night, as it happened, we were both here."

The Inspector hesitated for a moment, with a glance at the girl.

"Did he drink more than usual at dinner?" he asked, with a faint hesitation.

Evidently he might have spared his pains. It was Enid who replied.

"Rather less than usual, if anything. He wasn't drunk."

There was no mistaking the scorn in the tone. The implication was that usually Peter had got up from the table rather the worse of liquor.

"After dinner, can you remember what happened?"

"Immediately after dinner, I went out to a friend's house — Miss Hathern's. Perhaps you saw more of him, Harry?"

"He was in the smoking-room till ten o'clock," Harry took up the tale. "I happened to go in there to fill my case, and he was sitting at the window. He said nothing to me then. I went up to my own room and while I was up there, I heard the front door slam. I looked out of my window and saw him walking down the drive. That was the last I saw of him."

"You have two cars, haven't you?" the Inspector asked.

Enid nodded.

"Yes, we've a two-seater — I took that to go to Miss Hathern's — and an Austin Sixteen-Six."

"Then Mr. Thursford didn't take the saloon, did he?"

"No," Harry explained. "I don't know why he didn't, but he left it in the garage. As a matter of fact, that's why I looked out to see him go. I'd promised Mr. Mackworth to go across and sit up with him to listen to America on his set, and I wanted to know whether my uncle had taken the car or not. If he had, I'd have had to walk over to Mr. Mackworth's and I wasn't very keen on that. It's a longish walk, especially when one comes home at three or four in the morning."

"When did you get to Mr. Mackworth's?" the Inspector asked casually.

"Just before eleven o'clock. The phone message from the police station caught me there about three in the morning, just as we were thinking of shutting down for the night."

"There's one point I'd rather like to know about, but perhaps you can't tell me anything to help," Severn explained, turning to another subject. "Can you remember

anything about any letters which he may have received
yesterday?"

He surprised a glance passing from one to the other
as he spoke, and a slight lifting of the girl's eyebrows as
though she had hoped the question would not be asked
but was prepared for it, now that it had come.

"He got nothing but some bills and advertisements by
the post at breakfast-time," she explained. "I saw him
open them, and I remember that there wasn't a private
letter amongst them. The post didn't call again until
lunch-time. Only one letter came then, for him."

"You saw it, perhaps?"

"Yes, I was at the front door when the postman came
and I took the letter from him myself and handed it on
to my uncle."

It was perfectly evident that Enid Thursford realised
that in some way this letter was important. It was equally
obvious that she meant to volunteer nothing about it.

"Did you recognise the handwriting of the address,
by any chance?" the Inspector asked in as careless a tone
as he could muster.

Enid Thursford hesitated for the fraction of a second.

"No," she said.

Then, seeing the next question trembling on Severn's
lips, she decided to forestall it.

"The address was typewritten."

"What sort of envelope was it?" Severn persisted.
"Square? Oblong? Cream-laid? Bluish? Or what?"

This time there was no doubt about her hesitation. Nor
was there much doubt in the Inspector's mind as to the
cause of it. Enid Thursford wasn't pondering over
whether the envelope was square or oblong. She remembered that quite well. What she was trying to gauge

was how much he knew and how much she could suppress without actually lying.

"It was a sort of squarish-oblong envelope, rather bigger than ordinary note-paper size. About five inches by four, I should say. It was bluish paper."

Exactly the same as one of the samples he had taken from Viola Langdale's store, the Inspector recognised gleefully. Then a possible reason for Enid's hesitation occurred to him. She was a friend of Viola's. She must have recognised the envelope perfectly well, as it was the kind that Viola evidently used in her correspondence. Given the fact that Harry's engagement had just been broken off, and also her knowledge of her uncle's character, it was reasonable enough to suppose that she would hedge on the subject of that letter. She might be loyal to her friend and anxious to keep Viola's name out of the affair as far as possible; or she might merely be concerned to do as little dirty-linen washing in public as possible. He had got what he wanted, and there was no need to push the matter further, except for one point.

"Did you see your uncle open that letter, Miss Thursford?"

"Yes, he opened it immediately I gave it to him."

"He expected it, perhaps?"

"I don't know whether he expected it or not. He didn't seem surprised at getting a letter. Why should he be?"

"Well," said the Inspector bluntly, determined to get at the facts. "Did he seem pleased with it when he read it?"

"How should I know?"

But the Inspector was paying attention to her face rather than to her voice, and it was plain enough that he had hit the bull's-eye. Peter *had* been pleased. And that fairly identified the letter as the one found in his pocket-book after his death.

"You haven't the envelope, I suppose? Or the letter itself?"

"No. Our maids are given orders to collect anything of that sort at once when they see it and put it in the kitchen fire. The envelope, I mean. My uncle put the letter in his pocket after he'd read it."

"What did your uncle do after lunch, can you tell me?"

"He went to the bank, I believe." Enid explained. "He mentioned at lunch that he was going there; and after lunch he took out the Austin and went off in it. When he came back again, I saw him counting a packet of notes. He had tea with me at five o'clock, and after that he went up to his own room — for a nap, I expect. When I saw him again, he was dressed for dinner."

From her manner, Severn inferred that she attached little importance to the notes; and from this he guessed that she had no idea of the contents of the letter.

"When did you get home from Miss Hathern's?" he asked.

"Oh, I don't know exactly. Shortly after midnight, I should think. I didn't leave her house till close on twelve o'clock, I know. I was in bed and asleep by the time your telephone message came."

The Inspector pondered for a moment or two, trying to recall any point he had missed, but he could think of nothing.

"I don't want to have to bother you again," he said, apologetically. "There may be some other matters, but . . . Who was your uncle's lawyer? He would be able to tell me about the business side of things, if I happen to want anything of that sort."

"Mr. Roade was my uncle's solicitor," Harry Thursford answered. "He'll know about all that side of things, I expect. My sister and I are trustees — so my uncle told us. You see we're all that's left of the family."

The Inspector had now got as much as he expected. He had confirmed his other evidence more strongly than he had hoped; and there seemed no point in worrying his two witnesses further. He got them to put their signatures to his notes, and then took his departure.

As he walked down the drive to his motorcycle, he thought over the personality of the late Peter Thursford. Severn was not a sentimental man, but even his insensitive feelings had sensed the atmosphere in that house. A man must have been more than usually disagreeable when his two remaining relatives felt nothing but a relief at his disappearance. An alcoholic petty tyrant — he recalled what Enid Thursford had said about the old man's insistence on company at dinner — must have been a constant irritation. On Harry Thursford, Severn wasted little sympathy. That resignation from the Syndicate was common property by now, and Severn felt only contempt for a youngster who with a prize of £40,000 at stake, had cracked under the strain. The Inspector would have been only too glad to run the risk at that price. And, as he reflected, Harry Thursford must have been rather a poor type if he preferred to put up with his uncle instead of going off and making his own way in the world. It would need a very keen sense of the main chance to keep a man in these leading-strings. Enid Thursford's case was different. An untrained girl could hardly get a living in these days; and she simply had to stand her uncle as best she could. But even the unimaginative Severn could see what hatred and contempt any decent girl must have had for old Peter. She could hardly be expected to shed many tears over him. The Inspector thought all the better of her because she refused to make any pretence about it.

His next objective was the house where Viola's maid was staying with friends. Constable Tarporley had been able to furnish the address, and the Inspector was lucky enough to find the girl at home. As by this time the overnight tragedy was common talk in the place, he did not think it necessary to finesse much in his inquiries.

"You've been with Miss Langdale for a couple of years, haven't you?"

"Yes," the girl agreed, "I've been with her two years last May."

She looked at Severn with a slightly militant air, and then added:

"And if you think you're going to get me to say anything against her, you've come to the wrong shop. She's been kind to me, and I like her, so it's no use your coming here trying to get me to run her down. See that?"

"I see that," said the Inspector gravely. "But what I happen to want is just facts. They won't hurt her, will they?"

"No-o-o," the girl admitted though with more than a little suspicion in her drawl. "Ask away, then. But don't you think you can get round me and make me say things I don't want to say; for I shan't. See?"

"I want to ask about Mr. Harry Thursford, first of all," Severn began.

He wanted to induce the girl to talk freely, and he guessed that on that subject she would be eloquent enough on her mistress's side.

"Oh, that thing?" the maid said, contemptuously. "Ask away, then."

"You don't like him, evidently," was the Inspector's comment, made in a tone which suggested that he shared her own views. "Has he been much about the house lately? Since the engagement was broken off, I mean."

"He's been round every day, sometimes twice a day. A perfect pest, he's been, I can tell you. 'Not at home,' I'd say every time. Once he wouldn't take no for an answer. He just pushed past me into the drawing-room. Much good it did him! She'd gone out earlier in the afternoon. But do you think that satisfied him? Not a bit of it! He'd got in, and he stayed on there, waiting for her to come back. I knew she'd gone to play tennis and wouldn't be back for hours, so I just let him sit. I had my tea and went into the garden at the back to have a read. I never expected he'd stay that long; but he hung on until Miss Langdale came back. I told her about it, and she went into the drawing-room with her racquet in her hand. She was flushed a bit, and she looked just lovely."

"Yes?" interjected Severn, surmising that there was more to come.

"Much good he got by it! Miss Langdale's a perfect lady, but when she gets angry, she gets cooler and cooler, and she can say things fit to cut you to the bone, if you've got any feelings at all."

"I suppose the door was left open when you heard all this?"

"I didn't need to go listening at keyholes, if that's what you're kindly hinting at, Mister. I was in the garden and the drawing-room window was open. You could have heard him fifty yards away or further, and she's got one of these clear voices that don't need raising to make themselves heard. I didn't cock my ears to listen, but I couldn't help hearing."

"I suppose he wanted Miss Langdale to get engaged to him again?"

"You'd have thought so," said the maid, pertly. "And

not made much mistake, either. As good as a stage play, it was, with him getting more and more eager and excited, and her that cool and contemptuous all the time. It takes a real lady to carry it off like that. I'd have flown out at him, if it had been me. But she just got icier and icier the more he talked."

"And what happened in the end?"

"Oh, she dismissed him. I can't give you the exact words, but it was something like this: 'I'm not going to be troubled in this way any longer. If you come here again, I'll shut up the house and go away where you won't be able to make yourself a nuisance to me. I'm going to give my maid instructions that if you come to my door again, she's to ring up the police and get you removed.' "

"And what did he say to that?" inquired the Inspector with more than professional interest.

"He just said 'Viola!' Like that! Full of yearning, his voice was. Do you know," the maid added reflectively, "I think, before he showed up so badly, it must have been real nice to be made love to by him. Almost as good as some of the love-making on the talkies. Real passion in the tones, you know."

"And then?" the Inspector prompted, with a certain zest.

"Oh, she just cowed him. He went away like a beaten dog. But it didn't last. He was back again, the night before last. I'd put the door on the chain just in case of accidents. She was in the drawing-room. And when he wouldn't go away I went to the telephone in the hall and called up the police — with my finger on the clip, of course, but he couldn't see that. So at that he took fright, and went away. Miss Langdale had heard it all, but she said nothing to me about it. Then, yesterday morning, she gave me some money and told me to go to my friends here until she sent for me again. She did some packing in the morning — just a suit-case. And after lunch was over, she ran me down in her car to save me carrying my suit-case."

"She gave you no address?"

"No. If I didn't know it, I couldn't tell it. Not that I'd have given it away to Thursford. She needn't have been afraid of that."

"Had you a key of the house?"

"No. Miss Langdale asked me for mine — there are two — and I fetched it to her from where it usually lies on the salver on the hall table. She took it with her, I expect, just in case her own went a-missing. She once lost her keys and we had to get a fresh lock put in; and since then she's been extra particular about keys."

The Inspector thought for a moment before putting his next questions.

"Did Mr. Falgate ever come about the house?"

The maid shook her head.

"Not in my time."

"Or Mr. Redhill?"

"Mr. Redhill's been up once or twice. Not a regular visitor, though."

"Mr. Checkley?"

"Mr. Checkley's been up several times, at bridge-parties, and that sort of thing. More like an acquaintance than a friend, I'd say Mr. Checkley was."

"And Mr. Peter Thursford?"

"Him that's dead? No, I never opened the door to him in my life."

"Mr. Wendover?"

"He comes about once in a blue moon. I haven't seen him for months. Now Mr. Wendover's a real gentleman, if you like. Always so polite and got a sort of way with him, if you know what I mean."

The Inspector switched off to a fresh subject.

"Do you keep track of your empty bottles? Soda, and such-like?"

The maid stared at him in some surprise.

"Oh, I see what you mean. Do I know how many empties we've got just now? No, I don't."

"Talking of bottles," the Inspector said carelessly, as though the idea had just crossed his mind, "a friend of mine was telling me about a decanter he saw in a sales-room the other day that was very valuable. A rounded thing, shaped something like this, he said." (Severn made an illustrative gesture with his finger in the air.) "Anything like that amongst your crystal at the Cottage by any chance? It might be worth a lot of money."

The maid shook her head decidedly.

"We've got nothing of that sort. Square-sided, ours are. The kind that fit into a tantalus."

After getting the maid to put her signature to his notes, which she did suspiciously and with marked reluctance, the Inspector took leave of her and went back to the police station.

Here he found awaiting him a number of reports for which he had asked, and among them was one stating that no tyre-marks had been detected in Speedwell Lane. The dry weather and the rough road-surface had allowed cars to come and go without leaving a trace; and even Falgate's car had left no print.

On his desk, Severn found a letter from the Chief Constable asking him to forward immediately complete reports of the proceedings at the inquests, copies of his own notes and of witnesses' statements, prints of Willenhall's photographs and his own, with the corresponding films, photographs of all the documentary evidence, and, if possible, the latest album in which Willenhall stored his negatives.

"Phew!" the Inspector said to himself as he read over the list. "If he's going to take a hand in the business, I'll have to hurry up in case he gets ahead of me at the last moment."

But he was not actually perturbed. The reports which had just come in dealt with the question of alibis, and as he glanced through them he had seen his case clarifying very considerably.

He decided to charge Falgate with manslaughter and to arrange that bail should be refused. If Falgate were the murderer, then with him under lock and key, there could be no further crimes. If, on the other hand, the murderer was not Falgate but another member of the Syndicate, the risk of a fresh murder would be too big for him to take, since only Redhill, Checkley, and Wendover were left on the list of free agents, and Wendover was obviously out of the question. That left only the mysterious Mr. ABCD in play; but Severn was beginning to think that he knew something about the identity of that individual.

Following on what he had said to the maid, the Inspector paid a further visit to Azalea Cottage and examined the store of empty soda-water bottles for traces of Falgate's fingerprints. Not altogether to his surprise, he found nothing to correspond with the prints which his prisoner had allowed him to take.

CHAPTER XVI: THE ALIBI PROBLEM

WHEN he made a fresh appointment with Wendover at the Grange that evening, Severn had two objects in view. In the first place, he wanted to test the convincingness of his own arguments on someone, so as to discover if he had overlooked any weak points. Wendover had a soundly critical mind, he knew; and the Inspector had no fear that anything which he said in confidence would be gossiped abroad. Wendover could be relied on to keep his mouth shut. In the second place, the Inspector was anxious to know how much time he had in hand. Quite obviously, the Chief Constable was taking a direct interest in local affairs, since he had asked for all the documents. He might descend in person at any moment. But if he came, he would certainly stay with Wendover at the Grange; and Severn hoped to learn if any suggestion of the sort had been made.

He had not even the trouble of fishing for this information. He had hardly sat down before Wendover gave it to him unasked.

"I've had a wire from Sir Clinton," he said, knowing that the news would interest the Inspector. "He's coming down to stay with me over the week-end."

"This week-end?" Severn demanded, taken aback by the proximity of the Chief Constable's arrival.

Wendover had little difficulty in reading what was in the Inspector's mind, but he was too tactful to make a direct reference to it.

"You're bringing a charge of manslaughter against Mr. Falgate, I hear," he said, as though turning to a fresh subject. "Well, naturally that's not triable at the sessions, so I've no more to do with it than the man in the street. In any case, I'd have kept off the Bench on account of my connection with the Syndicate."

Severn made a slight gesture of agreement.

"That's one reason why I came to see you," he explained. "I knew you'd have nothing to do with the affair, so there's no harm in discussing it with you. I'd like a plain opinion, in confidence of course, about the bearing of some evidence that I've collected."

"You want to try it on the dog before trying it on the jury?" Wendover suggested in a slightly ironical tone.

He was obviously torn between the desire to exercise his detective powers and a doubt whether he should take any part in the matter at all.

"Well, it won't do any harm to listen," Severn pointed out. "And if you find a flaw in the business, then it's all the better for everybody, isn't it? It would save somebody a lot of unpleasantness and keep me from putting my foot in it in public," he added candidly.

"There's something in that," Wendover admitted, as he pushed the whiskey decanter towards the Inspector. "Go ahead, then. It's strictly in confidence and quite informal, I understand."

Severn nodded and, after pouring out some whiskey and soda, he produced from a capacious pocket a mass of papers, which he spread out on the table between them.

"One feature of this business, from start to finish," he began, "is that all the documents concerned in it have been typewritten. There are six of them: that first threatening letter that your Syndicate members received; a letter from Willenhall to Harry Thursford fixing an appointment on the morning of the affair up at the Gape; a letter from Willenhall to Checkley about that recipe for a sweetmeat; the second threatening letter; a letter from Miss Langdale to Falgate; and a letter from her to Peter Thursford. I've got the whole lot of them here.

"Now it struck me, as it would have struck anyone, that something might be got by identifying the machines on which these letters were written — the individual machines, I mean. It didn't look very hopeful in some cases; but one might as well be thorough when one was at it, I thought. So I set about it; and, as it turned out, I happened to strike it lucky."

"How did you tackle the business?" inquired Wendover, who took an interest in such details.

"Well, the first thing obviously was to find out what I could about typewriters belonging to people in that Syndicate of yours. One must make a start somewhere, and that would at least clear the ground. I didn't go and ask to see the machines, of course. That might have caused trouble, and besides it'd have given the show away at once. So I had to go about it indirectly."

Severn took a sip from his glass before exposing his method.

"I've got a good few acquaintances scattered up and down the country, and amongst them I picked out a set that I could trust and that wouldn't ask questions. Under my instructions, Mr. Brown (we'll say) would write from Middlesborough to Falgate and ask him to quote a wholesale price for some artificial silk fabric, with a lot of questions about quality and guarantee and so forth — anything that would draw a longish reply. At the same time Mrs. Brown would write to Checkley asking for the name of the nearest shop where she could get tins of his toffee, and enclosing a stamped envelope for reply. Then Mr. Jones, over in a village nearby here, would write to Coniston and ask for a quotation for hiring a couple of motorbuses for an afternoon — a Sunday-school picnic or something of that sort. And Mrs. Jones would inquire from Thursford's cinemas whether they made a reduction for quantity when a dozen seats were booked at once for a party. And Mr. Robinson of Liverpool would write very worriedly to Redhill's place asking if they stocked anything between the white and the cream shade in enamels and if so, would they kindly send him a sample of it. And so on, and so forth. Of course I had about a dozen people writing to each firm in the hope of getting a sample of writing done on every typewriter in the offices. It took a bit of arranging, but it paid me better than I hoped."

"But that only covered office machines," Wendover pointed out. "What if the machine had been used at home?"

"I managed that, too," Severn explained, with a certain pride in his ingenuity. "For instance, Mr. Smith would present his compliments to Mr. F. Halstead and make inquiries about the character of Sarah Wooton, who left his service in 1927 and is now seeking a position as housekeeper to an invalid gentleman. It was easy enough to get the names of servants from our constables. Or else Mr. Snooks would write, in a rather worried tone, about a beggar who is pestering him and who has given Mr. Halstead's name as a reference because Mr. Halstead is a brother of his. That generally drew a very blunt letter in reply," said the Inspector with a reminiscent smile.

"Deuced ingenious," Wendover admitted, though not

in a very hearty tone. "You didn't put your collaborators on my track, by any chance?"

The Inspector shook his head decidedly.

"No, of course not. I knew you hadn't a typewriter."

Wendover, who had expected a different reason, concealed his feelings as well as he could.

"Well, go on," he invited.

Severn spread out his papers, picked out two specimens, and handed them across to his host.

"I'll begin with the easiest. That's a note from Miss Langdale to Mr. Falgate. And here's a specimen of the characters of her machine on some of her own paper. The machine's an Underwood portable. If you compare the two, you'll see that both paper and characters are identical. By the way, that document isn't public property yet."

Wendover hardly heard him. It was the contents of Viola's letter and not the details of the characters which fixed his attention. "A dreadful position . . . hard pressed. . . ." So old Thursford had been right in his guess about her financial condition. But why on earth had she turned to Falgate, of all people? She might just as reasonably have appealed to Wendover himself for assistance in her straits. Falgate? The man she had turned down. Wendover couldn't see his way through it.

The Inspector was watching him closely, fingering a second sheet of paper as though not very sure whether to hand it over or not. At last, as Wendover laid down the papers he was holding, Severn decided to show him it.

"This is another letter from Miss Langdale, to Peter Thursford."

If the first note had been a surprise to Wendover, this new one took him completely aback, as his face betrayed. So neither scruples nor even fastidiousness

244

had stood in her way after all. She had struck her bargain with old Thursford — "bring the money in notes" — just as the old blackguard had expected that she would. It was like her — in some ways. And yet Wendover, with his rather chivalrous outlook on women, was deeply shocked by the transaction. Surely a girl could have found some easier way out of her difficulties than *that*.

Then a thought struck him. He picked up the letter to Falgate and compared the times of the two appointments: Falgate at 10.30 P. M., old Thursford at 11.30 P. M. Evidently she had tried Falgate first; and if he had helped her, old Peter would have found the door shut in his face an hour later.

Wendover had no great liking for Viola Langdale, but at the thought of Peter Thursford he felt an almost physical discomfort. How could any decent girl touch a thing like that?

His interest in the Inspector's case-building was quenched; but Severn gave him no time to think out any further implications of the two letters. Breaking in on Wendover's brief brown study, the Inspector pushed across a fresh document.

"That's the letter from Willenhall to Harry Thursford, making the appointment for their walk to the Maiden's Well," he explained. "And here's a letter from Mr. Halstead, written on the same Corona typewriter. Mr. Willenhall must have used Mr. Halstead's machine when he wrote to Harry Thursford. There's no doubt about it being the same machine. If you look at the 'W' 's in 'Well' and 'way' and 'Crowland' and 'well' in Willenhall's letter, you'll find that in each case the left side of the 'W' is heavier printed than the right-hand side. That means that the type is 'off its feet' as they call it. You know that the type-face in an ordinary typewriter isn't a plane surface. It's curved concave to fit the convex curve of the platen — the roller that holds the paper — so that when the machine's in proper adjustment you get uniform pressure over the whole letter when it comes down on the platen. If the machine gets out of adjustment, the two curves don't coincide as they ought to do, and you get a strong impression of one part of the letter and a weak impression of another part where there hasn't been complete contact. If you look at the letter I managed to draw from Mr. Halstead, you'll see exactly the same defect. In Willenhall's letter, again, you'll find that the 'K' 's are 'off their feet' in the same direction: the left-hand sides are strong and the right-hand of the letters is weak. Same in Mr. Halstead's letter. I've checked up four of these peculiarities in each case, and that puts the thing beyond all reasonable doubt."

Severn seemed rather disappointed that Wendover showed so little interest in his demonstration. To make quite sure that he was being understood, he selected another document.

"This will let you see what I mean. This is a Corona machine also. It's the letter we drew from Mr. Harry Thursford. Now if you'll glance at the 'W' 's and the 'K' 's in this one, you'll see at once that they're quite different from those made by Mr. Halstead's machine. Both 'W' and 'K' are 'on their feet' in Mr. Harry Thursford's typewriter; they're evenly printed. You couldn't palm off the work of the one machine as having been done on the other."

"I can see that," Wendover admitted, a trifle absently.

He was still occupied with the problem of Viola and that miserable old satyr. Why, in Heaven's name, hadn't she applied to some decent person, if she was in such a corner? Why have gone to Peter Thursford of all people? And he tried to evade the answer which suggested itself at once: "Because old Thursford would pay up handsomely on the spot and be glad to do it."

"This is a specimen of work done by Redhill's typewriter," the Inspector explained perfunctorily. "It's a Royal. I'm showing it to you merely for the sake of completeness, for it doesn't correspond to any of the documents."

He handed the paper over. Wendover stared at it with unseeing eyes for a moment; then, realising that his abstraction was impolite, he pulled himself together.

"Now I'm coming to the most important points of all," said Severn with a touch of asperity in his tone. "Here's your copy of the first threatening letter which was sent to the members of your Syndicate. It was written on a Remington; the tails of the 'y' 's and the hook of the 'j' are the easiest points to go for in that identification. Here's the second threatening letter. Same thing: Remington again. Here's a specimen of the Remington's work — a letter from their head office in London. You see the same characteristics there."

Wendover's politeness now made him, if anything, over-eager to pay attention to what the Inspector was saying.

"What I want you to look at specially in these next specimens," Severn went on, having assured himself that he was being followed with attention, "is the shift-key work. You know what I mean? The key that lifts the carriage so that a line of capitals is printed instead of a set of small letters. Well, suppose that goes slightly out of adjustment, what's the result? Your capitals will all be just a shade higher or lower than your ordinary letters. The same result would come about if an operator had a habit of not pressing down the shift-key to the full when he worked it. You see that?"

Wendover nodded without saying anything.

"Now look at the two threatening letters," Severn directed. "You see that whenever there's a capital, it's just the merest shade out of alignment. You'll notice it quite readily in 'The' and 'This' and 'That's' at the start of paragraphs in the two letters. The bottom bar of the 'T' isn't in exact alignment with the two bottom bars at the feet of the legs of the 'h.' "

Wendover examined the specimens carefully.

"It's a very minute difference," he objected.

Severn produced another set of exhibits from his pocket.

"Here are some very much enlarged photographs I've made of the two letters," he explained as he laid them out on the table. "It's plain enough in them. And I think you'll see that in each case the error of the machine is exactly the same. I've made some measurements on these enlargements, and the two sets tally precisely. There's not the least doubt in my mind that these two letters come from the same Remington machine."

"I don't see much in that," Wendover objected, testily. "If you'd told me they came from two different Remingtons, *then* I'd have been surprised."

"Just a moment," the Inspector begged. "While you've got your eye in, I want you to look at this other set of photographs showing the same combination 'th.' Now are these from the same machine as the others, or from a different Remington?"

Wendover scanned the various specimens closely for a long time. He did not wish to run the risk of making a slip and disgracing himself in Severn's eyes.

"They're all from the same machine," he pronounced at length. "No one could mistake it — if this test of yours is sound, of course."

"Here's a fourth specimen," Severn said, pushing another photograph over. "Same or different?"

"Identical, undoubtedly," Wendover decided, after a prolonged examination.

"Yes, identical, as you say," said the Inspector, grimly. "I've no doubts about it. And now I'll tell you where these specimens came from."

He arranged the four photographic enlargements in line.

"*This* one was taken from the first threatening letter. *That* one I photographed from threatening letter No. 2. And now this third one is part of a letter we drew from Checkley by our inquiries."

"Checkley? You mean Checkley was the author of these threatening letters?"

The Inspector wanted his main surprise to break on Wendover immediately, so he ignored the interruption. He put his finger on the fourth print.

"And this last one. *I took that from the letter Checkley said he got from Willenhall, the letter making that appointment at Brookman's Farm on the day that Willenhall was killed at Hell's Gape.*"

Wendover started in his chair.

"The devil you did!" he exclaimed. "Do you mean to say that Checkley typed a letter inviting himself to meet Willenhall that morning, and pretended at the inquest that he'd got it from Willenhall?"

"Looks like it, doesn't it?" Severn pointed out. "I don't see how you can explain it any other way. You identified the thing yourself, and I was careful not to give you any information that might bias you. The paper's the same as the others, too, same water-mark."

"But the signature? That's not typewritten," Wendover objected.

"Traced," said Severn tersely.

"How do you know that?" Wendover demanded.

"Easy enough, once I'd got the suggestion," Severn explained confidently. "I had one genuine specimen of Willenhall's signature — the one on the letter addressed to Harry Thursford and written on Halstead's typewriter. I put it under a microscope, and I found that the part *'illenhall'* was written in one sweep, without lifting the pen at all. That's what one expects; most of us write the major part of our signatures at a swoop, if the name allows it. Try your own."

Wendover pulled out his fountain pen and a piece of paper and scribbled his normal signature several times.

"Your practice is just the same as Willenhall's," the Inspector pointed out, as he examined the process. "You write *'W'* first. Then you lift your pen. After you've started the *'endover'* you don't lift your nib off the paper till you've finished the signature. You write the seven letters all in one sweep without hesitating or breaking the line."

Wendover made one further trial to verify this.

"Now here's an enlargement of Checkley's forgery," said Severn, producing yet another photographic print. "If you look at it, you'll see that the pen's been arrested no less than five times in the course of the nine letters in *'illenhall.'* Besides, look at the edge of the line; it's all serrated, showing that the pen moved slowly and hesitatingly. Compare that with the clean edge and straight sweep in Willenhall's actual signature — here's an enlargement of it. You don't notice these things in the unmagnified original; but when one makes an enlargement, they fairly stare at you. A child couldn't miss them."

Wendover studied the two prints in silence for a time, paying particular attention to the points to which Severn had drawn his attention. In the enlargement, the spots where the forger had arrested his pen while he studied the ensuing part of the curve were plain enough.

"Here's something else," he pointed out as he glanced up at last. "If you look at the point here, where Willenhall's signature shows a thick line, I think you'll see that the forger had to go over his work twice. His first attempt wasn't thick enough to match and he had to make a second run-over to broaden out the line."

The Inspector agreed, evidently pleased to find that Wendover had been able to detect evidence of his own to satisfy him.

"There was one thing in these threatening letters that set me thinking," he pointed out. "In fact, it was that that made me tackle the whole identification question thoroughly. If you look at both of them, you'll see that the money's described in both words and figures. It's 'ten thousand pounds' and then in brackets and figures '(£10,000).' That disposed straight off of the idea that these letters were a mere kid's joke. The phrasing looked as if it was meant to suggest a kid's joke, but when you get sums of money in both words and figures, no kid ever thought of that. That's a business man's way of doing things. It's second nature with some business men to do that; and here it slipped out quite unconsciously."

"And in the case of a man who thinks a lot about money, it would be more apt to slip out; is that what you mean?"

"Well, Mr. Checkley's mind runs a bit on money, doesn't it?"

Wendover, having had time to recover from his initial surprise at the Inspector's results, now found a source of some wonder in his own psychological reactions. The discovery that Checkley was in the affair up to the neck and might even be the murderer of Willenhall, had not given him anything like the shock which he had suffered when Severn handed over Viola's letter to Peter Thursford. But he was given no leisure to pursue this course of auto-psychoanalysis. Severn had other fish ready for him to fry and was evidently impatient to get on with the work.

"That's one side of the business," he said, pushing the prints and documents aside. "Now here's another aspect of it. I've been going into the question of alibis very thoroughly, because that's obviously one way in which one can eliminate innocent people from the problem. For instance, take your own case as an example. You were with Sir Clinton when the Hell's Gape affair happened. At the time Coniston went smash you were dining at Silver Grove and didn't get away from there until after Coniston was dead. On the night of Peter Thursford's death, you had a stag-party here at the Grange, and two of your guests stayed on until half-past twelve. Apart from everything else, these facts clear you completely. You see what I mean?"

Wendover saw also that the Inspector had evidently been making very careful inquiries into what he regarded as his own private affairs, and he was not altogether pleased by this revelation.

"Go on," he said, shortly.

Severn appeared to miss the abruptness in Wendover's tone.

"I've gone over the whole lot — everybody likely to be mixed up in the business — in exactly the same way, without any preconceived ideas," he pursued. "I needn't give you details in each individual case, but unless I could establish a man's alibi by independent witnesses I've reckoned him as having no alibi. I mean in no case do my results depend on any statement by the man himself; they're corroborated every time by some outside evidence, or else it counts as no alibi. These alibis could be sworn to in court. You see what I mean?"

"Yes, go on," said Wendover rather testily.

"Well, here's the result," Severn explained, putting down yet another sheet of paper. "I've headed the column I, II, and III. I. is the Hell's Gape affair; II. is Coniston's smash; and III. is the business at Azalea Cottage — old Thursford's death. If a person has a clear alibi, I've put a cross in the column. If I can get no proof of an alibi, I've put a dash in the column."

Wendover turned the sheet round and examined it with keen interest.

	I.	II.	III.
Wendover	+	+	+
Falgate	+	—	—
H. Thursford	+	+	+
Checkley	—	+	+
Redhill	+	+	+
Miss Langdale	+	—	—

Wendover pounced on one item immediately.

"Miss Langdale was at the Thursfords' house that night when Coniston came to smash. Why do you allow her no alibi when you give one to Checkley and Redhill who were there also?"

"Because Miss Langdale drove away before Coniston left. No one was with her in her car, therefore I've no independent evidence as to where she went or what she did."

"Oh, very well," Wendover acquiesced grumpily. "Have it your own way."

He returned to his study of the table for a moment and then looked up with considerable relief on his features.

"What you seem to have established, Inspector, is that none of these people is the murderer. Each of them has an alibi for at least one of the affairs."

"That's so," Severn agreed cheerfully.

Then he added in a meaning tone:

"But supposing it wasn't a single-handed job, what then?"

"What's that?" Wendover demanded.

"Well," said the Inspector slowly, "Suppose that two people had a hand in the business. Each of them could have a sound alibi for at least one of the affairs, couldn't he?"

Wendover's eye went back to the tabular document in front of him. In the light of Severn's suggestion, the crosses and dashes told a plain tale; but Wendover struggled against drawing the obvious inference. The Inspector, seeing his hesitation, put the thing into words in the plainest fashion.

"If there's anything in what I said, then Checkley must have carried through the affair at the Gape. Everybody else has a sound alibi. Besides, Checkley needed some excuse to account for being up at that out-of-the-way spot and so he forged that letter of invitation from Willenhall, about the recipe. I've had the countryside combed for that old woman with the Herb Suckit stuff. She doesn't exist. She's just an invention of Checkley's, a pure myth."

This was news to Wendover. Severn gave him no time to comment on it, however.

"But Checkley didn't commit either of the other murders," he went on. "Therefore, somebody else must have been mixed up in them. And that somebody will have no alibi in Coniston's case and Peter Thursford's case. Only two people on the list fit these conditions: Falgate and Miss Langdale."

Wendover cast back to a point which he had left aside at the moment it first occurred to him.

"Because a person hasn't an alibi which can be sworn to in court by an independent witness," he objected, "it doesn't necessarily follow that that person was on the spot and committed the crime, does it?"

"No," the Inspector agreed at once, "it doesn't. But in the case of Peter Thursford, Falgate *was* on the spot."

"What's your evidence for the alibis of the other people on the night of Peter Thursford's death?" Wendover inquired.

The Inspector ticked off the points rapidly.

"Peter Thursford's appointment at Azalea Cottage was at 11.30 P.M. and my constable found his body at a quarter past midnight; so he must have been killed between those two times. You had a stag-party here which lasted till half-past twelve. Harry Thursford reached Mr. Mackworth's house at 11 P.M. and was still there when the police rang him up in the small hours. Checkley and Redhill went out to play tennis at Mrs. Satterton's and stayed on there till well past midnight, playing bridge."

"That seems sound enough," Wendover admitted, though with a certain reluctance. Then he added, in a tone of relief, "Since you've pinned Falgate down as being on the spot when Peter Thursford died, Miss Langdale doesn't come into the affair? Your two criminals would be Checkley and Falgate, on that basis?"

"It was Miss Langdale's letters that brought both the men on to the spot," Severn pointed out soberly. "And Miss Langdale's vanished. I can't get on her track."

Wendover thought he saw a point which had escaped the Inspector. He broke into an uneasy laugh.

"Where's your motive?" he demanded, scornfully.

"Motive?" the Inspector echoed guardedly. "There's no need to establish a motive. You know that quite well. But" — he paused for a moment as though thinking rapidly — "I'm not so sure about there being no motive. Some time ago I talked about Mr. ABCD, you remember, the fellow who bought himself into your Syndicate without giving his name. It's just on the cards that what I should have said was *Miss* ABCD. I don't know," he added hastily in response to Wendover's obvious disapproval. "I'm merely taking every possibility into account. You asked for a motive, and I'm suggesting that a motive could be found even in an unlikely case. It's a possibility."

"Rubbish!" Wendover retorted angrily. "I know roughly what that girl's financial position is. These shares cost £6,400, you remember. It would have strained Miss Langdale's resources to raise a sum like that in fluid cash."

The Inspector pondered over this for quite a long time. When he spoke again, it was clear that Wendover's idea had taken root in a way quite different from what its author desired.

"Perhaps that's why she's got so devilish hard up, all of a sudden. That's an idea, that is. Thanks for giving me it."

CHAPTER XVII: VIOLA LANGDALE

ON thinking over that interview between himself and Wendover, Inspector Severn began to regret that he had ever sought it. Quite obviously they had not seen eye to eye, especially in the later stages. To the Inspector, the whole affair presented itself as a mere puzzle to be solved, like a chess-problem, without any regard for the feelings of the pieces on the board. Wendover, on the other hand, seemed to be unable to forget that these pieces were human beings with whom he had personal contacts. Naturally enough, when two people looked at the same thing from standpoints so far apart, they could hardly be expected to agree in their interpretations of what they saw.

Another point caused the Inspector some annoyance. He had counted on having his case complete as soon as he could lay hands on Viola Langdale and put her under examination. But unfortunately she had vanished with her car, leaving no trace behind her; and it was obviously going to take time to track her down. Now he learned that the Chief Constable intended to make a descent the next week-end. Severn would have given a good deal to be able to present a conclusive report, then, on the whole affair; but he saw no chance of that now.

Just as he was beginning to despair, however, a god descended from the machine in the guise of Constable Tarporley. While off duty in the afternoon, Tarporley had chanced to encounter Miss Langdale's maid; and in the course of casual conversation he had picked up from her the news that her mistress was returning for dinner that very evening. The girl had received a post-card with instructions; and when the constable came across her in the village she was buying some provisions to take with her up to Azalea Cottage. The unsentimental Tarporley had refrained from offering to carry them for her. Instead, with the hope of a good mark in his mind, he had gone straight to the police station and given his news to the Inspector.

Severn, thus rescued at the last moment from his difficulty, decided to run no risks. For all he knew, Viola might take fright as soon as she arrived and might depart as unexpectedly as she had come. It would be well to be on the spot at the moment of her arrival, he concluded; and in a very short time he was on his way to Azalea Cottage to wait there for her.

He had long to wait, for she did not arrive until just before dinner time. He heard her motor stopped at the gate and then driven into the garage. A couple of minutes later, she came into the drawing-room just as she had got out of her car.

"Inspector Severn, isn't it?" she said, coolly. "My maid told me you were waiting. Can I do anything for you?"

The Inspector could not make out whether this off-hand manner was natural or assumed. She certainly appeared in no way perturbed, but merely curious to know what brought him there. He made up his mind to take the bull by the horns and see if he could catch her off her guard.

"I've come to ask some questions about the death of Mr. Thursford," he explained formally.

"Mr. Thursford? Dead? Which Mr. Thursford?"

The tone of surprise was perfect, Severn had to admit. Well, if she wanted to take that line, he had no objections to leading her on.

"Mr. Peter Thursford."

Severn kept his eyes on her face, hoping to read something in her expression; but she defeated him completely.

"Oh, Mr. *Peter* Thursford. Is he dead? Well, Mr. Severn, I don't quite see how I can help you. I know nothing about Mr. Peter Thursford beyond what everybody else knew. Why do you come to me?"

She sat down on the chesterfield and pointed to a chair.

"Sit down, Mr. Severn, and tell me all about it."

The Inspector seated himself, but he had no intention of following her programme.

"I'm rather pressed for time," he said, apologetically, glancing at his wrist-watch. "If you don't mind, I'd like to ask one or two questions first."

Viola stared at him and an expression of perplexity deepened on her face.

"I don't know what you're getting at," she said with apparent frankness. "What have I got to do with Peter Thursford?"

"When did you see him last?" the Inspector demanded, without paying any attention to her question.

"When did I see him? Do you mean when did I meet him last? I don't know, really. A week or two ago, or perhaps longer. You see, Mr. Severn, there's been . . . Well, to put it plainly, his nephew and I were engaged, and now we aren't engaged. Naturally I haven't seen any more of the family than I could help."

"Then you've had no communication with him — Mr. Peter Thursford, I mean — within the last fortnight, or possibly three weeks? Could you make it more exact than that?"

Viola reflected for a few moments, as though running over her memory in search of facts.

"It's three weeks on Monday since I saw him, and then it was only in the street."

"You've had no communication whatever with him since then?"

"None whatever," said Viola in a rather offended tone. "May I ask, Mr. Severn, what all this is about? I know nothing about Mr. Peter Thursford. If he's dead, I'm sorry, of course. But he wasn't anything more than a mere acquaintance. Hardly even that, for I didn't like him. What have I got to do with the matter?"

"I'm sorry I've got to ask these questions," Severn apologised. "In a case of this sort we have to get all the information we can."

Viola fastened on the expression.

"A case of this sort? What sort?"

The Inspector was beginning to lose patience. Bluff was all very well in moderation, but this pretence was so shallow as to be a mere waste of time.

"Mr. Peter Thursford was killed just outside your gate, there."

He made a faint gesture towards the garden, but kept his eyes on her face.

"Out there?" She seemed completely surprised. "When did this happen?"

"It happened the night you went away from here."

"What happened? I mean, how was he killed?"

"In a motor smash," said the Inspector, rather disingenuously.

"Oh, that was it?"

Her face cleared as a thought crossed her mind.

"I see," she went on. "You thought he was in my house that evening and that perhaps he'd . . . well, got too much whiskey? Is that it? No, I never saw him that evening. In fact, I don't understand what he was doing here at all."

Severn saw his chance of the transition from one subject to another.

"Mr. Falgate was there at the time. Perhaps you invited *him* that evening."

"No, I didn't," said Viola with a certain show of bluntness.

"When did you see Mr. Falgate last?"

"Weeks ago."

"And you've had no communication with him since?"

"None whatever. Really, Mr. Severn, you seem desperately inquisitive about my private affairs."

The Inspector decided that the time had come to spring his mine. Of course the girl didn't know that these letters had fallen into his hands. She thought she was quite safe in bluffing. Very well, she could take her medicine.

The tone of his voice changed and became uncompromisingly official.

"Now be careful, Miss Langdale. I'm asking a plain question. Have you, within the last ten days, had any communication, direct or indirect, with either Mr. Peter Thursford or Mr. Falgate? Yes or no?"

Viola stared at him as though he were some strange animal, but she did not lose her coolness.

"You seem to be forgetting your manners, Mr. Severn. I'm not accustomed to be spoken to in that tone. And I'm not accustomed to having my word doubted. I've said 'No' once. Surely that's enough."

"I'm afraid not," Severn said downrightly. "I've given you your chance, Miss Langdale, and you wouldn't take it. Very well. Look at this."

He crossed over to the chesterfield and showed her the letter to Falgate, holding it in his own hand lest she should try to destroy it. As she read it, he kept his eyes on her face and had no difficulty in seeing that she was completely taken aback. When she had gone through it, she looked up at him with something like fear in her face.

"What's that?" she demanded, with much of the coolness gone from her voice. "I know nothing about it. I never saw it before. I didn't write it."

"That's easily proved," the Inspector suggested in a gentler tone. "You won't mind copying it on your machine, perhaps, and then we can compare your copy with the original. That would settle it, wouldn't it?"

Viola made a half-protest, but Severn overbore her objection. She went over to the typewriter and took down the letter at his dictation. When she had finished, she handed the copy to him, and he made a pretence of comparing it with the original. Then, without commenting on them, he showed her the letter to Peter Thursford. As she read it, he could see her flushing.

"Somebody seems to have gone to a lot of trouble to discredit me," she said, bitterly, as she came to the end "You don't imagine that I wrote that, do you? I'm not such a fool as to put a thing like that on paper, to fall into the hands of Tom, Dick, and Harry, as it seems to have done. That's obviously the work of somebody . . ."

Severn interrupted her. It seemed needless to let her involve herself in aimless lies which could help neither her nor himself. He beckoned her to the window where the light was good.

"Now, just look at these two documents, Miss Langdale. Here's the one you typed just now. You see the letter 't'? It's just a shade above the level of the rest of the letters, isn't it? Same here, and here, and here. Now look at the 't' s in the letter I showed you. Same defect in the 't' s there; they're all just a shade above the proper level, exactly as in your copy. Look at the 's' s. In each document, the lower loop of the letter 's' is weak. Finally, the 'd' s in both documents have lost a bit of the ceriph — the little horizontal tick at the bottom of the vertical line of the 'd'. It's useless to pretend that that letter and your copy of it came from different machines. They were both typed on that Underwood portable of yours. And the letter to Peter Thursford shows precisely the same defects."

Viola seemed dazed by this damning evidence.

"I don't understand it," she muttered.

Then her coolness seemed to return again.

"I never wrote either of these letters," she said, keeping her voice firm by an obvious effort. "I don't understand what's been going on. But I never wrote anything even remotely like that kind of thing. I never wrote to Mr. Peter Thursford in my life, not a line. I haven't written to Mr. Falgate for months — years, I should say."

Severn was quite unimpressed. This was what he expected her to say, once she had begun to deny her authorship. She had to brazen the thing out now, even in the face of the facts.

"I'd like to see your signature — no, don't bother to write it now," he added as she picked up a pen from her desk.

Obviously she would be on her guard and would write something slightly different from her normal signature. He thought for a moment or two before he hit on a fair test.

"Have you any book with your name written on the fly-leaf?"

She reflected for a moment. Severn guessed that she was calculating whether she could venture to risk the test.

"A newish book," he added quickly.

People changed their signatures sometimes, and he did not want to give her the chance of producing an old book with an out-of-date signature in it. His glance ranged round the room and lighted on a tiny bookshelf. Walking over to it, he picked up book after book until he came to one in which her name was written, then another, and a third.

"These will do," he said.

On the first fly-leaf he found "V. Langdale" which he compared with the signature of the letter to Peter Thursford. The second book had the inscription "Viola Langdale" and he compared the writing of the Christian name with the signature on the letter to Falgate. The third book had "Viola Langdale" inscribed in it also, and again he made a minute comparison. So far as he could see, the signatures on the letters corresponded — as closely as any two signatures do correspond in practice — with those on the books.

Without comment, he showed the writings to Viola.

"I don't care," she said, obstinately. "I didn't either type or sign these letters."

She bit her lip, evidently in great perplexity.

"I don't understand this," she broke out at last. "Why should anyone want to make out that I wrote these things? It's beastly, suggesting the things that letter hints at! I've a right to know more than you've told me, Mr. Severn. Where did you get hold of these letters? I simply can't make head or tail of all this. How did they fall into your hands?"

"Yes, I expect you'd like to find out as much as you

can. But you're not going to," was the Inspector's mental comment. Aloud, he took a different line.

"Let's drop these letters for a moment, Miss Langdale. I think I can clear the thing up quicker if you'll tell me your movements on the afternoon and evening of the day you left here. That may help to put me on the track. It's a serious thing, this kind of letter-writing; and I'm anxious to lay my hands on the person who's responsible."

Partly by his words — though they were purposely non-committal — and partly by his tone, he seemed to be enlisting her as a helper now, instead of treating her as under suspicion. To his satisfaction, she responded to the treatment. She seemed to have not the slightest objection to giving him any information he wanted.

"Begin at the afternoon, you say? Very well. I had lunch at the usual time. Then I took my maid and her suit-case down into the village in my little car. She was going to stay with friends there while I was away. I came back here, finished my packing, had some tea, washed up the tea-things, looked to all the window-catches, and then went off with my own suit-case in my car."

"What time would that be?" Severn interposed.

"Oh, about five o'clock or so. I didn't look at my watch."

"Where did you go?"

"I was going to London. I drove on until about dinner-time, and then I had dinner at a small hotel on the road. I can't remember its name."

"No, I bet you can't," was the Inspector's sardonic comment to himself. "I know that inn quite well. When you come to look for it, it's address is The Back o' Beyond, on the Road to Nowhere and you never can remember anything about it afterwards."

But Viola's next words shattered his hopes.

"When I got to London, I put up at the Enterkin Hotel near Hyde Park Gate, where I always stay when I'm in London. They know me there. I'd telegraphed for a room from a post-office on the road."

"When did you get there?" the Inspector asked with a last effort.

"Oh, about half-past nine or so."

That finished it! If Viola was in London at 9.30 P. M. on the night that Peter Thursford was killed, she could not by any possibility have been on the spot, here, when he died. The Inspector could make a good guess at when people were telling the truth; and Viola's story certainly gave him the impression that it was accurate, now that she had come down to definite, checkable details. If she were lying, she would never have taken the risk of mentioning a particular hotel and saying that it was one where she was well known. That could be checked. And it would be checked, too. Severn would see to that.

"What took you to London?" he inquired casually.

"I'm getting some dresses there," Viola said curtly, as though the subject were displeasing in some way. "And I had to go up to get fitted some time. I took the opportunity of going then."

"And you never heard of Mr. Peter Thursford's death?"

"How could I?" Viola demanded in a surprised tone. "I don't read newspapers when I'm in London. I've plenty of other things to do. And I'd left no address here, so no one wrote to me. Of course I didn't hear about it. And you're the first person I've seen — except my maid in passing — since I got back here. I think you'd better tell me what's happened now."

She paused abruptly, as though something had passed through her mind.

"Oh, I begin to see! You thought I was mixed up in it because of those letters? Is that it?"

Severn took refuge in a short narrative of Peter Thursford's end. When he had finished, Viola was silent for a few moments.

"I see," she said slowly. "And these letters were found on Mr. Peter Thursford and Mr. Falgate? That's very strange. Let me see the things again, please."

She examined them deliberately, both typescript and signatures, and then handed them back.

"You're quite right. The typing is the same as my own machine's, and these signatures are exactly like mine. But these letters weren't written by me, Mr. Severn. I never saw them until you took them out of your pocket. I can't imagine who's done this."

"Just one more question," said Severn. "Why did you not leave your London address when you went there? You knew where you were going even before you left here, I suppose."

Viola looked at him reflectively. Her coolness had come back to her again.

"Is it essential that you should pry into my private affairs? Well, then, I went away from here because I was being pestered by somebody and I wanted to stop that. If I'd left my address, I might have been followed and bothered again. That's why."

Severn had no need to push his inquiry further. The maid had told him about Harry Thursford's persistence in coming to Azalea Cottage after the engagement had been broken off. Viola's whole story hung together perfectly with the other evidence which he had.

He retired in good order; but as he walked back to the police station, his feelings were anything but pleasant. In some ways that interview had been disastrous for his self-esteem. He had gone to it with the certainty that Viola Langdale held one of the keys of the mystery; and now he was left puzzled as to her real position. Her story tallied perfectly well with all the other facts which he had about her movements; and he was quite prepared to admit that investigation would probably confirm her statement that she was at a London hotel at the time Peter Thursford was killed. But that didn't mean she was entirely cleared. These letters might be genuine after all, in spite of her denials. She might not have been on the spot, but she might have acted as decoy to bring Peter Thursford to the place where he met his death.

At the police station, he got out his microscope and examined the signatures on the decoy letters; and as he did so, he vented his feelings in a heartfelt oath. There, plain enough, he could see the work of the forger revealed: the hesitations of the pen, the wavering edges of the lines, even a faint retouching at one place where the first tracing had been unsatisfactory. What a fool he had been! Cocksure of the identity of the typewriter itself, he had neglected to put the signatures through the test. Just at the critical point he had given thoroughness the go-by, deserted his principles, and missed an essential fact in the case.

Very much shaken in his confidence, he began to wonder if he had not made some mistake about the typewriting itself. Again he went over the documents: the letter to Falgate, the letter to Peter Thursford, his own impressions from the Underwood portable, and Viola's copy taken at his dictation. It was with a sigh of relief that he put them down at last. No, he'd made no mistake there. The whole lot of them came from the one machine. And what was more, the blackness of the ribbon-impression was practically the same in them all, which showed that all of them had been written within the last few days.

A final test occurred to him. This time he would be thorough in every detail. When these typescripts had begun to bulk largely in his case, he had gone to a public library and taken out Osborn's *Questioned Documents* to familiarise himself with the proper procedure in the identification of typewriters; and now a case described in that book came back to his mind. Typewriter ribbons have their individual characteristics also. No two of them are woven exactly alike. Eagerly he set about his new test.

Taking the letter to Falgate first, he put it under his microscope and examined one of the capital "I" 's. Magnified in this way, the line which to the naked eye seemed uniform was now revealed as a series of spots with very minute spaces between them, each spot corresponding to the impression of one of the horizontal threads of the ribbon. Where the type-face encountered the gaps between two adjacent threads, no impression had been left on the paper. Fortunately for the Inspector, the ribbon was a well-worn one, which made the test easier.

Severn counted the dots in the stalk of the capital "I" and found thirteen of them, which showed that the ribbon had been woven of a texture containing thirteen threads in the height of a capital letter. Turning to the letter to Peter Thursford, he found thirteen threads there also, and the same number in his own impressions and in the copy which Viola had taken down under his dictation.

"Well, that's clinched," he assured himself in a more cheerful tone. "Same paper, same typewriter, same ribbon: there's no doubt about *that* point, anyhow."

And now his interview with Viola Langdale appeared in a better guise. He had been on the wrong track at the start; but none the less he had got the information he really needed to advance his case. He took out his table of alibis, changed the dash at Viola's name to a cross in the third column, and examined the result.

	I.	II.	III.
Wendover	+	+	+
Falgate	+	—	—
H. Thursford	+	+	+
Checkley	—	+	+
Redhill	+	+	+
Miss Langdale	+	—	+

If it was a two-handed business, then Checkley and Falgate between them could have managed it: Checkley being responsible for the affair at Hell's Gape and Falgate being the killer of Peter Thursford and Coniston. And quite possibly Coniston's death was accidental, after all. That was just on the cards.

He turned up the letter of invitation which Checkley had produced to justify his presence at Hell's Gape. On re-reading it in the light of his new knowledge, he was almost disgusted to think that he had ever been deceived by it. The old lady, the family recipe, the cottage that couldn't be located — the whole affair was so obviously a fake from start to finish.

"Herb Suckit!" the Inspector snorted, almost indignantly. "As if anybody in their senses would call a stuff by that name! I must have been demented when I took that seriously."

Checkley would find it difficult to account for that spurious letter. He had over-reached himself by producing it, for beyond his own statement there was nothing to prove that he had ever been near the Gape on that fatal afternoon.

The case against Falgate was plain enough, so far as Peter Thursford's death was concerned. But here the Inspector had to admit that there was a very big loophole for escape. A motor smash was such an everyday affair in these times; and the jury might take it into their heads to treat the thing as manslaughter. Still, now that he had Viola Langdale's evidence, the Inspector thought he could make that position untenable. There were too many flaws in Falgate's story: the Yale key that couldn't be found, the decanter that didn't exist, and the lack of his fingerprints on any soda-water bottle in the stock at Azalea Cottage. These would be awkward matters for his barrister to explain away.

Severn opened a drawer and took out some of the other exhibits which he hoped to use in court at no distant date. Sir Clinton had returned those sent to him, almost at once. The first thing that came to hand was the long strip of positive prints taken from Willenhall's negatives of the Maiden's Well. The Inspector searched for the corresponding prints taken from his own films, put the two side by side, and contemplated them with the satisfaction of an artist.

"That was a neat bit of photographing, though I say it myself," he pronounced judicially. "I've got his viewpoint to a hair, except that the big stone in the near foreground looks a shade broader in his print than it does in mine. Dashed little, though. The only one where I'm much out are the ones that are twins to his photos of Harry Thursford. He's got a lot more of the near foreground into them than I've got in my print. But the essentials are O.K. in mine, and that's the main thing."

He scrutinised the shadows in the prints and satisfied himself that they reached exactly the same points in the two versions. It had cost him no little trouble to get his pictures correct, and he was proud of his accuracy.

"It's a pity Willenhall didn't use his autographic gadget on this roll. If he'd only been thoughtful enough to jot down the time when he took that last exposure, it would have saved me a lot of bother. Well, perhaps there's more satisfaction in working things out oneself."

He pulled out the strip containing the photographs taken by Sir Clinton and rubbed his finger along the roughened edge of the film.

"I remember he found it stiff to screw up the roll, when he took these last two exposures. I wonder what Willenhall would have said if he'd known that film would be used on his own dead body. Rummy, to think of that."

His eye passed to the three exposures made by Willenhall immediately before the catastrophe.

"He was a good photographer, that's plain," he commented as he scanned them with the appreciation of a connoisseur. "That's a good bit of work, whether you look on it as a picture or a photograph. Let's have a look at some of his other stuff."

When he had applied for the negative album required by Sir Clinton, Willenhall's executors had forwarded a whole series of little oblong volumes in which were stored all the negatives taken by Willenhall during his stay with Halstead. Fortunately Willenhall had put the dates on each film with the autographic device, so that the Inspector had found no difficulty in picking out the most recent series to send to the Chief Constable. He now drew out one or two of the remaining albums and began to examine negatives in them, here and there, making a mental running commentary as he did so.

"Standing Stones. That doesn't offer much chance of the picturesque, anyhow. But one could have made a good guess at the time it was taken, if one had to, from the length of the shadows — he's got them very clear. . . . What's this?" He turned the film round and referred to the autographed description. "Oh, yes, '*Spinney, Heatingham, 2 June.*' . . . And here's one of Heatingham Abbey. Must be rather pretty in a positive. . . . And this looks like Halstead's garden." He referred to the inscription. "Yes, that looks like Halstead himself by the rock-pool. . . . And here's one of a girl . . . '*Miss Langdale, 3 June.*' She's a cool card, that girl."

CHAPTER XVIII: THE DIAL OF AHAZ

ON the following Friday, Sir Clinton arrived at the Grange for dinner according to his promise; but although Wendover fished for his views about the various cases which were under investigation, the Chief Constable refused to be drawn.

"I haven't got sufficient information yet," he declared at last, in answer to a blunt question. "Severn's done extraordinarily well in collecting facts; but I want to see one or two things with my own eyes before I can make up my mind. By tomorrow night, if the morning's fine, I hope to get what I want. If the weather's bad, I'll have to wait until Sunday."

Wendover glanced up at the barograph on the mantelpiece.

"It looks as if the good weather might last for a bit yet," he judged. "But if you're going out on the prowl tomorrow morning, it's a bit of a nuisance; I shan't be able to go with you. I've got some urgent business in the morning; it's just cropped up and I can't postpone it."

He was much disappointed by the turn of events, as he had been looking forward to seeing what line the Chief Constable's investigation would take.

"If you don't mind, Squire, I'll have Severn up here after dinner tomorrow — weather permitting — and he can go over the whole affair from his point of view. You'll be back by then?"

Wendover agreed at once.

"It must have been rather an uncomfortable time for

you, Squire," Sir Clinton commented. "Now that it's over — at least I hope so — I may as well tell you that I've had a watch kept on you lately. You see, since you were the one obviously innocent person in that Syndicate of yours, your death wouldn't have narrowed the circle of suspicion; and therefore you were the most likely person to be knocked out. I couldn't spare the men to watch everybody; but your case was the most urgent one."

"I'd never thought of that," Wendover confessed. "Now you put it forward, of course it's plain enough. But I don't remember seeing your 'shadow' on my heels anywhere."

"I imported a man or two from another district," Sir Clinton explained. "There wouldn't have been much point in having you dogged by people you knew, would there? You'd have spotted my guard at once and probably raised a howl at being given special treatment."

"That's so," Wendover had to admit. "I shouldn't have cared to be singled out for special protection. It would have looked a bit like favouritism, seeing that you're a friend of mine."

"No doubt," Sir Clinton agreed, drily.

Next morning proved to be clear-skied, and Wendover went off on his business errand with at least the comfort that the evening would bring him a good deal nearer an understanding of the problem of the Syndicate. As soon as he had gone, Sir Clinton in his turn set out, armed with a kodak of the same pattern as the one used by Willenhall. His car took him up the road to the point nearest the Maiden's Well which he visited for a short time to take photographs. Then he turned back to the village, called on the druggist and made arrangements to have the films developed immediately and rough prints of them made, without waiting for them to dry. His next port of call was the police station, where he spent some time in looking over back records of minor crimes. Finally, he paid a visit to Azalea Cottage. Miss Langdale was out, but he interviewed the maid, sent her into the garden, and, while she was there, copied out both the decoy letters on the Underwood portable. That done, he returned to the druggist and collected the prints which had been made from his films. He seemed well satisfied with his morning's work when he returned to the Grange for lunch.

In the afternoon, Sir Clinton refused to discuss the case with Wendover on the ground that it was not yet quite complete; but it was plain enough from his manner that little remained to be done, and his host could not understand why the Chief Constable insisted on going for a walk instead of finishing his investigation at once.

"Severn's got the stuff," was all Sir Clinton would vouchsafe. "He'll bring it up when he comes tonight. Then we shall see. By the way, Squire, would you mind if I put your wireless out of action temporarily in the cause of law and order? I may have to, but I promise not to do any real damage to the set."

"I've no objection," Wendover assured him at once.

But the proposal left him completely puzzled. It was of no use questioning Sir Clinton, for quite obviously he meant to divulge nothing until he had the Inspector there. Wireless? What on earth had wireless to do with the case? And why should it be necessary to put his set out of order? Wendover gave it up.

He fidgeted through the afternoon and during dinner, until Sir Clinton had to enter a mild protest against his lack of connected conversation; but at last they left the table. Wendover made his way to the smoking-room, while Sir Clinton went upstairs. When he returned, he put down on a table at his elbow a packet of photographs, some small tools, a short coil of insulated wire, a rubber pad, a pair of nippers, a copper plate with a binding-screw attached to it, a yard-stick and a pencil-shaped copper rod partly covered with rubber tubing from which another length of insulated wire protruded. A rubber glove completed this collection, at which Wendover stared in perplexity.

Severn's arrival put an end to his speculations. The Inspector had with him a small bag from which he proceeded to unpack a mass of papers and photographs, some of which Wendover recognised as being the ones which Severn had exhibited to him on a previous occasion. Sir Clinton drew the table up so that it stood in the centre of their three chairs and allowed them all to see the documents on it without stretching.

"Congratulations, Inspector!" Sir Clinton said heartily. "These notes you sent me were gems of completeness, and your report on the whole affair was a model. I don't think you've left me with a question to ask, in spite of my natural inquisitiveness."

Severn made no concealment of his pleasure at this commendation.

"Well, if you can say that, sir, I'm satisfied and a bit more."

"Just run over your conclusions, will you? I'd like to be quite sure you haven't come across anything fresh since your final report."

Now that Viola Langdale was out of the question, the Inspector had no fear of offending Wendover's prejudices. In fact, he was rather glad to be able to soothe his susceptibilities. Severn had, as he promised himself, checked Viola's story about her arrival at the London hotel and had found it perfectly accurate. She was quite well known there, and he easily obtained confirmatory evidence from the hotel servants. As he explained this, Wendover's hackles obviously subsided.

"I told you Miss Langdale had nothing to do with it," the Squire pointed out, but he said it more to justify his own acumen than in depreciation of Severn.

"So your idea is that Checkley and Falgate have been working this affair together?" Sir Clinton asked, when the Inspector had gone over his evidence.

"I don't see how you can make anything else out of it," Severn said dogmatically.

"I was just wondering where the theft of three one-pound sample tins of toffee came into your tale," said Sir Clinton innocently. "Perhaps I was dozing when you dealt with that point."

"I don't quite understand, sir," said the Inspector, helplessly.

He was accustomed to Sir Clinton's peculiarities, but this particular irrelevance confused him. He suspected that the Chief Constable was making sly fun of his passion for detail.

Sir Clinton brushed the matter aside.

"Well, well, we'll not bother about it just now," he said in a business-like tone, as though he regretted his jest and wished to cover it up. "Your point is that this was a two-handed affair. Checkley went to Falgate one fine day and said: 'Hello, old cock, what about doing in one or two of our fellow-Syndicateers and scooping a bigger share of the money?' And Falgate, being an intelligent fellow, caught his meaning at once, and replied: 'I'm on. Where do we begin?' Do you know, Inspector, that bit of dialogue doesn't sound to me quite natural. And even if you paraphrase it, I don't feel it gets any more natural in the process. It would take a bit of nerve to put forward a proposition of that kind, between friends, no matter how much you wrapped it up in re-fined English. It has been done, of course; but it's hardly a common sort of arrangement. I'd rather see something simpler."

"Facts are facts, sir," the Inspector protested stub-bornly.

"I'm not disputing your facts. The trouble is, I don't care for some of your inferences."

"But that alibi table of mine's based on facts. If you don't dispute them, then I don't see your point," Severn complained.

Sir Clinton did not reply directly.

"A sound alibi is the best defence that can be put up, I admit. But on the other hand, an unsuccessful attempt to prove an alibi generally damns an accused person in the eyes of a jury. If you break a man's alibi you don't necessarily prove him guilty on that account, but you discredit him considerably, all the same. Therefore it's obvious that we've got to overhaul these alibis very thoroughly from every point of view."

"I've done that already," said the Inspector in a rather resentful tone.

"Then there's no harm in my running over them again," the Chief Constable pointed out placidly. "Let's take the case of the Hell's Gape affair first of all."

Wendover saw that the Inspector was rather per-turbed by this persistence. Sir Clinton never wasted time, and if he proposed to "run over" the evidence, it was plain enough that he had something in view beyond what Severn had elicited.

"There's one form of alibi that has interested me, off and on, for some years," Sir Clinton began, reminiscently. "It was bound to be tried, sooner or later; and I've often thought over how it could be done and how it could be defeated if it was tried. There's a very neat suggestion about it in Barry Pain's *Problem Club* yarns. He devised a practically unbreakable alibi based on photographs; but it needed two men to work it, which would be rather a large order for an actual criminal case."

"I've read that," Wendover interjected. "Given the premises, it would be absolutely conclusive. But it needed two men, as you say."

"I looked on the thing in this way," Sir Clinton went on. "An alibi depends on establishing two factors: place and time. Take the case of a murder. The murderer wants to prove that he wasn't on the spot when the crime was committed or that he was on some other spot when the murder was done. The second alternative's obviously the more convincing of the two. Now obviously a man can't be in two places at once. If the murder was committed at noon at a certain place, the murderer can't prove that he was at another place at midday except by employing a witness to commit perjury or by misleading his witness with a doctored watch or clock. A single-handed crime bars out the perjured witness; and nowadays the altering of a watch would hardly convince anyone.

"How can you get round that? Suppose you change the *apparent* time at which the murder was committed. Meet an honest witness at eleven o'clock; go off and commit your murder at noon; fake the evidence to prove that the murder was done at eleven o'clock; and there's your alibi."

"Yes," the Inspector admitted grudgingly. "I dare say."

Obviously, from his tone, he was dismissing this idea as having no connection with his own actual case.

"That brings us to the photographic alibi," Sir Clinton continued briskly, without appearing to notice the Inspector's attitude. "The essence of an alibi of that sort is that it must contain, in the photograph itself, some definite evidence of the time the picture was taken. One could include a clock-face, for example, with the hands at the appropriate time. But I don't think that would convince a sceptic. He'd see immediately that one can shift the hands of a clock or a watch to suit the purpose of the photograph. Something rather less obvious is wanted.

"A sundial suggests itself as the next possibility. But it would be a bit difficult to arrange a snapshot of a sundial without dragging improbability in a bit; and sundials aren't usually in places where murder can be safely committed. But the sundial notion set me thinking about shadows, for after all any shadow will serve the purpose of establishing the time at which a snapshot was taken on a given day. You did it yourself, Inspector, and very well, too, with that series of photographs you took."

Severn did not seem altogether pleased with the compliment. He was now evidently perturbed by Sir Clinton's line of argument. Then, as something crossed his mind, he brightened up again as though he had detected a flaw in the Chief Constable's reasoning. Whatever it was, he kept it to himself for the moment.

"Speculations of that sort have been in my mind for long enough," Sir Clinton went on. "And that afternoon, up at Hell's Gape, they came up again, merely casually, I admit. These big fangs of rock, you remember, throwing their shadows on the cliff-face: it was a kind of natural sundial. Here was just the sort of thing that would serve the purpose of anyone looking for a photographic alibi. If one could shift the shadow back on the cliff-face, in a snapshot, it would fill the bill exactly — the very thing I'd been thinking out long before as a purely theoretical stunt. That was why Isaiah's miracle came into my mind at the moment. *'He brought the shadow ten steps backward, by which it had gone down on the dial of Ahaz.'* I don't pretend I suspected anything then. That big natural sundial merely brought to mind my old speculations and recalled the passage in the Bible. Something else turned up then. It didn't make me suspicious; it merely lodged in my mind for future reference. Did you notice anything when I screwed up the film of Willenhall's camera after each exposure?"

"It seemed to turn a bit stiffly," Severn interjected promptly. "I noticed you had trouble with the screwing. And when I came to develop that film I found, just as I expected, that one edge was a bit frilled, or scalloped, or whatever you call it, with rubbing against the disk at the end of the roller. The film had been put into the camera just a shade off the straight."

"Ah, you spotted that? So did I, naturally. In the old days, that sort of jamming used to happen at times because one had to be careful to get the paper straight when one threaded it through the slot in the spool. That's cured, now, because the Kodak people put a fold in the paper which makes it easy to see whether you've got it straight in the slot or not. You could hardly go wrong if you tried. And yet Willenhall — an expert with his kodak — put that film in slightly crooked. It struck me as curious; but after all, it's a thing that might happen even to an expert, once in a blue moon. It got docketed in my memory and that was all. What really did impress me, as I told you at the time, was the obvious fact that a good deal of money would be diverted as a result of Willenhall's death. But I wasn't very suspicious about it at the moment. It was just a factor that one couldn't quite brush aside."

Apparently Sir Clinton's argument was moving away from the point which had roused the Inspector. Wendover noticed that he was staring in some perplexity at the array of miscellaneous articles on the table. The Chief Constable picked up the yard-stick and cleared a space on the table-top.

"Now, you might let me have that strip of film, Inspector, the one with the two snapshots of Willenhall's body which I took."

Severn hunted in his bag and produced the negative strip which he handed over to Sir Clinton.

"And the white paper I asked you to bring," the Chief Constable added.

The Inspector brought out a roll of paper rather longer and wider than the negative film and handed it across. Sir Clinton shifted an ash-tray across to the Inspector's elbow to make room for the sheet of paper, which he proceeded to spread out on the table.

"You don't mind my sticking a drawing-pin or two into your table-top?" he asked Wendover.

"Not a bit," Wendover agreed. "It isn't polished. The marks won't show."

He was too interested in the coming demonstration, whatever it might be, to care about slight damage to his furniture. Sir Clinton lightly pinned down the long strip of film on top of the white paper, so that the five negatives appeared as black oblongs while the paper showed through clearly at the transparent edges of the celluloid strip. Taking a pencil from his pocket, the Chief Constable put a fine point on it.

"Now if you look at this," he reminded them, "you see at this end the three photographs of Hell's Gape which had been taken before we arrived. Then there's a blank exposure, which comes out almost transparent. And finally, there are the two snapshots of the body which I took myself."

Wendover and the Inspector, bending over the table, could see the objects as he enumerated them:

"Watch what I do," Sir Clinton directed, as he laid the edge of his yard-stick accurately along the lower edge of the three left-hand negatives and ruled a faint line on the film, continuing it towards the right. He then shifted the yard-stick over to the lower edges of the two right-hand negatives and ruled a second faint line, which he continued to the left until it cut the first pencil-mark.

"Now, Wendover, you're the impartial referee here. Have a good look at these two lines and then draw a rough diagram of what you see. You needn't bother about drawing to scale or anything like that. Just a very rough sketch will do."

Wendover examined the film carefully for a time before making his report.

"The two lines aren't continuous. Is that what you mean? They look like this, if one exaggerates the thing a lot."

He drew a very crude sketch to illustrate his meaning.

"That's good enough," Sir Clinton said. "You see the thing too, Inspector? The three negatives of the Gape lie in one line, whilst the blank exposure and my two photographs of the body lie in a second line which isn't parallel to the first one but cuts it at an angle. That's what I wanted to bring out. As you see, they're so nearly in line with each other all the way along that unless you were looking for it specially you might not notice that they were out of the true. What do you make of it?"

Severn evidently saw where this was trending; and in his reluctance to admit the thing which cut at the root of his case, he hesitated long enough to give Wendover his chance.

"I see what you're driving at, Clinton. That's damned ingenious! You mean there was some monkeying with that spool of film after the first three exposures were taken on it? They were all taken one after another and they're all in line as they ought to be. Then the film was taken out of the camera and put back again slightly out of the original adjustment, so that the second set didn't quite align with the first trio. Is that it?"

He broke off with a rather disappointed air.

"I don't quite see what follows from that, though, except that there's been some hankey-pankey."

Severn could not resist the chance of scoring over Wendover.

"You mean, sir, that the first three photographs — the ones of Hell's Gape — were taken with another kodak of the same pattern and were substituted for the actual spool in Willenhall's camera?"

Sir Clinton nodded.

"Yes, since all No. 1A kodaks are standard, a photograph taken with one of them is indistinguishable from a photograph taken with any other. What apparently happened was this. These three snapshots of the Gape were taken with another kodak — a No. 1A, of course. After three exposures had been made, the camera was opened in the dark and the film was rerolled back on to the spool. Then, after Willenhall had been murdered, the spool actually in his camera was removed by the murderer and this faked spool was put in its place.

"Now, just consider for a moment. As you know, it's almost impossible for a careful person to get a roll-film askew into a kodak in these days. And yet, as I spotted at once when I began to roll it up, that film had actually been mishandled in that way. Flurry, and extreme flurry at that, is the only thing that would account for it. That's what I started from when I began to look into the thing. Willenhall had no reason to be flurried, if one judged from the photographs he took. Therefore, someone else had put the film into the kodak, and put it in when he was pressed for time. I didn't need to go the length of ruling these lines, even. The mere fact that the film was crumpled at the edge told the story just as plainly. Remember that the one risk the murderer ran was of somebody turning up before he got clear away. And before he went, he had to change the films. You can guess that he must have tried to do it at top speed without bothering much about accuracy. And of course, if I hadn't chanced to take these two photographs, no one would have noticed the stiffening of the screw."

"Why didn't he complete the six exposures on the roll?" Wendover demanded. "That would have made him safe."

"Because it looked much more natural to leave half the roll unexposed. It was meant to put us off the idea of substitution, which might have suggested itself if a complete forged roll had been inserted. The half-finished roll was bound to suggest that Willenhall was cut off in the middle of his photographing and that strengthened the importance of the snapshots as a guide to the time of his death. That's how I read it myself."

"But these photographs might never have been developed at all," Wendover objected. "What good would they have been to the murderer then?"

"I rather suspect he banked on the Inspector's keenness as a photographer, which is fairly well known round about here," Sir Clinton said slyly. "Obviously he would want to know what pictures were on these last films, if only for purposes of the inquest. If not, the development of the pictures could always have been called for if it came to a trial."

"Wait a bit till I get this straight," Wendover interposed. "You mean that these photographs — the last three — were taken by the murderer himself at some earlier date, when the shadows were in the positions corresponding to those for one o'clock on June 13th? So there's no proof at all, now, that the murder did take place about that time?"

"Exactly. All that these pictures show is the state of things when the murderer took his snapshots. They've nothing whatever to do with the time or date of the murder itself. There's some subsidiary evidence as well. Perhaps I'd better give you it now. In the first place, I got hold of Willenhall's collection of negatives which he took while on his visit. The Inspector got them for me. Every one of them had the autographic imprint on it; he'd printed on the film in every case a note of the subject. These last negatives don't bear any imprint. Why? Because the murderer didn't dare to risk forging Willenhall's writing with the autographic device. Is it likely that Willenhall would have diverged from his invariable practice of autographing his snapshots in just three cases? Not a bit of it. Again you have something that throws doubt on the genuineness of these films.

"Then there's that tip of a walking-stick which the Inspector spotted in one picture. It was the murderer's walking-stick. But as the snapshot was probably taken a week or so ahead of the murder, the stick wasn't at Hell's Gape at the moment when Willenhall was killed. The murderer had it with him when he took these photographs and he happened to include its tip in one of them because it was too small an object to be seen in his view-finder when he snapped the shutter. But that's all the part it played in the case."

Wendover had no difficulty in following up this hint. Checkley had no stick with him when he went up to the Gape, since he came in a car to Brookman's Farm. But he might quite likely have had a stick with him when he walked up beforehand to take the spurious snapshots.

"You might give me that set of positives: the four of the Well and the two of Hell's Gape which came on one strip of film, Inspector," Sir Clinton requested. "And also your corresponding set of six."

Severn dived into his bag and laid the prints on the table. The Chief Constable picked out the pair of snapshots representing the Well, those which the Inspector had designated B.1 and Y.1 when he described them at the coroner's inquest.

"Just have a look at these two prints, Wendover," said Sir Clinton, pushing them across the table. "Can you see any particular difference between them?"

Wendover scrutinised the two photographs for some seconds.

"They're both taken from what seems to be the same viewpoint," he said at length. "The only difference I can see is that the stone in the foreground is broader in one picture than in the other."

He took a match from a stand on the table and, using it as a measuring-rod, made certain of the difference between the two photographs.

"Yes, that's all I can see. The stone's appreciably broader in the original picture than it seems to be in the Inspector's copy."

"I noticed that myself," said Severn defensively. "But that was as near as I could get the thing."

"I took some photographs myself this morning," Sir Clinton explained as he fished a couple of prints from a packet on the table. "I took a tripod stand with me, and a measuring tape. This photograph here was taken with the camera at forty inches above ground-level. It's much the same as your picture, isn't it?"

He handed his print to Severn who compared it with the one he had taken himself.

"Your one and mine are practically identical," he said, after he had compared the pictures of the stone in the foreground.

"Here's another version taken with the camera only thirty-six inches from the ground. Compare it with your Exhibit B.1. from the roll found in Willenhall's pocket."

"It's exactly the same, so far as the breadth of the stone in the foreground's concerned," the Inspector admitted, looking rather mystified.

"What height was Willenhall?"

"About my height — say five foot eleven," Severn guessed.

"Then if he had taken this photograph B.1. on the spool found in his pocket, wouldn't he have held his kodak at about the same level as you would hold it yourself — about forty inches off the ground? Wouldn't he have produced almost exactly the same picture of the stone in the foreground as you did? Obviously. But the stone in the foreground of B.1 corresponds to a photograph taken with the camera at three feet from the ground. What do you make of that?"

"You mean it was taken by a man four inches shorter than Willenhall?" Wendover interjected eagerly.

"Yes. The lower you place a camera, the more you tend to broaden out the picture of the near foreground. Now that broadening of the near foreground is characteristic of every picture in that set of six. Not one of them was taken by Willenhall. They were all taken by a man about five foot seven or five foot six in height. In fact, they're all fakes, just like their successors in the next spool."

"But hold on a minute, sir," the Inspector broke in. "If that's so, then these photographs . . . They fit Harry Thursford's evidence to a T. . . ."

"So much the worse for Harry Thursford," Sir Clinton answered, with a certain grimness in his tone.

"But that won't wash, sir." Severn was evidently excited, and Wendover guessed that now he was playing the card he had held back for a while. "In that lot there's a snapshot showing Harry Thursford sitting beside the Well. He couldn't have held the camera and taken his own photograph from twenty yards away!"

Sir Clinton seemed quite unperturbed by this reasoning.

"Look at the foreground," he suggested. "The camera was close to the ground when that film was exposed.

There's more lateral extension of near objects than in any of the other pictures. That snapshot was taken with the camera propped up on a bank less than three feet high. You'll admit that, at least?"

Severn inspected the print, compared its foreground with those of the others, and grudgingly admitted that the facts supported the Chief Constable.

"All the same, that snapshot must have been taken by a second person," he contended. "I know a man can photograph himself by setting up his camera, opening the shutter, and then placing himself in the scene. If you give a long exposure, it looks all right at the first glance. But it gives itself away because the background appears through the figure when you look closely. Now in this photograph, Harry Thursford's figure has had the same exposure as the rest of the film. There's no sign of background appearing through him, either."

"You think it can't be done?" Sir Clinton queried. "Well, here's a picture of myself in exactly the same setting at the Well; and I had no assistant."

The Inspector subjected the new print to a most minute examination.

"Nobody held the camera?" he demanded.

"Nobody. It was propped up on a bank, just as I told you."

He produced from his pocket a little cylindrical object which he put down on the table before the Inspector.

"This is a Kodak Self-timer. They advertise it as 'a handy little device which enables the photographer to include himself in the picture.' It presses the button at any time from half-a-second to one minute after it's been set, and so allows plenty of time for the operator to join a group. It fits on to the release of any kodak, I may say. Do you see now how Harry Thursford managed to get his own picture, just as if Willenhall had taken it?"

Severn had to admit the possibility of the method.

"Then the whole lot of these three rolls of film were just spoof pictures taken by Harry Thursford and not by Willenhall? And they weren't taken on that day at all, they were prepared beforehand? That's your case, sir?"

"Yes. Harry Thursford substituted them for the real rolls which he took out of Willenhall's pocket after the smash. Obviously he had to make the whole series consistent."

"And I walked right into his trap," the Inspector commented savagely, "just when I thought I was being extra smart. And . . . I had the whole of the evidence in front of me all the time! I noticed the foregrounds, I spotted that the last roll wasn't autographed although the rest were, and I knew about the stiffness of the camera-screw and the roughening of the edge of the film. I *have* made a hash of things!"

"It just happened that I'd amused myself with thinking out the notion of a photographic alibi," Sir Clinton pointed out. "I had the advantage of you there. And it was your fact and photographs that helped to clinch the business, Inspector. I shouldn't let it worry you."

Wendover interjected the result of his private reflections.

"This what you meant when you said that an unsuccessful attempt at an alibi is damning?"

"I'm afraid Harry Thursford may have some difficulty in explaining away these photographs now," Sir Clinton agreed. "You see, we can prove they weren't taken by Willenhall. But Harry Thursford swears that Willenhall took them. And what's more, they fit Harry

Thursford's story to a minute, almost. I suspect that the jury will regard both snapshots and story as fakes. The one thing collapses and brings down the other thing with it. And the resources of science are not yet exhausted. With your permission, Squire, I'm now going to do some temporary damage to your wireless set over there."

Severn opened his eyes at this apparently irrelevant suggestion; but he was still too sore to risk any vocal comment. Sir Clinton picked up the insulated wire, the copper stylus, the copper plate, and his tools, and then, pulling a small table close to the wireless set, he set to work.

"What I'm doing won't harm the set permanently," he explained. "I'm merely cutting a wire in the grid-circuit and joining one of the broken ends to this copper plate. The other broken end goes to this copper stylus. When we're finished, I'll replace the broken wire again and you'll be able to hear all about the 'depressions centering over Iceland' and the 'ridge of high pressure approaching from the Atlantic' just as usual. And meanwhile, Inspector, you might hunt out the original of that letter from Willenhall to Harry Thursford. I've only seen a copy of it, hitherto."

Only a few minutes were required for Sir Clinton's arrangements, and when they were complete, he put on the rubber glove to insulate his hand while he manipulated the stylus. The copper plate he laid on the table with the rubber pad beneath it, and then, taking the letter from Severn, he placed it flat on the surface of the metal slab.

"I came across this dodge in a book on forgery by Captain Quirke, the Free State Government's expert," he explained. "It's a very refined method of testing for erasures in a document. First of all, we bring the wireless set into oscillation, so that there's a constant howl from the loud-speaker. We'll just have to risk your wireless license, Squire. If the Postmaster-General comes down on you for oscillating, I'll try to clear your character."

He brought his stylus down on to the surface of the letter and moved it to and fro.

"You can hear that the pitch of the loud-speaker's howl remains practically unchanged? That's as it should be. Now it's not difficult to see what my arrangement amounts to. The copper slab and the metal stylus have the sheet of paper between them; so the whole arrangement forms a makeshift condenser in the grid-circuit. So long as that condenser has the same value, the howl will keep the same pitch. If the condenser alters in value, then the howl will change too. You see that? Well, a sheet of paper is practically homogenous, so that no matter where I put down the stylus, the value of the makeshift condenser will be practically the same. But if I happen to light on a spot where there has been an erasure, then the paper will be thinner than elsewhere, the value of the condenser will be changed, and the howl will alter in pitch. Let's see if I can hit it off."

He moved the stylus to and fro over the surface of the document, and at one point there was a perceptible change in the note from the loud-speaker.

"That's got it!"

He examined the point on which his stylus rested.

"Yes, I thought so."

Without showing them any more, he laid down the stylus, shut off the current, and came back to his chair.

"That document, you remember, Inspector, was the letter from Willenhall to Harry Thursford, typed on Halstead's Corona machine. The signature was genuine, and everything pointed to it being all right. It made the appointment with Harry Thursford at Crowland Corner at 10.15 A. M. easily. All the evidence that the story told by Harry Thursford. But now we know that Harry Thursford's story is a mere pack of lies; and we have to fall back on other evidence. Willenhall left the village at 9.45 A. M. He could have got to Crowland's Corner at 10.15 A. M. easily. All the evidence that he wasted time on the road is based on photographs which we know are fakes. Therefore it's reasonable to assume that he got to Crowland's Corner at 10.15 A. M.

"But Harry Thursford had to make the time 10.45 A. M. to fit his story. There was one extra bit of evidence he could forge. He could use his own Corona machine to alter one figure in the genuine Willenhall letter — change the '1' into a '4.' It's such a very minor change that it could be done easily enough without leaving any really visible trace. The typewriters were of the same make, so that the style of figures would correspond exactly. It only meant scrupulous care in the erasing and fitting the new figure into exactly the right spot. And by that means, Harry Thursford established, on the evidence of Willenhall's own letter, that they had met at Crowland's Corner at 10.45 A. M. instead of 10.15 A. M. He gained half-an-hour; and he accounted for that with the fake photographs which went to show that Willenhall had pottered about the Silver Grove grounds between 9.45 A. M. and 10.45 A. M. when he reached Crowland's Corner.

"In erasing the figure '1' and substituting the '4,' he made the paper a shade thinner. That was what made the loud-speaker change its note when I put the stylus over that spot on the document. You'd better try it for yourselves."

The Inspector and Wendover followed his directions and were able to detect the area of the erasure quite distinctly.

"That will be another detail which Harry Thursford will find it very hard to account for," Sir Clinton commented. "And now," he turned to the Inspector, "we come to that theft of three one-pound sample tins of toffee from the Checkley sweet-meat factory. That looked like a greedy small boy, didn't it? It was meant to look like that. But would a greedy small boy with a dirty nose-rag be so very careful not to leave any fingerprints? I admit the spread of education and all that sort of thing, but still . . . it stuck in my throat when I read the case in the archives. Particularly as I'd been looking for some burglary at Checkley's house or at his office."

"What made you think there must have been a burglary at Checkley's?" Wendover demanded.

"Because the letter about 'Herb Suckit' fitted in so neatly with the times according to Harry Thursford, and I knew that Harry Thursford's times were fakes. Therefore it was unlikely that that letter was a sound bit of evidence. It had undoubtedly been written on Checkley's Remington, as the Inspector proved. Therefore someone must have got at Checkley's typewriter surreptitiously. Burglary was the obvious way to manage that."

"You mean that Harry Thursford was the burglar of Checkley's place and that what he was really after was to type out the threatening letters and the 'Herb Suckit' production while he was on the premises. The theft of the toffee was a blind, merely?"

"Exactly. Here's one bit of confirmatory evidence. There are no dates on the threatening letters or the

'Herb Suckit' letter. Why? Because the writer didn't know exactly when he would need to use them. He couldn't risk a second visit to Checkley's, so he simply omitted the dates and talked about 'tomorrow' or 'next Friday night' which would fit any date on which he liked to use the documents. What he was after was to throw suspicion on Checkley via the typewriter, and to lure Checkley up to Hell's Gape on the day of the murder."

Sir Clinton seemed about to add something, but changed his mind.

"There's another point in connection with the letters on the Checkley Remington which you may have noticed. I'll come to it later on in another connection, though."

Wendover took advantage of the pause to put in his word.

"Could you give us in a nutshell what really did happen? I see most of it, but I'd like to have it put together."

"It's not really complicated," Sir Clinton pointed out. "Here's the rough chronology of the business. Harry Thursford burgled Checkley's place and typed those letters. The threatening letters were a mere blind and could be sent off on any date that suited him. The fact that they came from Checkley's machine would direct suspicion on to Checkley if investigations were made. He had a talk with Willenhall and offered himself as guide to the Maiden's Well, suggesting 10.15 A. M. as a good time for them to meet at Crowland's Corner. Willenhall agreed. Then Harry Thursford set about manufacturing his alibi by taking all these photographs with the shadows properly gauged. He'd have used these in evidence at a trial, according to his plans. Then he got Willenhall's note asking him to meet him at Crowland's Corner at 10.15 A. M. He at once despatched the 'Herb Suckit' invitation to Checkley, knowing that it could not reach him through the post before the morning of the murder, and that there was no chance of Willenhall and Checkley running across each other before Willenhall started off for his appointment.

"At 10.15 A. M. he met Willenhall at Crowland's Corner, and a question or two would bring out whether Willenhall had met anyone as he came through the Silver Grove grounds. He hadn't, as we know now; and that left the way open for Harry Thursford to go on with his scheme. If Willenhall had chanced to meet someone, the scheme would have been risky owing to a possible discrepancy between the time Willenhall was seen on the road and the times deducible from the faked snapshots.

"Then they went up to the Well, where presumably Willenhall took some photographs which Thursford afterwards suppressed in favour of his own fakes. After that they went on together up to Hell's Gape, reaching there about 11.15 A. M., I should imagine, if one reckons out the distance they had to walk.

"Up at the Gape, I suspect that Harry Thursford made some pretence of having had an early breakfast and got Willenhall to offer him a sandwich. That was to get the sandwich-case into the evidence and lend further colour to the idea that the death occurred about lunch-time.

"As to the murder itself, there are any number of ways of luring an unsuspecting man to the edge of a cliff where one good shove will send him over. Then Thursford probably made sure he was dead. After that he took all the 'genuine' rolls of film out of Willenhall's pockets and substituted his own fakes, refilled the camera with his half-used fake film, and cleared off in time to meet Miss Langdale at noon, according to previous arrangement. He had to be at that little dell with plenty of time in hand, for if she had got there first, she would have seen that he came down from the Hell's Gape direction. You can understand now what a devil of a hurry he must have been in when he was inserting that last roll of film into the camera, and how easily he could make the mistake of putting it in slightly off the true.

"That left him on velvet. The snapshots dated the murder at after half-past one, instead of at 11.15 A. M.; and at 1.30 P. M. he'd been in Miss Langdale's company for a solid hour. His alibi was perfect, on the evidence. And on the other side of the Gape, the unfortunate Checkley, lured there by the faked 'Herb Suckit' invitation, was toiling up the slope in nice time to be suspected of the murder at half-past one.

"All that remained was to alter the 10.15 in Willenhall's invitation into 10.45 — the change of a single figure — and Thursford had what seemed to be a perfectly cast-iron alibi. But unfortunately for him, the more cast-iron his alibi was, the worse plight he's got into now that the alibi's gone west. He's far worse off now than he would have been if he'd no alibi at all. The thing breaks down on so many points that no jury could fail to convict."

CHAPTER XIX: THE REST OF THE CASE

IN the past, Wendover had goodhumouredly endured sundry examples of Sir Clinton's irony at his expense; and now he thought he saw his way clear to getting some of his own back.

"*Hamlet* minus the Prince of Denmark," he commented sardonically. "Everything there, except the motive for it all. May I point out that Harry Thursford resigned from the Syndicate after Coniston's death? He stands out altogether now. If he committed these murders, why did he resign?"

Sir Clinton pulled out his cigarette case, took out a cigarette, and lit it before replying.

"Why did he resign? Why, I suppose he did it to hoodwink people like yourself, Squire."

"But what's the motive behind the whole affair? What does he gain in the business?"

"He gains a half-share in his uncle's cinema business, since he and his sister are old Peter's heirs. And I'm not in much doubt that he gains over £60,000 from the shares he bought up from Redhill and Checkley under cover of all that mystery-mongering. Once we get him under lock and key, the Inspector can overhaul his bank account and I shall be very much surprised if we don't find some trace of notes drawn out to finance these cash transactions of his. The whole of that business was fishy from start to finish. No firm of bookies would ever have indulged in pseudo-melodrama like that, you know."

"So he was your Mr. ABCD," said Wendover to the Inspector. "You had the right end of the stick there, if you can prove it."

"I don't think there'll really be much difficulty about that part of the business," Sir Clinton assured him. "Harry Thursford's one of these clever fellows who over-reach themselves by being just a shade too clever; and I've not the least doubt we shall find the same trait in his financial manœuvres. Damn!"

The abrupt ending was due to his twitching his cigarette and sending some ash on to his trousers. He got up hurriedly, put his cigarette on the ash-tray at the Inspector's elbow, and dusted his clothes vigorously.

"I hope the damned stuff hasn't burned a hole anywhere," he said anxiously, as he inspected the cloth. "No, it seems all right. And now, let's get on to the Coniston affair. That was a much neater business than the Hell's Gape murder. It was a far riskier thing to try; but once it came off, it was absolutely unprovable against him. At least, I can't prove how it was done, though I've a fair notion of how he managed it. But it's an interesting variation in the alibi problem, for in it he actually had a real cast-iron alibi with no faking about it."

"You don't think you could bring it home to him?" the Inspector asked in a rather disappointed tone.

"No, not strongly enough to convince a jury. In fact, I'm only making a guess at the method. We don't need to prove it. The Hell's Gape affair will serve our simple needs, so far as hanging him's concerned. But about Coniston. Just try to recollect, if you can, what happened just before Coniston set off that night. What was the last thing . . ."

F-F-F-F-T-T!

The Inspector jumped in his chair as a big flash leaped up from the cigarette at his elbow and a puff of blue smoke caught him in the eyes.

"Nothing like a practical demonstration," Sir Clinton said calmly. "You wouldn't have been so impressed if I had merely described it to you. Having jumped yourself, you can guess how Coniston behaved when that loaded cigarette went off right in his face. Of course he was startled and blinded temporarily and at that speed he was almost sure to swerve. The slippery road did the rest."

"Of course, that was why I thought of fireworks," the Inspector interjected in a chagrined tone. "I smelt the gunpowder fume in the car and I found the cigarette end. But it looked quite normal, not burst or blown up in any way."

"Look at that one there," Sir Clinton suggested. "You'll find it's quite normal too. The blaze-up simply blows the end off and doesn't leave any trace on the rest of the paper."

"I see," the Inspector admitted, after examining the stub. "Now I remember what happened. Harry Thursford egged Coniston on to try this race home — had a bet on him, which would put Coniston on his mettle because he was a good sportsman and wouldn't let a friend down. Then Harry Thursford got hold of Coniston's cigarette-case; passed it round the group so as to empty it; put in his doctored cigarette which he had ready; and handed the case with the single cigarette back to Coniston, who naturally lit up since everyone else had done so. And the cork tip made sure of which end he'd put in his mouth, so the gunpowder could be lodged quite near the other end, ready to go off after a couple of minutes smoking. Is that it?"

"More or less," Sir Clinton agreed. "Of course he used genuine Ardath cigarettes and extracted some of the tobacco from one end. Then he planted a pinch of gunpowder and refilled the paper tube with tobacco. He must have wasted dozens of cigarettes before he produced one that would pass muster. It's no easy job, I can tell you from experience."

The Inspector rubbed his chin doubtfully.

"I'm inclined to agree with you, sir, that a jury would be a bit chary about taking our word for it. Lucky that there's no need to prove each of the cases. One's enough."

Sir Clinton nodded, and lit another cigarette.

"The next thing Harry Thursford did was to resign from the Syndicate. That meant losing £40,000; but it also meant that it apparently removed him completely from the list of possible suspects. I've a sneaking admiration for him, over that. There's a certain boldness in the conception, you know. And he could afford to do it, since his actual share was even then bigger than any of the rest of you had. He seems to have carried it off well in his acting, and taken you all in.

"Unfortunately, from his point of view, that produced repercussions which he hadn't foreseen. Miss Langdale broke off her engagement. And from what I've heard about Miss Langdale, I gather that she has a rather sharp tongue when she's vexed. I think she was vexed by Harry Thursford's resignation from the Syndicate — which, of course she did not clearly understand — and she probably said what she thought about it — and him — very plainly. When some men are turned down, they turn nasty."

"Revengeful, do you mean?" Wendover demanded.

"If you like the word. Now take the affair of Peter

Thursford. What actual evidence is there? First of all, Miss Langdale seems a truthful witness, and she says she has had no communication with either Falgate or Peter Thursford for a long time. That bars out the possibility that she had talked with Peter Thursford and agreed to sell herself for a definite sum, cash down. Peter, by the midday post on the day of his death, gets a letter which causes him to go to the bank and draw some money. The letter found on his body mentions no definite sum of money. It simply says: *'Bring the money in notes.'* This makes quite clear that the letter found on Peter's body wasn't the letter he got by the midday post, in which there must have been a mention of a definite figure. I suspect that the midday letter was a much spicier production, putting a definite price on her favours, and it probably contained an injunction to bring the letter with him when he came to Azalea Cottage, so that she could be sure it was destroyed. He brought it with him; and the murderer took it out of his pocket, replacing it by the one you found, Inspector.

"The letter to Falgate I'll deal with in a moment or two. He got a letter purporting to come from Miss Langdale, and I think it was probably in the terms you know already.

"Neither of these letters which you found, Inspector, had a date on it. It was the usual 'tonight' phrasing which needed no date, just as was the case with the threatening letters and the decoy letter to Checkley. Obviously these things were prepared beforehand and couched in terms which would allow them to be used whenever occasion suited.

"They were both written on Miss Langdale's own paper with her own Underwood portable machine, but the signatures were forged. Someone must have had access to her typewriter. There was no burglary in this case. Since Harry Thursford is the person under suspicion, the question is simply: Had he access to her machine for long enough to type out these letters?

"Look at his procedure. After the breaking-off of his engagement, he made himself an insufferable nuisance to Miss Langdale by haunting her house at all times, under the pretext of trying to get her back and begging her to renew the engagement. Sooner or later, he was bound to hit on a time that suited his purpose. I think you actually got a note of the very occasion, Inspector."

"You mean that day he called and forced his way into the drawing-room when she was out and when the maid was up in the garden, sir?"

"Yes. I tested the point today with the maid's help. From where she was sitting on that afternoon it was impossible to hear the typewriter at work. That was when he produced his fake letters on Miss Langdale's machine. But this haunting of the premises had another object. He wanted to drive her away from the place for at least a day; and he succeeded in doing it, as you learned.

"The next thing is: Where did the Yale key come from? The one which figured in Falgate's story but which never reappeared, I mean. You learned from the maid that one Yale key was left on the hall-table. Harry Thursford could easily have taken an impression of it that afternoon when the maid was in the garden; and with a wax impression to work from, it's easy to file a Yale key to fit a given lock. That would give Harry Thursford access to the house any time it was left empty. And that afternoon he did a second stroke of business; he forced Miss Langdale to threaten that she'd leave the place if he came to the door again. He knew she was a girl who'd stick to what she said, so he'd got it in his power to make her decamp at any time he chose. As you know, he did come back again, and she kept her word and cleared out. She sent her maid to friends in the village and she herself left in her car in the late afternoon.

"Turn to Falgate next. If Harry Thursford is the criminal, then Falgate's story may be quite correct, so far as it goes. The first point in it is that he went to Azalea Cottage by appointment at 9.30 P. M. That was the time fixed in the letter he received, he says. But the letter found in his pocket made the appointment for 10.30 P. M. — an hour later. Except for that, the letter in his pocket was identical with the one he said he received by post. He states that he entered the Cottage by means of the Yale key sent to him in the posted letter and the rest of his story is consistent with the idea that he was induced to help himself to some drugged whiskey.

"At the same time, his story fails to fit the facts which you established, Inspector. The position of the tea-table, the type of whiskey decanter, the lack of his finger-prints on an empty soda-water bottle, and the disappearance of the typewritten invitation to have some whiskey: these points all tell against him. But every one of them can be accounted for if one assumes that young Thursford had access to the house and could clear things up a bit when Falgate had fallen into his drugged sleep after drinking some whiskey. And you'll notice that all these points tended to give the impression that Falgate was lying. The murderer's idea evidently was to entrap Falgate into telling a true story which would appear demonstrably false on almost every testable point.

"On this basis, if Harry Thursford was the murderer, he must have paid one visit to the Cottage after Miss Langdale left, to arrange the table, set out his own whiskey decanter with some drug in it, type the invitation, and so forth. Then, afterwards, he must have paid a second visit, while Falgate was asleep under the drug, to clear everything up and remove his own decanter, soda-water bottle, etc.

"Now comes the problem of Harry Thursford's alibi. He arrived at Mackworth's at 11 P. M. and he had a sound excuse for staying there until well into the small hours. If he committed the murder, then Peter Thursford must have been killed before 11 P. M.; and Harry Thursford's problem was to suggest that the old man had not been murdered until after 11 P. M. when he himself had an alibi. He had to bring Peter Thursford to Azalea Cottage about half-past ten, and he had to suggest in some way that Peter didn't arrive at the Cottage until after 11 P. M. There you have the obvious reason for this hankey-pankey with the letters.

"The real letter which Falgate received by post fixed his appointment at Azalea Cottage at 9.30 P. M. just as he declared, I believe. He went there and fell into the trap of the drugged whiskey. By 10 P. M. he was probably insensible. Suppose Harry Thursford arrived then. The drawing-room curtains were not drawn, and Thursford could see for himself whether Falgate was insensible or not, without giving himself away by entering the house. All being well, he could get in, draw the curtains in case anyone else turned up by accident, clear up all the whiskey, etc. and take the decanter to his own car. Then, with Falgate unconscious, it would be easy enough to take the Yale key out of his pocket, and to replace the posted letter by a second edition naming 10.30 P. M.

as the time of his appointment instead of the real 9.30 P. M."

"But what's the point in that?" Severn demanded.

"Just another touch to make Falgate seem to be telling a pack of lies about his doings that night," Sir Clinton returned. "Friend Harry is a master of detail. I take off my hat to him there. Didn't that very point make you suspicious yourself, Inspector?"

Severn acknowledged this rather shamefacedly and waited for Sir Clinton to continue.

"I expect Harry Thursford had parked his car somewhere farther along the road, out of sight. Falgate's car was standing at the gate. It was, if you remember, an Austin Sixteen-Six, exactly like the Thursfords' own car. Harry went out, swung Falgate's car round till it was standing across the road at right angles to the pavement. Then, I suspect, he got into the driving-seat and waited for his uncle to come along."

"But Peter Thursford wasn't due until 11.30 P. M.," Wendover objected.

"How do you know that? Half-past eleven is mentioned in the letter that the Inspector got in his pocket, I admit. But I've proved to you already that that letter was a fake and not the one Peter had received by post. Half-past ten at the latest was the hour fixed in the real letter. Nothing else will fit the facts.

"My theory is that Peter came along the pathway — it isn't even a pavement — and found Harry apparently leaving in his own car after a visit to Miss Langdale. Naturally, Peter would want to get Harry away immediately. You can imagine the rest. Harry would make some excuse to get the old man round to the back of the car: 'Just see if that spare wheel's all right, will you? I thought I felt it loose as I turned the car.' Something of that sort. And as soon as Peter got in between the car and the wall, Harry would drop his toe on the accelerator with the reverse in, and — well, quick acceleration is one of the points of these cars. Peter wouldn't stand a chance.

"After that, all Harry had to do was to get at Peter's pocket-book, grab the money — just to make things a bit more complex — take away the real letter of appointment and substitute the fake which post-dated Peter's arrival to 11.30 P. M. Then he had to drag out Falgate, who was too heavily doped to know what was happening; push him into the driving-seat of the murder-car; and then go off in his own car to Mackworth's. He arrived at Mackworth's at 11 P. M., and there was the letter in Peter's pocket to show that he had reached Azalea Cottage only at 11.30 P. M. and therefore could not have died until at least half-an-hour after his nephew reached Mackworth's house."

"And you worked the whole thing out on that basis?" Wendover asked. "You hadn't anything else to go on? It looks rather like a leap in the dark, if you ask me."

"I had something else, as it happens," Sir Clinton assured him. "There was one scrap of evidence which linked together the Willenhall murder and the Peter Thursford affair and made it practically certain that they were done by the same hand. You've had it in front of you all the time, both of you."

Wendover and the Inspector exchanged glances of discomfiture.

"I'll make it easier," Sir Clinton said, chaffingly. "Everyone has some peculiarity or other when he uses a typewriter. It may be the number of spaces in the indention of the first line in a paragraph, or the spacing after a full stop, or striking one letter in mistake for another, or the length of the line, or anything of that sort. Whatever it is, you find him always doing it, because it's second nature to him, no matter what machine he's using."

The Inspector hurriedly turned over the various documents in the case, while Wendover endeavoured to get a glimpse of them.

"Punctuation sometimes suggests something," Sir Clinton hinted slyly, when Severn seemed to draw blank.

The Inspector caught his meaning at last.

"Oh, I see. There isn't a comma in the Willenhall-Checkley fake invitation . . . Nor in the threatening letters . . ."

"Nor in the decoy letters supposed to have been written by Miss Langdale either. That's the important point. If they were written by the same person who wrote the 'Herb Suckit' fake, then you have the link between the two cases. And obviously they were. Therefore Harry Thursford was at the bottom of the Azalea Cottage business. And therefore his alibi in that case was a fraud. But his alibi began at 11 P. M., so the murder must have been done before that. And hence it's possible to unravel the whole tangle, as I've shown you. I don't say I'm correct in every detail; but I think I'm near enough. In any case, it's a bit academic, for we shan't need to drag in either the Coniston or the Peter Thursford affairs. We can bring the Hell's Gape murder home to him quite clearly."

"I'm glad of that," Wendover declared frankly. "Miss Langdale needn't be dragged into the business then. Awkward for her to have that letter read out in court, you know. A lot of old wives would chatter and 'wonder whether there wasn't something in it after all.' That young scoundrel must have been eaten up with spite and rage when he planned to bring her into the affair.

The worst of it was, he had probability in his favour over one thing. Old Thursford would have behaved just like that, if he'd had the chance. I overheard something once that showed up the old man completely on that subject."

Sir Clinton made no comment on this, but turned to the Inspector with a business-like air.

"We can prove the case without adducing a motive, of course. But as soon as you get young Thursford under lock and key, you'd better take steps to examine his bank account. I don't see how we can miss finding evidence there to connect him with these transactions in the Syndicate shares. Then you'd better search his house and see if you can find a No. 1A Kodak. Most likely he's got rid of it, but it's worth looking for. And if you can trace any purchases of films by him, it would be just as well to know about them."

He paused for a moment, considering a course of action.

"And now, Inspector, I think you'd better be off at once and arrest Harry Thursford without wasting time. If you want a warrant, Mr. Wendover can give you one. We must let Mr. Falgate out of gaol at once, now, and we can't do that till we've got Thursford locked up. He might hear of Falgate's release and take fright if we gave him a chance. I'll see about releasing Falgate. Mr. Wendover will lend you a car to follow up Thursford in case he happens to be out at a friend's house tonight."

In a very few minutes everything was arranged and the Inspector departed on his errand.

"I'll borrow the second car, if you don't mind, Squire, and go down myself to see about Falgate's release. If you've no objection, I want to bring him back here for a short time. We'll have to explain things to him, more or less, so as to avoid any squalls on his part or even incautious talk. I think I know what note to strike."

"What one?" Wendover asked curiously.

"Well, I'll tell him we want to keep Miss Langdale's name out of it all," Sir Clinton said with a faint smile. "He's not the same breed as Thursford, you see, Squire. Although she turned him down once, he was ready to hurry to her side as soon as he thought she was in a tight place. I think we can persuade him to keep his mouth shut by saying it's in her interest — as, of course, it is."

He paused again, and his smile seemed to become a cynical one.

"I expect this is the first time you've had a financial interest in the date of a hanging, Squire."

"What d'you mean?" Wendover demanded uncomprehendingly.

"Well, your share in the Syndicate's worth £60,480 at present. If the High Court over there drags out its procedure until after Thursford's execution, why . . . then your share will be worth £80,640. There'll only be yourself, Redhill, and Falgate left to split the £241,920 between you, then. A tidy little sum for each of you. What do you mean to do with it?"

"You're a gruesome devil," Wendover protested angrily. "As to the money, I don't need it; and I'd feel — well, I couldn't touch it. It's hardly clean cash, somehow. I've made up my mind to give it away in charity."

He smiled in turn, evidently tickled by the thought that occurred to him.

"There's a police fund, isn't there, for providing supplements to pensions of debilitated Chief Constables and other small fry? I'll give some of the money to that, Clinton. Now, say 'Thank you!' nicely."

THE END

〉〉〉 If you've enjoyed this book and would like to discover more great vintage crime and thriller titles, as well as the most exciting crime and thriller authors writing today, visit: 〉〉〉

The Murder Room
Where Criminal Minds Meet

themurderroom.com